Praise for
FREEDOM'S LANDING

"Exciting and totally convincing... There can only be more action in the sequels McCaffrey presumably plans."
—*Booklist*

"McCaffrey has created another set of winning protagonists and a carefully detailed, exotic background."
—*Publishers Weekly*

"A brand-new series that has 'classic' written all over it."
—*Romantic Times*

"Not for nothing do her fans call the author 'the Dragon-Lady' ... Along the way she crafts a sci-fi adventure that will please followers of the genre, and of the author."
—*Dayton Daily News*

"There are enough problems and mysteries involved in establishing a colony to keep things interesting, and to promise intriguing developments to come in this new series."
—*Locus*

"The narrative hits an admirable groove."
—*Kirkus Reviews*

Books by Anne McCaffrey

*not science fiction–fantasy

freedom's
CHOICE

Anne McCaffrey

ACE BOOKS, NEW YORK

FREEDOM'S CHOICE

An Ace Book / published by arrangement with
the author

PRINTING HISTORY
Ace/Putnam hardcover edition / 1997
Ace mass-market edition / June 1998

The Penguin Putnam Inc. World Wide Web site address is
http://www.penguinputnam.com

Check out the Ace Science Fiction/Fantasy newsletter, and much
more, at Club PPI!

ISBN: 0-441-00531-4

ACE®
Ace Books are published by
The Berkley Publishing Group, a division of Penguin Putnam Inc.,
375 Hudson Street, New York, New York 10014.
ACE and the "A" design are trademarks
belonging to Penguin Putnam Inc.

PRINTED IN THE UNITED STATES OF AMERICA

10 9 8 7 6

*This book is affectionately
dedicated to Jan Regan,
who is more like Lessa than Lessa was.*

*Exercising racehorses is the nearest
thing to riding Dragons
on this good earth.*

PREFACE

When the Catteni, mercenaries for a race called Eosi, invaded Earth, they used their standard tactic of domination by landing in fifty cities across the planet and removing entire urban populations. These were distributed throughout the Catteni worlds and sold as slaves along with other conquered species.

Since slavery did not sit well with many of the first-world countries, the conquerors met with considerably more resistance than had been anticipated. The size and general brutality of the Catteni soldier had inculcated sufficient fear and obedience to inhibit active resistance on many of their previous invasions. However, since many M-type planets had been discovered by the Eosi, the Catteni were advised to round up dissidents and felons alike, deposit them on whatever M-type planet was currently available for occupation, and let them fend for themselves.

Not all M-type worlds are suitable for colonization but, since the Catteni had quantities of expendable personnel, they could use an empirical method of discovering which were fertile and friendly, and which con-

tained dangers making them inimical. A check was kept
on the survival rate of the inadvertent settlers. If few
remained alive, the world was abandoned. If the survival
rate was high, more deliveries were made. When the
imposed population had made the world tenable, the
Catteni would install an overlord and exact a percentage
of the gross planetary product. Any dissenters to this
procedure were then rounded up and deposited on yet
another potential colonial world.

Botany was one such colonial world on which the
Catteni, emptying holdings cells on Barevi and Earth,
dropped several species to see how they survived—each
other as well as the native, but as yet unidentified, denizens. Humans, Deski, and Rugarians were the "colonists" in the first drop.

The Catteni outfitted each of the unsuspecting colonists with durable clothing, a blanket, and a packet of
dry rations. The "shipment" spent the voyage in a form
of suspended animation and were deposited on the planet
along with knives, hatchets, and rudimentary medical
kits.

On Botany, however, a former staff sergeant took
charge of those dropped with him, and, warned by one
of the nonhuman species, they managed to avoid the
local avian predators.

Zainal, the one Catteni who had been shanghaied in
that shipment, vaguely remembered other problems on
this planet from a cursory reading of the original exploration report. Although some of the stranded people
wanted to revenge themselves by taking the Catteni's
life, Kris Bjornsen forestalled the attempt, suggesting
that he knew more than anyone else did about the planet
and they'd better keep him alive for a while. Sergeant
Chuck Mitford saw the wisdom in that, and also took
the Catteni's advice to seek higher, stonier ground if
they wished to survive. In a forced march to the safety

of the nearby hills, Mitford realized that Zainal could be useful for quite a few reasons.

Establishing a base camp, hunting for edible life-forms and foods, occupied every one of the survivors under Mitford's command. The settlers discovered that this planet was not as unoccupied as the Catteni report suggested. In fact, it seemed to be a planet extensively farmed by mechanized, highly sophisticated machinery, operating without any "live" supervision. On a scouting mission, Kris Bjornsen and Zainal encountered more humans as well as representatives of the four other races dumped on Botany.

In order to save those of the Deski species from dying of malnutrition, since Botany did not produce one of their basic dietary requirements, Zainal forced a confrontation with the Catteni captain of a second transport dumping a new load of settlers. He also sent back the message that this planet was obviously an agricultural subsidiary of a heretofore undiscovered race.

Then he was summoned to a covert meeting with another Emassi—a high ranking Catteni official—with an offer to be returned to his rank and duties: an offer he summarily rejected.

By then, there were sufficient technicians and engineers available to redesign some of the available equipment into useful appliances and machines, supplying communications and other assistance to the settlers.

Using the aerial maps reluctantly supplied him, Zainal led a group to what might be a command center on the planet. However, it had obviously not been occupied for a very long time, though a garage held several aerial devices and smaller missiles of a homing device design. One of these was deliberately launched by Dick Aarens, in the hope that the actual "owners" of Botany might return and help the colonists against the Catteni.

PROLOGUE

PART ONE

The satellite logged the departure of a missile from the surface of the planet under observation. It analyzed the components, attempted to correlate the information within its memory banks, and found no match. The unusual speed and approximate direction of the device was also noted as it headed north and east toward the farther edge of the Milky Way. Just as the missile reached the heliopause of the system, it disappeared. A scan produced no debris; no ion or any other trace of what had powered its drive could be detected. The missile had vanished: a fact that was unacceptable to the monitoring program and caused a functional error which required internal investigation and repair. Although its earlier tracking was recorded, the satellite did not, due to the anomalies, immediately forward the data to its servor.

Consequently, without a requisite emergency code, the information went through several processings before the anomalies were noticed. It was then immediately reported to the proper authority. A team was dispatched to correct the malfunction. None was found even after a complete overhaul and maintenance check of the satellite. The data was therefore suspect as a malfunction in itself, rather than the recording of an event. The planet was, after all, a penal colony; the exiles were equipped with the barest essentials for survival and no technological equipment whatever. It was only by chance that the report was ever seen by persons with the essential information to realize the significance of the sighting, and the mysterious disappearance of the homing device.

PART TWO

"You say that he *refused* to answer the summons?" The speaker scowled at the Emassi captain.

As they were also father and son, the son was accustomed to his sire's scowls: he almost enjoyed the reaction, knowing that Zainal's refusal to return and accept the duty imposed on his rank and family would further blacken his brother's previously spotless reputation in their father's estimation.

"He was chosen," Perizec continued, bashing one huge fist onto the pervalloy worktop. "He cannot refuse the summons."

"He did," Lenvec said with an imperturbable shrug of one shoulder. " 'I'm dropped, I stay.' You know the convention."

Perizec crashed both fists onto the worktop, bouncing everything on it, scattering the files from the desk rack. "An Eosi matter has precedence over any Catteni convention! You know that!" The scowl deepened, pulling down the heavy mouth and jaw, darkening the gray-toned skin. "He has known of this duty since he was presented to the Eosi. Dropped or not, he is to return to accept that duty." The fists banged emphatically again. Then Perizec's eyes narrowed to slits through which his yellow pupils flashed with anger. "How did he come to be dropped on that felon planet?"

Lenvec shrugged. He knew that his father was well aware of the whole circumstance but he repeated the report.

"Zainal engaged in a fatal brawl with a minor transport officer. The crew sought vengeance and Zainal escaped in a flitter. It was hit and crashed in the western hunting grounds. No trace was found of him then. He seems to have been picked up along with dissidents who were gassed during a riot, and so was included in the slave shipment. He made his presence known to a second drop crew. Your office was alerted and I made the run to retrieve him. He refused . . ."

"I know, I know," and Perizec flicked thick fingers to end the recital. "He must return. The duty is required of him. We cannot avoid the choosing." Perizec frowned, deep in thought. "See to it that the crew who arranged his deportation are sent to the same destination. They will ensure that he is ready to be collected when next you land there."

"A thought, sir," Lenvec began. "Catteni would not be popular on the planet and may even be prevented from finding Zainal."

Perizec regarded him with anger. "Zainal survived. You said yourself that he was a member of some sort of team."

Lenvec shrugged. "Zainal is, after all, Emassi, sir, and as clever a man as you yourself . . ."

Perizec grunted at the filial compliment. "He is also Catteni and would resist attempts to eliminate members of his own race."

"He might not be in a position to do so. He may also wish to eliminate the crew for having put him on that plane in the first instance."

"They will have to be 'rewarded,' " and Perizec's smile was unpleasant, "for their part in his exile. See to that. And let us find among the Emassi two or three of Zainal's hunting friends. Them he would certainly protect, would he not?'' Lenvec nodded. ''They will see to it that he is willing to leave when next you land.''

''Am I to transport them there?''

''By no means. That would put Zainal on his guard. When is the next mass transportation scheduled?''

Lenvec consulted his wrist unit. ''In twenty-two days.''

''Choose the men . . .''

''A female, too, sir, if I may suggest it. He's been a long time without . . . companionship.''

''An excellent notion,'' and Perizec grinned back at his son. ''You have someone in mind?'' Lenvec nodded. ''They will all be rewarded.'' He reached to the files and methodically began stacking them in order as he continued speaking. ''This must be completed as expeditiously as possible. I have told the Eosi that Zainal was sent on a special assignment and is unaware of their need of him. We have been granted a respite, but their anger will fall on us all if we do not present Zainal within a reasonable period of time.''

Lenvec nodded. Since Zainal had been acceptable to the Eosi, there had been no need for Lenvec to be presented. Nor would he wish to be accorded such an Eosi ''honor,'' since he knew exactly what it entailed. However, he might yet find himself the substitute, if Zainal did not present himself. The honor of the family was at stake. Failure to comply with an Eosi demand brought disaster and disgrace to every blood relation.

''Keep me informed, Lenvec,'' Perizec told his son by way of dismissal.

As Lenvec saluted formally, pivoted smartly, and left the office, Perizec began to consider how to punish the stupidity of a mere freighter crew who had presumed to place an Emassi among transported dissidents. He enjoyed deciding on the exact and perfect punishment for their presumption and shortly was able to issue the necessary orders. Once the rumor was circulated, few Tudo or Drassi would dare to repeat such treatment, no matter what the cause. That this abrogated one of the main tenets of Catteni discipline did not bother Perizec. His rank had privileges, and he exercised all frequently.

CHAPTER 1

As he was supposed to do, the Deski immediately informed the camp leader of what he had heard on the height above Camp Rock.

"You heard a ship come down?" Worrell asked, rubbing his face hard in an effort to comprehend what Coo was telling him.

"Come down," Coo said, nodding vigorously, "not big. Not you-zoo-al," he added, struggling with the syllables.

"Not usual?" Worrell repeated while Coo nodded with a Deski-style grin which Worrell was now accustomed to. "You mean, not a drop?" Coo shook his head and then nodded, to be sure he was understood.

Worrell sighed with relief. The damned Catteni had speeded up their deposits of "colonists" over the past month to the point where there was barely time to assimilate each new delivery.

"No drop. No long down. Come," and Coo gestured with his thin, oddly knuckled digits, swooping them down to close with his other hand, pause briefly, before elevating it again. "Go. Soft." And now he put a hand to his ear and pretended to listen hard.

Instantly Worry began to fret. His nickname was less a contraction of his surname than a description of his chief trait.

"A quick drop, then. A few people at the most. Only what kind?" he asked himself more than Coo. "Nearby?"

"Not near-near." Coo dropped his head, orienting himself, then shifted his feet slightly to the right, so that he was facing due north. The Deski ability to know where they were was an extremely useful trait on Botany. They could get themselves back to the main settlements, like Camp Ayres Rock, from any point, so it had become common practice to include at least one Deski in every scouting expedition.

Now Coo extended both long, double-jointed arms, kept the right one facing due north, and angled his left arm almost due west. "There. Not near-near."

"Really?" Worry rose and patted Coo's bony shoulder. "Real good, Coo. Thanks."

"Good job done?"

"Beaut job, Coo." Worrell turned up the light so he could see the map hung on his wall. Much of the continent it represented was still blank but, over the past few wintry months, details had been added by scouting teams. "If we're here, Coo," and Worrell put his finger on the cave system of Camp Rock, "how far west?"

Coo extended his head toward the map on a neck that seemed elastic, put one digit on the camp, and then slid it in the appropriate direction. "No more far."

"Really?" Worrell felt anxiety bloom in his gut. The point Coo had indicated was where Zainal and his team had met the scout ship: the one sent to take him back to his duties as a Catteni Emassi. "Thanks, Coo. You'd best get back on duty."

"I go." And the Deski slipped quietly from the room.

Worrell glanced briefly at his timepiece. Dawn was too far away for him to send a squad to check the landing site. The night crawlers would be all too eager to catch anything that traveled aboveground. Not even a large team, stamping heavily, would escape those winter-hungry denizens.

Then Worrell chuckled to himself. If Catteni had indeed landed someone for some purpose . . . like getting in touch with Zainal again . . . they'd've had a welcome they didn't expect.

"Serve 'em right, too," Worrell said, though he was not by nature a vindictive man. In a considerably more cheerful mood, he returned to his bed and went soundly back to sleep.

Worrell would have liked to have Zainal to send down to investigate the reported landing but he and Kris Bjornsen were out with their team on another long scouting trip: looking for more caves, or barns, or rocky terrain to house the settlers continuously supplied them by the Catteni. So he sent for Mic Rowland, one of the Fifth Drop group. He'd been a stuntman for the movies and could be trusted to observe, be discreet, and get himself and a team out of trouble. Worry told him about the late-night landing and where Coo thought the ship had touched down.

"If a Deski said it landed there, we'll find some signs." Mic was far too accustomed to working with all-sorts, as he called them, not to appreciate talent wherever it was found.

"Even scout ships leave a stench behind them," Worrell agreed. "Take a party of those newbies with you. Give 'em a chance to hunt."

"Sure thing," Mic said with a businesslike nod.

Worrell grinned when he saw Rowland tag the first five people in the breakfast line whose new-looking coveralls marked them as the latest drop. He did let them eat first before he took them off.

Worrell knew the trip would do them good. So many got to Botany still full of their Earthside sabotage activities and how many Cats they'd injured or killed and other kinds of derring-do, and they needed to be taken down a few pegs to the realities of Botany. Fortunately more were adapting well to the new world than Worry would have expected.

What worried the Australian, and the other camp managers, was the indisputable fact that the Catteni were making more frequent deposits of dissidents. Zainal had been surprised, too, and had suggested, slyly, that it was because Earth was showing far more rebellion than any other race the Catteni had subjugated. So there were more rebels to be exiled. So far the colony had been able to absorb quantities of both human and alien species, though they had followed Zainal's suggestion to let the belligerent and uncooperative Turs go off on their own in the small groups in which they arrived. However, the population of Botany had risen from the original drop of 582 to nearly 9,000.

Worrell worried all day over what Mic Rowland would find. He also widened the perimeter guard, in case of infiltration, warning them vaguely that someone had seen Turs prowling about. It was possible, in Worrell's view of human frailties, that even some specimens of Mankind could have been brainwashed into cooperating with their Catteni masters, and try to slip into the colony to cause trouble. That actually made more sense to him than a secret landing of Catteni, since they would be instantly noticed. So far Zainal remained the only one of his race resident on Botany. And he had barely escaped being killed that first day. Which was fortunate, since he had proved so helpful in the first days, and ever since: even to rejecting a chance to leave.

Mic Rowland returned with enough game to justify

the hunt. Dismissing his weary group, he caught Worrell's glance, jerked his head toward Worrell's office on the height, and moved quickly to join the camp manager there. He dropped the rocksquats with the cooks, but not the sack in his right hand.

Once they were private, Mic upended the sack on the table and grinned at Worrell's surprise.

"Boots?"

"That was all that was left. And not the same sort they issued us," Mic said, "much better made. And this." He took from his chest pocket a very thin plate about seven centimeters long, and maybe two thick. "I'd say it was a comunit, or some sort of call device. Maybe even an implant. I rubbed the gore off." Then he picked up one of the boots, which was scored as if something hot, or very strong, had twined around it, leaving deep grooves. He twisted the heel and the whole lower part of the shoe swiveled free, showing a compact kit of small tools embedded in the material of the thick sole. "There's something in each boot." He picked up the smallest pair and opened the sole of one, revealing its contents to Worrell. "This looks like a drug injector." He opened the other, which contained two small vials. "And the drugs."

"Drugs? Yes, well, I'll give that stuff to Dane." Worrell counted eight boots in an effort to defuse his mounting anxiety. "Dropped a team, did they? To do what?" Though Worrell had an awful suspicion his first guess might prove correct. Would Mic know?

Mic shrugged. "You been here longer. An educated guess would be they were after Zainal." When he caught Worrell's sharp look, he grinned. "I heard. Damn few would have stayed if they had a chance to leave."

"Hmmm. No other . . . remains?"

Mic shook his head. "Some bits of metal, probably from whatever they were wearing but even Catteni material is edible by the crawlers. Boots are just a touch too tough for 'em.'' And he flicked his fingers at one. ''Big mothers wore 'em. Big even for Catteni. They have goon squads, too.''

''One pair is much smaller. *Would* they have sent a woman with them?''

Mic shrugged. ''Who knows what Catteni will do.'' He closed his lips on whatever he had been about to add and shrugged again.

Worrell could very well imagine what had been left unsaid. Before his deportation, Worrell had seen enough of the higher-ranking Catteni women to know that Kris Bjornsen was a lot better-looking than the best of them. Many disapproved of her liaison with Zainal but no one had the gall, other than Dick Aarens, to complain or dispute it.

''Thanks, Mic. Did the others notice?''

''Couldn't fail to, not with those empty boots scattered around. I don't think the newbies noticed that the footwear isn't the same stuff we have. So I'm reporting a missing patrol to you. Right?''

''Too right,'' Worrell said, ''and I trust you rammed home the lesson?''

''Never miss an opportunity like that, Worry.'' And Mic left with a big grin on his face.

Worrell made a mental note that Mic was ready for more responsibility. First he dialed Zainal's team number for them to report in and then got in touch with Chuck Mitford.

''Well, put 'em in a safe place, Worry,'' Mitford said, ''until either Zainal or I can have a look-see. Just give the medical junk to Dane. He might know what it is and maybe have a use for it. I suppose you better send those tools down here to Narrow for the engineering types. They could use some high-quality stuff despite some of the new items they've been able to turn out recently. I'll have to figure out a way to explain their . . . ah . . . acquisition." He contradicted himself a moment later. "I don't have to explain anything, do I?"

"Sure don't, sarge."

Worrell grinned at the comment. In one of the recent drops there had been several ex-admirals, ex-generals, and assorted other brass, most of whom, when they had a chance to recover from the trials of their journey, were quite willing to refer respectfully to Mitford as "sergeant." Those who didn't soon learned how much was owed that sergeant, or found themselves settling into perhaps less amenable campsites. No one—except someone on sick call—shirked assigned duties and everyone took a turn at hunting, preparing food, sentry, and whatever other duty they were thought capable of managing. When he hadn't anything else to fuss about though, Worrell worried that some sort of high-level executive type might try to bounce Mitford out of his current eminence. Of course, if Mitford decided on his own to step down, that had to be entirely his option. So far, Mitford's management—and he had listened to suggestions from just about everyone in the first couple of drops—had worked pretty damn well.

"Sarge, should we worry about human infiltrators?" he asked, hoping to have such a notion knocked down.

Mitford's snort made the diaphragm of the portable phone vibrate, and Worrell began to relax.

"Not unless they can run faster than a crawler can grab. And if there were four Catteni, they'd've been heavy enough on those big feet of theirs to have alerted every scavenger four fields over." There was a brief pause. "Worry, you can't actually believe any human being would work *with* the Catteni, do you?"

"There've been traitors, renegades, spies, quislings in every war, sarge. Why not this one?"

Mitford cursed briefly but colorfully. "You could be right. Damn it. Only why send in infiltrators by special delivery? You could as easily send 'em in a regular drop.

Anyway, why mess us up? Zainal says the Catteni prefer colonies to prosper so they can come in and take over when one gets going well.'' Pause. ''Furthermore,'' and Mitford's tone was adamant, ''they'll have their work cut out for them if they try that tactic on *my* planet.''

Nor would anyone dispute Mitford's use of the possessive pronoun.

''We'd be with you four hundred percent, sarge.''

Another brief pause. ''I'll tell Easley we'd better be double careful checking IDs on the next drops. Right?''

With that he cut off, leaving Worrell not quite as anxious as he had been: no one was going to take over ''my planet.'' He grinned at the outrage in Mitford's voice. Scouts had come across the remains of several rough camps in the hills, above the level the night scavengers inhabited, and the skeletons of those who hadn't survived. But everything was much better organized now, especially the drops. Peter Easley, a former personnel manager of a huge international firm, had been responsible for that. His second morning on Botany he had sought Mitford out and made suggestions on how to simplify and speed up the influx, and how to catch the signs of those still in trauma, needing counseling. He'd deferentially organized additional men and women experienced in crowd control and personnel handling and passed on recommendations of other specialists that Mitford might want to interview himself. Mitford had turned the whole problem of drops over to Easley. The complexity of resettlement, after another of Easley's sensible recommendations, had gone to Yuri Palit, previously a UN resettlement manager for displaced persons. There were now enough degree engineers, aviation and production-line mechanics, and inventor types to keep even Dick Aarens from getting cocky while speeding up their output.

With enough hand-held communication units available, scouting teams could report in to Mitford on any unusual occurrences, as Worrell had just done, and the sergeant had actually been able to keep "business hours."

"I'll get enough time yet," Mitford had recently confided to Worrell on a trip through Camp Rock to Camp Silo, "to lead a recon group myself."

"Is that what you'd really like to do?" Worrell had asked, since that was the first time he'd ever heard something akin to a complaint from the man.

"All this brand-new world and everyone else is getting to see it first!" Mitford had flung his hand up in frustration. "Well, I get closer to it all the time." Then he'd grinned. "And I get less and less paperwork to do."

So now Mitford had more time to spend to organize the teams and send expeditions in every direction, trying to locate more bases, especially to replace Camp Rock, which was established just above a deep gorge that showed the scars from centuries of spring flooding. Zainal and Kris Bjornsen were on just such a scouting mission, hoping to find a site that was not an installation of the "Mech Makers" or "Farmers," as many people were beginning to call them because of the agricultural emphasis of the planet.

Worrell packed the boots back into the sack and he peered more closely at the plate. There did seem to be round indentations on one end: possibly touch points. He counted nine—as many as a numeric pad. He was sorely tempted but decided against any whimsical experimentation. He'd sent out the recall sequence, and Zainal and Kris should be back in a few days.

The team was at that time in a state of exultation, for they had managed to complete a difficult ascent up an irregular cliff mass and now looked down into a long valley that bore no traces of the neatness which typified the land the Mech Makers farmed. Their ascent had been a quick decision, prompted by certain anomalies that both Zainal and Whitby, the mountaineering expert of the team, had noticed. The first was a stream bubbling vigorously from what seemed like a solid rock face. Investigating, they found the stream had bored a channel through the stony barrier.

"That's not the kind of rock that water erodes," Whitby said. "It was carved somehow."

The second curiosity was that the high mound of rubble that barred their way couldn't, in Whitby's estimation, have been caused by a natural landslide or depression, and he called their attention to the top of the cliffs, which did look shorn.

"Could have been an earthquake," Kris had suggested.

"We've seen no other subsidence on our way here," Basil Whitby had said, shaking his head, glancing along the cliffs on either side. "Not a landslide, not with that kind of stone." Then he grimaced at the tumbled rocks of the barrier.

"Don't see any kind of road leading up here," Sarah said, swinging around to be sure.

"As if mechanicals left any tracks with those air cushions," Joe Marley reminded her, and she made a face at him. "Not even a mark where a big mother would have parked for a time."

"Animals do leave tracks," she replied.

"And we haven't seen many of them lately, now have we?" he said in good-natured sparring.

"There have to be other animals than loo-cows, rocksquats, night crawlers, and those vicious avians. Even I know that much about ecological balance."

"Maybe," and Leila Massuri's tone was cautious, "that barrier's there for a good reason." She and Whitby were the new members of the Kris-Zainal team. Leila contributed more to the pot with her crossbow prowess than to discussions.

"Keeping something in? Or out?" Joe asked, accepting the premise.

"We find out," said Zainal, and began to pass out appropriate equipment for scaling the barrier. Though the air cushion of their all-terrain vehicle allowed it to traverse very rough terrain, the gradient of the rocky obstacle in front of them was too acute.

They were far better equipped now for explorations than they had been in the initial days after being dumped on Botany. Leila slung her crossbow across her back, and made sure that the quarrel pouch was fastened, while Kris loaded her pouch with pebbles for her sling and slung the rope coil Zainal handed her over one shoulder. Whitby had fashioned himself a proper climbing pick, which he slid into the loop at his belt, stuffed pitons into thigh pockets, and secured the short compound bow and quiver of arrows to the harness on his back. Sarah and Joe had slings as well as boomerangs, a utensil that was becoming more popular: Fek and Slav armed themselves with lances and hatchets. They all carried blanket rolls and small sacks with food and water.

The climb up the irregular and often shifting cliffside had taken most of the morning but the view at the top was more than worth the effort. Below them lay a peaceful valley, obviously undisturbed by the agricultural mechanicals that dominated the slopes behind them. At the narrow end of the valley they could see a distant waterfall, its descent a murmur as it fell into a small lake. The stream leading from it meandered down the far, lower side of the valley and blundered into the cliff, answering the question of its origin. The valley floor was interspersed with flat grasslands and some of the odd-looking thickets that in their season would bear edible berries. But the most unusual feature was the little groves of what Kris called lodge-pole trees: straight tall trunks that flattened at the very top into a thick crest of narrow branches fanning out, and were covered in needles during the warmer weather. Specimens did grow in some of the hedgerows that lined the mechanicals' fields but only as single trees, not in copses like these, and certainly not as many groves as could be seen from their vantage point. A pungently scented breeze cooled their sweaty faces.

"It's as good as Shangri-la," Sarah McDouall said, beaming down at the valley. "It's lovely. So peaceful, so . . ."

"Secret?" Joe supplied. "I wonder what else we'll find down there."

"Why, there's space for hundreds here," she said, ignoring his implicit pessimism.

"Hmmmm," Zainal murmured, obviously sharing Joe's caution. "Slav?" he asked the Rugarian, who was shielding his eyes as he surveyed the valley.

Slav shrugged.

"Fek?" Zainal turned to the Deski, who showed no exertion from the difficult ascent. The Deski were such natural climbers that Kris had wondered if their home planet was nothing but perpendicular surfaces. Actually, their oddly shaped hands and the soles of their feet became slick with a sort of adhesive substance which gave them purchase on sheer surfaces and their unusually jointed arms and legs permitted them to assume postures that would have broken human limbs.

Fek had assumed her intensive listening posture, almost as if her hearing organs were extending themselves from the side of her head, wide open to experience the slightest of sounds.

"Wind. Water. Small noises," she said, shaking her head to indicate a lack of obvious danger. "No livings." Without waiting for Zainal's signal, she started to descend. He shifted the heavy coil of rope he carried, rubbed the sweat off his face, and followed.

Fek found the easiest descent for the rest of the party, zigzagging down some of the sheerer boulders, which she would have managed quite easily with her natural advantages. But she, too, stopped where sheer-sided stone angled sharply outward.

"I'd say that looks like something was meant to stay in there," Kris said.

"Twenty-five meters slanted at fifteen degrees or more," Whitby said. "So we rappel down." He unloosed his pick, found a piton, and started hammering it in, while Zainal removed the coil from his shoulder to rig it for the drop.

Once again, Kris thought as she took her turn at the descent, *That silly survival course comes in handy in my new life on Botany.* All of them, even Fek, grinning for all she was worth as she rappelled, made it safely to the floor of the valley.

"Leave," Zainal said when Whitby would have released one of the three ropes used. "We may need to get out quickly."

Leila immediately armed herself with her crossbow and looked around warily.

"It's full daylight, Lee," Kris said, reassuringly. "So even if our thudding on the ground here aroused anything, we're safe as long as the sun shines. Me, I'm for that stream."

One bend of the meandering water was not far from them and, though Leila did not put up her crossbow, they all approached the stream. Sarah as team medic used one of the testing strips on a cupful.

"Potable," she said, and dipped her cup back in to bring it full to her mouth, though she sipped carefully.

The other humans did likewise, then rinsed their sweaty faces in the cooling water. Fek and Slav, who never seemed to need much water, remained alert, listening and looking for any dangers unseen from the height. Then both knelt to take a sample mouthful directly from the stream, as they preferred to drink.

"This place looks almost too good to be true," Sarah

said, breaking off a branch from a nearby shrub and smelling it. "One of the burnables, and growing all over the place," she said with an expansive gesture of her hand up the length of the valley. They could just make out the waterfall through the copses of lodge-pole trees. "Plenty of stone, too, ready to build from," she added, jerking her thumb over her shoulder at the rocks behind them.

"Not bad at all," Joe Marley said, already closely examining a handful of the ground vegetation and discarding the varieties he recognized. He was the team's botanist.

"It is very pretty place here," Leila Massuri said in her careful English, her contralto voice making inflections almost musical. She gazed around her with an almost dreamy smile on her unusual face. She was Maltese by birth, corralled by the Catteni in a demonstration raid in Marseilles. "So why was it blocked off?"

"We look closer," Zainal said, and he pointed at Joe, Sarah, and Whitby. "You go right with Slav. Rest of us go left and meet at falls."

Zainal gestured for Fek and the rest to accompany him as he waded across the stream, not more than knee height at this point. Once on the other side, they spread out in a loose line, checking the ground, noting which of the low bushes would bear fruit in season, and generally sizing up the environment.

"No rocksquats. That's odd," Kris said when they had been traveling a few moments. She pointed to rocky projections where the stupid but tasty creatures would be likely to perch, since they enjoyed the sun.

"There were some," Zainal said, and pointed to a little heap of bones just visible through the branches of a low shrub.

"No night crawlers then," Leila Massuri said with a shudder. She was a Fourth Drop and remembered all too keenly that the person next to her had been absorbed by a night crawler before her horrified eyes just as she was waking up.

"I'm not sure I like the possibility of more omnivores," Kris said, although, in truth, they hadn't seen much in the way of other hostile creatures in their considerable travels, except for the aerial marauders which either Slav or Fek warned them about. They camped in the vehicle or on rock heights to avoid earthbound scavengers.

"Things do die of old age or of falling off high places," Leila suggested.

"This stream gets swollen, to judge by the height of these banks," Kris said, pointing to them.

"Spring melt," Whitby said. They could not see the higher ranges, now hidden by the unbroken line of cliff surrounding the valley; mountains which were snow-clad all year round. Sarah McDouall had quipped that it must have annoyed the mechanicals to have so much unusable uphill land. Whitby's face had had a hungry look on it as he had surveyed the towering peaks.

"Never did get to the Himalayas," he had murmured, "but those buggers'd be great fun."

"Later," Zaïnal had said, but grinned as if he understood the mountaineer's yearning.

Now the Catteni stopped to squat beside dried dung, partially covered by dirt. Grooves did suggest the claw marks of an animal of considerable size.

"Old," Zainal said, finding a stick and poking the droppings.

"Big," Kris remarked, and looked around the glade.

Zainal picked up the desiccated patty and dropped it into the sack he kept for fire makings. Then they all continued on their sweep, more vigilant now. More dried dung was found but all examples seemed to be old and Kris was somewhat reassured.

"Reminds me of a place I went to once in Yellowstone Park," she said when they reached the far side of the valley, and its stony barrier. Craning her head, she peered upward, looking for cave entrances, but saw nothing, not even a ledge to give access to even the most agile creature. "We could use this wall for backing and build outward," she said. "If we could get one of the vehicles to maneuver through the pass so we could transport all that stone someone dumped across the pass."

"We'd need explosives to move the lower rank," Whitby said. "They were planted there to stay."

"To keep *what* in?" Kris asked with a shiver for whatever that might be.

Zainal shrugged but, by the way he was examining everything, Kris rather thought he could see the valley as a human settlement, too. The valley could accommodate several hundred folks, leaving plenty of elbow room. Of course, first they had to find out why the valley had been so tightly sealed.

Despite that consideration, she found herself looking for likely home sites. Imagine, a proper house at ground level . . . maybe even steps to a sleeping loft . . . one with plenty of headroom. She glanced over at Zainal's large figure quartering the ground ahead, searching, searching. Considering how much time he'd spent in space, he seemed completely at ease on planetary surfaces. He looked over his shoulder and beckoned for her to join him.

More bone, larger ones this time.

"A six-footed animal. Too small for loo-cow," and he held up what looked like a handful of thigh bones, then a smaller one that fit neatly into a clean socket. Rubbing his fingers across the bones: "Chewed, too." He pointed to obvious tooth marks. "Wouldn't want to meet that on a dark night."

Kris grinned, as much for his use of the slang expression as for a sentiment she could immediately share. He fiddled with the bones, making her hold the front set of legs, trying to get a size on the animal. The skull had been smashed into fragments, including the jawbone, although a scattering of molars and pointy teeth did not suggest to Kris that this had been a herbivore.

"That should please the biologists," Whitby said, joining them. Leila and Fek peered over his shoulder. "They said there had to be other carnivores for ecological balance." He picked up a fragment of the cranium and tapped it. "Hmmm. Thick. And yet crushed like a melon. Wouldn't like to meet what did it."

"A sentiment we all share," Kris remarked dryly, letting the bones fall out of her hands. Several smaller ones shattered. "Been here a long time if they're that brittle."

"Hmmmm," was the response from Zainal.

"Caves, possibly?" Zainal added.

"Haven't seen any yet," Kris said cheerfully, and then Zainal had them spread out again to search.

Though they came across more scattered bones, some in advanced states of decay, nothing else came to light. They reached the lake first as the other scouts were finishing their explorations of the other side, which was wider at the point.

Suddenly Joe let out one of his earsplitting Australian howls and gestured broadly for them to come on the double to the cliff wall where he was standing. Zainal strode into the stream without a second thought but Whitby pointed to a convenient scattering of rocks and boulders to get the rest of them across the water. Zainal was up to his chest in the center of the stream but he was already running toward Joe and the others before the rest managed to cross.

"I don't like the look of this," Joe said, holding aside branches so that the skeleton, grotesquely draped on the scattering of rocks, could be seen.

"It's human," Sarah said. "Or was." She was pale under her tan.

Kris peered briefly, enough to see that the skull was human but not all the rest of it. No leg or arm bones, just the torso. Slav and Fek looked and nodded.

"Bird," Fek suggested, gesturing the swoop of the predatory avians.

"Could be," Joe cleared his throat and let the bushes fall back.

Suddenly they all were craning their necks back to scan the top of the precipice.

"Ah, they'd have attacked before now if they were nearby," Joe said. "You haven't heard anything, have you, Fek?" he asked.

Fek shook her head and pointed above her head. "I hear high."

"We do know that the avians always come down from the mountains when they attack," Sarah said, her color returning, as she and the others, moved toward the cover of the nearest copse of trees.

"I listen good," Fek added, touching both ear holes.

"We found some piles of other bones, all old, some even partially embedded in the dirt," Joe said. He sighed as he let his gaze rove across the valley. "Too bad. It'd be a great place to set up a permanent headquarters."

Zainal was shading his eyes from the now noon-high sun to look at the straight cliffs that formed the boundaries. He shook his head. "We must know why," and he pointed back to the barred pass. He clapped his big hands together, startling everyone, so he grinned. "There are fish in the stream. Let's catch and eat. We have time."

So far all the brook and lake denizens had been edible with the one toxic exception of a multilegged bottom-hugging worm that appeared only in stiller water.

The dung that had been collected gave off such a stench that they doused the fire with water and started a new one in a fresh place, using windfall branches. Whitby outdid everyone else by catching the orange-gray scaled fish with his bare hands. They all ate their fill and there was enough cooked fish left over to save for the next day.

Worrell and Chuck Mitford were enjoying a few pints of beer by the fire when they both heard a growling bark. With no dogs on Botany, the unexpected noise had both of them reaching for their daggers while Mitford roared for a sentry's report.

"Nothing's moving, sarge," the call came back. "And First Moon's bright enough to see klicks in all directions."

A second bark, which had at least three syllables to it, sounded again, with a hint of impatience. Instantly Worrell reached for the pouch in which he had put the thin plate that Mic Rowland had discovered.

"How did Leon say you operated one of these things?" Worrell whispered at Chuck.

Chuck took the object from his second in command and depressed the first button. "Tikso damt. Chouma," he said in a guttural voice as if he were expectorating rather than speaking. He put the unit down on the table beside them and glared at it.

"Didn't know you spoke any Catten, sarge," Worrell said, impressed.

"Whoever it is wants a report. I told him later. And to be quiet," said Chuck Mitford. "At least I hope that's what he'll understand I said. Where's Zainal?"

"Still hunting safe places up in the hills."

"I'll see can I reach him," Mitford said, and connected his unit to the aerial socket that served Camp Rock, high up on the cliff. He let it ring awhile. "Asleep or out of range. Well, let's keep after him until he does answer. Come to think of it, Leon Dane knows more Catten than I do. At least enough to stall them until Zainal gets back."

Leon Dane was on duty, but not occupied, when Mitford and Worrell went to the infirmary caverns. He had already been given the injector and drugs but had put them aside until Zainal could tell him what he might know about the contents of the vials.

"So someone's looking for those the midnight beasties ate up for us," Leon said with a faint grin. "Someone forgot to brief the landing party about Botanical life-forms. Served 'em right. D'you think they were here to collect Zainal?"

"Only reason I can think of for them to send four," Chuck Mitford said with a snort. "That wouldn't have been enough of a guerrilla gang to do doodly against us but sufficient to snatch a man. Zainal did mention that he was wanted back home for a duty of some sort he'd rather avoid. Maybe they want him badly enough to come after him."

"Lemme see the unit," Dane asked, and Chuck handed it over. "Oh, that's the idiot kind. Already preset to its destination. So what do you want me to report?"

"Do they give a damn if the team landed safely?" Chuck asked.

"I doubt it."

"Then let's say that they're hiding out. Haven't located Zainal . . . no, make it target personnel."

"Emassi?" Worrell suggested, and Chuck nodded agreement to the change.

Leon scribbled what looked like hieroglyphics on a sheet of paper.

"You can write it, too?" Worrell asked, more impressed.

"A little," Leon said with a wry grin. In his professional capacity as a surgeon, working on injured Catteni under the eyes of their medics, he had been in a very good position to pick up the language as well as aid the subversive elements in Sydney. "Most of what I learned is either medical or military. I can't ask for my aunt's pen on the table or order a meal. But I can spout real good Emassi-like orders." He scribbled something else, this time in English. "How does this sound, sarge? 'Emassi not here. Moving to find. Report tomorrow this time. Do not contact.' "

"That sounds about right. They'd hide from our people during the day," Chuck said, thoughtfully. "That'll give us some time at any rate. You can say that much?"

"Too right," Leon said, grinning broadly. "Most fun I've had all week."

They all went outside and up to the top of the Rock for a clearer message. The moon shone down on the trio.

"Right out in the bright light, too," Leon said, shaking his head and grinning. Then he sobered, depressed the appropriate send stud, and, with his free hand clutching at his throat, growled out the message in a hoarse whisper.

He released the stud, counting. He shrugged. Depressed the stud and repeated the message. This time a single word answered his effort.

"What was that?" Chuck asked.

Leon gave him a conspiratorial grin. " 'Kotik.' Means 'Accept.' Nothing about doing a good job or anything but Catteni don't expect thanks, do they?" He handed the unit back to Chuck Mitford. They were starting back down when he had a sudden thought. "Hey, maybe I should have sounded feminine. You did say you think one of the victims was a female?"

"One set of boots was much smaller," Worrell said. "But," and he scrubbed his head, "I don't think women lead many Catteni commando units."

"No," and now Chuck's tone was smug, "though they might just have sent along someone Zainal might be glad to see about now . . . as bait."

"Guessed wrong, didn't they?" Leon remarked in a level tone.

It was when Kris, Sarah, and Leila decided to have an afternoon swim that they found more skeletons, gleam-

ing white bones in the shallows among the thick water
reeds that grew there.

"That does it," Sarah announced, refastening her
coverall. "Makes me wonder what the fish we had for
lunch had for lunch."

Leila looked slightly nauseous.

"Sarah!" Kris exclaimed. Medics often had displayed
a ghoulish sense of humor. She did have to swallow
before she added: "We'd better see what kind these
are."

Zainal waded in to fetch some of the nearer skeletons,
which were identified as loo-cow, rocksquat, Turs, and
another human skull, still partly attached to its neck. It
was Leila who found the odd scales and quills. No one
had taken any more than a glancing look skyward for
any hovering avian predators but everyone agreed they
didn't seem to be feathered, so perhaps they used the
lake for bathing or in a grooming ritual.

"But they could just fly in and out. That barrier
wasn't for them," Sarah said, frowning over the puzzle.

"It must have been something real bad for the Farmers to want to keep it contained," Kris said, trying not
to shiver. She glanced up to see the position of the sun.
"I move we get back to the vehicle and out of here. I
don't want my next place of residence to be that lake."

So they put out the fire and retraced their steps to the
barrier.

"Start up," Zainal told the others. "Whitby, with me.
I look closer at stream . . ."

The two trotted down the other end of the valley. Kris,
Leila, and Slav made the first ascent on the ropes. When
Kris gratefully reached the top, she could see Zainal and
Whitby having quite a gawk where the stream went
through the bluff. The water boiled up over whatever
outlet there was for its flow and made a wide pond at
cliff base. She wondered what Zainal had hoped to learn
from scrutiny. As soon as Fek, Sarah, and Joe joined

them, they continued on up the cliff, reaching the top just as Zainal and Whitby surmounted the slanted barrier and began to unhitch the rappel equipment. The others started down to the vehicle but Kris waited for Zainal and Whitby.

"Well?" she asked as Zainal pulled himself up beside her.

"Something could swim through underneath," he said.

"Have to have been damned desperate to take such a risk," Whitby added, "unless you've some amphibious species here you haven't told me about yet."

"On Earth large carnivores will swim," Kris said.

"On Earth," Whitby agreed, nodding as he mopped his forehead and face. He looked back down at the daunting rock face. "If whatever it was had nothing left to eat, even the fish, possibly it would take such a risk. But I would still rather not meet whatever it was. Let's take a look at that aerial—"

His words were broken off by the loud buzz of Zainal's portable.

"Worrell here. You guys all right?" The Aussie was shouting into the speaker.

"Yes, all right. Deep in a valley all day," Zainal explained.

"Oh. Well, a problem dropped in here the other night," he said. "And you're needed back as fast as you can make it, Zainal."

"What sort of problem?" Zainal asked but Kris thought from the twinkle in his eyes that he had some idea. "They look for me?"

"We think so. Only they weren't briefed proper."

"Night crawlers?" Zainal asked, and grinned when Kris shuddered.

"You bet," and Worrell sounded pleased. "And someone's asking them questions on the portable com-unit that was about all that was left of them . . . barring the shoes. Leon told whoever called that you weren't here and they were still looking.''

"You want me to give myself up?''

If Zainal hadn't been grinning like a loon, Kris would have gasped.

"Hell no, Zainal,'' and Worrell's tone was indignant. "Chuck's got an idea.''

"I wonder if we have the same one,'' Zainal said, winking at Kris. "We come as fast as possible.''

"Find anything good?''

"Tell you when we get there.''

Worrell disconnected and Zainal replaced the unit in its pouch, fastening the flap.

"Should I know what I just heard?'' Whitby asked respectfully, but his curiosity was apparent.

"Why not?'' Zainal said with a shrug, and nodded to Kris to explain.

Whitby had breath for a good chuckle over, "I drop, I stay,'' and Zainal's demonstration about the night crawlers and showing the hand unit that proved the planet possibly had another owner.

The question which Whitby did not ask, nor did Kris volunteer to answer since she didn't know it, was what duty was so important that Zainal had to be abducted by stealth.

They had reached the ground now.

"We go back to camp as fast as we can,'' Zainal said.

"We're five days away,'' Joe protested.

"We took side trips up here,'' Zainal reminded him. "We take turns. Drive all night.''

"Hey, it sounds important.''

"Dirty work with cross feet?'' Zainal asked.

"Cross*roads*,'' Kris corrected in spite of realizing that he was being deliberately obtuse.

"Sticky wicket, huh?'' Joe said, and neatly finished recoiling the ropes. "Let's move out. I'll drive first. I've had a breather.''

Both Slav and Fek liked to stand up in the front of the load bed of the vehicle, hanging on to the frame, staying alert and watchful. Sarah and Leila sat in the wide front seat with Joe. Kris, Whitby, and Zainal arranged themselves on the bedrolls in the back. Zainal then slid down until he could put his head on Kris' shoulder, folded his arms, and promptly went to sleep in the smooth-riding air-cushioned ground machine.

CHAPTER 2

They arrived back in camp rock by sunset of the next day, having pushed the vehicle to the limits of its panel-supplied power. Joe was of the opinion that the two full moons had been bright enough to keep the power levels high but Whitby and Leila had argued the point. It made an interesting discussion during the long hours of the trek, when they halted only long enough for natural requirements and to bag a few rocksquats. Joe turned out to be correct about the power, though the vehicle had slowed down considerably.

The sentry hailed them on their approach and rang the bell so that Worrell and Mitford were awaiting them in the parking area, one of Camp Rock's newer amenities. A big hauler and a small runabout, reserved for Mitford's use, occupied the space.

"We heard the transport," Zainal said as he swung down from the driver's seat. "Another drop?"

"Yeah, another thirteen hundred reluctant colonists," Mitford said with a grimace.

"Your species shouldn't be so difficult to manage," Zainal said with a grin.

"We also had to answer another message," Mitford said, showing his teeth.

"Tell me," Zainal said.

"We'll just unpack," Joe said tactfully, and gestured to the others.

Zainal caught Kris' arm as Mitford and Worrell started up the stone steps that led to the height's office. The two-roomed stone building had been built on a leveled-off area, well above any spring flood that might rampage down the gorge that split Camp Rock. Aerials and solar panels were attached to the slated roof of the good-sized facility. A desk, occupied as much by Mitford as Worrell in his capacity as Rock's manager, commanded a view down the length of the camp from the main window. From the other, smaller one, the view was across sloping stone to the first of the Farmers' fields.

Mitford gestured for all to sit on the stools and benches provided. "Leon's coming," he added. "Lemme fill you in."

Zainal nodded.

"The unit buzzed off shortly before we heard the transport angling in for a landing."

"Usual field?" Zainal asked.

Mitford nodded. "They've got that much right at any rate. Leon got a message that suggested the commando group was to meet with the transport and deliver your unconscious body. Certainly there was a group hanging around near the hedges doing nothing, apart from peering around and listening to their wrists a lot."

"What did you say back?"

"Leon told them the search continued."

Zainal frowned slightly. "What words did he use?"

"I knew the right ones," Leon said, entering just then and leaning against the doorframe to catch his breath from the climb. "I always had a team watching me operate on any wounded Catteni. I got used to some of the distinctions Emassi made. So I adopted a hoarse whisper in case it was the female who was to report." Zainal shook his head, his expression inscrutable. "I said," and Leon put one hand on his windpipe to alter the sounds he made, " 'Mekichak Zainal obli. Tik escag eridi. Tikso tag.' " He removed his hand to speak less growlingly. "Which, I think, translates into, 'Moves Zainal much. Hear he returns soon. Report then.' " Leon raised an eyebrow at Zainal.

It wasn't often that the big Catteni burst out laughing as he did now, grinning broadly and obviously also enjoying some sort of a personally satisfying private joke. "You don't know it, Leon, but I am always moving a lot. You said exactly what they will believe. Where is the unit?"

Leon slid it out of a chest pocket. "Since I'm the only one who knows enough Catten to answer, I've been in charge of it."

The communicator looked much smaller in Zainal's large hands and could be slipped into a pocket or down a boot. He examined it carefully, his smile broadening again.

"This is very good. Very good," and Zainal's eyes sparkled with amused triumph.

"These were found in a boot," and Dane very carefully laid the other three items on the table.

Zainal held one vial up to the light and snorted. "Vikso. In very small doses, it will be useful to you, Dane. Makes muscles weak," and he pretended to sag like a limp string puppet before he handed it back to the surgeon.

"So, they knew they'd have to knock you out," Chuck Mitford said, tipping back in his chair and folding his arms across his chest. "Care to tell us why they'd go to this much trouble over you?"

Zainal chuckled again, still very pleased, and seeming to ignore the question. "This will be useful," he said, and waggled the unit before he replaced it carefully on the stone slab that was the sergeant's worktop. "Now we can set traps. Two would be the most we could get."

"Two ships?" Kris caught on first, though Mitford's chair returned to all four legs as he leaned across the desk, looking so eager and hopeful that Kris caught her breath.

"Two?" Worrell exclaimed, amazed at the audacious prospect.

Zainal nodded, leaning across the table toward the sergeant. "You have captured me. You, Kris, will speak this in a message, but I have fought hard and killed two. You need fast scout before vikso," and he tapped the vial, "wears off. They must land where Emassi scout met us. They must land silent," and he dropped his voice to a dramatic whisper, "with no lights and walk to edge of field to help you move captured Zainal."

"But I don't know enough Catteni."

"You will when you send message," Zainal said, and the look he gave her told her she was in for it now. After all, she'd been teaching him English: turnabout was fair play. "*You* will have made my capture."

"Me?" Kris looked around the room at the others, grinning at her almost maliciously. "Cut it out, you guys," she said with an edge to her voice.

"At ease, Kris," Mitford said, understanding her flare of resentment, and then focused his attention back on Zainal. There was no question that the sergeant would do much to possess a useful spaceship but he was not totally reassured by such sketchy details. "So you get them out of the scout, and preferably disposed of by the night crawlers, and then what?"

"We have one scout vessel."

"And no reprisals?" Mitford was extremely skeptical.

"No reason because the ship will take off . . ." and everyone exclaimed at that, and Zainal glanced about, grinning again. "It leaves to make them believe what will happen next." He turned to Kris. "You will manage to make one more message . . . and then . . ." He slid one finger across his throat and grinned.

"You overpowered us again?" Kris rolled her eyes incredulously. "Boy, will they buy that?"

"Buy it?" Zainal asked. His command of idiom and grammar was increasing but not yet as good as his accent.

"Believe it," she substituted.

"On Barevi I showed you I am difficult to catch."

Kris laughed. "All right. So I manage a message out before you kill me . . ."

"And I alter course . . ."

"*You* alter course?" Mitford asked, suspicious, narrowing his eyes and staring hard at Zainal.

"Certainly, so that moon hides ship to get back here." Then Zainal grinned again. "I will bring Kris with me . . ." and Mitford glowered more deeply, "and Bert Put and the woman, Raisha Simonova—who flew in space from your planet. They learn to use the ship. It is very simple to fly. You may come, too," he added with another grin and a bow to Mitford.

"Thanks, but no thanks," Mitford said with a wave of his hand and a fleeting expression of distaste. "I'll stick to good ol' Terra Firma. But taking the spacers is a damned good idea."

"I'll go in your place, sarge," Worrell said, raising his hand, his expression avid for the experience. "If I could . . ." he added hopefully. "We don't want too many people in on this, do we?"

Mitford shook his head, fretting over flaws in the plan, then caught Zainal's eyes again. "Your guys won't come looking here for the scout?"

"Scout does not leave much trail and they will not be quick to look around here," and he circled his finger in the air, meaning Botany. "They will start looking where I have friends to hide me. If they come back, the scout will be hidden with other metallic stuff at Camp Narrow.

It will not be noticed in a scan.'' Then, after a moment of silence when the others were thinking the plan over, he added, ''The last place they will look for me is here!'' He pointed an emphatic finger at the ground as he grinned at them.

''Well, I'll buy that,'' Mitford agreed in a droll tone with the beginning of a smile on his lips.

''It will work,'' Zainal said with such conviction that Mitford began to straighten up from his crouch across the table. The Catteni paused, a smile tugging at his mouth. ''Then . . .'' and he had everyone's attention, ''the next transport ship to arrive will be surprised and we will have two to use.''

There was a long moment of surprised reflection but Mitford broke it.

''Your people can't be that stupid,'' Mitford began.

''No?'' Zainal said, raising his eyebrows with a sarcastic expression. ''The transport uses only Drassi. Not Emassi. The transports that come here are all in bad condition.'' He grinned again. ''Used over often. So if the ship explodes after takeoff . . .'' and he spread his hands at such a simple ruse.

''The ship will explode?'' Mitford asked, jutting his chin out.

''An explosion can be made with metal left in space to prove accident. That is why it is very necessary to get the scout ship first. It can dump garbage into space. Then, we have two ships.''

''Only one of them is not in good shape,'' Mitford pointed out.

Zainal shook his head in denial. ''Many people here are trained to work with machinery. I am not just pilot. I know how to . . .'' Zainal tapped an impatient finger on the worktop as he searched for a word. ''To . . . repair as well.'' He grinned. ''I have faith in your people, Mitford. Have faith in me.''

''Jesus, Zainal, I do, believe me,'' Mitford said forcefully, slamming both palms flat on the table. "And I think that goes for all here." That vote of confidence was immediately seconded. "And it would be great to know we're not stuck anymore on..." He paused, looked surprised, and then laughed. "You know, I'm not as eager to leave Botany as I used to be." He brushed away that candid remark. "Won't the Emassi retaliate on Earth when they've lost both a scout and a transport here on Botany?"

"I don't think they would." Leon Dane spoke up with a wry grin. "The Catteni I met considered us a short step above aborigines. Our sabotage and revolts are annoyances that will stop when the leaders are all rounded up and dropped here."

"Or elsewhere." Zainal disconcerted them all by that qualification. "There are other planets that need to be ... tested for occupation. Not this one alone. I do have one worry," and he glanced at Worrell.

"I'm almost glad to hear that," Mitford answered drolly. "What?"

"That Lenvec, who came for me in the first scout ship, speaks to a higher commander that we have technology not sent with us, that this planet is in use. That is another reason to capture me again."

"How big are the odds he's done that?"

Zainal looked dubious. "He can be persuasive but," and now he gave a snort, "many Catteni believe only what they like to believe."

"Just like some humans I know," Leon said in a caustic tone.

"So, we might even have something to defend ourselves with if the Farmers come looking for us," Worrell said, looking relieved.

Zainal shook his head. "Only scout has weapons. But two is better than nothing and there are other uses for a scout."

"Our own exploratory missions?" Mitford asked.

"I myself will like to know who the other owners are. Don't you?" asked Zainal. "Also, it is not the Catteni who are your real enemy. It is the Eosi. Who farms this planet, who left that command tower, may be stronger, wiser and better than Eosi." He leaned back then, watching Mitford's expression changing as he absorbed this concept. "I do not want Eosi controlling my people anymore. Or yours. This is the first time I think there is the chance to end Eosi."

"Well, I'll be fucked," Mitford murmured, dropping his shoulders as he relaxed in complete surprise at Zainal's plan. He began to grin, and a laugh started in his belly, a laugh that was joined by Leon Dane's yowl of approval and Worrell's expression of sheer, incredulous delight.

"So that's what you hatched up on the way back here last night," Kris said, eyeing him drolly.

"Isn't that taking on one helluva lot?" Mitford asked, but the gleam in his eye and the jut of his jaw suggested a measure of approval.

"Yes," and Zainal shrugged, "why not?"

Mitford slapped the table again and gave another burst of laughter. "Yeah, why not?"

"We can *try* . . ." Leon said, swatting his thigh with one hand in emphasis. "By God, I want to!"

"Do you think we should?" asked Worrell, hitching his pants with his elbows. "I mean, they may be mad enough at *us* for what we've already done to their neat agricultural enterprise . . ."

"But who put us here in the first place?" Kris asked. "Only why do you have to pretend the transport explodes? And why do you have to be careful returning the scout to Botany?"

"We must joke the satellite."

"Joke?" Mitford raised his eyebrows, "Oh, fool."

"Satellite?" Worrell exclaimed, anxiously.

Zainal held up the slim unit. "They have one because

this relays the messages. A satellite is standard for any colony planet. It sends in reports. It must send in the right ones so we . . . ah . . . fool it.''

''Clarify one point for me, will you, Zainal?'' Mitford asked, and when Zainal nodded, ''Why do they want you so bad for that duty you don't want any part of?''

Zainal gave a harsh laugh. ''I was chosen for it by Eosi. They can choose someone else now.''

''Just what *is* that duty?'' Mitford asked at his bluntest.

The change in Zainal's posture and face, though subtle, sent chills down Kris' spine and caused Mitford to recoil slightly.

''Eosi use your body.'' Then, with a second almost imperceptible change which emphatically told Kris that Zainal would not elaborate on that subject, he went on. ''So, do we take the scout ship?'' His expression altered back to his usual bland one as he looked around at the expectant expressions of Kris, Dane, and Worrell before settling his gaze on Mitford. ''That much is possible but we must act tonight. Kris must learn what to say. I need Bert Put and woman. Is that possible?''

''Can do,'' Mitford said, and reached for the handheld, tapping out the code for Camp Narrow. ''Yo, Latore? Send Bert Put and Raisha Simonova up here on the double, will ya? Something's come up. We need them before . . .'' and he glanced at Zainal, who held up two fingers, ''second moonrise. Okay?'' Then he paused, his eyes flickering with rapid thoughts. ''We'll call this Phase One, and all of it stays among us.'' The other nodded. ''Phase Two we'll talk about if Phase One works.''

''It will work,'' Zainal said with absolute confidence.

''Phase Three . . .'' and Mitford pointed a finger at Zainal, ''is going to need a lot more thinking.''

Zainal was in total agreement.

''Damn it, sarge,'' Leon Dane said staunchly, ''even

the mere notion of . . . Phase Three . . . puts heart in me. Think what it can do to the general morale.''

"I do,'' and Mitford's voice had dropped to a growl, ''and I don't want even a whisper of a happy smile on your faces when you leave here. We're doing well enough right now, better all the time, and I don't want to have to deal with false hopes. Let's take it a step at a time.''

"Don't you mean a phase at a time?'' Kris said.

Actually she wanted to cheer wildly for the surge of hope that Zainal's master plan had given her. Securing the first ship would be a big enough coup. Hijacking a transport would prove to everyone on Botany that they could get their own back on the Catteni. She wasn't at all sure about Phase Three, but having two spacegoing ships gave them a positive advantage in finding whoever did own Botany. Would a Catteni scout ship be able to keep up with the monstrous leviathans sent by the Farmers to collect the harvests of Botany? *First,* she told herself firmly, *get it, then dream.* And if *they* were a species that resented having their supply planets taken over by another spacefaring power, maybe Phase Three would happen. And both Earth and Catten might get free of Eosian domination.

"Right,'' and Mitford gave her an odd smile, ''hijacking spaceships sure beats sitting around waiting for the next drop-ins.'' He caught Zainal's eyes and began ticking details off on his fingers. ''You teach Kris what to say to get the scout down here by second moonrise?'' Zainal nodded. ''So, if the scout buys it, they come down, leave the ship . . . only how'll they know you're there to be picked up? I can't volunteer anyone at night out on a field . . .''

"Air-cushioned vehicles attract no night crawlers,'' Zainal reminded him.

"On the way back,'' Kris added, ''we found out that the full moon's enough to keep power up.''

"Good point," and Mitford went on. "So we've got stand-ins far enough up the field . . ."

"Vehicle will move toward Catteni," Zainal said, nodding. "But not fast because they carry heavy load." He thumbed his chest. "Me."

"Good . . . so there's enough time for the night crawlers to attack. What about the Catteni shooting 'em? That Lenvec Emassi saw what night crawlers do on his last trip here."

Zainal shrugged. "Winter night crawlers are very hungry, very fast, and grab feet. Or we can be humane," and he grinned as he saw the reaction to the word, "and kill before they know. We have fast and silent weapons. Lance, crossbow, slingshot."

"Won't they leave a man on board?" asked Mitford.

Zainal shrugged. "I am drugged. It will take two, three to carry me. If is one, once we open hatch, it is over for him." He tapped the knife at his belt.

Mitford made an approving sort of grimace. "All right . . . everything goes according to plan and you, with your crew, take off and do your disappearing act. One small detail. Kris might be useful to lure the pickup squad down, but if you are overcoming a crew, would you not kill off the female first, the one who drugged you?"

Zainal slowly nodded his head, perceptive enough to know what Mitford did not spell out. "Leon speaks Catteni. I cannot talk because they have record of my voice. Leon can give final message."

"Point," and Mitford looked at Kris. "You understand, don't you?"

Kris did, and did not bother to hide the bitterness she felt for such a suggestion.

"You will go to space another time," Zainal told her, looking from Mitford to her.

"Now, wait a minute, Mitford," Dane began in protest.

"Leon will speak the necessary dying words," Zainal said firmly, his eyes still holding Kris'. "It reassures."

"It had better," and Kris glared fiercely at Mitford. How dare he imply that she and Zainal would be so selfish as to take the ship for themselves if both were on board.

"Why do you need Bert and Raisha?" Worrell asked.

"They need to have a first lesson in flying a scout. More people who know is better." Zainal put an odd smile on his face. "And soon."

"I'll buy that," Mitford said, shifting his eyes anywhere but in Kris' direction. "Phase One is green for go . . . and definitely top-security. Use your team, Zainal, for the driving and . . . the executions. Slav and Fek see well in the dark. I'll send Bert and Raisha to you as soon as they get here." Then, in a complete change of voice and manner, "Did your patrol find anything interesting before you were recalled for this?"

Astonished by that business-as-usual switch, even in Mitford, Kris glared at him.

"A very interesting valley," Zainal said, rising and popping the unit into his pocket before he picked up the sack of empty boots. Leon took charge of the medical items. "Let Joe and others debrief." Then he held out his free hand to Kris. "Now, you must to learn to speak like Catteni female."

"After all you've done," Leon Dane muttered, exiting behind them. "Surely he can't doubt your integrity."

"Not to worry, Leon," Zainal said.

"I do all the worrying," Worrell said, but his tone made it obvious that he felt Mitford's precaution of keeping Kris out of space unnecessary.

"Don't worry about tonight," Zainal said, sounding, to Kris' ears, far too cheerful considering what he had just set into motion.

Then Kris found her mind going back to the echo of his colorless voice saying, "Eosi use your body." Small wonder he wanted to avoid that duty. She knew without a doubt that he would have hated possession. And yet, his original comment on "that duty" had indicated that it was considered an honor for an Emassi, and one they undertook with some pride. Had Botany wrought a great change in him, or was it simply that he now had an escape from such a hideous future? Then she began to wonder how deeply the possession went: Was just the body used as a vehicle for these mysterious Eosi? Or did they subsume the entire personality, leaving nothing of the original man? Or . . . what?

"Don't think about it," Zainal said softly, touching her elbow as they reached ground level. "I do not mean Mitford." Then he hailed the other members of their team, obviously waiting a turn to report to Mitford. "Go on up. He's waiting to debrief you."

"We're in our usual abode," Sarah told them as she followed Joe up the steps. "We've already put your gear there."

"Good. We have a small job to do at second moonrise. I tell you later."

Kris knew Sarah was dying to ask why Dane and Worrell had been in Mitford's office for an ordinary scout debriefing.

"We swim first?" Zainal asked as they made their way to their quarters in Michelstown cave.

"You bet. I think better cleaner," Kris said, and besides, not only could she use the immersion in the cold waters of the lake to reduce her anger but she also needed the privacy with Zainal . . . if they had the lake to themselves.

They did, and there were clean overalls in their quarters to change into. Zainal put the Catteni communicator carefully in the pouch with his portable unit in his fresh clothing before they left for their wash.

. . .

He seemed eager to make this a special occasion, too. They spent time soaping each other and then swimming exuberant lengths against the lake's deep current within the roped safety area before emerging to dry each other off. That led to a chance to release tension. In moments like these, Kris wondered just how much Zainal really did deviate—no, differ—from other Catteni and even Emassi. She knew that her association with Zainal was not universally accepted. There were incidents of spitefulness with each new drop but gradually, over the past months, that had altered—with very few exceptions— as most Botany settlers learned just how much they owed to Zainal's presence on the planet. Xenophobia was not encouraged by Mitford or Easley or any of those involved in introducing this world to its new residents.

Her pleasurable ruminations were rudely interrupted the moment they started back up the stairs to the main cavern, as Zainal barked sounds at her.

"We're starting already?"

"Second moon rises soon. You must be ready."

"I gotta know what the sounds mean, Zainal," she complained.

"Get the sound right and then I tell you meanings," he said, and repeated the four staccato syllables again. She did her best to imitate . . . though the combination of fricatives was enough to choke her. She'd already noticed that characteristic of the Catten language. Sort of like German with a French accent . . . or maybe guttural French with a very bad German accent, and a little Chinese for seasoning.

She managed to get the first set of syllables to his satisfaction by the time they reached the main cavern. Food was still being served and they stood in line for their portions, which they took to the privacy of one of the lookout levels, out of earshot of those who were enjoying their meal outside in the mild evening. Botany's primary had not yet set but the first moon was already above the eastern hills, a pale ghost in what was left of the sunlight. That reminded Kris that time was a constraint.

Because she had always learned better using visual aids, Kris took a sharp pebble and scratched out the phonetics of what Zainal coached her to say . . . as well as she could. Just when she thought her mimicry was accurate, Zainal would shake his head.

"What's the matter with that?"

He shook his head again but patted her shoulder. "You don't sound . . . mean."

"Mean?"

He growled out the words she now knew meant, "Report. Found Zainal. He fought hard. Two dead. He is drugged. Land where Lenvec did. No lights. Meet in field."

She tried again, as deep in her throat as she could, still realizing that even that wasn't perfect.

"Look, I'll growl a whisper. How'll they know the difference?"

"They might." Then he held up his hand. "What was it that Leon did to sound hoarse?"

"Grabbed his throat," and doing that, she repeated the phrases once again, hoping she wouldn't accidentally strangle herself.

"That's it," Zainal said, bringing both hands together in a clap of approval. "Now, listen . . ." and he rattled off a sentence of which she understood three words, "report," "dead," and "land."

She told him what she understood.

"You may be asked. You must know what to answer to any question."

"What about 'I don't know'?"

"You must sound as if you do know all. So, say first, 'Chouma'—'quiet'—as if you can be overheard. Then 'Schkelk' . . ." and Kris sat upright with surprise because she knew what that meant.

" 'Listen'?"

Zainal grinned with surprise as he nodded. "Say it as harsh as you can because you are dealing with a stupid person."

"I heard it said that way often enough on Barevi," Kris said in a rueful tone, and then spat the word out with appropriate venom. Zainal laughed and gave her hand an approving squeeze.

"Just use that tone with all the words and they will not argue with you. You sound almost Emassi. After 'Schkelk,' you repeat the original message to be sure they heard you right the first time. Next you say, 'Kotik?' in the way which means they are not to question you again."

"Got it."

He drilled her and drilled her until her voice became hoarse enough without a need to strangle herself. She was surprised to see that First Moon was bright and high when he finally said she was good enough.

He took out the unit and held it up. "Now!"

"Now? You mean, we do it tonight?" She panicked. She wasn't ready yet. "But Bert and Raisha . . ."

"They are here. I saw them drive in. I brief them, too. So we send message now. All is fresh in your mind. And mouth."

He pressed the finger pad and, much too quickly for Kris' peace of mind, a voice responded. Kris gulped and began her well-rehearsed message, overriding one question with as harsh a "Schkelk" as she had ever been given. Zainal nodded assurance, wagging his hand to reassure that the interruption meant nothing. She said, "Chouma," as nastily as she could, and went right into the prepared speech again. By this time she was so scared that her final "Kotik?" came out every bit as savage as the worst Catteni guard's.

An almost meek "Kotik" plus two syllables she

didn't understand was the response and Zainal depressed
the disconnect button.

"Baby, you were great!" And Zainal tousled her hair
and pressed his cheek against hers with great affection.
That had become his special caress for her.

"But what was that last bit?"

"Your name. You are, or were, Arvonk."

Kris made a face. "Awful name."

"Useful to know."

"They answered awful fast."

Zainal considered that. "They want Zainal bad. They
are there till they get me."

"In a bigger ship?"

"The scout is ship enough for this errand."

"They're *not* getting you!" she said, jumping to her
feet.

"No, they are not," he agreed equably, and took her
hand as they made their way down and across to Mitford's office.

Mitford must have been watching because the group he
had been speaking to were abruptly dismissed. Surprised, they passed Zainal and Kris on the way up the
steps. Bert Put, his lean face alight with anticipation, an
Raisha Simonova raced across the gorge to catch up.
They didn't until Zainal and Kris entered Mitford's office.

"You got the message through?" Mitford asked.

"They come. Kris spoke like good Emassi." Zainal
was grinning with obvious pride as he held the door
open for her.

"I had to say it often enough to get it right," she said
gruffly, and, with instant solicitude, Mitford offered her
a cup of the herbal tea that everyone had come to enjoy.

Bert and Raisha came in and took seats, but so ten-
tatively that Kris knew they had no idea why they had
been summoned.

"Have you spoken to your team yet, Zainal?" Mitford asked.

"Not yet. They will do what needs to be done with no problems."

Mitford grunted and scratched the back of his head. He still did not look Kris in the eye. Which somewhat appeased her.

"May I have paper?" Zainal asked, and Mitford quickly supplied him with sheets and a pencil. With his usual quick sure strokes, Zainal sketched what had to be the interior of the scout. Bert's eyes grew rounder and wider while Raisha watched with avid fascination.

"The interior of a Catteni scout?" Bert asked, incredulous eyes on Zainal's face. "How?" he demanded, and Raisha sat right on the edge of her stool.

"You said nothing to them about Phase One, sergeant?" Zainal asked as he continued to detail the layout.

Kris covered her grin with her hand because Zainal had suddenly turned pure Emassi and Mitford reacted by sitting straight up, exactly as a subordinate should. He did spare one droll but respectful look in Zainal's direction before he spoke.

"Bert, Raisha, we mean to catch us a scout ship tonight," he said, and both gawked in disbelief. "A few nights ago a Catteni ship landed four commando types on a field at night."

"Oho!" Raisha said, and turned pale.

"That would have been their first mistake," Bert said with a smug grin.

"Their second was in thinking it would be easy to find Zainal," Mitford said. "Fortunately night crawlers left boots and some other inedible pieces of equipment. So we can lure the scout back down."

"You mean, like tonight?" Raisha shifted forward on her chair, inhaling with deep delight.

Kris couldn't resist jumping in then. "I told them to

land silently, with no lights, to meet me and an unconscious Zainal. That I needed help moving him as he'd killed two others trying to escape before I could zap him." Raisha looked slightly confused. "One pair of boots was a lot smaller. Cherchez la femme."

"Oh, gotcha!" Raisha said. "Only how do *we* avoid the night crawlers?"

Mitford went through the rest of Phase One and the two gave a small round of applause when he finished.

"Look, I did a lot of training but only one short shuttle flight," Raisha began anxiously.

"I only had two but one as navigator," Bert said, though both were clearly dying to go on despite their inexperience.

"You'll do good," Zainal said, so convincingly that both demurred. "A scout can carry six at most. Four were set down. I think only two remain. Both can be told to come help Arvonk, the contact," and he pointed at Kris. "Maybe not. So, if we have to get in fast and kill, inside is like this."

He walked them through the tight passageways of the scout ship and then using the drawings he had also made of the control panels, talked them through the short preflight sequences. He mentioned the colors of the relevant toggles and drew diagrams of the icons above other controls. They concentrated so hard Kris could almost see them absorb words and drawings into their heads.

"We take Leon, who speaks Catten, to give last warning of trick by Zainal and then . . ." Once again he used his finger across his throat and grinned. "I will show you how to circle moon and glide to land." He turned to Mitford. "We hide scout and then I work you hard to learn how to pilot Catteni vessel."

"You will?" Bert's eyes were nearly popping out of his sockets but Raisha assumed an aura of complete calm confidence and gave a little sigh.

Zainal had certainly made two people very happy. "Study hard now. Kris and I prepare our team."

CHAPTER 3

For a plan that had been so hastily put together, it could not have gone more smoothly. Kris was shaking badly when the comunit buzzed but Zainal had rehearsed her in two more phrases.

"Arvonk," she said, hand on her windpipe, and added in harsh Catteni, "See you. Glide in. Chouma." Which she added on her own.

They could just make out the ship in the gleam of the rising moon as it settled silently in the corner of the field. A brief glint of muted light was cut off as the hatch closed.

Zainal was pretending to be one of his own captors, Kris the other, while Leon, being tall, was plainly leaning against Zainal as if unconscious. Joe Marley, face blackened, hunched over the controls of Mitford's usual air-cushion machine and eased it forward at a slow walking pace.

The first surprised burst from the Catteni was the signal for Fek and Slav to rise from their crouching positions and dispatch both intruders with silent lances. Then Joe increased the power of the vehicle and they whizzed down the field to the scout. Zainal hit the exterior release and Bert and Raisha bolted through as soon as the hatch was wide enough. It was Leon's turn now.

"Stolix Zainal," he called out, trying to sound triumphant but listening to be sure there was no sound of another person on board.

Zainal pushed past, knife at the ready, and strode with no stealth at all toward the bridge in the prow of the small spaceship. Those listening outside heard him slide a panel.

"Were only two," he called back.

"Permission to come aboard, sir?" Bert asked, not quite facetiously as he adhered to protocol.

"Permission given," Zainal said, and Kris heard the relief in his voice.

"I just want a quick look," she said, and followed Raisha and Bert down the passageway. She wondered if scout crews were chosen because they were physically small enough to maneuver in such enclosed spaces. Zainal certainly had to walk sideways.

Raisha was already seated in one position, with Bert running his fingers lightly across this and that panel as if confirming the briefing Zainal had given them. The look on his face made Kris gulp. He was having a hard time believing that he was actually preparing to go into space again—not as an unconscious passenger this time. She envied them.

"Kris, one last message," Zainal said, turning her toward the controls. "Say, 'Arvonk icts, stolix Zainal. Escag. Klotnik.' "

She muttered them over to herself and then Zainal pointed to the speaker grille and threw a toggle up. She almost forgot to grab her throat but the fact that she could say the words with authority lent a certain vibrant triumph to her tone. "What did I say?"

Zainal ruffled her hair. " 'Arvonk here, have Zainal. Return. Out.' "

"Out sounds too much like 'Kotik, accept.' "

"Not to Catteni listener. Now, out. The satellite must record the takeoff." He escorted her down the cramped aisle to the hatch, one large hand on her shoulder. At the hatch, he put his cheek against hers, pressing hard before he hit the open button.

Dazed as she was by the night's success and the prospect of being without him for a day or two, she remembered to step carefully down onto the air-cushion platform. She lifted one hand to her cheek, feeling his against hers. Joe drove off.

He was picking up speed when Fek abruptly shouted, "Stop!" Surprised, Joe braked so quickly his passengers had to grab at each other to remain upright and in the vehicle. Fek leaned over the side, peering down at something Kris was very glad she could not see as clearly as the Deski could. With a grab as deft as Whitby's fishing, Fek wrenched something aboard that clattered as it fell. She reached down again, arm at full stretch and her other hand clutching Joe, and got hold of something else. A ray of light illuminated a field that writhed and seethed, for it was a hand beam she had retrieved. Kris groaned and turned her face away. The night crawlers bumped in futile search at the floor of the vehicle.

"You see, Slav?" she asked, grinning the triangular Deski smile as she focused light on the other side of the vehicle, and the other victim.

"I see. I get." And Slav made two equally speedy retrievals. One he held up for Kris to see in the light, and his smile was the broadest she'd yet seen on a Rugarian face. "Stunner." And, in a sudden, unexpectedly juvenile manner, leaned the barrel across his arm and made the hissing sound of a stunner blast.

"Can we leave now?" Joe Marley asked in an edgy voice. He didn't wait for an answer, pushing the control bar hard over. "We could have waited until morning. Crawlers can't digest metal."

"I want tonight," Fek said with uncharacteristic firmness.

"And stop shining that thing around," Joe added testily as they sped up a field which writhed and glistened.

Mitford was waiting in the parking area, as if he didn't quite trust the participants to keep the night's event to themselves. Kris knew herself to be on an adrenaline high so his presence had a certain sobering effect on her. He gestured for them all to go through the silent camp, up to his office. He had thoughtfully provided beer and the salty pretzel-like snacks. Rugarians and Deski rather liked beer now and then but they were careful not to drink much or often. It had some sort of an effect on their metabolism—not a hangover, according to Leon Dane, but something similar—that they did not cope well with.

Kris took a long pull on her beer to settle her stomach, and noticed that Joe did, too. Mitford just waited, knowing from the look of their faces that the hijack had been successful.

"I'd say by now I've been killed and Leon is dying," she began. "Otherwise it all worked out just as we planned . . . with a little diversion from Fek and Slav." She shuddered as the two now dropped the retrieved equipment on Mitford's desk.

He only glanced at the hand beams, which Kris thought would have been more useful than stunners. But, of course, weapons would come first with a military man. He picked the stunner up, turning it over in his hand, checking the controls and snapping something shut. "That's the safety on—now—but you guys wouldn't have known." He almost patted it when he put it down, and took up the other to render it harmless.

"Bert and Raisha looked as if they were having Christmas," she went on. "I had a peek around once Zainal said the coast was clear." Mitford nodded. "Rather cramped. Good thing Leon isn't an inch taller."

Mitford nodded again. "He will be back, you know."
Mitford nodded one more time.

She finished off the beer, took a handful of the pret-
zels, and stood up. "I'm worn out," she said. "Good
night, and thanks, Joe, Fek, Slav. We're the best team
on Botany!"

Mitford nodded.

It was only when she turned over in her bed that Kris
realized she still had the comunit. A lot of good it did
her even if it was a link with Zainal up in the scout ship,
faking the next step of Phase One. She slipped it up onto
her shelf and then let herself fall deeply asleep.

Mitford took her and the unit down to drop field the
second day, when Zainal could be expected to return.
Camp Rock vibrated with rumors, although everyone
connected with Phase One had done their best to act in
a normal fashion. To make sure she gave nothing away,
Kris had to pretend she'd sprained her ankle. Sarah kept
busy getting cold water to reduce the swelling. Joe, Fek,
and Slav worked on servicing their big exploratory vehicle or writing reports. Leon Dane was reported to have
gone off with Zainal, Bert, and Raisha to be at some
emergency at Camp Shutdown. But the rumors persisted.

"We'll still surprise them," Mitford said as he pulled
the little air-cushion runabout up against the hedge.
They'd seen a few of the avian predators on their way,
so he took what cover there was. "I hope."

"We're alone, sarge, so I'll give you a piece of my
mind on that stunt you pulled . . ." Kris had the satisfaction of seeing Mitford flush with embarrassment.
"You had no right to insult Zainal that way . . . and even
less right to use *me* as his surety. I came awful close to
hitting you . . ." She cocked her fist in demonstration.

"Goddammitall to hell'n'gone, Kris Bjornsen," Mitford recovered sufficiently to snarl at her, "I had to! I
do trust Zainal, quite likely more than I've ever trusted

another human being . . . and he is human to me . . .''
Mitford's response was as fervent as hers had been and
his eyes were sparking. ''But I can't take any chances.
With him or you.'' He let out a deep snort, rubbing his
hands through his close-cropped hair in a gesture of ex-
asperation and, oddly, impotence. ''And I need *him*
more. *We,*'' and he meant the colony, ''need him more.''
Then, in one of his swift mood changes, he grinned at
her, impudent and oddly melancholy. ''I would have
liked to be where he is now with you . . .'' He held up
both hands quickly in defense. ''Don't take me up
wrong, Kris. But you're a fine woman and Zainal's the
only man I wouldn't try to muscle out.''

It was Kris' turn to be embarrassed. She had vaguely
known that Mitford fancied her, though after he kept
sending her out with Zainal, she had to decide that she
had imagined it.

''I'm sorry, Chuck,'' she said, all her previous aggravation dissipating. ''It sort of happened and you kept
throwing me at him . . . more or less.''

''More,'' and Mitford let a wry expression touch his
rough features. ''because I shouldn't. And you were the
only one *I* could trust to keep him alive until the rest of
them figured out he was far more valuable alive than
dead.''

''We owe you a lot, sarge,'' she said, and touched his
arm lightly and gratefully. ''But you still made me real
mad yesterday.''

Mitford laughed, stretching his legs out the side of the
parked vehicle.

''Yeah, well, sometimes, I gotta do what I gotta do,
and there was no time to call in some of the brass we
got around here now.''

''Ha!'' Kris grinned back at him. ''You wanted to do
this one yourself without any brass involved. But I
strongly suspect you really better let the others in on
planning Phase Two . . .''

"And Phase Three," said Mitford, turning his head slightly to gaze off down the field, its ground cover matted down by the frequent landings of the transport ship and unconscious bodies. He scratched at his head again and looked back at her. "I'd be stupid, real stupid, not to get the strategists in on Phase Two. But this first one . . . That," and he jabbed his thumb into his chest, "was for me! And you," he added magnanimously. "In fact, I'm sort of phasing me out."

"Oh come now, Chuck . . ."

"No, I mean it, Kris. We've got nearly nine thousand here now. I knew what I was doing for five hundred and eighty-two, even two thousand, but . . . goddammitall, I want to be the one finding the good stuff, not leave it up to you and Zainal, or the Doyles or that Scandinavian crowd. Me, Chuck Mitford, wants to have some of the fun."

"Who'll you have on your team?" she asked, as much to cope with his surprising announcement. She knew very well that the colony had trained men, like Easley and Rastancil and governors like Ayckburn and Chavell, but Mitford had made the colony *work*.

"It won't be the same without you in charge. Not at all," she said with deep regret.

Now he touched her arm lightly and winked. "You won't know I've been gone until I get back. Frankly, my dear, I'd rather someone else who really knows how to plan big pushes carried the can on Phase Two and Phase Three. But you can bet your last nickel, I'll wangle some part in it."

"You wouldn't be you if you didn't."

"Hell, Kris," and he was serious again, "I made a promise to the folks when I took command Day One that somehow we'd get free." He looked off into the distance of morning mist–shrouded fields. "Free, yes. Leave? I'm not so sure about that now." He looked around him at a landscape that no longer seemed alien and unreal.

"I wondered," she said, encouragingly.

"If we could come to some sort of an agreement with the landlords, either or both, this'd be a great place to build up without all those damned minorities messing up their own landscapes. It'd be a fresh start for everyone."

"We've already made one, you know."

He nodded and knuckled his nose. "That I do. But free. I promised that and now we've got a chance to deliver."

"Phase Three might mean leaving here if the brass does buy Zainal's master plan and free Earth, and Catten, from those Eosi."

He gave her a narrow-eyed look of pure devilment.

"Hell, gal, there's at least one more war in this marine. I'm not at all sure of the combat zone or the weapons and you better believe," and he waggled his finger at her sternly, "that I'm not going to be the only one to debrief that Zainal, article, clause, and all the fine print. There's an awful lot we don't know about the Catteni— not to mention the Eosi."

"And our landlords, the Farmers."

They both heard the faint rumbling sound from above, followed by a more vigorous rustling as Slav, Fek, Joe, Sarah, Whitby, and Leila pushed through the hedgerows just beyond them.

Kris managed one startled glance at Mitford, wondering if their very private conversation had been overheard. He winked and pointed to the team, who were panting as if they'd been running a good distance.

"Fek hear," the Deski said, grinning. "Scout comes."

Slav pointed and they could see the speck in the sky that rapidly increased in size. The noise became not louder but clearer. Suddenly more avians than any of them had ever seen at one time swarmed around it: some bodies dropped as oak seeds might, flittering and twisting groundward; some dropped more quickly as disparate sections, while those left alive did astonishing aerial maneuvers and flew away as fast as they could.

"That's handy to know," Mitford said with an approving grunt, and climbed out of the runabout. He stood, arms crossed on his chest, his eyes narrowing as he watched the ship's steady approach.

Was Zainal piloting, Kris wondered, or had he let Bert? Whoever it was made a very neat touchdown about twenty yards from the onlookers with a final burst of steamy exhaust from the portside thruster. The hatch moved open and Raisha jumped down, grinning radiantly. She snapped a salute to Mitford, which he returned.

"Mission accomplished, sir. All present and accounted for." Then she threw her right arm in the air and let out an exceedingly unmilitary yell.

With everyone else, Kris moved toward her, trying to peer around for a sight of Zainal, and Bert, too.

"That Zainal . . . he even let Bert land her," Raisha cried, shaking hands with everyone, even Fek and Slav, who were now accustomed to that odd human habit. "You should see this place from outer space, sarge. It's even more beautiful than Earth. I know that sounds like heresy but it's true! And we know where the satellite is, so Zainal says there'll be an easy way to avoid it by taking different windows out because it's positioned geosynchronously for this area. No way of telling how long it's been up, so it's possible that, even if it was in geosynch with this landing area, it might not have seen the Farmers' ships."

Kris grinned at Raisha, recognizing the high she was on, but Kris also kept looking for Zainal.

"Oh, he's still explaining some of the finer points to Bert. You'll have to drag them out of there," Raisha said. "Sarge, we got good views of the other continents during our landing orbit. It looks like only one other one is being farmed as intensively as this. It'd be smart to have a look and see if it isn't wiser to transfer everything to an unoccupied continent and just put the farms back to the way they were before we got here. Just think how that'd confuse the Catteni.''

"Easy now, Raisha," Mitford said, grinning at her babble.

"Oh!" She looked over to the others. "I should just debrief to you, shouldn't I? But they all know about Phase One, don't they? It's . . ." and she stopped, took a deep breath, brushed sudden tears out of her eyes. "It's just that once the Catteni took over, I never thought I'd make space in a real ship." She dashed more tears from her eyes and made an obvious effort to control herself. "One helluvan astronaut I'm making."

"You did just great, ma'am," Mitford said in military tones, and that did the trick.

"Thank you, sergeant. I appreciate having had the honor to go."

" 'Where no human has gone before.' " Kris heard herself repeating the *Star Trek* phrase.

Mitford inched closer to the open hatch but Kris reached it first.

"Zainal?" she called, damning herself for acting like a possessive female.

"On the bridge!" He sounded elated, too.

As Raisha had said, he was still explaining to Bert yaw and roll procedures and which toggles and handles were used in which situations.

"You landed her on a dime," Kris said, looking from one to the other, and it was Bert who smiled proudly back at her.

"Zainal insisted. Damn near wet myself," he said, but Kris only laughed at him. "There seem to be only so many ways to arrange controls and panels, so it wasn't actually that hard. Not that Zainal wouldn't have taken

over if I glitched . . ." He pointed to the right-hand position at the bridge. "Mind you, those predators coming
at me like F-88s were scary . . ."

"I don't think they'll be back anytime soon," Kris
said. "Those that lived to fly away."

"They don't appear when transports do," Zainal said,
thoughtfully.

"The scout makes a sort of whistle . . ." Kris suggested, and he nodded. She wanted to do something
more than stand there with both hands at her sides,
something to show Zainal how very, very glad she was
to see him. She wished Bert anywhere but on the bridge.

Then Zainal stepped to her side, pulled her so that
their cheeks touched and his lips brushed her ear before
he stepped back. "I go debrief to Mitford." He turned
back to Bert. "Go through the sequences. We must put
her out of sight before we close her down." Then he
pushed Kris around and down the narrow passageway.
"We now know much more about Botany that is useful
to know."

All Kris could think of was that he was back and
Phase One complete and Mitford was willing to go to
Phase Two. As she stepped out onto the field where she
had lain unconscious and vulnerable nine months ago,
she could scarcely believe the change in fortune. And
all because she'd rescued a fugitive Catteni.

As Kris discovered, while the curious—and they came
in droves down from Camp Narrow—inspected the
scout ship, Zainal's debriefing with Mitford dealt more
with the details of what he had observed of the rest of
the planet during the landing orbit than with the flight.
He had piloted in the initial stages, past the satellite,
given the scout some rolls and yaws.

"To look out of control," Zainal said with a grin,
"and then I went behind the moon and out of the satellite's range." Of Bert and Raisha, he said, "They

know more than they think they do. Well trained. Able to drive while I looked. The scout makes fast ... sketches ...'' He looked inquiringly at Kris, who supplied, ''photos.'' ''Yes, photos, details of other continents. Got very close on last pass.'' Zainal grinned. ''Much better than what we were given.'' And he paused, twitching one eyebrow in irritation over the earlier reluctant handouts.

''Raisha said something about only two continents being farmed.''

Zainal nodded. ''One is empty but greening. Other not too good, I think. But I am not farmer.''

''You want us to shift our living space?'' and Mitford waved over his head to mean the campsites the colonists now occupied, ''and keep us out of trouble with the real landlords?''

''Land ...'' and Zainal separated the two words in puzzlement, ''lords?''

''The race which first claimed this planet.''

''Ah, landlords. Yes. This is considerable. A people who could make a prison of that valley we explored do not act as Catteni or Eosi do. They kept something in there, or kept something from getting in. That is not how Catteni or Eosi work.''

''Nor even humans, if you look at history,'' Mitford said in a droll tone, crossing his arms on his chest again.

Then, out of the corner of his eye, Zainal gave Mitford a long look.

''Phase Two, sarge?''

Mitford chuckled, dropped his arms to slap his hands on his knees. ''You found weapons?''

''Enough to overpower stupid Drassi,'' Zainal said almost contemptuously.

''Things are getting more and more interesting, aren't they?'' Mitford said to no one in particular.

Someone nearby cleared his throat and Kris looked over her shoulder at a group of men she vaguely remembered were formerly military and naval brass. Instantly she was alarmed for Mitford's sake. She didn't want him summarily replaced by newcomers who figured they knew more about running this world than Mitford. It was Peter Easley who had cleared his throat.

"Sergeant, when you have a chance, we'd like a few words with you?"

"More than a few and your being here saves me sending for you," Mitford said, stepping down from the driver's seat. "Have you met Emassi Zainal and Kris Bjornsen yet?"

There was a formal shaking of hands all round, hands which Kris noticed were callused and hardened by "civilian" labors. She noticed that everyone was respectful to both her and Zainal and told herself that she was imagining "hostile takeovers." The cordiality of all nine did not seem forced. Their comments ranged from "Well done" to "A terrific boost to morale here."

"What Earth rank is 'Emassi' equal to, Zainal?" Mitford asked, and winked at Kris.

" 'Emassi' is captain," Zainal informed Mitford, regarding him blandly. "Emassi outranks sergeant," he added, and grinned.

"Beg pardon," Peter Easley said, leaning forward politely, as if he thought he had missed something.

"Old joke," Mitford said. "Have you been in the ship yet, gentlemen?"

They all nodded and grins widened.

"Might we get filled in on the details?" asked a silver-haired man—one of the generals, Kris thought. His eyes traveled from Zainal to Kris to Mitford and then Easley. "The implications of such a capture are staggering. Rastancil, Major General," and he added with a rueful expression, "retired."

"As I said," Mitford began, "I was going to send for you as soon as I could report that Phase One was successful." He gestured toward the ship, frowned briefly as there was a scuffle at the hatch. Cupping his hands over his mouth, he let out his parade-ground voice. "EASY DOWN THERE! OR NO ONE GOES IN! LATORE, DOYLE, MAKE 'EM FORM A PROPER LINE. Sorry about that," and he turned back to the brass. "It is successful and I think it's time I turned the matter over to Tactics or Strategy or whatever you want to call an appropriate body."

"Sergeant, if you got this much done," Rastancil said, "you've more than earned the right to sit in on a Phase Two, if you mean what I think you do."

Mitford nodded sharply. "A Phase Two and a Phase Three." He gestured to Zainal again. "Yeah, we do need to talk." More sharp yells of protest from the spaceship. "Lemme handle this first," he said, and slipping back into the runabout, his expression ominous, he circled down to the crowd around the hatch.

"Just what had you in mind for Phase Two, Emassi Zainal?" one of the naval men asked. He had a definite British accent, so Kris placed him as Geoffrey Ainger.

"I am Zainal, no more Emassi," he said. "I will tell you about Phase One."

"Then do it up at Narrow, why don't you?" Kris suggested as yet more people swarmed across the field to set eyes on the space vehicle. "I'll wait here for the sergeant."

"We will all wait for the sergeant," Easley said, but he gestured to a point farther up the field, well out of the traffic from camp to the parked ship, where there was a slope up to the hedgerow, providing seating.

If there were one or two men who cleared their throats or raised eyebrows in surprise at that firmly delivered suggestion, Easley was so deft at easing them the way he wanted them to go that they all complied. When they got to the spot, Zainal crossed his ankles and sank gracefully to the ground. Kris sat beside him and Easley on Zainal's other side, facing the others as they made themselves comfortable. He gave a concise report of Phase One, from the first report by Coo to the moment it landed. Kris was particularly proud of his English, maybe not perfectly grammatical, but concise.

When he was finished, a balding, stockily built man with a weather-beaten face and a fine scar from jaw to temple, held up his hand. "Why would you have been the object of such a concerted kidnap attempt, Zainal?"

"How much do you know of Eosi?"

"More than I like but not enough to understand why they'd hunt out one man," was the reply.

"You are the American general, Bull Fctterman?" A nod answered Zainal's question and Kris gave him full marks for having sorted out names and ranks. Zainal kept himself informed of what sort of people had been dropped, and knew, from Mitford's report, of the presence of military and naval officers. "Then you will know that Eosi command Catteni maneuvers." Fetterman wasn't the only one who nodded. "They pick Emassi to make longer their lives."

"Say what?" Bull Fetterman assumed a posture and an expression that had undoubtedly given him his nickname.

"They subsume the Catteni totally," Kris said. "Zainal would have become a zombie . . . or worse. . . . He wouldn't be dead but he wouldn't have any personality left. Like Heinlein's Puppet Masters' yarn."

"And the first scout came to take you back because you'd been chosen?" Easley asked.

Zainal nodded.

"I heard it was some sort of honor," Rastancil said, though his expression suggested he didn't consider it so.

"It is." And then Zainal grinned. "But I was dropped. I stay." He made a scissors motion with his big hands. "I am off the honors list."

Easley blinked and grinned. Rastancil did, too.

"But it was duty?" Fetterman said.

"Not once I was dropped here," And Zainal pointed emphatically at the ground.

"Someone has to take your place?" asked a black officer—late forties, Kris judged his age.

"Another male of my line. There are several," Zainal said with a shrug.

"What about reprisals here?" another man asked. Kris thought he was Reidenbacker. She'd been reviewing in her mind all the names and occupations on drop lists and was putting them now to faces.

"The last place they will look is here," Zainal said.

"You're sure of that?" Admiral Scott asked, his tone barely civil.

"He's got a point, Ray," Rastancil replied. "If you were deserting, the last place you'd go to is the place you deserted from."

"I do not desert," Zainal said with a slight frown. "I was dropped. I stay."

"Then that's some kind of duty or just a personal preference?" Scott wanted to know.

"Zainal is referring to the fact that no one placed on one of these trial planetary occupations is ever released," Kris said firmly and trying not to glare at Scott. "This is essentially a penal colony, you know. Zainal *refused* the option to leave because that would break another rule: only because it suited his superiors. If they'd retrieved him before he was sent off with us dissenters, it would've been another matter entirely. But they let him get sent." She added that, whether it was true or not, just to make sure Scott wasn't going to call Zainal a deserter or coward or anything like that.

"We concede the issue," Rastancil said, smiling.

"So we can be sure we won't be in for any reprisals because you brought the scout here," Scott added.

"I think we've established that that is unlikely," Easley said, trying to end that topic, "since Zainal deliberately took a course that would take him out of this system on his departure. Ah, here's the sergeant."

Mitford cleared the look of irritation from his face as he stepped down from his runabout.

"Damn Aarens claiming he had rights . . ." he muttered to Kris as he hunkered down beside her. "Finished discussing Phase One?"

"Indeed we have . . ." Easley began.

"Could we have a written report for the record?" Scott asked.

"One's all we got paper for, sir," Mitford said with no apology. "Kris, can you do it for me? So, Zainal, if you'll describe Phase Two just as you told it to me three nights ago . . ."

Zainal suddenly rose to his feet. Even though most of the brass were sitting on a slope, his new position required them all to look up at him, as neat a bit of strategy as Kris had ever seen.

"The transports that make the drops come more often. Your planet is giving Catteni trouble they did not expect. The ships are not in good repair. We have weapons now. We can take a second ship." He held up one hand to forestall questions that goal provoked. The gesture was one of such dignified command that even Scott subsided, scowling. "We take transport. Then scout takes load of metals from mechs and bomb and explode in space far enough up there . . ." He extended his hand upward. "Satellite is geo-syn-chron-ous," and if he sounded out the syllables, he had them in the right order. "Can only see this side. Will see explosion." He made the scissors gesture again.

"Now don't try to tell me the Catteni will let that go without some sort of an in-depth investigation!" Scott said, making no attempt to disguise his skepticism and disapproval.

"Not if crew's last message tells of . . . system's failure." Zainal had to work to find the words, but he found the right ones.

"Two famous last messages and each time a ship disappears?" Scott said, openly scoffing.

"Only Drassi are on transport ship. No big loss," Zainal said coldly. "Catteni . . ." and he laid an emphasis on the word, "do not worry over small casualties. Ship or Drassi. You should know that by now."

"Does that mean you, a Catteni officer, are willing to let *us* kill Catteni?" Scott demanded, watching Zainal with narrowed eyes.

Zainal gave a shrug. "War makes casualties. You know that. I know that. Or," and he let a wry smile play on his lips, "do as Catteni do. Let crew go free, those that remain alive. If they are not found in one whole day," and he lifted a finger, "they live and join us. They are dropped. They stay."

Kris hastily covered her mouth with her hand but she scanned faces to see who understood Zainal's wit. More got it than didn't. These guys were sharp enough. Scott seemed the only hard critic.

"You did know about that Catteni rule, didn't you, admiral?" Mitford asked very politely.

Scott gave him a curt nod.

"With respect, sir, in case no one mentioned it," the sergeant went on, "Zainal was shanghaied aboard that ship in contradiction to that rule. Just in case any of you wondered why he didn't feel he had to comply with any further orders from Emassi."

"Thank you for explaining that, sergeant," Easley said. "I think that should clear up any lingering doubts about where Zainal's loyalties now lie. To return to Phase Two, what good does it do us to have a ship that may not be useful? Even if Zainal believes we can disregard reprisals."

"I think of the Farmers," Zainal said, and all eyes were on him again. "With two ships, we can send one with their transport . . ."

Scott dismissed that notion with a snort and looked away.

"Now, wait a minute, Scott," Fetterman said. "I'm not entirely clear on these Farmers or Mech Makers or whatever you want to call them." Then he turned back to Zainal. "You *want* them to know we're squatting on their land?"

"Squatting?" Puzzled, Zainal looked down at Kris for an explanation.

"Slang for taking over lands or a place that you don't own," she said quickly. "Actually, that's Phase Three." Before they started arguing over Phase Two, Kris wanted them to have some grasp of the scope of Zainal's plans. "Forming an alliance with the Farmers against the Eosi because if they can farm a planet without any sentient being in charge, Zainal thinks they may have a sufficiently sophisticated technology to help the Catteni get out from under the domination of the Eosi—and stop being made into zombies and doing things because the Eosi order them to be done. Like take over Earth."

"Whoa, there, young lady," Fetterman said, but he was grinning and so was Rastancil, while Scott looked more annoyed than ever. "Pretty ambitious, if you ask me."

"The longest journey starts with the first step," she said in a firm but clear voice, and gestured back over her shoulder at the spaceship. "Step number one."

"Kris has a point," Easley said, once again taking charge as he seemed able to do almost effortlessly. "Until this morning none of us would have remotely considered the possibility of hijacking a Catteni ship . . ."

"Having a damaged transport's no damned good . . . for going after Catteni or Eosi or these Farmers," Scott said, standing up.

"But transport allows us to shift a lot of people to one of the other continents that the Farmers are not using," Mitford said, beginning to let his irritation show.

"It's another step to owning ourselves instead of being a goddamned Catteni colony they think they can just walk into and take over when it gets on its feet. That's the usual plan, isn't it, Zainal?"

Kris watched Mitford winding himself up and looked anxiously in Easley's direction, but the man was watching eagerly as if he wanted Mitford to sound off.

"Well, a scout's a start on our Botany Defense Initiative and I'll back Phase Two with every man and woman that's been following me the past nine months." Then Mitford caught hold of himself, took a deep breath. "If we pull that off, too, then we can reevaluate the situation. And there's more than just the Catteni to worry about. There're the Farmers and how they'll take to us being dropped here on their prime real estate without their say-so. Now I know I've mentioned to you that most of us are beginning to think we ought to leave the Farmers' installations alone and find our own. That's why I have scout parties out all over the continent."

"Hold it there a minute, sergeant," Rastancil said, getting to his feet. "Thought you dismantled all those mechanicals so that the Farmers would come and see who was vandalizing their planet."

"That was the only option open to us *then,* sir. But we've been having discussions about that," and Mitford gestured to Easley, Fetterman, and up the hill toward Camp Narrow. "Nor was I the only one who wanted to get off this planet *then.*" He paused. "I'm not so sure I want to leave now. And I know a lot of others have had second thoughts like me. But that," and he pointed back toward the scout ship, "alters everything. Or . . . hell, you should see that as well as I can." And he ended with his arms at his sides, waiting for reaction.

"Definitely the situation has changed," Easley said, and heard murmurs of seconds to that. He seemed to be appraising the moods around him. "Phase Two seems feasible but, as Sergeant Mitford says, it's going to need some intense planning and good timing . . . even with weapons at our disposal. I suggest that we adjourn and discuss ways and means.''

"Scout hides," Zainal said, and pointed toward Camp Narrow.

"You're going to fly it in?" asked a man with a rather rakish mustache as he got to his feet, brushing off the seat of his coverall. "I'd like permission to be aboard, sir. I was mission control on the last shuttle project. Trained as a test pilot. Gino Marrucci.''

Zainal looked to Mitford, who nodded. Then Zainal looked to Scott. "You come, too?''

Someone stifled a chuckle but Scott, controlling his expression, stood up. "I would like to.''

"Ship only holds eight at the most," Kris said, though she'd hoped to be one. "You have to go, sergeant.''

"Then you do, too," Mitford said, jutting out his chin.

"One more," Zainal said. "Air force man?''

"I was air force," the black general said, getting to his feet. "John Beverly.''

"That's settled then," Peter Easley said. "Shall I drive your runabout back to Camp Narrow, sarge? And be sure that garage's . . . or should I say, hangar's . . . ready.''

"Good idea," Mitford said.

Zainal pivoted and, without looking back to see who followed, led the way back down the field.

"Always meant to go see the display at Houston but never found the time," Mitford said conversationally to no one in particular in the group walking in step with him. He grinned as Kris made a hasty leg change to match strides with the others. "Happens all the time with us military types.''

"Okay, okay," Joe Latore was saying when he saw the phalanx moving in on the spaceship, and gestured for those in line to see the ship to make way. Grumbling started until Mitford swung into view, when it was replaced by cheers for Zainal and Mitford.

"We're gonna fly this baby up to Narrow now," Mitford said. "You'll get a chance to look inside later."

"You mean, the Catteni are goin' to be lookin' for it?" a man asked in a nervous tone.

"Naw," Bert said, appearing in the open hatch. He grinned when he saw the delegation, and jumped to the ground, waving those behind him from the last tour to make a quick exit. "Why would a Catteni in his right mind want to live on Botany if he could get off?"

There was good-natured laughter, as those still hoping to see inside the prize began to drift back up the hill.

"Gentlemen." Bert waved the new group in. "Shall I . . ." he began to Zainal, as if he anticipated being replaced.

"You must watch me do it," Zainal said. "These watch, too."

"I'll bet they do," Bert murmured low enough for only Kris and Zainal to hear as they passed him.

Kris stepped up, into the hatch, ahead of the brass. She wasn't going to be left behind this time. Mitford did give precedence to Scott, Beverly, and Gino Marrucci. When they reached the bridge, Raisha was in the second seat and hastily got to her feet.

Zainal gave her a nod and then pointed to Bert to take her place, while he folded himself into the pilot's chair.

"Secure hatch, Raisha," Zainal said, and looked at the arrangement of those standing in the cramped space of the small bridge. He nodded and gestured for them to stay where they were.

Kris inched closer to Mitford, who was just behind Zainal.

"You watch good?" Zainal said to Bert, who nodded as Zainal's fingers moved in slow sequence over toggles and switches. "Got that?"

"Yes, yes . . ."

A quick glance around and Kris saw that Bert was not the only one memorizing the sequence. Beverly and the test pilot were the most eager but Scott's expression was less critical.

"Ve-ry smooth," Beverly said. He was the first to be conscious of the vertical takeoff.

"It is extremely maneuverable craft," Zainal said in an instructional tone, two fingers of his right hand on the grip. "One of its biggest . . ." He tipped his head back, toward Kris, for her to give him the word he needed.

"Assets," Kris supplied.

"Ass-*ets*, not asses?" Zainal asked, blank-faced.

"You pick up too much bad language, man," she muttered as everyone else grinned.

"In space as well?" asked Beverly.

"Better in space," Zainal answered, as he depressed a button on the panel in front of him and began a horizontal forward movement, skimming safely above the heads of those moving back to Camp Narrow.

"That satellite won't see the movement?" Scott asked.

Kris wondered if the admiral would ever give Zainal any slack.

"Not that kind. Very basic and geo-syn-chron-ous," Zainal replied, twitching one shoulder. "I use only . . . guide . . ." He craned his head about, for Kris' help.

"Guidance," Beverly supplied. "Thrusters? Or rockets?"

Zainal made a gesture with his free hand as if pressing the earth away from him.

"We'd call 'em thrusters, I think," Beverly said. "Do they move?" and he rocked his hand to indicate different positions. Zainal, flashing a look at the signals, nodded. He was watching the landscape closely.

"Is there much fuel left?" the test pilot said, looking over the gauges and dials. "Which one?"

"This one," Bert said, and tapped it—a needle point just a shade over a halfway mark.

"Reason two for Phase Two. Transport will have fuel," Zainal said.

"How far will what there is take us?"

Zainal shrugged. "Not back to your Earth."

"What sort of fuel do you use?" asked the test pilot.

Zainal rattled out some Catteni sounds and then grinned at the pilot.

"Can't make here." He made another correction, moved a toggle, and the pilot gasped.

"You're gliding in?"

"No need to waste fuel," Zainal said, and pointed his finger just as the entrance to Camp Narrow appeared in the hillside.

There were a lot of people watching now, waving their hands, mouths open though no sound penetrated the scout.

"Fraggit," Mitford muttered, his face pale, as he grabbed for something to hang on to as the scout seemed to slide down a corridor that had once seemed much wider.

"Easy as pie, sergeant," Beverly said, grinning broadly as they headed inexorably toward the target barn's wide-open doors.

"It'll fit?" Mitford asked, taking a firmer hold on the ceiling handle he had found.

"No problem," Bert said.

Kris sympathized with Mitford. She tried not to hold her breath. The flight vanes on the rear of the fuselage must be just clearing the sides of the alley. Then she noticed someone encouraging the forward motion with hand gestures as he backed toward the barn. Zainal held up one hand, caught the man's attention, and gestured him to stand aside. With the slightest possible touches on the thrust handlers, Zainal lifted the ship above the cliffside, and with equally delicate movements, turned the scout around, lowered it, and began backing it into the barn. The ground crew leaped in front and now made pushing gestures, as he stood to one side so he could judge when to wave off.

"No rear mirrors on this thing, huh?" Mitford murmured in Kris' ear, but he had color back in his face now that they were nearly parked.

The wave-off came and, with one final adjustment, they felt the scout ship settle to the floor.

To Kris' surprise, the observers clapped their hands, even Scott.

"You'd've been a great Atlantis pilot," Marrucci said.

Zainal stood up, squeezing up against Mitford and Kris in the cramped space. "Bert, show Marrucci how to shut her down."

"Can we watch?" asked John Beverly.

Zainal shrugged, looking at Mitford.

"Sure, why not," the sergeant said, and eased himself toward the passageway to give the others more space. But he looked over his shoulder to observe that Scott stayed as well.

"Did it go well?" Raisha asked from her position in the passageway. "I couldn't see a thing with all the bodies in the way but I felt it turn around."

Zainal undogged the hatch and stepped out into the barn, giving Kris a hand down first, and then Raisha.

"Can this be locked, Zainal?" Mitford asked in a low voice because the man who had acted as ground crew was loping up to them.

"There are six of these," Zainal said, showing Mitford the small grayish-brown rectangle in his hand. "I have hidden three. Bert and Raisha each have one. Is that right?"

Mitford looked thoughtful, almost sad. "For now but

I think the flyboys and the brass will decide who gets
to use this baby.''

"Baby?'' Zainal asked, turning to Kris. "Is that like
'boy oh boy,' and 'man oh man'?''

"Ships are generally referred to as 'shes,' female,''
she said, grinning. "And special ships are 'babies.' Spe-
cially good ships!''

"That's a lot of baby,'' Zainal said, with suspicious
laughter glinting in his eyes as he looked down the
length of the scout.

"Hey, Zainal, that was some sweet job of piloting,''
the crewman said, running up with his hand out for
Zainal to shake. "I used to be flight deck officer on the
George Washington . . .''

"Aircraft carrier,'' Kris explained.

"Boy, you landed that baby as sweet as if you'd been
backing her into this hangar all your life!''

Zainal gave yet another of his shrugs. "I had to learn.
And pay for holes made.''

"Didja?'' Somehow that pleased the man. "Need any
more help with her, I'm your man. Vic Yowell's the
name.'' He gave Zainal's hand another shake and then
went to prowl around the vessel.

"All that brass isn't going to take the ship away from
us, are they?'' Raisha asked, keeping her voice down
and her eye anxiously on Mitford.

"Listen up, you lot,'' Mitford said, catching them
with a stern glance, "that ship makes this a whole new
ball game. I know General Rastancil by reputation—he
has a good one. I heard good things about General Beverly . . . don't know about the navy, but I do know,'' and
he waggled his finger at them, "that there'll be some
changes and we gotta be flexible. So let's go with the
flow. Right?''

"Where I flow, you go,'' Zainal said, poking Mitford
in the shoulder with one finger with each word.
"Right?''

Mitford gave a short laugh but Kris knew that he appreciated Zainal's statement of loyalty.

"I don't know about you lot, but I need some chow about this time of day." He walked out of the hangar.

"Me, too," Raisha said. "I didn't like Catteni shipboard rations. They tasted like cardboard wadding."

"Healthy," Zainal said as he took Kris by the arm to follow the lead.

"*Will* we get to Phase Two?" Raisha asked over her shoulder.

"For fuel we must," Zainal said.

"So if I get a chance to learn to pilot the scout, I could pilot a transport vessel?"

"You can now," Zainal said, grinning at her surprise. "Drassi need very simple controls."

"Say, Zainal," Mitford asked, "how many ships do you think we can hijack before they stop landing here or your destroyers come to have a look?"

Zainal just grinned.

They had finished with the noontime meal when Bert and the others who had stayed on in Baby, as the ship was unimaginatively called, joined them at their table. Marrucci and Beverly were full of questions for Zainal about the performance levels of the ship, its cruising range, cargo capacity, weaponry, and maintenance requirements. Kris translated terms as well as she could, with help from both Bert and Raisha when she bogged down over unfamiliar words and meanings. Mitford sent someone for paper and pencil.

"Would you have such a thing as a manual?" Ray Scott asked at one point.

"What good would a Catteni manual do us?" Kris asked, almost defensively although Scott's attitude had modified considerably since the docking hop.

"Diagrams," Scott said, and Kris was ashamed to have missed the obvious.

So Zainal told Bert where to find the service manuals in the pilot compartment. The day became a session of terminology and translation. Engineers were sent for to decipher the schematics while Zainal struggled to explain with his inadequate technical vocabulary. For Kris there was only guesswork, but she came up with appropriate ones more often than the others did. Zainal did know the basic maintenance routines and checks required since he had often flown this type of craft and had had to make repairs.

Worrell arrived at one point and took Mitford off with him. Reidenbacker left later on and took Fetterman with him but Kris was far too occupied with spatial and aviation words to do more than register that there were other faces where those men had sat. There was also no question that the capture of Baby was the best thing that could have happened on Botany at that particular moment.

It was full dark before Zainal suddenly shook himself and stood up.

"I can talk no more tonight."

Then everyone became solicitous and grateful and said that by all means he should get some rest.

"You, too," he said to Raisha and Bert. "No sleep last night. Not good. Minds must be rested to learn how to fly Baby." He caught Kris with one hand, Raisha by the other, and gestured for Bert to follow them out.

There was a brief lull in the various conversations as they stood, but by the time they reached the door these had picked up again, and sheets of Zainal's meticulous diagrams were being passed around along with the manual.

All four walked wearily to one of the less crowded end barns. A "people" door had been cut into the larger one and a narrow entry area established before three aisles sectioned off the floor space. Screens of woven reeds divided areas into living spaces, affording a certain degree of privacy. Single pallets stuffed with fluff weed, spare blankets, a rough box to hold possessions, and two stools made up the furnishings of the one Zainal and Kris took. He moved two pallets together. Kris got her boots off, emptied her pockets of the comunit and items she hadn't realized she still had with her, and lay down. Zainal covered her with a blanket, before removing his boots and settling down beside her, reaching out to grasp her hand before he took one deep breath and fell asleep at the end of it. She wasn't far behind him.

Still unaccustomed to Botany's longer diurnal period even after nine months, and despite the excitements and exertions of the previous day and night, Kris found herself waking before sunrise. Zainal was awake, too, lying on his back, hands behind his head.

"What's up?" she asked in a low voice.

He released one hand, curled his arm around her head to stroke her cheek. "Thinking."

"Good thoughts?"

He nodded.

"Share them?"

He rubbed his knuckles against her cheek: she could see his teeth in a smile in the dim light. "I must outthink Catteni."

She caught his hand, holding it against her cheek as she turned toward him, her lips closer to his ear. "Then there could be trouble over the scout."

"Not here yet." She could feel his cheek muscles lifting as his smile broadened. "Lenvec may not be . . . fooled. Or it is 'joke' this time?"

"Fooled. Why?" She tried not to stiffen against him in concern but he sensed it, far too aware of her body language now, and his hand flattened soothingly against her head.

"He does not wish to do Eosi duty."

"Is he the other male you meant yesterday?"

She felt Zainal's shoulder twitch and the rumble of amusement in his chest. "He is next but may not be chosen." That seemed to amuse him even more. "He has life mate and several childs already," Zainal added as if that should be a consolation.

"Children," she corrected automatically. "Don't you?" she heard herself ask.

"No chosen has life mate but I have two males. Too young to be chosen."

"So if Lenvec is chosen, we don't have to worry?"

"He did not say how soon the chosen must go. If there is time, maybe. He will be commanded where to search first." Then Zainal paused, and she sensed he deliberated on whether or not to continue. He stroked her head slowly. "Maybe . . . he gets better satellite over Botany."

"Higher-tech? More sophisticated?"

Zainal nodded. "But even that will take time." And she felt his laugh. Felt him stop, too. "I must be very careful."

"Shouldn't we tell Mitford all this?"

Zainal gave his head one shake. "Not now. He has enough troubles with—what did you call them—the brass? Beverly, Scott, Rastancil, them?"

"Yeah, they're all brass, admirals, generals: Marrucci was a colonel, I think. Watch out for Scott."

Zainal grunted agreement and surprised her by smiling. "I like a good fight."

"You mean, convincing Scott you're all right for a Catteni? Or getting Phase Two and more fuel for the scout?"

"Both." He gave her hand a warm squeeze. "This gets interesting."

"Don't get smug, Emassi Zainal."

"Me? Never. This Catteni bastard watches his step."

"Zainal! Where did you pick up that language?"

"Is it not correct?"

She knew he was teasing and laughed. "I'm damned glad you know as much as you do, particularly right now . . ."

"For the brass-heads."

She giggled, ducking her head into his chest to muffle the sound. "Brass-heads"—she must remember to tell that to the sergeant.

At Lenvec's insistence, which was beginning to annoy Perizec both as patriarch and commander, he listened to the record tape and replayed the satellite's recording of the scout's takeoff, the suddenly erratic course which straightened into a dive toward the subject planet's second moon, disappearing beyond the satellite's visual limitation.

"But analysis proves that is *not* Zainal's voice. None of them are. What has Personnel said about Arvonk?"

That was the one flaw in Lenvec's arguments. "There is none of Arvonk, who was only a woman and not in service as Emassi. She was used because Zainal had chosen her several times for intercourse."

"There are no other Catteni down there. Who else but another scout could have responded?"

"Some of the Terrans have learned our language."

Perizec snorted. "But not how to operate comunits."

"Zainal could teach them." Lenvec spoke through his teeth with aggravation—an unwise attitude to show his senior and parent, but he had absolutely no doubts that Zainal had somehow escaped capture: had probably piloted the scout off the planet. And then, for reasons Lenvec could not understand in a Catteni Emassi who had been chosen to serve the Eosi, Zainal had returned to the planet. He had not taken refuge anywhere in Catteni space because everywhere he would be hunted: nowhere would he find asylum.

Zainal's taunt "I drop, I stay" was like a pulse in the back of Lenvec's brain. What good did it do Zainal to go back to the planet, no matter what technology had been found there? Could Zainal know the origin of the original occupants of that planet? Was that why he took the scout? What good would such a move do?

"He has somehow made friends with the Terran dissidents," Lenvec went on, desperate to persuade his father to believe him. "Now he has transportation. He has some plan in mind."

Perizec dismissed that consideration as he rose. "For all the good it will do him."

"Sir, for the honor of the family, insist on a second orbital satellite. Geosynchronous does not have sufficient capability to keep a watch on his next moves."

"Next moves?" Perizec regarded his son steadily and with such malice that it was all Lenvec could do not to recoil from such scrutiny. "*Your* next move is to attend the Eosi Selection. No further delay is possible. Is that understood?"

"Maybe the Eosi will not be so blind," Lenvec said in a bitter tone, and when the nerve whip suddenly appeared in his father's hand, he braced himself for the blow. Despite that, the agony rocked him to his knees.

He had to be helped by his life mate to his quarters, where she disobeyed the protocol that required the recipient to endure a whiplash by administering a nerve block. Clern stayed by his side until the medication took effect. Which was more than she ought to have done but did not, as she had probably hoped, appease his bitter resentment sufficiently for one final sexual interlude. Lenvec could think only what he had been deprived of because Zainal had been the chosen of their bloodline. The opportunities and promotions that Zainal had enjoyed because he had been the chosen. Eosi liked their "subjects" to have rich experiences to bring for them to enjoy, to use as guides in their manipulation of their subject species. Lenvec had had to be satisfied with a circumspect life, learning to manage the family estates and accepting simpler rewards than Zainal gathered. Lenvec had even had to rear Zainal's children with his own, since being chosen kept Zainal from having a mate. That was the one privilege Lenvec had had which Zainal did not. And now Clern had to be set aside because Zainal had escaped.

During those long last hours of his single being, Lenvec toyed with suicide but the dishonor would have deprived Clern of wealth and protection, and his sons of their inheritance, which would be considerable. If he could have also deprived his father of honor by taking his own life, Lenvec might well have murdered himself.

His hatred of Zainal, his sense of betrayal, his keen awareness of the injustice done, consumed Lenvec, even when, supported by a blood pride he had not known he possessed in such depth, he was accompanied by Perizec to the vast complex reserved for Eosi. He entered with the three other Catteni being presented by their fathers, and Lenvec's resentment flared and deepened. *They* had been chosen: *they* had had the privileges Zainal had enjoyed and he had been denied. But he had as large a measure of Emassi pride as any of them and so he went, seething with hatred and the now deeply embedded ambition to somehow get even with Zainal.

That kept his back straight, his knees stiff as he faced the Eosi Mentat who would engulf him, making him no more Lenvec but all Eosi. A fearsome entity even to an Emassi who had seen what Catteni became when subsumed by Eosian Mentats: that shining immensity in a giganticized Catteni form. That one thought, of eventual triumph, sufficed Lenvec as the subsumption occurred. It kept him from screaming as two of the others, previously willing and proud young men, did as they were engulfed.

Certainly the intense emotion intrigued the Eosi as it settled into the strong new body, and the shell it had been using drifted like the dead thing it had been for centuries onto the highly polished floor of the chamber. Quite unusual, in fact, for the Eosi had made such transfers frequently and was delighted by a novel experience as the last of the personality which had once been Lenvec totally dissolved within the Mentat.

The shell, crumbling into dust, was swept into a receptacle and returned with proper ceremony to Perizec, who waited with other fathers to receive the discarded husks. Of them all, Perizec was the most relieved. He had greatly feared that Lenvec would be found unacceptable, and the dishonor to their bloodline would have been catastrophic. But honor had been served and their family would continue to supply young men to the Eosi and reap more worldly rewards than other, less favored families.

However, Perizec must still discover where the cowardly Zainal was hiding and make sure he paid the price of his evasion. Perizec smiled at the thought of a suitable execution. Private, of course, but the event could be enjoyed by Clern, who had been deprived of her mate, and should be seen by Zainal's sons so that they would have to live with his dishonor as their lifelong penance.

He took the receptacle of his great-grandfather's dust to the family crypt and placed it in the niche prepared for it. He looked at the array of ancestors who had done their duty. Then did his final task: listing first Zainal and then Lenvec as dead. Too bad he could do nothing punitive to Zainal's sons, but that would expose the reason why Lenvec had had to stand in for his brother. There were other, subtler ways to make them pay for their father's defection.

Quite a considerable galactic distance from the Eosian home planet and its expanding sphere of influence, the homing device arrived in the slot designed to receive it on the huge moon installation where such devices were processed. When no message was displayed, the container was routinely overhauled for the malfunction. Such homing missiles were rarely dispatched without cause. No malfunction was discovered. The device had been well engineered and had always operated within its design parameters. The lack of any message was unusual. The container was sent to Processing to identify its point of origin. Since that planet was not one in any sense critical, or even very important, the errant device was shunted to the agency that, from time to time, investigated anomalies. The appropriate galactic coordinates were tagged for investigation during the next regular maintenance circuit.

CHAPTER 4

If those intimately connected with Phase One slept, it became obvious to Zainal and Kris when they quietly exited their quarters at dawn, that others had not.

A weary duty cook had propped her chair back against the wall, her head lolling to one side as she caught what rest she could while the knot of men and women at the table farthest from her murmured urgent conversations and passed papers back and forth.

Though Kris and Zainal had entered the mess hall quietly, their arrival immediately curtailed the discussions. Almost every head turned to see who came in.

"Zainal! Kris!" Peter Easley half rose from his seat and beckoned them over. "Grab something to eat and drink, will you? And join us?"

The cook slept on, snoring slightly, so Kris and Zainal helped themselves to the food kept warm in the pans and the tea in the kettle.

Kris identified not only Scott and most of yesterday's brass but others, obviously called in from the other camps for this session.

"You started something, Zainal," Peter said, rising

and gesturing for Zainal to take his place, while he hooked over chairs from the next table for Kris and himself.

"Phase Two?" Zainal asked, settling himself, and eyeing the mass of papers and charts and lists that littered the table. He sipped.

"You bet," Easley said while several men at the other end of the table resumed their interrupted debate. "I sent Mitford off to bed at third moonrise. He couldn't keep his eyes open."

"How can *you* then?" Kris asked.

"Oh, I caught a coupla hours before we changed guard," and Easley winked at her conspiratorially.

She was somewhat reassured although she had not previously considered Easley, for all the help he gave Mitford during drops, as a surrogate for the sergeant.

"We have discovered a lot of droppees have had military training, and more than enough have commando, SAS, or similar training in their own countries so that we can have our pick of the force to make Phase Two successful," Easley explained in a low voice. "What is needed now is information from you on—"

"What weapons there are aboard the scout," Scott interrupted, "some idea of the interior of a transport ship and what weapons they'd have so we can properly train our personnel."

Zainal took a sip of the hot beverage and gestured that he be given paper and writing implement.

"Breakfast first?" Kris said in a caustic tone, lifting a spoonful from her bowl of porridge. "Army ... and navy, I'm sure ... still function better when fed."

"Miss Bjornsen," Scott began ever so politely.

"Knock it off," Zainal said in a very quiet voice, but he gave Scott a brief, warning look, before he began to sketch the long void of a transport ship outline, sipping as he did so. "Twenty crew, only Drassi armed with weapons. Others have nerve whips ... ." Zainal gave

Scott a long look. "You know about nerve whips?"

Scott nodded slowly and it pleased Kris to no end to realize that he had had at least one incident of intimate knowledge with that persuader.

"Crew carry on back," and Zainal demonstrated tying the whiplash to a handle and slinging the imaginary item to his back. "People unconscious no problem." He outlined the bridge area, the main crew quarters, where they seemed to sleep stacked nearly as closely together as their passengers would be, and then indicated the engine room, air plant, and other essential elements of the transport, including cargo areas that did not have oxygen. That left an empty midsection across which Zainal now drew a series of parallel lines.

"Sleepers don't need much space. Empty one deck, remove, shift upward, empty two deck . . ."

"We were crammed in like sardines then," Easley remarked with a bit of a shudder. "What do they use to keep us in suspended animation?"

"Asleep?" Kris whispered, because she knew Zainal would recognize those words.

"Eosi make. Not even Emassi know in-gre-di-ents," Zainal said with one of his indifferent shrugs.

"So we would have to get the guards, storm through here to secure the bridge . . ."

Kris didn't recognize the voice, nor identify the slight accent, must less the long nonwhite finger that had done the walking, and looked up. The slender man had angled in beside Scott and Fetterman. He grinned at her and touched a nonexistent hat brim.

"Hassan Moussa, late of the Israeli forces," he said.

"No," and Zainal shook his head. "First they unload, then we do not risk lives. They will not expect attack. With dropping done, they are also tired. We stun those outside, maybe all will be. *Then* we . . ." and Zainal grinned at Moussa, "storm through to bridge and surprise Drassi."

Moussa wasn't the only one who chuckled at Zainal's suggestion to let the Catteni unload.

"I'm reliably informed that not everyone is unloaded with any caution," said the British Ainger.

"I will be there, of course, to see," Zainal remarked.

"Hey wait a minute," Kris said, and she wasn't the only one to see the folly of that.

"Not when the Catteni tried to kidnap you . . ." Rastancil said, frowning.

"Drassi will not know that," Zainal said, "but they obey Emassi orders anytime."

Open disagreement broke out and, after listening a few moments, Zainal began to eat his porridge, ignoring the dispute.

"He tells us he's a kidnap victim . . ."

"A transport was slated to pick him up the first time, wasn't it?"

"Can we really trust him?"

"If it's that easy to take the transport, why hasn't anyone tried?"

"You haven't seen bare hands against nerve whips, have you?"

"So, if Drassi and Emassi never mix, who would recognize him?"

"And the risk is better than the twenty-five percent casualties."

Kris identified Leon Dane's voice. "Leon can make like an Emassi from the shadows," she said, broadcasting her suggestion over the other voices. That stopped them. "It's the tone they respond to, not the figure."

"Good idea," Zainal said, licking his lips. "He sounds Emassi. Could . . . fool . . . me." And he cast a mischievous side glance at Kris as he continued to eat his breakfast.

"We can decide on that stratagem later," Scott said firmly. "If you've finished," he addressed Zainal, who had indeed just emptied both bowl and cup, "let's go through the numbers . . . of the crew . . . again.''

"One Drassi captain," Zainal dutifully ticked off on his fingers, "one Drassi navigator, one Drassi com, one Drassi engineer, four more to take turns, and twelve to unload.''

"That makes twenty. Do all unload?"

Zainal nodded. "Off-duty help, so sixteen unload. Others relax here," and he pointed to the bridge. "Not much security," he added. "Stand from here," and he put his finger on the portal, "and stun all."

"Stun?" The look on Scott's face was ludicrous.

"Why not? Killing weapons messy."

"And wasn't it decided," Kris got in, "that they'd at least have a chance to run for it?"

"Why?" The mood around the table turned ugly.

"Because then we're not the same as Catteni," John Beverly said, raising his voice above the vengeful babble.

"General, I don't think the population here will appreciate leniency," Bull Fetterman said.

"I don't see why not," Hassan Moussa said with a vulpine grin. "It could provide some sport."

"Now, wait a bloody minute." Kris felt her breakfast roiling about in her stomach. "We are not Catteni. We are human beings . . ."

"They can be tried as war criminals," Moussa said, still grinning, and looked down at Zainal to see his reaction, but the Catteni was adding details to the sketch, apparently oblivious to the moral issue.

"Take a camp vote," Yuri Palit said, standing up at the end of the table.

"That's always assuming that we take the damned transport in the first place," Beverly said.

"Now wait a minute, general . . ."

"Beverly, if we can't overpower twenty—"

"Referendum!"

"Everyone needs to know—"

"Those guys murdered—"

"We don't have to do the same—"

Kris got up from the table, taking her dishes and Zainal's before she heaved up breakfast listening to such vengeful talk. She *did,* she told herself as she stalked to the cleanup area, understand why they wanted to take it out on any Catteni they could, but the slaughter still made humans no better than Catteni and polluted this new world, and this fresh start, with all the old hatreds and prejudices that bubbled just skin-deep and could be sublimated by attacking a new species-victim.

She almost threw the dishes down but spotted the still-sleeping cook and siipped them quietly in the warm dishwater to soak. Possibly, if she had to, she could kill a Catteni in cold blood. She hadn't minded when Fek and Slav had killed the kidnappers but her blood certainly hadn't been cold then—it had been frozen with fear that the ruse would be uncovered and Zainal taken. All the arguments were specious. It was the principle that was important. And more important here on Botany than at any other time in her life . . . even when she had feared rape by the brutish Catteni steward on Barevi.

"Kris!" Zainal's voice had not been pitched loudly but he stood at the exit and beckoned to her. The "strategists" were so involved in arguing points of honor, law, principle, integrity that his departure had not been noticed. Except by Easley and Rastancil, who hurried toward him.

"Zainal?" Easley's quiet voice held a note of apology and Rastancil's expression was entreating.

"We will see what weapons and other useful junk is on scout," Zainal said. "That is next step to take to prepare for Phase Two." He exited first, turned to wait for Kris, Rastancil, and Easley, and added, "You are men of sense."

He strode at such a pace that even the long-legged Easley had trouble keeping up. Abruptly he stopped, staring ahead as the predawn sky outlined the hangar, which Kris realized had acquired the most peculiar outline. Zainal snorted and walked on.

"What'd they do to it?" Kris asked, though she thought she knew the answer.

"Mitford suggested we disguise the contents," Easley said. "Just enough in case someone should scan. All they'd see is metal hunks. Roof'll take the weight. The engineers checked."

The moment they cracked the inset door, a shadowy figure got to his feet and challenged them: in Vic Yowell's unmistakable tones. He even had a lance at the ready. "Who's there?"

"Zainal, Kris, Easley, and Rastancil," Zainal said, taking him literally.

"Oh," and Vic let out a relieved sigh. "More damned people poking their noses in," and he changed his voice to a whine. "I didn't get to see it when it landed . . ." He altered tone again. "I want a lock on that damned door."

"No one could get into the ship, Vic," Kris said.

"I told 'em that but they wanted to see the outside at least if they couldn't see in."

"Go get some proper sleep, Vic," Easley suggested. "We'll need you later on and I appreciate your taking charge here."

Vic gathered up his blanket and pallet and grinned as he passed them.

"Never thought I'd have a chance to land anything ever again. Don't want it messed up."

Rastancil gave him a genial slap on the back as he went, and when Vic had closed the door behind him, the hangar was dark again. Rastancil cursed but Easley turned on a hand beam. Kris recognized it as one that had been lifted from the kidnappers' bodies.

"You're quick," she said with a grin up at Easley.

"Spoils of war are meant to be used," he said.

Kris wondered if the man was ever out of sorts. He'd been up all night arguing with brass-headed types and his equanimity seemed not the least bit strained.

"You always this way?" she asked.

"Which way?"

She could see his so innocent grin in the light.

"Zainal calls them brass-heads," she added, since he wasn't answering her question.

"Brass-heads?" He chuckled. "Indeed, indeed."

"Lord, I can't even get you to commit yourself to a joke."

"Oh, I commit myself, Miss Bjornsen. Believe me, I do."

The hatch opened and lights inside came up, surprising an exclamation out of both Easley and Rastancil.

"Do *not*," Easley murmured, lowering his head to Kris' ear, "let them get Zainal's control away from him."

"He isn't planning to let them," she whispered back under the noise of Rastancil stumbling up into the ship. So Easley had committed himself—and to the right people—she thought, hauling herself up inside the ship. It had been easier from the air-cushion vehicle.

A low noise started, and Kris felt fresh air drawn in past her.

"You can vent to the outside?" Rastancil asked.

"Air is . . . old," Zainal said. He made a gesture of a spinning blade. Then he indicated for them to go toward the stern rather than the pilot's compartment. They'd only taken a half dozen steps when he stopped and pulled at handles set flush in the wall.

The closet he had opened was stocked with an assortment of ordnance, much of it unfamiliar to Kris but Rastancil sighed with unadulterated delight and, looking to Zainal for permission, picked up a rifle-type affair with a thick cartridge case and a stumpy muzzle. Zainal pointed and named what each knob or toggle did.

"Safety, power up is red, white is empty. Make thin or fat spray of . . ." He turned to Kris.

"Bullets?" She made a space between thumb and forefinger. "Metal? Kill?" Zainal closed the distance to almost very thin. "Needle?"

He nodded.

"Oh, I heard about them on Earth. They started using toxic tips just before I was rounded up. Nasty." Rastancil carefully returned the weapon. "Any single-shot, revolver-type weapons?"

Zainal frowned. Kris made her hand into a gun shape and enunciated a single "Pow!"

"Stunner," Zainal said, and touched the rack of eight. Then he laid his hand on their neighbor, a thick long barrel. "Ground-to-air." Then nodded toward the bow. "Space stuff up front."

"What sort of armament do you have?" Rastancil said eagerly.

Zainal gave a little laugh. "Space, air-to-ground, small satellite to mark places. Not much. This is fast, and moves well."

"So you count on its speed and maneuverability more than its ordnance?"

Kris wondered which words needed translating but Zainal was looking at Rastancil and then gave a brief nod. "Yes, speed and . . . other word . . ." He did look at Kris now, flipping his hand and fingers.

"Flexibility," she supplied.

"Any telepathy in your family, Kris?" Easley asked.

"None, but I've been partnered with Zainal since we were dropped. I know what words he has learned . . . and he's got a very good vocabulary," and Kris stressed that, "so it's less guess and more acting as synonym finder."

Easley chuckled. "I suspect he understands far more English than people think."

"I don't suspect," Kris replied, and she meant that as a tacit warning. "I know."

"I shall keep that remark under my . . . hair, since my wardrobe does not run to a hat."

Whether or not Easley might just be jollying her along, Kris sensed that Peter Easley was on Zainal's side and wanting to be considered a friend.

By the time Zainal had revealed the other goodies the scout contained—like very high-powered binoculars with thermal readings and nocturnal settings; a variety of comunits, emergency lights, beacons, maps, and the completed photos that he had taken on the way in; as well as hand cameras, Catteni-style exploratory equipment, compasses, ropes, backpacks, winter and summer gear, thermal suits, and a lot of other gear that would see the scouting teams far better equipped—her head was reeling with such riches. Mitford would go bananas! There was even diving equipment and two watercraft, dismantled and packed for transport.

"Sail! Or powered?" Easley said, coming alive with interest at their appearance. He diagrammed a sail in the air and made a putt-putt noise for the power.

Zainal grinned. "Both."

"It's Christmas!" Kris said, wanting to clap her hands together.

"Well, to a degree," Easley amended, but he was grinning, too. "You've done so well with so little, don't let all this stifle ingenuity. There isn't even eight of everything."

"There's eight of everything we'd need for Phase Two," Rastancil said in a sober tone, eyeing the weapons cache.

Zainal nodded but he was far more interested in Kris' reaction to the photos he offered her. She wasn't quite sure why she would be interested in mountains and valleys, until his index finger touched first one, then another point.

"Oh, more dead ends, like the valley we found?"

He nodded. "Many."

"All empty?" she asked.

Zainal shrugged one shoulder and grinned. "We go see?"

"What?" Easley wanted to know, peering over her shoulder.

"Our scouting project," Kris said, not wanting to go into much detail.

"Oh, blind valleys like the one your team discovered, which Mitford told me about?" Easley and his face wore a hopeful expression, soliciting their confidence in him.

"Is a thing kept in? Or out?" Zainal said, giving it.

"Out would be my educated guess, considering the nocturnal horrors Botany has," and Easley gave a little shudder.

"You've seen them?"

He pretended a repugnance that was probably sincere. "Don't care to, either, but then I never go . . . went . . . to horror pictures, either."

Rastancil craned his neck, nodding approval at the prints. "Very clear! What sort of camera equipment do you have on board?"

Zainal chuckled. "I let experts tell me. Baxter says he was cameraman on films . . . no, filums."

"Films," Kris said, as clearly as possible.

Zainal grinned. "Whatever. I push button and later," and he nodded to the slot in the wall, "picture comes out. Show these to Mitford, Kris, please."

"We can both show him," she said.

Zainal shook his head. "My duty is here today, show-ing off."

"Show me around a couple more times, Zainal, and I'll spell you," Rastancil offered.

"Many will want grand tour," Zainal said, his eyes sparkling with such open amusement that Rastancil re-garded him with surprise. "I learn much from Kris," he said, dropping a proprietary arm across her shoulders.

"Ah, yes, well," Rastancil said, ducking his head in what Kris thought was as close to embarrassment as a brass-head was likely to get. "There wouldn't be an inventory of what's on board Baby, would there? I know it'd be in your language but we've got a couple of personnel down here now who learned to read Catteni."

"Come," and Zainal beckoned Rastancil to walk forward to the pilot's compartment. "You take a good look around, Kris, Peter," he added, pointing to the other doors along the narrow hall. "Familiarize yourselves."

Easley was shaking his head respectfully as Zainal followed Rastancil.

"He's quite a guy. I'd never have thought a Catteni had an active sense of humor."

"Maybe they just never had the opportunity," Kris said, and slid back the first door. "Phew! This needs an airing. What slobs!" Clothing was thrown about floor and bunks while used cups and plates, attached to the surface of the table, had not been collected for washing. There was a blank screen and a hand control unit which Easley picked up, examined, and replaced, as the markings meant nothing to him. There were four bunks, wide enough for Catteni bulk, and all unmade and messy.

Easley did look into the nearest locker, pinched his nose, and shut it up. But he glanced in at the others. "Some of the gear can be useful. Especially the uniforms for Phase Two. Once they've been washed."

There were two more compartments, one with three bunks, and one—the captain's, Kris thought—with one, which also contained command equipment. A viewer plate like the one she'd seen the steward on Barevi use, and racks of the disks used in it. Easley homed in on that. He was familiar with such things, neatly inserting a disk and turning on the viewer. A Catteni voice in monotone added comments to whatever was printed in the glyphs.

"Well, very interesting, I'm sure," he said, clicking it off and absently returning the disk to its rack. "Now where did they eat and wash?—if they did."

One of the doors in the captain's unit slid back to disclose what had to be a shower compartment, complete with what Kris thought resembled a urinal, and another odd opening. Well, Catteni had much the same alimentary requirements as Humankind. Easley gave a mild grunt when he peered in over her shoulder.

There was another unit next in line down the passageway which would accommodate two at once. The galley was just beyond it, almost the last door in the passage.

"One-butt, at that," she said, looking at the "kitchen" side and its equipment. A table with padded seating around it was evidently where the crew ate, if not in their rooms. But the place was neat and tidy. Even clean. Ah, but Raisha had said that they'd eaten aboard the ship so she had probably also cleaned it up.

"Wonder what's back here, though," Easley said after the briefest glance in the wardroom, turning his attention to the final, large door that took up the end of the passageway. It was dogged tight with large Catteni glyphs in white.

"If empty is white on Catteni guns, would it be caution on equipment?" Kris asked.

The moment Easley put his hands on the toggles, an alarm sounded.

"Don't enter." Zainal's voice issued from an intercom right above their heads. "Please," he added.

"He's not totally assimilated, is he?" Easley remarked. "Let's see what they're up to. Unless you want to clear out those lockers. We might need clean Catteni uniforms."

Kris gave him a stern look. "We might but I think it would count as a morale booster for others to see just what slobs the Catteni can be."

"Point!"

"What I really want to do is itemize all that lovely gear I hope we scouts have first pick of," she said, rubbing her hands together. "Damn, I've no paper."

"Voilà," Easley said, taking a wad of small sheets out of one thigh pocket and a pencil from his chest pocket.

"Hey, the comforts of home. Mitford can't operate without a pad and pencil, either."

"Where do you think I got them?"

Sharing a grin over that, Kris and Easley began to take stock. They were interrupted by a clanging on the open hatch.

"Who's on board?" an irritated voice demanded.

"Scott?" Easley called back.

"With Fetterman, Reidenbacker, and Marrucci," and the four men climbed on board, crowding the passageway. "Didn't see you leave, Easley."

Easley smiled, ignoring the implied accusation. "Decided to inventory what's here before the crowd gathers. Rastancil's forward with Zainal, doing printouts or something operational. I have six only of what looks like pack frames," he went on to Kris, and put the first one back in its slot.

When they heard the newcomers moving forward, Easley grinned at Kris.

"Took 'em long enough to miss us, didn't it?"

"I wonder," she replied, grinning back at him, "if they ever reached any conclusion."

"Oh, probably not until they've gone over Baby with a fine-toothed comb. The Catteni don't seem to stock such items, do they? Not even toothbrushes or soap."

"I found what looks like liquid soap, remember?"

"Oh yes, drawer nine."

The inventory turned out to be the pleasantest part of the day.

CHAPTER 5

Once that was finished, Kris went to Mitford. Easley, who had initially gone forward to see how Zainal was faring, ran to catch up with her halfway to the barn where Mitford held office in Camp Narrow.

"The compartment's jam-packed back with those who need-to-know. I'll wait for a quieter time," Peter said.

Kris gave a snort. "No matter what he explains, they'll still need him to fly the thing."

"I expect so," Peter replied equably.

Chuck Mitford's eyes bugged out when he spread out the pages of available equipment. He was flabbergasted when he saw the aerial photos.

"Clearest recon photos I ever saw," he said, amazed, picking up one after another and scanning them.

"Look, here . . . here . . . and here," Kris said, pointing out spots on the various photos. One was quite close to Camp Narrow although it was in an area that had been lightly explored. "More of those dead-end valleys. Zainal thinks they have, or had, a purpose."

"If they didn't before, they may now. Especially as we've got enough personnel—*and* the equipment," and

Mitford's voice rang with satisfaction, "so a team could hang around, safe enough, and see what comes up." He tapped the near valley with his index finger. "If we can secure this area—" He broke off as his shoulders convulsed in a shudder. "I want us *out* of the Farmers' facilities. I got a hunch about 'em."

He gathered the inventory sheets into one neat pile and the photos into another one. "Anyone seen these yet?"

"No," Easley replied, "you're in charge of exploration. And were I you, I would secure these supplies for your teams and start sending them out."

Mitford grinned crookedly. "Appreciate the advice, Peter." He turned to Kris. "The rest of your team's doing KP but they should be finished by now. I'll just rev up the load bed trundler and secure those supplies. Any weapons?"

"Some but I'd leave them where they are until Zainal drills us in their use," Peter said. "Some of 'em'll make right nasty holes in people. You know," and he scratched his head, contorting his features as the sort of prelude that Kris decided was his way of leading up to utterance of a diplomatic suggestion, "we might take a page from the Catteni book of colonial administration and drop the next bunch of Turs into one of those valleys. Come back in a few weeks and see how they've got on." He paused. "Or better still, dump any Catteni prisoners we take in them. A bit of turnabout's fair play."

Mitford stared, frowning at Peter Easley. "You a bleeding heart or something?"

"It was Yuri Palit's notion, actually," Easley replied, slightly abashed. "I mentioned that you'd discovered the one. I don't see the need for gratuitous violence or killing. There's been quite enough of that. I'd rather we humans fell on the side of the angels than the Eosi. Besides, it rounds things out," and he made a cage of the fingers of both hands, rotating one around the other, "and they get back a little of what they've been dealing out besides supplying us with guinea pigs for whatever might lurk in one of those valleys."

Mitford was unconvinced. "They want this referendum first, don't they?"

"I think you'll have trouble getting the notion of lenience across to any one who's tangled with a nerve whip," Kris said.

"I can see it for the Turs, Easley," Mitford allowed. "I've never liked just turning them loose. They're dangerous and, if there're enough of them, they constitute a menace." He rubbed his jaw. "Actually, we could use valleys as a detention facility. That's less messy than staking a guy out at night for the crawlers." Then, with a shrug, he dismissed that topic and split his attention between the photos and the inventory.

"The print won't fade," Kris said, pulling his sleeve. "Let's go get what we need before someone else requisitions it."

"Damn well told," Mitford replied, and Easley and Kris had to run to keep up with him.

Vic Yowell was back on duty, standing squarely in the inset door, his expression inscrutable until Mitford leaned out of the driver's side of the trundler.

"Open up, will ya, Vic. I've requisitioned some of the gear on board to outfit my scouting teams."

Vic took no exception to that and pushed the main door back. So Mitford reversed the vehicle right up to the hatch, the load bed almost level with it. With Joe, Sarah, Whitby, Leila, Pete, and Mitford working quickly and quietly, Kris checked off the items they were taking from the inventory list. They soon had emptied the passageway lockers. While the others were stowing the last acquisitions, Mitford took a quick look at the arsenal and closed that compartment firmly.

Temptation, step behind me, Kris thought.

Just then Scott appeared in the forward end of the passageway.

"What're you doing, sergeant?"

"Looking at the arsenal sir. Could be useful."

"Pete and I have just finished the inventory of the lockers, admiral," Kris added, holding up the pad.

"Good idea, Bjornsen. Carry on."

"We will," she said jauntily, and, stifling a giggle at her deception, she followed Mitford out.

"Get what you needed?" Vic asked as the flatbed silently moved out of the hangar.

"I think so," Mitford said, and elbowed Sarah before she laughed loud enough for Vic to hear.

They had their loot all neatly stored at the back of Mitford's office covered with Catteni-issue blankets. The rest of Kris' team went to get some lunch while Mitford called in Judy Blane, who'd been a cartographer. He wanted to match the photos to their appropriate areas on the map. Meanwhile, Mitford called in the recon squads he wanted, ordered travel food from the kitchen, and was ready to equip them as soon as they reported in.

"Before the brass-heads find out where it's all gone to," Kris said when the sergeant paused briefly.

"Brass-*heads*?" He chuckled. "Zainal?" She nodded.

"Are you going to lead a group this time, sarge, and get out of their way?"

He shook his head with a rueful smile and grimace. "Naw, not this time. I figure I better hang around."

"I can't say I'm not happy you will, Chuck," she said, tilting her head toward the hangar and the "brass-heads" occupying it. "But you deserve to get out of here for a while and clear your head. You've done more than your share. You need some R and R."

"I'll go after Phase Two's complete. And don't you worry, Kris. No matter what they decide in their conferences and brass-headed strategy meetings, they need Zainal more than he needs them. Or us.'' Then he leveled a cocky grin at her. "With the exception of you . . . Bjornsen.''

"Scott doesn't trust him at all,'' Kris said, perching on the edge of the worktop.

"The admiral doesn't trust anyone,'' Mitford said with a snort, folding his arms across his chest. "For starters, he's stuck on dry land, which isn't really where he functions best. But distrust's not altogether a bad habit.''

A knock on the door, which opened without his permission, disclosed the first of the teams he'd called in, Ninety Doyle's. The Scandinavians arrived, breathlessly eager, before Mitford could brief Ninety's squad on the current situation. Kris left him to it and eased herself out of the now crowded office and went to get some lunch.

Part of the original strategy-and-tactics group were still busy at the end table and those coming in to eat left a sort of no-man's-land of unused tables around the area to maintain their privacy. She picked up her lunch of soup and fresh bread and made her way to where Sarah, Joe, Leila, and Whitby were sitting.

"Are we going to get to use some of that beaut gear?'' Joe asked.

"We won't be going out . . .''

"Until the brass start believing Zainal?'' Sarah asked in caustic voice.

"Oh, I think they believe him,'' Kris said.

"It's trust that's lacking,'' Whitby added when she paused.

"I would rather wait until Zainal comes with us,'' Leila remarked in her quiet but firm way, and sipped soup.

"Besides which, I wouldn't want to miss Phase Two for anything,'' Joe added. "Got any update on that, Kris?''

She shook her head and gave a little snort, jerking her thumb toward the earnest knot of men at the end table. "They have to make up their minds first."

"Whaddya bet they'll end up doing what Zainal suggested in the first place?" Joe asked, looking around the table.

"Just so long as they make up their minds before the next transport gets here," Sarah said. "It could come any day now, too, judging by the frequency we've been getting drops lately."

"You'd think they were planning World War Three," Whitby said, entering the conversation, "instead of a minor commando action."

They had just finished their meal when the rumble of male voices was heard, heralding the arrival of Scott, Fetterman, Rastancil, Beverly, Marrucci, and Zainal. Zainal halted at the door, surveying the room, spotted Kris, and, cocking his finger at her, indicated she was to join them at the strategy table.

"I've been paged," she said, cleaning the corners of her mouth of any traces of soup with two fingers and brushing bread crumbs off her front with the other hand as she rose. "Hang about, will you?"

"Over at Mitford's, dear," Sarah said, also rising. "I don't want to get sucked into another session of KP just because we're all sitting here looking as if we're doing nothing."

"Which we are," said Joe, but he got up, too, and as Kris joined Zainal, they all left the mess hall. Peter Easley passed them on his way in, sauntering in that easy bent-knee gait, pausing to exchange a few words and a laugh.

As he came up, he winked at Kris.

"There you are, Easley," Scott said. "When can the next transport be expected?"

"Anytime now," Easley replied indifferently.

Every one turned around to stare at him.

"They come when they have a full load, evidently," he said, and looked to Zainal, who shrugged.

"Last one was eight days ago. Sometimes there's twenty-one days between drops." He dismissed that concern with a flick of his fingers. "Deskis hear the best. Deskis spread out . . ." and now he waved his big hand, splay-fingered, over the map that occupied one end of the long table. "They hear. They report."

"And they have been using the same field they dropped us in?" Scott asked.

"Lately at any rate," Easley said, grinning at Zainal, "ever since Zainal had a little word with them."

"Can the Deskis be trusted?" Rastancil asked.

"With what?" Kris asked. "Hearing or reporting?"

"Do they *know* how to use comunits?" Scott asked, ignoring her remark.

"The ones we have even your grandmother could manage," Kris snapped back, "begging your grandmother's pardon," she added, making herself grin at Scott's indignant reaction.

"Are they capable of giving a detailed enough report, though?" Beverly asked, slightly more respectfully. "I mean, I've never heard them use more than one word."

"What more is needed? 'Hear ship. Comes down near. Comes down far. Your way,' " Zainal said, and Kris was delighted to hear him effect the odd tonality of the Deski voice.

"A Deski did all right warning us about the scout," she added. "And telling Worrell exactly where it had landed."

"Point," Beverly said. "So we can count on their ears . . ."

"And eyes," Easley added. "Deskis and Rugarians are also blessed with exceedingly acute night vision."

"Send a human along if you're worried," Kris suggested.

"No need," Zainal said, and then took out of his coverall a sheaf of pictures, evidently second copies of the ones now being examined in Mitford's office. He spread them on the table, while some of the other tacticians exclaimed and reached out for one to examine. Zainal found the one he wanted. "This is the line I flew in."

It had been taken at an altitude of the descent well above the cliffs in which Camp Narrow was located but showed the fields leading to what was now called the Drop Field. The scope of the photo included the third drop area, and the boggy swamp where Zainal had lain, wounded by the toxic thorns.

"Drop made here, too." He put his finger squarely on the little patch of field.

"But all the others have been made here," and Easley pointed to the Drop Field.

"Good cover for troops in those hedges. We can improve on it, though," Fetterman said, indicating the three upper sides.

"And move forward when enough crates have been positioned," and Rastancil tapped a pencil on the spot where the supplies were usually unloaded.

"There are some spare Catteni uniforms on the scout . . ." Kris said. "They'll have to be washed first, but I saw them in the lockers. So guys stocky enough could actually get on board easily."

"Catteni don't talk much when unloading," Easley said, having watched the procedure often enough in his official capacity as inflow officer. "Most don't even carry whip or stunner."

The whole procedure was then gone over and over until Kris felt her stomach rolling. She hated meetings where the obvious got repeated and repeated and no conclusions made. Once, when she shifted impatiently, she felt Zainal, who was sitting next to her, press his leg against hers and she settled for a little while longer.

Then orders were issued for Deski teams—Easley, Beverly, and Rastancil backed Zainal's assurance that the aliens would manage such a duty without a human counterpart—to spread out in a wide circle around the sprawling human settlement, equipped with comunits, to report the first rumble of an approaching transport ship. They were given extra rations and blankets and a translation in Deski by Zainal of their orders, in case they hadn't understood Beverly's. They had grinned broadly enough when they listened intently to the black general but they hiccuped with amusement after Zainal's remarks. Kris saw that he was smiling back at them, but his face was serious as he turned back to the brass-heads.

"Now, we wait," he said.

"No, now we train the assault forces," Scott said, and he marched off with those who were assisting him in that. The others drifted away, gathering up their notes and maps and papers, and leaving, probably to get some sleep.

"You cleared equipment?" Zainal asked Kris as he guided her to the buffet table to get some lunch.

"Everything that looked useful—except the dirty uniforms."

She asked for a cup of the herbal tea and joined him at the table he took, set at the opposite end of the mess hall from the conference area, in an unoccupied corner. All day and night, people drifted in and out of the mess hall, eating whenever their duties permitted. Kris noticed Aarens coming in, arguing with a man she recognized as a senior design engineer. Aarens had lost a lot of his arrogance, though he still maintained a unique position as a clever adapter of useful gadgets from the Farmers' materials.

"By now the sergeant probably has sent most of it out with the scout teams he called in."

Zainal grinned slightly. "Did he go?"

Kris shook her head. "He's got the right to be in on Phase Two."

Zainal nodded. "He is."

"Oh, was that decided in the scout?"

"I believe so." Something else about this morning amused Zainal, and although she tried to get him to tell her, he shook his head.

"Not to worry," he said. "He is in his office?"

"Probably." She stood as Zainal did. When they had carried their dishes to the weary young woman who was handling that chore, they made for Mitford's office.

Although he called a cheery "Come in" when they knocked at the door, he was not alone. A rather officious-looking young man with a receding hairline, holding a clipboard fashioned from a piece of supply crate, was jotting notes down as fast as he could write. Glancing to the back of the office, Kris noticed that the equipment, which had reached nearly to the ceiling when they finished unpacking it that morning, was down to a single level in most places.

"I'm in charge of recon groups and I sent all of them out, properly equipped for the first time. You tell Admiral Scott that we took nothing else." Mitford flipped an indolent finger at the neatly stacked inventory sheets Kris had made. "All signed out or accounted for. Not a damned thing *he'd* need for an assault force or training. Ah, Zainal, come to brief me on the overall picture? Well, this in-die-vid-jual's just leaving. Aren't you, son?"

"As I told you earlier, *sergeant*," the man said in an icy tone, stressing the rank. "I was Admiral Scott's aide in the resistance . . ."

"And still no doubt an admirable aide in this one," Mitford said, "but, lieutenant, we're all droppees here on Botany, ain't we, Zainal?"

"We dropped. We stay." Zainal held the door politely open for the lieutenant to leave by.

As soon as he was gone, Mitford dropped his chair on all four legs and whistled softly. "Damn fool. Scott, too. Not a fragging thing he'd need, and my teams do."

"Good on you, sarge," Kris said, chuckling as she settled down on a stool. Zainal pulled one up closer to the desk and she let him tell Mitford what had happened so far.

As occasionally happens with well-laid plans, and just about the time everyone in Camp Narrow started to get real antsy from the waiting, a Deski called in to the command post in the dim light of false dawn five days later. Mitford happened to be duty officer on that shift.

"Comes now. Bad noise. Bad smell," she said. "Wrong noise."

"What could she mean by that?" Beverly asked. He'd jumped out of his cot in the duty office and was hunched over the hand unit which Mitford had politely tilted so the general could hear the report, which Mitford asked Tul to repeat.

"Let's ask Zainal." He rose and shook awake the runners who'd been stationed in the office for this contingency. Each of the youngsters knew who he was to waken and where they were bunked. Then he turned to the diagram on the wall which showed the position of each Deski. "Hmmm. Tul's here," and he pointed. "If it was coming in properly, we should have heard from Fek." He moved his finger, and drew it in a straight line down to the Drop Field. "Off course?"

Beverly ran a straight line from Tul's position and wound up klicks away from the usual area. "We'd better get vehicles ready."

He was gone before Mitford could remind Beverly that they had plenty of leeway to get to a different position, and still mount the rehearsed assault.

Narrow was not the only camp alerted. The Deski followed Zainal's orders to contact Narrow first, and then their camps. Worrell called in to ask for instructions. Even Camp Bella Vista, up in the hills, had been included in the contingency plans that the brass-heads had made. Well, it was something to do to keep busy until Phase Two actually started. It had!

Fek's report came in a moment before Zainal, Kris, and the rest of their team arrived.

"It comes. Noisy," Fek said.

"Where is it headed, Fek?" Mitford asked.

"You," she answered.

"Thanks, Fek. Keep listening. Tul said the noise is wrong."

"Is." Fek agreed, and Zainal nodded to indicate he had heard and understood.

"Kris, find Beverly and tell him it's headed here after all," Mitford said. "He'll be at the main garage. Why would a transport be making a 'wrong noise,' Zainal?"

Zainal cocked his head. "I told you ship's not in good condition. I must hear noise to make a guess. I go up!" He pointed to the roof of the office.

A ladder had been affixed in one of the alleys between barns to reach the cliffs against which they were backed.

Mitford swore but stayed on the comunit desk for any further reports.

Two more Deski listeners reported in, also remarking on "wrong noise." A runner came back and Mitford beckoned him to the desk and the comunit while he went outside to listen. There was so much noise now, with men and women running up and down, seeking their assigned vehicles, getting their gear on, that he gave up and went back inside.

His comunit went off again. This time it was Zainal.

"I hear wrong noise, too. Ship in trouble. Drive is bad."

"Fraggit. We need an operational ship," Mitford said, hopes blasted by the news.

"Not to worry. Attack plan may need change."

"Not if Scott has anything to say about it and he *is* in charge of Phase Two."

"Phase Two is my idea," Zainal said, and the co-munit went dead.

It wasn't long before everyone could hear the transport, wheezing and rumbling and giving off hoarse metallic shrieks, landing lights blazing and onboard sirens audible. The surface force made it to the Drop Field, and into their assigned positions, before the ailing transport came into view, barely skimming the lodge-pole trees and skidding to a stop, rather than landing. As many landings as Mitford had already seen, some bouncing several times, others skidding to a stop, this was the worst. He dreaded to think of the unconscious bodies being thrown around inside the shallow decks.

Steam poured out of the base of the transport. The main hatch opened and Catteni, coughing, sneezing, staggering, made a disorderly descent from the vessel. All of them. Mitford counted twenty, which Zainal had estimated was the usual crew complement. And they were running as fast as they could, away from the ship.

Zainal ran into the light, waving a stunner and barking orders. He pointed to one of the faster runners.

"Get him!" he called in English, and roared louder in Catteni.

The vanguard did not slow and Zainal left off a stun bolt, hitting the Catteni in the head—a mortal shot—and got the next two in the legs. They fell, moaning in frustration. That was enough to halt the others and make them turn around, hands in the air. He barked another order and they reluctantly retraced their steps, their eyes wide and frightened, darting anxiously from Zainal to the hulk they had somehow managed to land.

Zainal called out a question. He got a response and immediately gestured for those hidden in the shadows to come out.

"Ship's circuitry in overload. May blow. We must get people out. Dane, Chavell, Rastancil, take control of them. Scott, we need every man you have.'' He raced up the ramp, Kris and the rest of their team right behind. He went to controls set just inside the main hatch, throwing open the lid, which was hot. He was muttering or cursing in Catteni. ''Schkelk!''

She felt herself go rigid with attention at his Catteni ''Listen.''

''They will not breathe, Kris. No air. You pull down this type,'' he said, pulling the flat lever, ''to open the hatch. Push up to close. This one to change decks. Got it? Good! BERT! MARRUCCI! YOWELL! DOWDALL! Come with me! I go to bridge. Things can be done. I need engineers, any mechanics, pilots. AARENS!''

Looking over her shoulder, she saw the deck part its horizontal doors, and lights came up to reveal the pitiful mounds of people who had been thrown about in the landing. She didn't need to shriek for rescuers: they were already running up the ramp and ducking into the fetid level. The frightened Catteni crewmen were back, too, each encouraged by a settler holding a stunner on him to unload the passengers.

The evacuation began. Catteni managed to lift two or three bodies while their captors managed one in a fireman's hold. More help arrived as the ship trembled and shuddered and made the most hideous and frightening of metallic noises while steam hissed out from unlikely places. Kris' right hand was caught in a gush just behind the control board. Whimpering from pain, she licked and then blew on it.

''Got them all out,'' someone yelled at her.

''No, you haven't,'' she yelled back. And switched decks. The smell that issued was appalling. Those going in to rescue coughed and gagged but they kept at their grim task.

Men carrying tool kits hurried past her, kits bearing Baby's markings. Then a group raced aft, Zainal shout-

ing instructions about gauges and controls at them. The
heat and the smells were almost more than Kris could
manage, even as close as she was to the outside, and her
stomach heaved in rebellion. Her hand was really hurt-
ing. She leaned around the open door, inhaling the
fresher air outside. She managed to filter some of the
stench by drawing the front of her coverall over her
mouth and nose, hunching down in a cramped position
to do so.

"Got that lot." Yuri stopped by her side, his face a
dirty mask, his coverall blood-smeared. "How many
more to go?"

"Two more decks." She worked the controls although, with the noise the machinery made, she wasn't
sure if the mechanism would shift decks at all. The metal
must have warped in the heat. But slowly the third deck
level was accessible. "Have many survived?"

"Others tend them."

"We should salvage the cargo, too," Kris said.

"Cargo? The living first." Yuri dismissed her suggestion with a wave and ran into the newly exposed
deck, ducking under the half-raised hatch.

Suddenly the levels of noise from around the ship
seemed to abate and some were silenced. More men and
women ran around, both aft and forward, some holding
tools, carrying hoses and other equipment she realized
they must have found in the transport.

One more tremendous gout of steam erupted from the
deck plates beneath her feet and she jumped and skipped
about, trying to find someplace not burning-hot. As soon
as she could get the machinery to turn to the last deck,
she darted in to help unload. The heat was almost un-
bearable. How long had these unconscious people endured such temperatures? Or had they?

She slung an arm over her shoulder and hoisted a
body, a woman's, and staggered out and down the ramp.

"That way. Make it to the next field," she was told,

a hand turning her in the proper direction. The sun was up and she could at least see where she was going. There were only two bodies in the field, one Catteni, one unidentifiable, and both dead. She staggered along, more conscious now of the sting in her steam-burned hand and very tender feet. The hedgerow had been cut down and boards put on either side over the ditches. This field was covered with bodies. Many of them, she thankfully saw, were moving and being attended: water poured over them or cups held to their mouths so they could drink. The field was one cacophonous moan, with weeping woven in. She staggered until she could find a free spot to lay her burden down. And seeing the awful stillness in the gray face, she felt for a pulse in the neck. There was none and with a cry of despair she curved in on herself, weeping.

"Easy, Kris," a familiar voice said, and she looked up at Sandy Areson, who was holding a cup of water to her. "Drink." Her gentle hand smoothed the hair back from her sweating face and patted her shoulder. "We've saved a great many. Thanks to Zainal."

Kris started to rise. Maybe they weren't all dead on that level. But Sandy's hand held her down.

"Oh no you don't," Sandy said. "Hey, what happened to your hand? It's blistered."

"It is?" and Kris held it out and looked stupidly down at it. "So it is," she heard herself say as she slipped sidewise into unconsciousness.

It took several days for the events of the momentous morning to be sorted out. Of the 728 left alive, many were injured; broken bones being the least of the problems for the triage teams that checked over each survivor. All were dehydrated and that was almost the first need addressed. Internal injuries as well as concussions were more serious, due to a rough landing which had pitched the inert bodies of the passengers around the

shallow decks, piling up and injuring those beneath
them. Severe heat prostration had caused twenty major
and minor heart attacks and that had probably been the
cause of many more of the deaths. Of those from the
lowest deck, only forty-five survived; four humans, nine
Deski, twelve Turs, six Ilginish oozing green goo, and
fourteen Rugarians, who had almost all their body hair
singed off.

Even those who had suffered no major injuries needed
reassurance, proper food, and counseling in that order to
recover from their ordeal. The only true advantage the
consolers had was that they had been through much the
same experiences and really did understand how it affected people. Easley worked tirelessly in directing his
teams, asking only for the survivors' names and their
origin before turning them over to Yuri Palit's resettlement people, transporting the walking wounded to
calmer surroundings as soon as possible.

The injured were transported by the air-cushion machines to Narrow for emergency treatment. "Great ambulance service," Leon Dane commented, "nothing to
bump or jar 'em!"

The Tur contingent were unusually docile from their
recent horrific experience and pathetically grateful for
the water and soup passed out to them. The uninjured
ones—forty all told—were given such dire and terse
warnings by Zainal in their own language about the dangers of the avian predators and night crawlers that they
remained subdued as they were driven off to their new
quarters. Joe and Whitby headed the expedition with a
well-armed guard contingent. The first night out, Whitby
also arranged a demonstration of what night crawlers did
to a dead loo-cow, and that had kept them quiet the rest
of the trip. They did not even struggle when they were
lowered, with cups, blankets, knives, and generous supplies of the Catteni food bars, into the valley.

Zainal also won a second victory, aided and abetted

by Easley, Yuri Palit, and surprisingly, Mitford. The nineteen surviving Catteni crewmen were sequestered in the nearer blind valley which Ninety Doyle's team had explored. They had also had an object lesson before their departure. Zainal forced them to watch the night crawlers ingesting the bodies of those who had not survived the crash landing. He had also required Scott, Fetterman, Rastancil, and Reidenbacker to attend. It was a salutary lesson for each group.

"They expected to be thrown into the field last night, didn't they?" Doyle asked Zainal when the biggest air-cushion vehicle was finally free of its ambulance duty and the Catteni crewmen were loaded aboard.

"They expected death," Zainal replied. "They did not expect an Emassi to be in charge."

"Catteni better learn not to underestimate us humans," Doyle replied as he waved his stunner to speed up the loading process. The two crewmen Zainal had stunned were still not very steady on their feet but none of their companions lent any assistance. "Mean sonsabitches even to their own, ain't they?"

"One of their most endearing traits," Zainal said, in such a facetious tone that Doyle nearly missed the sarcasm.

As the vehicle glided silently off, the Drassi captain gave Zainal a look compounded of hatred, fear, and indignation that one of his own species was responsible for this total humiliation.

"He wanted to sear Zainal's skin off him," Sarah told Kris, and gave her shoulders a shake to rid herself of that memory. "Hope it doesn't turn out later that it would have been wiser to stake 'em out."

"No, we'd be no better than they are doing an eye-for-an-eye bit," she said, and then inhaled sharply in pain. Sarah was checking the blisters on her steam-burned hand. There was nothing to treat it with nor the very tender soles of her feet. The soles of her Catteni boots had melted on the hot deck plates, and had she waited much longer, the injuries might have been even more severe. Leon had seen her injuries, rueful that he had nothing, even from the medical stores of the scout, with which to treat the burns.

"I think there won't be any lasting damage, Kris," he said, gently laying her hand back in the sling. "Once that main blister has popped, it'll ease off and your body will take over the healing process. We do have that salve Patti Sue made up which the cooks all swear by, to keep the skin supple. Might ease the soles of your feet, too."

"I'm not complaining," she said. "Sarah was a little officious, taking you away from the ones who really need you."

"Oh, never fear, m'dear," Leon said, grinning. "We've got quite a list of specialists these days, you know. And a supply of the gas they use. It makes an effective anesthesia." He gave a little shudder. "Thank God. Some of the repair work would have been barbaric without it."

Kris had refused to go back to the Rock, wanting to stay near the hub of activity, and Zainal, and very eager to hear how they had kept the ship from blowing. Sarah and Leila kept her informed and helped her down to the main mess hall, where she could listen to the "hourly bulletins," as Sarah called them, updating those not involved with various aspects of what was going on.

Zainal and the engineers had managed to jury-rig the control board, venting the buildup to an explosion. A pump was found, disconnected from the ship, and dropped into the nearby stream. By combining all the hoses on the Catteni ship, the fuel tanks had been kept from exploding and the reduction in temperature had saved other systems from reacting to the intense heat.

"If they hadn't managed, the explosion would have altered the landscape considerably," Sarah went on, talking to distract Kris from her tender ministrations to the raw sole of her right foot. "But the fuel got saved and there's plenty for Baby now."

"So that's why the Catteni were running away as fast as they could," Kris said through clenched teeth. "Was the ship badly damaged inside? Can we make use of anything?" Granted all she had seen was just inside the cargo area, with bursting conduits and pipes and hot deck plates, but surely something was salvageable.

Sarah grinned up at her from bandaging her feet with sufficient fluff to form a protective layer. "You better believe it! The entire bridge!"

"Really!"

Sarah chuckled in a mock-malicious way. "Well, what there actually is of it. Anyone who's ever flown anything is wondering how the damned thing stayed in the air, much less made journeys out into space. However, Scott wanted it where it can be used. And the interior of the transport still stinks to high heaven, so it was dismantled and it's been reconstructed in the hangar. They've even got the communications up and running. And solar panels on the hangar to power it.

"Everyone's over the transport like ants, taking it apart. It's nothing but a shell now—which still stinks. The mechanics and engineers are having a field day with all these new treasures, even if most of the loot is second-hand, slightly damaged goods. But it's more than we've ever had to work with.

"Then there's real competition over who can sound more Catteni than another. More learned the language than you might think."

"I suppose that knowledge didn't make you all that popular on Earth," Kris mused. "But why is there a competition? You said the crew was sequestered in a valley." Kris tried to keep her concentration on what Sarah was saying, rather than on the painful dressing of her feet.

"Sorry, luv, I keep thinking you've been in on all the

briefings. The Drassi captain sent out a Mayday, or whatever Catteni call an emergency, to another transport, which said, and I quote, they'd get around to picking up the crew when they were on their way back to base. That is, if they survive the crash landing.''

"So that's why Scott wanted the bridge operational." Kris grinned, for it was easy to see what was likely to happen next. "So, have they reported they survived?''

Sarah nodded, grinning from ear to ear. "Leon did it. He's still the best but not for long.''

"When do they expect this rescue vessel?''

Sarah shrugged. "From what Zainal discovered in questioning the crew—the captain wouldn't say doodly to him—it's a bigger, newer ship, with a longer range and so we have to wait for another message from them when to expect them. So there's plenty of time to prepare, rehearse, and drill for their arrival.''

"A bigger, newer ship?'' Kris repeated. Then she chuckled to herself, thinking of Admiral Scott's bridge, being run from a hangar. "And we'll have three ships!'' She was so proud of Zainal that she wriggled in the bed.

"Scott's even acting as if Zainal's not so bad after all,'' Sarah said. "And he's got a committee working to find out something that will add the necessary gray tinge to human skin. Those loose uniforms they wear will camouflage who's in them but they gotta have gray skin. Leon's dying to take part but he's really too tall to play a Drassi.''

"So is Zainal.'' Kris began to worry again. Zainal was taking so many risks. A bigger, newer ship would be better captained and crewed. But then surprise was still on their side.

The dressings were now complete, she glared down at her feet. They'd better be completely healed. She had to be able to be at this second enactment of Phase Two.

CHAPTER 6

When Zainal spent more time explaining to the mechanics and engineers what the salvageable material had been used for, they could more knowledgeably adapt it to their needs. Once the bridge was sited and up and working again, Scott preempted him to translate the data on the transport's log files.

"Much is routine," Zainal said, scrolling at a fast pace through the entries.

"But we need to know where they have been, how long it takes, the protocols they use . . ." Scott said, scowling.

"I think I've found someone from the latest drop who can manage to translate routine reports," Easley said, once again diplomatically inserting his presence. "In fact, several someones who have a good working knowledge of the glyphs. Learned to help decipher Catteni documents captured during raids."

Beth Isbell was the only uninjured member of the three "someones" who were summoned. Sally Stoffers, a petite brunette with an extremely innocent expression, arrived on crutches for a broken leg, while François

Chavell had his left arm in a sling. Scott insisted on interviewing them first as to their Earthside activities. Once satisfied, he turned them over to Zainal, who tested their skills by having them read out loud from log entries.

"They read Catten well," Zainal said, passing all three.

Later Easley asked if he'd spoken truthfully or merely to get himself out of a very boring task.

"I said true. They can copy what they do not understand and I will translate . . . if I can," and Zainal grinned from Easley to Kris.

Scott next had him interview every male who had listed some understanding and speaking knowledge of Catteni in their drop interviews. With Kris' help, Zainal made a list in order of fluency and vocabulary of over seventy men. Scott then had his choice of those he felt would be most useful in the commando unit he was training to stand in for the transport's stranded crew.

"You're certain they're coming back for the crew?" Beverly had asked Zainal at the very beginning of this new venture.

"That was the message," and Zainal had shrugged. "They will not hurry to do so. The crew would be safe in ship, away from us who are dropped."

Scott might not have been certain of Catteni altruism in collecting a stranded crew but he was also counting on it as a replacement for the useless hulk in the Drop Field.

Zainal gave Kris a list of the most frequent commands, which she wrote down with phonetic translations, so that all could learn them, and learn the proper responses of both Drassi and ordinary crew commands. Rank had some privileges.

"Catteni crew don't talk much," Zainal said. "Just obey."

"They must also know what is being said so they can

act on their initiative if that becomes necessary,'' was Scott's reply.

"Not Catteni," Zainal replied, shaking his head.

"So long as the real Catteni obey, there's no problem," Scott said, a stubborn look coming into his eye.

"So the surprise will be even greater," Easley said, smiling at Scott, "and that will work in our favor, won't it?''

Scott gritted out a surly "Yes" and went back to the diagrams Zainal had contrived of what he thought the interior of the new transport should be. He hadn't, himself, had an opportunity to inspect any.

"Designed to carry more with fewer deaths," he said in summary. "Just being newer is improvement."

The engineers and mechanics in the meeting agreed to that.

"Some of the controls were wired together and I dunno what they used to keep the drive units operating," Peter Snyder said.

He'd been a jet-engine propulsion engineer and was fascinated by the Catteni drives: especially how they kept working in the state they were in. By using the schematics in the manuals, he and the other aviation and space-shuttle personnel were trying to reconstruct one working system from the remainders of four.

"To know how it should work, mainly," Snyder had said. He was an amiable fellow, medium in build and height, and usually either whistling or humming, on key, as he and his team worked to rebuild the engine. "We're in sort of no-man's land here, with bits and pieces we know worked in a high-tech society and should work if we reassemble them right, but we are working with the equivalent of early Iron Age tools. Aarens is miraculous, sometimes—if you tell him what you want a tool to do, he manages to provide one which does it. The problem is knowing what tool you need next and how long you'll have to wait until he can contrive it.''

Kris, now hobbling on crutches with well-wrapped feet and a bandaged hand, accompanied Zainal to the various meetings. She still seemed to be the necessary verbal bridge for vocabulary for him. Half the time, she was floundering for technical jargon even more than he was, but she was not about to admit that failing to anyone. Easley probably had guessed, but he was on their side. Kris would be very glad when she, Zainal, and their team could get back to what they were best at: exploring.

Sometimes it seemed to her that Scott resented what Zainal had had no reason to learn—as far as details of his own species' space drive technology went—while he was still forced to include the Catteni in all major meetings because of the little he did know and the insights he could provide on other details.

"Scott's got an incredible mind for detail," Easley murmured to Kris one evening during a long session.

"He comes across ultrasuspicious and snide to me," she whispered back.

"Suspicion is detail, too, you know, but I happen to know that he is impressed by Zainal."

"You could have fooled me," Kris replied, glaring at the end of the table where Scott, Rastancil, Ainger, Marrucci, and Beverly were crouched, heads together in inaudible conversation.

"But I don't," Easley said, his low voice vibrant with sincerity. "He knows a man of integrity when he sees one, and he sees Zainal as one. I don't think many of us had any idea of the role the Eosi play in what the Catteni do. So he's abandoned the position of detesting the Catteni for what was done on Earth, to come halfway to absolving the tool for the work it's been put to. Zainal's responsible for that adjustment without losing either dignity or respect in Scott's eyes."

Kris absorbed that speech, feeling a little better about what seemed like Scott's persecution of her lover. But only a little better.

. . .

Once again when the extra-acute hearing of the Deski sentries caught the first sound of the approaching vessel, they alerted the camps before the landing ship announced its imminent arrival on the communication band.

The "bridge" accepted the message with typical Catteni stolidity as Zainal had drilled them, reaffirming the coordinates of their downed ship's position. Though Leon had prepared a report of what had disabled the ship, he wasn't asked for it. Zainal had told him it wouldn't be required but had helped him learn the terms.

The camps in the line of the ship's descent—Bella Vista, Ayres Rock, and Shutdown—cleared away any signs of orderly living. All the air-cushioned vehicles were stowed out of sight and there was some concern over people, scouts and hunters, who might be seen out and about. Narrow, particularly, must appear deserted from the air.

"They will know from heat signs people are on the surface," Zainal had said, "but not what they are doing or what they live in. Wiser for them to see men out hunting."

"You mean they'll be counting noses?" someone had asked.

Zainal laughed at the notion. "No, just the presence of sufficient life signs to suggest survivors down here."

"So they can send us more?" Mitford asked in a sour tone.

"At this point, it's the more the merrier," Easley had said, grinning so infectiously that Mitford had smiled back.

The instrumentation on the bridge in the hangar was now working with an efficiency it had lacked for many voyages and the descent of the rescue vessel was easily estimated. The assault team, in position from the moment the first Deski alarm had come in, lounged about the downed transport: some were outside, others sitting on the ramp, while the "Drassi" would not appear until their counterparts called for them.

Camouflaged in the hedgerows and up the trees in strategic positions were sharpshooters with crossbows and lances. Zainal had had no information about the crew complement of the new transports. The "Catteni" to be rescued were armed with stunners, which might be all that was needed. Surprise was on their side.

The takeover of the transport ship was even smoother than the hijacking of the scout. The supercilious Drassi of the rescue vessel had been so eager to mock the stranded captain that he had been first down the ramp, the other Drassi staff following, while the crew began to unload what passengers remained. They were laughing and chatting, pleased to be on the last leg of this journey and going home. They were also looking forward to making the rescued Catteni work while they loafed.

Flat on her stomach in the next field, Zainal by her chuckling softly to himself, Kris watched as the Catteni Drassi strolled arrogantly across to the damaged transport.

The mock-Catteni crew had, of course, jumped to an appropriate alert stance, calling out—in an excellent accent, Kris thought proudly—to those inside that the Drassi captain was coming aboard. They followed in, a respectful distance behind, and one remained at the open hatch, leaning against it as the rescuers finished unloading the latest unconscious droppees. They had no sooner finished than they were called to come aboard the wreck.

"Now what do we have to do?" one Catteni demanded of another as they made their way across the field, or so Zainal translated for Kris.

"Probably dismantle equipment the beasts might use," the other said.

"Beasts, huh?" Joe muttered on the other side of Zainal. "We'll beast them."

Zainal translated the first part of the Catteni response. " 'Let's hope it doesn't take too long, then. I need my . . .' " And he refused to translate that rather long sentence to Kris. Considering the nasty way the two Catteni chuckled, she was glad he hadn't.

After the observers had waited anxiously for what seemed an interminable time, the mock-Drassi captain—actually Vic Yowell, who was not only the right size but had known enough Catteni to handle the necessary interchanges—appeared and with his men strode purposefully across to the newly arrived ship and up its ramp.

There was a brief interval before he reappeared, waving his cap and showing the difference between his Catteni makeup and his own skin color.

"It's ours now!"

The hedges sprouted humans, cheering and dancing with glee at the success of the second Phase Two assault. Then they hurried to attend to the newly arrived, 114 of them, all from Earth and in far better condition than many of the most recent arrivals. The Catteni prisoners were sent off to join their compatriots in the valley.

Yuri Palit, another mock Catteni with his skin back to its original shade, headed the guards who accompanied the prisoners. On the way they were given an example of night crawler activity and so descriptively warned of other dangers of Botany that they were thoroughly cowed by the time they arrived.

By the time the new transport had been gone over, Scott was actually smiling at everyone. This had been the maiden voyage of the KDL, according to its log and the look and smell of still-new equipment. Zainal, Kris, Bert Put, Peter Snyder, Rastancil, and Beverly were up all night translating manuals and understanding the improvements incorporated in its systems.

Best by far was the discovery of two small ships, capable of short-range planetary flight, and one large well-equipped ground vehicle, suitable for rough terrain, with exterior plating to resist many corrosive-type atmospheres. Looking at its specs on its control board, Zainal said that it was also probably "watergoing."

"Amphibious," Kris had murmured, and they had locked eyes and smiled. They would not have to risk using the scout, and being seen, in order to get to the other continents. This craft would hold twelve passengers and three crew and would transport them safely to at least the closest landmass. They'd better pick a day when the channel waters were calm, because she didn't like to think of being seasick in such confines.

But that sort of exploration was not in their immediate future. The next scenario to be played out was to take off in the brand-new transport, and head back toward Barevi, its base.

As many as could fit aboard entered the KDL 45A—which is how the glyphs on its side translated—and took off, and that about took in everyone who had worked in NASA or on air force jets from various countries. The decks could be arranged in a variety of heights and ways, according to cargo or passengers, awake or unconscious. Rather an ingenious arrangement, Marrucci and Beverly agreed, when Zainal showed them how to achieve various combinations. So the KDL could actually accommodate the many who had some reason, or claim, to make the journey. Some were going to have a chance in space; others had to learn how to manage the transport, and all would help jettison the traces of the sudden and complete destruction of a brand-new ship. Zainal had found log references to several minor incidents with the propulsion unit on the outward-bound journey: one severe enough for the captain to shut down the engines and send an EVA team to clear the tubes. That had been reported to their base, since it had delayed their touchdown at Botany to collect the transport crew.

Pete Snyder headed a team appointed to figure out just what malfunction could now result in a fatal accident. They had plenty of debris from the damaged ship—fortunately the components were all constructed of similar alloys. With a little ingenuity in their messages to their base, each describing further problems and then . . . a delayed-action explosion, sufficient detritus would be left floating in space to convince anyone who cared to examine it that the KDL had indeed, exploded on her way home. An appropriate outer panel had been taken from the old transport, and paint had been found in the KDL's supply bay to duplicate her glyphs. The bogus outward-bound voyage was scheduled to take a week, since Zainal wished to get beyond the system's heliopause, beyond the satellite's range, before conducting the explosion.

Kris had remained behind, her hand insufficiently healed for her to be useful on the voyage . . . especially when so many, like Raisha and other space-trained women pilots, deserved the chance. Truth to tell, she was tired from late nights and long sessions of translating. And then Mitford had asked for, and got, the land vehicle for his scouting teams. She'd be of much more use familiarizing herself with that piece of machinery than being a supernumerary on a space flight.

"They should be back by now, shouldn't they?" she asked Mitford as they were storing their equipment on the land-sea vehicle, nicknamed the Tub. When Zainal returned, Mitford was planning a trip, himself as leader, to cross the channel that separated this continent from its nearest neighbor. He was combining two teams for the project and was happier than Kris had seen him since he'd handed debriefing newcomers to Peter Easley.

"Yeah, in fact, they're three days overdue. But the destruction went off okay. You know that."

The link between the old transport's bridge and the

KDL was open and all the mounting hysteria, orders and counterorders, as the propulsion system "failed" had been duly followed by those on the ground . . . including the final bang. So that part had gone well.

The Deski sentries were ordered to keep their ears wide open, since their senses were trusted far more than the obsolete and erratic detection system on the bridge in the hangar.

Kris accompanied Mitford when they did a check on the prison valley and found the Catteni alive, but certainly not making any move to "settle" in.

"No initiative," Mitford muttered to Kris. "Just like Zainal said. Not even that pair of Drassi captains."

These seemed to be concentrating on a small space of dirt in front of them, but neither moved.

"Chess?" Kris asked, for they had that sort of concentration about them.

"Chess?" Mitford regarded her with surprise. "They haven't the wits for checkers, much less chess."

"Well, there's someone trying to fish," Kris said, pointing to the one man poised over the stream with a thin lance in his hand.

"So he is. Even Catteni get tired of those dry rations," he said, and turned away.

Yuri Palit, in his authority as head of resettlement, had gone to check the Turs and came back with the information that they had already made a few shelters, chopping down the lodge-pole trees. There also seemed to be several wounded lying in the sun: broken legs and arms and one with raw wounds visible down his side.

"Trying to climb out?" asked Astrid.

"How stubborn can Turs be?" Yuri Palit asked of Mitford.

The sergeant shrugged. "Damned stubborn. Leave 'em alone."

"And let them ruin that lovely valley?" Kris demanded.

Mitford jerked his head toward the photos that adorned his back wall, the ones showing the other closed valleys Zainal had seen on his way in. "They're others as well as the other continents."

"Now, about them," Astrid began.

Mitford held up one hand, grinning at the tall attractive Swede. "Gotta wait until Zainal checks us out on the amphibian."

Which reminded everyone that KDL was now six days' overdue. Kris tried to appear unconcerned, but possible disaster scenarios kept her awake most nights.

"What could have happened?" Astrid asked her the morning of the seventh day. "Surely they should be returning now?"

"That bang wasn't for real," Mitford said, avoiding Kris' eyes, but speaking as positively as if he had consummate faith in Zainal's return.

"There'll be a good reason, I'm positive," Kris said so firmly that Mitford shot her a quick look.

"Yeah, there would be, kid. I just can't imagine what."

"Asteroids, some technical difficulty, or operational problem, there could be dozens of good reasons."

"Yeah."

"It wouldn't be a good idea for him to get in touch and give it all away since the ship's been destroyed and that damned satellite would catch any message he sent."

"You're right there," Mitford acknowledged and then went to do something else.

"New satellite," Zainal told them as soon as the hatch opened to the crowd waiting so anxiously. "We go . . ." and he gestured a circuitous course. He looked for and found Kris at the side of the hatch. "Lenvec's work." He dropped down beside her, touching her cheek just briefly as the rest of the spacefarers exited, exultant in their shouts to the welcoming committee.

The biggest smile was on Scott's face as he came down the ramp, Beverly, Rastancil, and those who were now being called the High Command following closely.

"Mitford, Easley," Scott called out, and added other names, "meeting at nineteen-thirty at Narrow. Beggs!" The officious lieutenant Kris disliked so came running up to meet him, clipboard in hand. "I want all these men and women to make that meeting if humanly possible . . ." and he continued giving orders while proceeding to the nearest air-cushion vehicle and gesturing for it to take off toward Camp Narrow.

Zainal, taking Kris by the arm, steered her off to one side, away from the general jubilation around the hatch.

"Lenvec got them to put up a more powerful satellite spy?" she asked.

"Someone did. We had to time its orbits to sneak back in. KDL is very good at glide."

"You glided? From where?"

Zainal grinned at her astonishment. "Not hard. Your space shuttles did it. Catteni still better space jockeys."

"Jockeys?" Kris had to admit to herself that she didn't like him picking up slang from other sources— and severely curbed her reaction.

"Bert brought her down. Good man, Bert. Now, where can she hide?" Zainal frowned over that problem.

Kris looked up the field at the hulk still sitting there. "Put it there. They expect a wreck in that place. How much detail will the satellite be able to make out down here on the surface? The name glyphs?"

Zainal began to chuckle. "Why not? The KDL masses more but not that much more."

"Hiding it right out in sight always confuses a searcher," Kris said.

"Scott will agree?"

Kris shrugged. "That thing's too big to fit in any garage—except maybe the one we can't get into at the seaside. Who will come looking for it? You had us all excited, listening to orders and counterorders and all the hysterics . . ."

Zainal chuckled louder now, his yellow eyes reflecting his laughter, most un-Catteni-ish.

"And if you guys avoided the satellite's eyes on the way in, surely we've succeeded in deceiving them."

"Some one of your wise men said once," and he tipped his head back a moment, recalling the exact words, which he carefully enunciated, "that you can fool most of the people part of the time but not all of the people all of the time."

She had to smile at him, he looked so pleased with remembering the apt quote. And she was so pleased he was back, safe. "You think Lenvec is that vindictive?"

"Not think. I know. When I was chosen . . ." He paused briefly and then went on, "I was given privileges the chosen have. Lenvec was . . . jealous. If he is now to take my place as chosen, he will feel like he got robbed." He gave her a sideways glance, to see her reaction to his slang. She grinned at him. He was also speaking with a less guttural tone to the English words. Soon his accent would be indistinguishable from a native-born speaker.

"Hmmm, yes, if he's the jealous type, he would feel robbed. But maybe he's been . . . chosen already. How much of *him* is left in the Eosi?"

Zainal nodded his head slowly over that point. "I do not know that. Fortunately," and now he held his cheek down against hers, holding her tightly, "I was dropped and I stay."

Kris was not the only one who thought of keeping the KDL right out in the open. An artistically scorched glyph took the bright new KDL 45's place but there were, actually, no other options, even if they could find a Farmer facility big enough to house it. The ship was not just a trophy, gathering dust, although how it would be used was yet to be decided. Scott had approved Phase Two but who knew if the admiral, who seemed to have taken charge of the military aspect of the High Command, felt they should attempt Phase Three.

The KDL settled itself on the wreck, compressing its empty shell. The Deski sentries would give enough advance warning of any landings . . . should other transports be sent here . . . so that she could lift and settle down a few fields over, and be camouflaged from casual inspection. The Catteni rarely looked around during the process of hauling out their passengers and what few supplies accompanied them. A certain risk was taken, but Scott had come to agree with Zainal's assessment of the Drassi: Do as little work as possible and get back to base.

"You know, someone might just think it was odd that there have been three ships blown up in this area," Leon Dane remarked at the end of the final debriefing, "and decide it isn't worth visiting this sector of the vast Eosi-Catteni empire and leave us alone."

"I doubt that," Easley said with a sad smile. "According to the latest arrivals, Earth's resistance is growing, and the Catteni are still taking anyone they think might be a saboteur or ringleader into custody. We had a troop of Sea Scouts in the last group and all they were doing was holding their monthly meeting. We may end up with more of Earth's population here . . . and wherever else they've been dumped . . . than on good old Terra Firma."

"I just hope we can maintain a fresh-start approach on Botany and ditch the attitudes that made trouble back on good old Terra Firma," Mitford said, with good reason to doubt the ability of people to forget ingrained intolerance and bigotry. Three men and a woman were serving time in the stocks right now who had revived an old prejudice in an hour-long brawl. The injured would serve their sentences when they had sufficiently recovered. "The more people we get in, the more trouble we acquire."

"We've got four continents . . . well, two, if we leave the Farmers theirs," Leon said. "There's enough space for everyone, isn't there?"

"For some types, there's never enough space," Sarah said.

"Too right," Dane said, exhaling tiredly.

CHAPTER 7

Once the excitement of procuring and hiding the KDL calmed down, Scott and others of the High Command, military branch, spent hours debriefing the latest arrivals from Earth, trying to figure out world events from fragmented individual reports. Not much news was broadcast anymore in a world that once had twenty-four-hour news bulletin coverage.

"Disasters every time of the day or night," Kris had said.

"Do they do that on Catten or Barevi?" Sarah had asked Zainal. They were all sitting around their table after the evening meal in Narrow.

"Tell everyone everything? No," and Zainal chuckled at the notion. His gray hair had grown so long now that he was wearing it in a ponytail, a style that suited him better than most. Kris had offered to braid it, Amerind fashion, as she did her now much longer hair, but he had declined. "Only need-to-know is told." Then he gave a shrug. "And evenings of lies about new worlds and brave Catten."

"Recruiting?"

Zainal considered the word, squeezing Kris' hand to indicate he was going to figure that one out himself. "Yes, to join space army."

He got a thumbs-up for accuracy from the others at the table—their scouting partners and those from Astrid's six-strong team. They spent a lot of time together, learning how to drive the amphibious machine so that anyone could. The mechanics had been all over it, too, familiarizing themselves with its equipment, engines, systems, communications, and life support. While Mitford was ranked a senior in the High Command Committee now governing the settlers, he still had to get "proper clearance" to take such a valuable piece of machinery. He also needed Scott's clearance to take Zainal.

"They'll do anything, any damned thing, rather than let us function as a team," Mitford had ranted the previous night. "They've got both bridges manned, and the KDL working off solar power, and we still have the Deski perimeter listeners. Almost nothing can sneak up on us down here. If they really needed Zainal, Marrucci could fly over in one of those atmosphere planes now that he's learned how not to kill himself in it. And it doesn't leave the sort of trail visible to the spy sat."

Zainal wasn't exactly reassuring on that count because he didn't know how sophisticated the new satellite was, just that it was on a full global orbit, checking the surface of the planet once every thirty hours. He was positive that the reconditioned air-cushion Farmer vehicles would not show up on the satellite since they ran on solar power. The amphibious vehicle might possibly be visible—since it was no longer supposed to exist—so he had plotted a course and they would move only when the satellite was at another point around Botany's globe. It might take slightly longer to reach the coast, but once in the water, he thought, the Tub would be undetectable since water would not only cool its exterior but mask its emissions.

Kris' hand was still slightly red but her feet had healed, even if she was careful to keep a layer of fluff as an insole. And she dearly wanted to leave Camp Narrow, for Mitford's sake as well as Zainal's. She tried to convince herself it was just the wander-itch that made her restless, because she didn't think she had a trace of precognition in her, but she did very much want to leave. To go explore the neighbor continent.

Fully accustomed now to its new form, Eosi Mentat Ix was bored. It had returned to pleasures that its weakening former husk had been unable to perform, and now these no longer satisfied its seeking for unusual experiences. The new form had been relatively circumscribed, not having had the training of the young originally chosen from that bloodline.

That was when it remembered the animosity and bitterness of the Catteni mind when it had been subsumed. Ix accessed the memories. A brief exploration would discover if the entity's suspicions had been valid. Ix was somewhat startled to discover that a more powerful satellite had been put in position around the subject planet. The entity's traces grew alarmed within the Mentat as the most recent report was mentally gleaned from those on duty.

The scout ship had disappeared and no trace of it had been found anywhere in Eosi space: it had not refueled at any station, planetary or space. Nor could the satellite find that sort of metal shape on the subject planet. The matter of the wreck of the transport was resolved by the interchange of communications between the KDL and the downed ship. The KDL, the newest of the transport fleet, had taken off after discharging its cargo and had been tracked out of that solar system. By both satellites. And the tape of its final emergency and explosion was on record.

Ix carefully reviewed that tape, the details of the final

moments of the ship's life and the efforts of the crew to remedy the fault. Ix also reviewed the fault in the light of the KDL's sister ships now coming on line and found that such a back surge in the propulsion was indeed a possibility, however improbable.

The Eosi Mentat ordered a search for the log of the KDL, which should be found in the space debris. It was. Within the tiny fraction of Ix's great mentality an infinitesimal scream insisted that such events were suspicious.

Ix screened the orbiting satellite's records and found only the wreck that had been left where it had landed. Then Eosi Mentat Ix was called to a meeting of its peers, to determine what must be done with the increasing problems experienced by Catteni occupying forces on the latest planet they had subjugated. Such continued resistance was unique, even bizarre, and Ix was caught up in deciding what punitive measures to take that would completely solve this problem. However, all Eosi found themselves rather fascinated by the scope and originality of the opposition to their benign rule.

The general-maintenance orb reached the target planet and found its near space occupied by two technological items: one orbiting in a thirty-hour, total global pattern, and the other geosynchronous. These objects were thoroughly examined before the orb descended to a level at which it could investigate why a homing missile had been dispatched from the command facility without a message. The orb discovered some life-forms resident in the facility, for what purpose it was not programmed to discover, but their presence was noted. It proceeded on its orderly inspection of the agricultural facilities placed around the more arable continents and discovered anomalies throughout a large area, suggesting malfunction on an unprecedented scale of the indigenous equipment. Checking inventory against what should have been idle at this time of the planet's growing season, it could discover parts of the equipment but not in the usual form. This abnormality was duly noted. There did appear to be more life-forms than the natural propagation of the indigenous species would ordinarily produce. There was no possible way in which such a bovine species could damage, much less alter the machinery that husbanded it. The orb was programmed only for mechanical devices, inventory and supply: it did not examine life-forms. That was another department.

It completed the necessary circuits at the altitude programmed into it for the maximum efficiency of required investigations, sent its findings back to its home world, and continued on its scheduled maintenance cycle.

The Deski were covering their eyes, cowering, but still managed to report in to their bases that there was the most fearful noise in the air. The boards on both bridges reported a spatial object, traveling at an impossible speed, spinning about Botany at what Marrucci stammered had to be damned near the speed of light. Its manifestation on the bridge boards was of a continuous pattern of light, encompassing Botany.

"Then it can't be Catteni," replied Rastancil, watching behind Marrucci. "They don't have that capability . . ."

"Yet," Marrucci added, sotto voce.

The team at the command post reported a terrifying moment.

"I felt like I was being scanned by ETs," reported the generally sanguine Colonel Salvinato in a voice that shook noticeably.

"Well, you're not alone. Something's giving us a real going-over," Rastancil replied, which he hoped would reassure the colonel: his body still tingled from whatever it was that had touched him.

Salvinato reported in later that there were now two

homing devices where there had recently been only one.

"Replacements by matter transmitter?" Rastancil said, condescendingly.

" 'Beam me up, Scotty,' " Marrucci said, and this time he didn't lower his voice. "The Catteni also don't have anything that can do that."

"That *would* account for how the Farmers' ships managed to load up so fast," Mitford said, when he was called in to give his interpretation of the curious incident. "I felt it, too, like someone going over me with a mild electrical current." And then he smiled. "The Farmers have finally noticed us."

"Do we really want them to?"

Mitford thought that over for a long moment and then shrugged. "Beats me, general," he said. The generals had taken control of Botany out of his hands, but he still felt the responsibility. "It was the only option I had at the time. Still seems a good one. Only no one hung around long enough to speak to us. So, what happens next?"

Scott called an immediate meeting of as many of those from Camp Rock as had witnessed the fly-past of the Mech Makers'/Farmers' spaceship. Rumors circulated and with each lap of the scanner they doubled in improbability, stupidity, and frightfulness. It was now supposed to have infected everyone with a deadly disease that would kill off the entire population in twenty-four hours. Other rumors included the notion that the Farmers had counted them and would shortly come and round them up, process them in the abattoir, and ship them back as delicacies. Or, all of them were "marked" now and would be enslaved or converted into six-legged loo-cows or night crawlers.

There was certainly tension as the First Drop folk gathered in the mess hall at Narrow, late that afternoon. Benches (made of old machine parts, and these were the last places the arrivals sat) and stools formed a semicircle around a table at which sat Jim Rastancil, Geoffrey Ainger, Bull Fetterman, Bob Reidenbacker, John Beverly, Pete Easley, Yuri Palit, and the former judge, Iri Bempechat, who had recently taken over the disciplinary duties for work evasion or inadequacy. Ray Scott, with his insufferable aide, Beggs, taking notes and counting noses, rose when it was evident that all who intended to come had arrived.

"I hope none of you have suffered any repercussions from those ludicrous rumors started after our recent visitation," Scott began, with a rueful expression.

He looked directly at Chuck Mitford, who sat with Zainal on his right and Kris to his left, with Dowdall, Cumber, Esker, Murphy, and Tesco—his original assistants during the retreat from the First Drop field—ranged along the row: defenders who had made very certain that no hystericals got near the sergeant. Other First Drop took the second row, showing solid support. Patti Sue just behind him with Jay Greene, Sandy Areson, Bart, Coo, Pess, Slav, Bass, Matt Su, and Mack Dargle. More from the First Drop spread out behind them: Janet, Anna Bollinger and her son, the Doyles, Joe Latore, and Dick Aarens.

Mitford sat with arms crossed over his chest. "You and me both know the problem with rumors, admiral, but I'm not going into decline over 'em, scanned or not. Especially when everyone'll wake up tomorrow in the same shape they went to sleep in."

"Yes, that will solve the problem, but not the bigger ones we must seriously consider," Scott said. He looked at Zainal. "I take it that phenomenal display had nothing to do with either Eosi or Catteni spacecraft?"

"Absolutely nothing. The satellites' reports are going to cause a big stir. I know that much," Zainal responded. "The Eosi won't like to see what came. They will be very worried. Finally."

"You were a scout, weren't you, Zainal?" Bull Fetterman asked. "You ever encountered any traces of them in this galaxy?"

Zainal shook his head. "This is new solar system for Eosi and Catteni. Which is why *we*," and he emphasized the plural pronoun as he glanced around to include everyone there, "are colonizing it. What I know is that their technology is far superior to Eosi. I also do not fear them as I do Eosi."

"You don't?" Scott was not the only one surprised by that admission. "How do you arrive at that conclusion, considering what just happened?"

"Because of what just happened," Zainal said as if that should be obvious. "No one was injured by scanning. The homer was replaced. No, I do not fear the Farmers. A . . ." and he put his hand flat against his stomach, "a . . . gut feeling."

"Does anyone else share this . . . gut feeling?" Scott asked, more amused than patronizing.

"After seeing that valley, I'm inclined to agree," Kris said. There was something about the ambiance in the valley that she thought the entire team shared: its tranquillity, carefully saved and preserved by the blocked entrance. "These are not killers, like Eosi. They nourish this planet carefully."

"Why didn't they get rid of the night crawlers, then, I'd like to know," Dowdall said sourly.

"Very efficient in clearing up waste and garbage," Kris said.

"They made safe places to keep something in, or something out. Eosi do not do such things. The Farmers are very different from Eosi . . . and Catteni."

Lenny Doyle raised his hand, grinning. "I'd be a bit more apt to believe him if the Mechs . . . the Farmers . . . hadn't nearly chopped us up for the crates. But Zainal got us out before they could, and besides, the machines weren't programmed to know the difference between us and loo-cows."

Dick Aarens made a low disclaimer.

"Would that suggest the Farmers aren't bipedal?" Scott asked.

"No, it only suggests that the Farmers' machines were not programmed to differentiate between warm-blooded species," Kris said.

"Could the Mechs have been made in the form of their makers?" Janet asked, her eyes flicking around for reassurance.

Lenny began to guffaw at the notion, laughter he tried to stifle when he saw how he offended Janet.

"C'mon, Janet," Aarens said rudely, "spare us that religious tripe . . . made in their image? Shit, no! Every single piece of equipment on this planet is a masterpiece of design, using renewable power sources and with easy access for self-repair and maintenance. No one's been able to figure out what sort of alloy was used, but the machinery is practically indestructible."

"Until you came along," Janet said angrily, stung by Aarens' snide manner.

"That does not, however," and Ray Scott jumped in quickly, waving for both of them to sit down, "give us any insights into what course of action the Farmers might take when that orbiting whiz-ball of theirs reports that all the machinery in a good-sized section of their farmlands is no longer in operating condition."

Kris covered her mouth to hide her grin. She wouldn't have expected that sort of wry assessment from the admiral.

"Let us not digress into useless speculation," Scott said. "Will the Eosi do anything to Botany while they're studying the reports? Like a blockade?"

"Or at least stop shipping us more colonists?" asked Pete Easley in a plaintive tone.

"That is more likely," Zainal said.

"What I had more in mind is sending a team to investigate a planet that has been the last point of call for a scout ship and two transports."

"What about blaming the ETs for disappearing those ships?" asked Lenny Doyle.

"That would be too much to hope for," Jim Rastancil said, but he looked thoughtful.

"The Eosi do not care what happens to a colony like this one," Zainal said. "But they will not like what happened today when they see the reports. The Eosi believe that their technology is best."

"And they'll find it hard to swallow that it isn't," Rastancil said, quite satisfied with that turn.

"So, it's the Eosi who are your inventors?" Ainger asked.

"Yes. They supply the plans. Catteni build."

"You're sure they won't come after Botany because it has attracted such extra . . ." Rastancil asked, pausing for the appropriate term, "stellar visitations?"

Zainal considered this.

"How the hell can Zainal answer that, general?" Mitford asked with some acrimony. "The Eosi have been supreme in space so far. At least to hear Catteni tell it, and I heard all their tales when I was stuck in Barevi."

"There will be much worry and many meetings," Zainal said, obviously enjoying the thought of Eosian consternation. "You," and he gestured to those around the table, mostly the latest to arrive on Botany, "do not realize how low the Catteni are in their great minds and . . . selfs." He looked at Kris to see if he had the right word. "They will spend much effort and time trying to find out who sent that very, very fast space machine. *Not*," and he paused for emphasis, "why it should appear here around their penal colony."

"That's a relief," murmured Anna in the row behind.

"That's some relief," echoed Rastancil, sitting back.

"So we can put the Eosi response to this in the slow

lane, then,'' Scott said, ''but I doubt we can ignore the response of the Farmers.''

''He thinks by calling them 'farmers,' they won't scare us as much,'' Janet remarked to Anna.

Kris grinned over her shoulder at Janet but the woman was whistling in the dark: her eyes were scared and her chin trembled a bit. Anna Bollinger, who had left her baby son with someone for this meeting, looked even more frightened.

''I hoped to get their attention, admiral, as the one chance I saw—then—of getting off this planet and back home. Best scenario would be to make *them* notice the Eosi-Catteni combine,'' Mitford said.

''A bit naïve of you, wasn't it, sergeant?'' asked Geoffrey Ainger.

''Now, wait just a minute, Ainger,'' Kris said, sitting up straight with the anger that bit of condescension roused in her. She was not placated by Easley leaning over to murmur something to the British naval officer.

''My apologies, Miss Bjornsen. I forget how little you had at your disposal in the early days,'' Ainger said, elevating his butt off the chair. ''Sergeant Mitford, no offense intended.''

''None taken,'' Mitford said equably, and waved his hand, accepting the apology. The hand came down on Kris' leg, a reminder that he was well able to defend himself.

''It was at the very least what any noncom should do,'' Bull Fetterman said. ''Establish what escape route is possible to return to his regiment.''

''We established a lot more than that,'' Dick Aarens said, jumping to his feet. ''And we've done a damned good job of converting the Mech Makers' stuff to human needs. Give us some credit, damn it.''

''We do, I assure you, Mr. Aarens, especially since you contrived so many of the improvements . . .'' Reidenbacker began.

"We'd better stop congratulating ourselves," Mitford put in, "begging your pardon, sir, but I'd like to hear what Admiral Scott now has in mind."

Kris privately believed it was obvious from Scott's expression that he had nothing in mind . . . yet.

"What I'd like to hear again . . . friends," and Scott was having trouble finding an appropriately inoffensive group noun, "is exactly your impressions of the arrival of the leviathan you saw, collecting this planet's harvests."

"If you mean, were we scanned then," Kris replied, "no, we weren't."

"Hell, admiral, the ship didn't even know we were there," Jay Greene said. "It just sailed overhead like some sort of . . ." and he waved his hand above his head, "monstrous dinosaur."

"It didn't land?"

"Not that we saw," Mitford replied.

"Zainal led a group of us back here, because we thought that's where it hovered," Ninety Doyle said. "We weren't that far behind it when it took off again. There wasn't a bloody thing left of the acres of crates we had to climb to get out of here."

"So there was nothing in it of the speed and flexibility of what buzzed us?" Beverly asked.

"Nuh-huh," and Ninety shook his head emphatically. "Different thing entirely."

"We sort of thought at the time," Jay Greene said, "that it was preprogrammed to do its job. That there wasn't any life-form aboard it."

Rastancil whistled, impressed. "Totally automated?"

"And a culture which has patently invented matter transmitters . . ." Scott said, clearing his throat.

"That would have been the only way all that stuff could have been loaded in the time it hovered," Ninety agreed. "Just like on *Star Trek*."

"Then it is entirely likely that today's scanner is also totally automated," Easley said.

"We couldn't get any idea of the mass of the scanner," Rastancil said. "I was on the bridge when it began its orbit and the transport doesn't have much in the way of fancy detection devices . . ." He looked over at Marrucci, who had been in the scout.

The pilot shook his head, holding up his hands. "I couldn't figure out what to activate on the board." He looked at Zainal.

"The scout will not track such speed," the Catteni said.

"So, essentially, we must wait until the device sends its reports to the Farmers," Scott said, "and then await results."

"Isn't there anything we can *do* to save ourselves?" Anna Bollinger's voice had a slightly hysterical note in it.

"We can't just sit still and do nothing." Janet added her protest.

A slightly supercilious expression crossed Admiral Scott's face and Kris, who had started to like the man, changed her opinion again.

"If he asks her what she thinks we should do . . ." she murmured to Mitford, who once again clamped his hand on her leg in restraint as he turned around to Janet.

"There's a lot we can do, Janet, and that's why we're here. Now, we've done pretty well so far, haven't we?" he asked, and waited until she gave her head an unwilling nod. "So just hold tight a bit longer, huh?" Then Mitford turned back to the front table. "Since it's a fair bet that the scanner saw that we've altered all the machines that are supposed to be in the various garages and barns we've been using, why don't we start by clearing them out? I'd also recommend that we explore the nearer continent with the view of taking up our residence there

... that is, if we find the Farmers haven't set up shop there, too.''

Scott was nodding acceptance of these suggestions, and even Ainger looked less dour.

"There're all those closed valleys on this continent, blocked to keep something in, or something out. How many did we discover, Zainal?'' Mitford turned to his right.

"Several dozens. We must ask the map woman, Sheila, for details.''

"The caves are ours,'' Patti Sue said firmly, the last person Kris would have thought would speak up in such a meeting. "We've made them livable.''

"But we have trespassed,'' Janet said to her.

Kris didn't dare look around at Janet: what she was saying seemed so weird from a woman who was considered basically quite sensible. Maybe the scan had done something to some folks after all. She shuddered. She wasn't going to think there could be the least bit of truth in those asinine rumors, all products of insecurity and lack of self-confidence.

"If we give them back what we took . . .'' Janet went on and then, hearing Dick Aarens' contemptuous snort at that idea, she whirled around on him, pointing her finger. "You're the one who started taking their machines apart . . .''

"Janet!'' Once again Mitford called her to order, twisting around to face her. "You're not thinking this through and you're not a silly woman. You've been such a strength to so many who got here confused and scared.''

Sandy Areson had discreetly moved to sit on Janet's other side and now put a comforting arm around her shoulders, nodding once to Mitford to indicate she would take over now.

"What was done is done, and I doubt even the best of our mechanical geniuses could put all the parts back together again," Scott said in a conciliatory tone. "Not that that would be even remotely feasible, since we'll need every single thing we've contrived from their machinery to effect an evacuation of their premises. If that is one of our options."

"I think retreat in the face of overwhelming strength is usually considered a sensible course of action," Bull Fetterman said at his driest.

He got scattered laughter for his attempt to reduce the tension in the mess hall.

"Furthermore we can prepare places for everyone," Beverly said with a big smile, "if what I've seen of some of those valleys is any indication."

"The other continent's a better idea, General," Mitford said, rising from his chair. "Especially as we now have the Tub to do reconnaissance. Which I had planned to do anyway."

"Positive action is always admirable, sergeant," Scott said, "and I suggest you complete your plans and get them under way as soon as possible."

"Will Yuri's group start immediate evacuations, too?" Mitford swung halfway around, indicating Janet.

"You better believe it," but it was Reidenbacker who answered the question. He gave Janet an encouraging smile. She made a pathetic little sound in her throat but managed a brief smile, still twisting her hands nervously in her lap.

"They'd better consider that there'll be a lot more newcomers reacting like Janet," Kris murmured to Mitford. He nodded his head.

"Shouldn't we clear out all the things we've made?" Dick Aarens asked. "We need everything if we're going to function. And the scout? Where can we stash that now if we've got to clear the barns?"

Scott held up his hands. "Give us a few hours here," and he gestured to the specialists sitting behind him, "and we'll formulate the necessary plans and set up teams to implement them. Now, I know some of you have been upset by the whiz-ball we had this morning . . ." His label for the orbital caught everyone's attention this time, and he grinned to see its effect. "But we don't want to start another batch of rumors with those who still feel insecure here on Botany. Let's be careful how we discuss this meeting outside the mess hall, shall we? I ask all of you, by whatever you hold sacred, not to start a second wave of ridiculous rumors. We'll do as much as humanly possible to rectify our misappropriation of housing and effects. Certainly our first priority is getting people out of our landlords' buildings and to safer places, like the valleys. Equally important is preserving the equipment we need to conduct an orderly evacuation."

Chuck Mitford turned around to those behind him. "Keep in mind, folks, it's taken the Farmers more than nine months to discover we're here. I'd say we had plenty of time to get elsewhere and at least sweep the garages and barns clean before we leave. Right, Janet? Anna?"

"We can do it," Patti Sue said, so staunchly that Kris, remembering how fearful the girl had once been, could have cheered out loud at that vote of confidence. Both Janet and Anna responded to her remark and looked less despondent.

"Of course," Patti added ingenuously, "they might not come until the growing season starts, and we don't even know when winter ends, if this *is* winter."

Zainal got to his feet again. "I like the idea of moving us all to the other continent if it is okay," he said. "I think we should go soon. The airships can look at the other landmass. It may not be as barren as it looks from space. If it is, they can help us search."

Ninety got to his feet as soon as Zainal sat down. "There are a lot of those closed valleys, too, which obviously weren't used by the Farmers. Maybe we can put people in them.'' When he heard protests arise, he added, ''With stairs to get out when you had to. The valleys grow trees and bushes. We could transfer a lot of the stuff we've been growing to feed us to the valleys. And aren't the Turs and Catteni trying 'em out for us?'' He grinned broadly with a teasing glance at Zainal.

Mitford rose. ''I agree with Zainal, for what it's worth,'' he said with an unusual touch of humility.

''Sarge, you had the only idea feasible at the time. Don't have a guilt trip over it now,'' Kris said staunchly, and her remark was quickly seconded by many in the hall.

''We all helped,'' Joe Latore said, and turning around in his seat, looked straight at Dick Aarens. ''Didn't we?''

Aarens noticeably ignored him.

''Yes, but what happens if we move to the other continent,'' Anna Bollinger said, her face distorted with fear, ''and they come after us there?'' Janet immediately put a reassuring arm on her shoulders and glared around.

''Hell's bells, missus,'' Ninety said, ''there're caves all over the planet they'd never find you in. And probably caves across the channel, too, wouldn't you say, Zainal?''

Kris turned around, one hand going to Anna's knee. ''We know it's really your son you're worried about, Anna, but why borrow any more trouble than we've already got?''

''Which brings me to the subject of the Catteni contribution to our present crisis,'' Scott said. ''Zainal, what will your High Eosi do when the satellite reports that whiz-ball?''

''Worry,'' Zainal answered succinctly, his yellow eyes glinting with mischief.

Scott allowed a slight smile at Zainal's facetiousness. ''Would they come back to inspect Botany or set up a blockade of warships or something similar?''

"First, it will be discussed. Second, the satellite will be checked for faults that what it reported is true. Third, they may send someone to see what happened to us." Zainal obviously doubted his third point was likely.

"Fourth, what if they send us more colonists?" Sandy Areson asked.

Zainal considered that for a moment, dropping his chin to his chest.

"I think no more colonists come for a while now, Sandy."

"Especially since it's been unlucky for them to land on this planet," Aarens said, chuckling.

Zainal went on as if Aarens hadn't aired his wit. "They will not believe the speed of the whiz-ball."

"And they know that it did not originate in this solar system?" Scott asked.

Zainal nodded. "They will think a long time before they do anything."

"Good," Scott said, rubbing his hands together. "Then that will give us time to remove ourselves completely. As I understand Catteni colonial policy, Zainal, they might even abandon the planet as unsuitable. Is that right?"

Zainal nodded.

"So we might be all right after all?" Anna Bollinger asked, her tear-streaked face brightening.

"It is entirely possible," Scott said with considerable and sincere aplomb.

The upshot of the discussion was not a referendum after all, but the organization of scouting parties to check out every single one of what Ninety Doyle tagged "lonesome valleys." Small groups would be quartered in the valleys to discover any unusual denizens, though none had been seen in either of the other two inhabited places. Once Mitford had organized the basics of those explorations, he left a sheaf of instructions with Easley as "the manual" and roused the members of his combined team. They set off before second moonrise since the amphibious vehicle had lights.

It also had excellent suspension. Mitford slept his usual six hours as Zainal drove it over surfaces rough and smooth.

The driver sat in the center of this vehicle with seating for two on either side and control panels across the width of the command position. Zainal gave demonstrations to his relief drivers, Joe Marley and Astrid, conducting a running lesson on the vehicle's potential and what each control was supposed to show, what the various icons on the panel board meant.

"Have we got a periscope?" Marley asked facetiously.

"Third button on right, sun icon," Zainal said.

"Why didn't I guess?"

"We can drive deep, cannot use scope. Says the manual," Zainal replied.

"A man who will read manuals!" Sarah gave a sigh of exaggerated respect.

Joe gingerly tapped the "glass" of the slit window beside him. "How much pressure will this stand?"

"Enough. We will not go deep. Is more built for corro-sive atmospheres," Zainal added. "Which is to close vents, Astrid?" he asked, testing her memory of the functions on the panel in front of her.

"This one," she said, promptly pointing to it.

"Got it in one," Zainal said, and Kris, seated behind him, chuckled. He leaned back. "I learn new ones every day, don't I?"

"I, too," said Astrid proudly.

"You sure do, Astrid," Joe replied, grinning at her.

The point they were headed toward was close to five hundred miles from Camp Narrow, and the intention was to drive straight through to their destination with only brief halts to let air circulate through the Tub. It was such a new piece of equipment that it reeked of paint and oil and other strong odors and needed to have its air system flushed out, especially before they submerged. So they stopped from time to time, to brew tea and relieve themselves.

By midmorning the next day, the sea sparkled ahead of them. Visible without benefit of the binoculars was the irregular lavender coastline of the neighbor landmass. The water before them was calm, with gentle ripples curling over onto the beach.

"Further away than Dover from Calais," Astrid said, for she had traveled extensively in Europe in her college days.

Zainal said something in Catteni, flicked up his left hand when the number he wanted refused to come to mind. "Six or seven plus seven tens," he said.

"Seventy-six," Kris said. "And how fast will the Tub go underwater?"

"Not as fast as on land," he replied. "Half the speed."

"That's far from slow," said Joe, impressed, and peered at the sloping shoreline. "Shallow?" he wondered.

"We'll find out soon enough," Mitford said. "All aboard," and he called in Astrid, Bjorn, and Jan, who had been searching for clams on the pebbly beach.

They had no sooner reached the flotation point for the Tub when a quick ping began to echo from Joe's panel. "Sonar?" he asked, and then saw the gauge that was lighting up. "Or something like it. Are you taking us down, Skipper?"

Zainal shook his head. "Distance to bottom."

Water was reaching the slit windows now and covering two thirds of the main one and the slight movement of the waters could be seen.

"I forgot to ask," Mitford said, "does anyone on board get seasick . . . besides me?"

"Sarge? You can't," Kris said in mock alarm.

Leila, always attentive, rose from her seat and went aft. She returned with a large basin, which she offered to Mitford. He gave her such a disgusted look that she started to apologize. "I was only trying to be helpful."

"He's teasing you, Leila," Kris said.

"Maybe I'm not." Mitford said, staring down at the basin.

"Are you claustrophobic?" Kris murmured.

He nodded.

"Oh," she said in as sympathetic a tone as she could manage. No wonder he hadn't been so keen to fly in Baby.

"The way the Tub is moving, Sarge," Joe said in a very cheerful tone, "we'll be there in no time at all. No time at all!"

"Just think of it, Chuck . . ."

Mitford put a hasty hand on Kris' shoulder. "Don't . . . use that particular word, will you?"

"Ooops, but you are first to cross this channel, or strait, or whatever it is. Can we name it after you?"

"Huh?" and the sergeant regarded her with startled eyes. Then he realized she was trying to divert him and managed a grin. "I'll be all right. There's still some view left . . ." But the waves washed up over the windscreen and he hastily looked away from their activity.

The crossing was completed in just under two Catteni-style hours as marked by the timepiece set in the control panel. The Tub trundled out onto a sandy beach, dotted with the same sort of shrubs that grew on its neighbor.

"Clams, too," Astrid said, pointing to the air holes as they all emerged from the Tub, once again flushing out the newness smells. "We get some?" she asked Mitford.

"There's plenty of time," he said, shading his eyes to glance up the slope that led inland. Then he glanced down at the map he had taken from his pocket and unfolded it. "We're about here," he said, pointing and then cocking his finger due west. "Should be higher ground this way. Zainal, Kris, Astrid, Bjorn, Whitby, let's have bit of a recon," and he strode forward. "Joe, you're in charge of the Tub," he added.

When they reached the first height and had an overview, there were green-covered stretches in either direction and right back to the distant hills.

"Like loo-cow pastures," Bjorn said, pausing to dig a toe through the vegetation to the soil beneath. Little many-legged things burrowed deeper, away from the air. "Good dirt," he added, pinching some between his fingers and letting it sift back down. Neatly, he stepped on the divot he had made.

"Think the Farmers'd notice if we rustled some of their steers?" Kris asked, wondering what else was hidden in the soil here.

"No such insects in loo-cow pastures," Bjorn added. "Maybe no night crawlers, too."

Kris looked around her. "We should be so lucky." She tried to remember what she'd learned in geography about terrain. "This looks exactly like the landscape over there," and she pointed over her shoulder at the distant mainland. "Could there have been some sort of subsidence to separate the two . . . or maybe the gap just hasn't closed as it did on Earth in prehistoric days. Continents didn't used to be the way they are now, you know. Maybe this is a young land . . ."

"No, this is an old planet," Whitby said. "No volcanoes on those space maps at all and a lot of the hills are worn down. But this place does look just like the same sort of terrain that we left."

"Then why it is not farmed?" Astrid asked, her usually serene expression marred by a frown.

Mitford shrugged his shoulders and cleared his throat. "Who knows, but we'll keep in mind that, if it looks alike, it could be alike and we might have night crawlers

here, too. We'll bunk in the Tub tonight.'' Then he
swung his arm in a wide arc. ''Let's move out and see
if we can find a good place to park.''

In the four hours they searched, they caught only a
glimpse or two of small aerial life-forms, but no rocksquats.

''They wouldn't be down here where there's no rocks,
for starters,'' Mitford said when Astrid grew worried
about their absence. ''Not even any trees for the avians
either. Just bushes. Let's split up into two groups. You
head north, Zainal, with Kris, Coo, and Bjorn. You,
Slav, and the rest, we'll go south.''

Several times, Bjorn stopped to check the soil again.
It was good, black and moist, but not too moist, full of
small creatures to keep it loose. ''Plenty good for
farms.''

''Then why aren't there Farms here?'' Kris asked, almost aggrieved.

''We will find the reason,'' Zainal reassured her,
touching her elbow briefly.

''They farm well enough on the main continent. Don't
need this one,'' Bjorn said, but he didn't sound all that
convinced.

''And the closed valleys?'' Kris asked. ''They're even
more enigmatic.''

''Perhaps,'' and Bjorn considered his words, ''they
used them to keep animals in. Safe from the night crawlers.''

''Where are the animals now, then?'' Kris demanded.

''Eaten?'' Bjorn asked, his eyes twinkling.

''We will ask that question, also,'' Zainal said.

They had gone north and now swung wide on their
return to the Tub. Zainal had seen low foothills at a good
day's travel to the north but otherwise this coastal plain
was covered in low vegetation and bush. Good smells

wafted on the evening breeze as they neared the Tub's position.

Joe had wasted no time in digging for clams; Leila and Oskar had caught several varieties of fish and, having tested them in the Tub's small but efficient laboratory unit, found them safe for humans to eat. Sarah contributed some familiar edible roots and greens she found near a stream. Among the Tub's supplies were small cooking units, which were occupied by boiling pots of clams. A grill had been laid across stones for the fish and there was bread from Narrow among their supplies, so when Mitford broke out the beer, everyone was in an expansive mood.

The report of the unusual orbiting device was forwarded to the Eosi Mentat Ix, who had registered an interest in everything to do with the colony planet.

Ix snarled each time it replayed the record of the object, for the speed alone suggested a technology worryingly more advanced than the Eosi's. Ix demanded all records, especially those made by its new entity, for within the entity's fading mind was a memory of a visit to the planet. Ix drew forth all the relevant facts, including the presence of the Catteni it had chosen from the bloodline of its present, but not selected, entity. It examined what the entity had dismissed, the gadget that had been presented for inspection as proof that the planet perhaps had been or was occupied by another species.

Ix worried over all the little memories, having them repeated and repeated until every nuance was dragged out for inspection. The Mentat was pleased that Catteni had set up a second, more flexible satellite around the subject planet. Unfortunately this satellite only emphasized the incredibly fast global search that had been conducted by the alien orb, and the anger of Ix increased at the implications of technical superiority over the Eosi.

Logic suggested that the original discoverers of that

planet were reevaluating the world. What had it been programmed to discover? And why had this object, too, disappeared just beyond the heliopause of this solar system?

Ix summoned a meeting of those of its fellow Mentats who were sufficiently cognizant of their responsibilities to be useful in formulating a course of action. In lightning exchanges of information—as unlike the torturous communications with their subject Catteni as the orbiting object of the Unknown was unlike their own satellite units—it was decided the matter must be investigated in greater detail. All further shipments to the colony planet were suspended and the great number of recalcitrant Earth people would be sent to the secondary colonial venture.

Since it was the Ix Mentat's idea that the matter must be investigated, its peers decided that it must undertake the onerous journey, forgoing its usual pleasures and routines. Fortunately it could pass the tedium of the voyage in a suspended state but that amenity required some alterations to the newest and fastest Catteni warship. The delay annoyed the Ix still further and it amused itself thinking of ways to punish those beings which had been instrumental in causing its discommodation.

The Ix Mentat had just been awakened by the high-ranking naval commander of this jewel of the Catteni fleet when proximity alarms jangled fiercely all over the ship, which went into attack alert. The mass approaching the Catteni vessel was so large it could not be contained on the detection screen. Suddenly waves of force rocked the XZ as if it were a pod in a pond. The Ix, in a manner inconsonant with its dignity and size, grabbed for support until the buffeting subsided.

"Report!" it said in its cold and vicious verbal communication form.

"Most High Eosi, an unknown vessel has appeared . . ."

"You keep no watch?"

"It appeared on screen just as we passed the heliopause," the commander said, not daring to raise his eyes to the towering Eosi, "where other such devices have been seen to disappear." The commander had been well briefed on the problems of, and connected with, this colony planet, not to mention the extraordinary fact that the Mentat had not received its chosen of record but another in the bloodline.

"What is it?" the Ix demanded. "Can you not show it?"

The commander hastily called up on the nearest screen what had stunned his entire bridge crew. The monstrous ship was ten times the size of the AAI, which itself was three times the size of the next largest spaceship in the Catteni navy. The immense ship was obviously headed inward and at a rate of speed which would bring it to its destination thirty time units before the AAI, for all its vaunted improved propulsion system and cruising speed.

"Can you not attach a tracer to its hull before it gets out of range?"

Even as it spoke, Ix realized that the ship was probably out of range.

"It is already out of range for such an attachment, Great Eosi."

Ix fumed that the commander would waste its time stating the obvious. How *could* another species have developed such technology without the Eosi being aware of their existence? The Eosi had not bothered lately with anything more complicated than the improvement in propulsion and cruising range, their present navy having been deemed sufficient for all practical purposes. Such an attitude of complacence was no longer permissible.

"Watch it and record it. Do not fail for an instant."

"No, Most High Eosi, not for an instant," and the commander, relieved to have escaped with his life, strode as quickly as courtesy permitted away from the Eosi to the relative safety of his own bridge.

No one commented on his arrival or moved an eye muscle from whatever panel their duties bound them to.

Several hours later, the captain was awakened from an inadvertent doze by a stir and excitement, palpable on the bridge.

"Sir, the ship is . . ."

Wide awake, and staring at the view screen, the commander watched, awed, as the strange ship, magnified many times to keep it on the slower warship's screens, dipped briefly into the atmosphere of the subject planet, then bobbed up again and continued on its way to the other side of the solar system. Where, upon reaching the heliopause, it disappeared from even the most sensitive instrumentation.

The commander reported to the Eosi, who was ensconced on a huge chair in the cargo compartment which had been altered to provide it with the maximum comfort. The huge chair faced a large screen which had already shown the Ix everything the captain would have to report.

"The planet is of no importance in the face of this." The Eosi paused. "Return to Catten. At all possible speed," and its tone was contemptuous of such a torpid rate now that it had seen a velocity that transcended the best of Eosi capabilities. "This must be reported—and countered."

As the AAI passed through the heliopause of the system, a faint shock, like a low voltage of electricity, was felt by those awake. Only a nanosecond blip registered the shock on the bridge and it was dismissed as an anomaly.

Deski ears felt the noise in the air long before the huge vessel was visible. But, while frightened people ran for the nearest cover in the caves they still occupied and the valleys they were exploring, the noise did not increase. To those with binoculars the ship was visible more as a scintillating lozenge very high overhead. On the view screens of the bridges, the monster seemed to do no more than skim the very top of the stratosphere, skipping like a flat stone across a calm lake, before altering its course and flying off into space, taking its skull-shattering noise with it.

Scott blinked, cleared his throat, and managed to unclench his fists. He had been in the KDL's bridge, his eyes glued to the incredible astronautic event shown on the detection screen.

No one cared to break the silence, for no one quite believed what they had just seen, until a comunit beeped, an almost impudent noise considering the enormity of the recent event.

"That's about the size of the first one, Admiral," said Su. "I think we're lucky it was so high up. . . . What's that? 'Scuse me, sir . . ." and the connection was broken.

Dick Aarens came running full clip down the passageway to the bridge, catching himself on the doorframe to stop, his face ashen and the expression in his eyes as close to awe as he was ever likely to come.

"They did it, Scott. They did it. They've replaced every last fri—"

"Watch your language on my bridge, Aarens," Scott recovered enough to reprimand him. "What has been replaced?"

"All the Mech Makers' stuff, the farm machinery we disassembled. It's all back. Back in the abattoir and everywhere . . ."

Peter Easley, who had been just as flabbergasted as everyone else on the bridge, absorbed that news before Ray Scott or John Beverly did. "Good thing we got the main garage cleaned out then, isn't it?"

"It would have been very messy if we hadn't," Beverly remarked, and then he and Peter burst out laughing.

"Yes, but did they take the *parts* back?" Scott demanded.

"The parts?" Aarens was confused.

"I don't think so, Ray," Beverly said, holding up the comunit usually attached to his belt.

Aarens ran to the hatch but sauntered back to the bridge, a smug grin on his face. "The air-cushion's still there. Maybe the Farmer didn't recognize what I'd done to their material."

The newly devised com board of the KDL lit up with other incoming calls from Shutdown, Bella Vista, and the other three garage sites that had so recently been cleared of human occupation. Then the caves and the valleys that were now human habitations.

"They don't know we're here, then," was Worrell's reaction.

"And couldn't care less," said Jay Greene. "Hope the satellite caught that visitation!"

"You do?" Worry began to fret over what trouble that could cause back in Barevi or Catten or wherever the Eosi hung out.

The machinery was back, gleaming new models of every single unit that had been disassembled by the colonists, in pristine condition and arranged in the appropriate order in each garage, barn, or building. The solar panels that had been taken down and installed elsewhere for the camps' needs were also replaced and seemingly operational.

"Why aren't the machines moving?"

"It isn't spring yet. Not the time to farm."

"Weren't we lucky to have moved out in time!"

"No messages with the unpacking?"

"As if we could have read them?"

"Was Kilroy here or his ET counterpart?"

"*What* do we do now?"

Chuck Mitford, having seen the huge spaceship on the

Tub's screen as they made their way back to the head-quarters at New Narrow Valley to report, had one answer to that when John Beverly informed him of the arrival of complete replacements.

"Get into those garages and remove the anesthetic darts from the launchers before those machines are fully charged."

"Won't such interference be noticed?" Beverly asked.

"I sure hope not. We took the first ones out when they were down, but you'd want to do it before they get fully operational. Fill the reservoirs with water. That anesthesia damned near put paid to a lot of us on the First Drop. Lenny Doyle or Pess'll show you how. They've done it before."

"Any other suggestions, sergeant?" Beverly asked at his most respectful.

"Watch out for the avian predators. Those machines can call them down on anything that moves where it shouldn't."

"Anything else?"

"If I think of something, I'll let you know. But check with Cumber, Esker, the Doyle brothers, Mack Su, any of the First Drop who scouted for me."

Mitford had been sending back daily reports on their explorations. Now he turned back to his team.

"I thought for sure we'd have more than three weeks before anything happened," he said, scratching his head in a measure of anxiety. "Can we make a bit more speed on this thing, Sarah?" he asked, since she was the driver.

"Sure, but it's about to get bumpy again."

"We are not far now," Zainal said, peering out the front windows.

"How long would it take the Eosi to do something, Zainal?" Mitford asked, now drumming restless fingers on his knee with his free hand as he clung to a safety strap with the other.

Zainal shrugged. "I do not think they can move as fast as Farmers. Eosi are not automated. Nor do they have matter transmission."

"I sure hope it galls their souls to hell'n'back," Mitford said, grinning. "I sure hope it makes 'em squirm with envy and dismay."

"Just so long as they keep out of our hair," Kris added. She knew that despite Zainal's assurances, she wasn't the only one fretting over the possibility of Eosi reprisals on the colony. He would know better than she, of course, but it didn't keep her from worrying. She daren't even *think* how the Farmers might react in a direct confrontation with their uninvited tenants, though Zainal's point about the valleys' protection barriers was comforting—as far as it went with an unknown species.

New Camp Narrow was located in one of the closed valleys, south and east of the original cliff installation and itself suitably narrow but longer than most. It had been opened up by the simple expedient of blowing the barrier down with ingredients taken from Baby's arsenal. Zainal had instructed several miners and an ex–ordnance officer as to the explosive capability of the different substances in her lockers. The original notion had been to use such combustibles for mining operations, since the Farmers had apparently ignored the mineral and metal resources of the planet. Inside the appropriately long, narrow valley, Baby and the KDL were parked one beside the other: despite Baby's size in comparison to the larger, oblong transport vessel, she looked sleek, powerful, and far more dangerous. Parts of the wrecked transport had been utilized to make a fair-sized shelter nearby and the returning explorers had no trouble identifying it as headquarters from the flow of people in and out.

Small tents of loo-cow skins dotted the other side of

the usual valley stream and the carcass of a loo-cow was turning on a spit over a firepit. The rubble from the opening had been lugged across the stream for use in constructing homes. Several were as high as window height, with masons busy around them. A much larger building was already in use, its heavy stone pillars supporting a roof of slate that overhung to provide shelter from rains while half-built sides of rough timber gave the edifice the look of a forestry preserve facility. Tables, benches, stools, a few chairs, and a neat pile of blanket rolls suggested it was providing several functions, unfinished as it was.

As the explorers swung around to park and dismount from their vehicle, they were hailed by many but no one stopped working for more than a few moments.

"I wonder where they stashed the airplanes and all the air cushions," Kris said, noting their absence.

"This wouldn't be the only valley in use," Mitford said, stretching his legs. "Okay, Kris, Zainal, Bjorn, Whitby, Coo, we'll make the initial report. You got all the maps. Whitby? Yeah . . ."

"I have pictures," Zainal volunteered, showing the mass in one big hand.

"I have soil samples," and Bjorn showed the little case he had made for them.

"And I have the log printout," Kris added, wondering why Mitford was so antsy suddenly.

"Sarah," the sergeant said, turning toward her and Joe, "go see what the drill is here. Astrid, see if we can get some food. Slav, put water in the tank. Oskar, Jan, Leila, air the Tub out good, and maybe even give it a good wash." He waved toward the stream.

If the refinements of headquarters left a lot to be desired as they entered and looked around it, the essentials—including the yet again reconstructed bridge of the wrecked transport—showed it to be in good working order and array. There were even "offices," cubicles with reed-woven walls to afford some privacy. Old mech parts still doubled for stools, cupboards, shelving, and benches.

"D'you suppose the Farmers didn't *recognize* their own stuff?" Kris murmured to Zainal.

"Bring your group over this way, sergeant," called Scott, standing in the opening of one of the larger reed-walled compartments, on the far side of the bridge.

"Even has a ready room," Kris murmured, this time to Mitford.

"You're getting far too impudent, ma'am," Mitford replied, though he was also peering at the equipment. The Catteni who had once operated from this bridge had never kept it in such good order.

"Mitford, Kris, Zainal, Bjorn, Whitby . . ." Scott was solemnly shaking hands as he ushered them in. "Saw you coming," he added, "so John, Bull, and Jim asked to be in on the debriefing."

He sat at a desk that was really no more than several planks fitted together, rubbed smooth with some sort of polish to prevent splinters; two woven baskets sat on the surface. For in and out, Kris thought irreverently, but their presence was oddly comforting. Business as usual. The other brass-heads sat on Scott's side of the desk.

"It'd be a super place to settle a lot, if not all, of our people in, admiral," Mitford said, pulling the stool closer to his legs. Whitby was unfolding the map indicating the scope of their explorations as Zainal arranged the photos of the sites that looked suitable for habitation. "Though you look like you've settled in here well."

"Thanks, sergeant. It is indeed a pleasant place and there've been no indications of undesirable elements in any of the valleys we're utilizing." Scott had taken up one photo, and Kris nudged Zainal because she'd had a bet on with him that it'd be the one that took his eyes. "Now this is a magnificent setting," he said, and passed the picture to John Beverly on his right.

"Thought you'd like the view of the harbor," Kris said. "It's deep enough for an aircraft carrier."

"What would you know about draft, Kris?" Scott asked, but he was clearly in a good mood.

"The water's real dark down there," she said, grinning. "Too bad we don't have any big ships. Yet."

Mitford nodded to Bjorn to report now. "The ground is fertile, though it had not been tilled in many years."

"You mean it was, once?" Scott sat forward, dropping the second picture he had taken up.

Mitford pulled the telltale picture away from those overlapping it. "The Farmers always put their facilities on unusable real estate, rocky or sandy, or plain nonarable. Look at the way this cliff has been hollowed out. We could damned near hide the KDL in here. For sure, it'd take Baby and all our converted equipment. This whole area shows sign of previous usage. And we found another section further along that ridge that reminds me of the way the abattoir was set up."

The four bent their heads to examine the suspect photos and it was obvious they agreed with him.

"We found two more garage-type installations further up here," and Mitford indicated the positions on the map. "We didn't concentrate on finding any more because they had so obviously been vacant a very long time."

"We think we saw some likely spots on the other side of the bay," Whitby said, "but the terrain was too steep for the Tub, so we didn't cross the bay."

"Is it possible that the Farmers have just allowed the land to remain fallow because they have enough here?" Scott asked.

"It has been fallow many, many years," Bjorn said. "But the soil is rich and would grow everything we needed. Especially if we used the land as wisely as the Farmers do." He ended on an admonitory note.

"All we need is another shipment of replacements," Beverly said with a grin.

"Hell's bells, general," and Mitford grinned, "we saved everything we didn't use, so we've still got the plows and other farming junk. I'd heard none of the scraps were vacuumed up or beamed or whatever. We only have to mount plows and stuff back on the air-cushions and use 'em for their original function. No big problem!"

"That's true, though some will not want to give up their runabouts," and he winked at Mitford, "for plowing. What about the scavengers?"

"Nary a sign of them," Mitford said.

"And that's a puzzle," Whitby said. "We left out our garbage every night we were there—and found it still there the next morning. But the terrain is very similar to what we have here."

"No night crawlers on that continent?"

"None we could find, t'any rate." Mitford took up the recital. "We did find rocksquats, whole colonies of them up in the hills—and just as dumb as the ones over here. There were avians where the lodge-poles have grown up into forests. Perhaps the damned crawlers died of starvation." He grinned. "We can always rustle a few loo-cows from here and see what happens. There're none there that we could find."

"Many of the same root vegetables and berry bushes already grow there and other vegetation is similar," Bjorn put in, his expression glowing with pleasure. "And fish and clams . . ."

"Roasted corn would have gone so well with them," Kris said suddenly, and sighed. "I'm sorry."

Scott bent an understanding look on her and his lips twitched in a bit of a smile. "You're not alone."

"We may yet find something similar," Bjorn said, his wide face eager to please her. "We don't really have a complete catalog of the planet's flora."

"By the way, Mitford," Beverly said, "we disarmed the darts as you recommended. That's quite a powerful anesthesia!"

"Indeed," Zainal and Kris said in unison.

"That's right," and Scott turned to them. "You were caught and subsequently saved another, more fortunate group." He paused a moment. "If there are truly no night crawlers. . . . There are many valid reasons for shifting our operations to that continent."

Mitford leaned forward, circumscribing the area they had searched with his index finger. "It's great country, sir. It'd take quite a few trips in the transport, but it might be the smartest move we've done since we got dropped here."

"If we could be sure the Eosi aren't watching . . ." Scott murmured, and looked at Zainal.

"They will still be 'considering,' Scott," Zainal replied to the unasked question. "Eosi consider long and hard before acting. Here, we use transport at correct times so the orbital does not see—short trip. If thrusters are used carefully, in short bursts, the geosynchronous one will not show enough to read."

"Besides which," Mitford said with great satisfaction, "they don't even know we've got those ships. And if they've any smarts at all, once they've seen reports of that monster, they'll stay the hell away from Botany."

Everyone looked at Zainal, who looked right back around the table and then shrugged.

Not every valley being used as new accommodations was as far along in supplying shelter and amenities as the headquarters establishment. Nevertheless, the thought of picking up *again* and resettling was met with a certain amount of resistance, especially from the technical and engineering groups who intensely disliked a second displacement. They were already involved in various projects and didn't want to drop tools—even the ones they were making. However, the availability of the massive caverns, when they were having to put together sheds from primitive substances, did cause them to reconsider. Then, all of a sudden, they wanted to be the first to get over there and resettled.

The miners were less happy, especially Walter Duxie, the mining engineer in charge, since they'd already reached a good iron lode and wanted to continue working it. While the Catteni space mapping did show mineral deposits on the target continent, they were loath to leave one that was already showing results. So it was decided that they could continue where they were: they had an adequate workforce, which could take turns hunting and supplying their needs, and the nearby caves were already habitable. Judicious use of the KDL would bring ore to where smelting and fabrication processes would be handled.

"What about the fuel situation?" Beverly asked Zainal at one meeting. "What happens if we run out? We've scarcely the technology to make it even if the natural resources are available."

Zainal grinned. "I know where more supplies are kept. With captured ships, a trip to Barevi would not be too hard."

"You pirate," Beverly said with a laugh, and then had to explain the term.

"I will make a very good pirate," Zainal decided, pleased with the definition. "Not the only one, too."

"Hey, what else could you lift at the same time?" Su asked. He was head of one engineering group who found themselves constantly having to invent the tools that had once been always available.

"Depends on what you want," Zainal said.

"Hey, can I go with you and see what's on display at the store?" Su asked, and Zainal pointed at Beverly.

"Ask him. We will not need to go soon. Not much fuel is needed for short hops."

Nevertheless, Zainal kept a close watch on the gauge on the first trip and, having reached a minimum quantity within a safe trajectory, tried to shave minutes off thruster use to preserve every ounce possible.

Mitford had taken a full load of passengers in the Tub to start up the new location, leaving Zainal and Kris behind helping to organize who and what would go in upcoming KDL transfers. The farming community wanted to be among the next wave, as it was essential to plant as soon as the danger of frost was over. So far ''winter'' on Botany had consisted of cold, damp days interspersed with sunny cold days and a lot of early-morning frosts. No real storms, no snow despite cloudy days when the sky suggested blizzards to many who came from cold climates. The temperatures dipped very low occasionally, hampering work outside, but there was always something to be done in what shelter was available from the cold. The people who suffered were those used to tropical conditions and they were given extra clothing and first priority when rugs and long vests of rocksquat pelts were available.

Not long after Mitford had left on the first of many Tub trips, Sandy Areson, who ran the Headquarters Valley camp, came over to Kris where she sat, eating a quick lunch in the Big Building.

''Been trying to catch you alone ever since you got back from the other continent,'' Sandy said.

''Alone? That sounds ominous,'' Kris said.

''It is and it isn't,'' Sandy said, ''and I have to agree with the basic logic of it as far as spreading the wealth is concerned.''

''What wealth?'' Kris asked, puzzled. Wealth on Botany meant hours of additional work for the few ''extras'' that might be available, above and beyond essentials like food and shelter. Even she and Zainal had done stints of kitchen duty.

Although they were the only ones at the long table,

Sandy leaned closer to Kris and said, "Us," pointing to her chest.

"Us?" Then Kris shook her head as she caught on. "Us as in women . . . of childbearing age?"

"You got it," Sandy said, leaning back again and grinning wryly. "There are far more men than women on Botany and as there hasn't been a drop in four weeks, we're not likely to get more. So, if we want to keep up a decent genetic pool . . ."

"You mean, we're operating as if we'll never get off Botany?"

Sandy gave her an astonished stare. "We're dropped, we stay," she said, "or don't you listen to what Zainal says?"

Kris gulped. "I guess I've been naive after all. . . . I mean, we have the KDL. We could get off."

"And go back to Earth?" Sandy looked even more disgusted with her. "You been away from the camps too much, gal, and involved with that hunk of Catteni. Not," and she hastily put out her hand, "that I blame you. I didn't know they came in any variation of 'nice' . . ."

"People are considering him 'nice,' then?"

"Hey, spare me the sarcasm, Kris Bjornsen, and yes, lots of people have got it through their thick and intolerant skulls that Zainal is a lot more Botanical than Cattenical now. 'I drop, I stay.' " Sandy snorted in amusement. "Especially the brass-heads. But you two can't procreate. You do know that?" When Kris nodded, she went on, "And you're of an age to do so."

Kris felt a total rejection of what she knew would come next and leaned away from Sandy. She couldn't, she really couldn't, go with anyone else, even to increase the genetic pool of a colony she was working very hard to make secure.

"Now don't get all silly about it," Sandy said. "We've got enough doctors here now so you can just be inseminated with sperm at the appropriate time in your cycle. I did. I was one of the first," and now Sandy patted her abdomen. "Mind you, I chose the father."

Kris gulped again, feeling distinctly queasy at the prospect.

"Anna Bollinger's preggers, too, but she got formally hand-fasted to Matt before she did. Janet's too old. Patti Sue also did it the old-fashioned way, but I just wanted to warn you that you're on the list. It won't be like being unfaithful to Zainal at all."

"That isn't my problem," she said in a weak voice. "How can I possibly get pregnant until we're all settled and we know what the Eosi and the Farmers are going to do. What'd happen if—"

"Calm down, Kris," and Sandy captured one of her waving hands and held it firmly in both of hers. "You're one of the last on the list, I should say, because your talents are more valuable elsewhere than in the lullaby line."

Kris couldn't suppress her agitation. She hadn't planned on having kids for years! She was barely twenty-two, or thereabouts, since she'd lost a lot of subjective time on the way to Botany and hadn't a clue what month, day, or year it was. Then she didn't think she'd make a good mother anyhow. She'd never liked babysitting jobs in high school or college, unless the kid was asleep. When one woke up and screamed at her, she never went back to that family. She didn't think she had an ounce of maternal instinct in her.

"Anyway, we're going to set up crèches and minders who are maternally inclined, so once a baby's here, you can ignore it completely if that's the way you feel about motherhood."

"That is just the way I feel," Kris said, trapped. Which she didn't add. "When did this get decided? This is the first I've heard of it." She started to get angry now. She hadn't minded or complained of any of the duties she'd been asked to perform on this alien planet. She'd welcomed the opportunities to show her flexibility and stamina and develop skills she'd never have used in a normal life on Earth.

Sandy kept smiling at her. "In case you're interested, you're going through the same phases that others have—including Astrid—before accepting the inevitable."

That jolted Kris. She hated reacting in an expectable way. Sandy chuckled now and patted her shoulder.

"It won't be soon and it won't be as bad as you expect. But I figured you mightn't have been told. You've been out on scouting parties, so you missed the great debate and no one's had the courage to tell you about it."

"Who stuck you with the duty? Did Mitford know?"

"I volunteered. Mitford was too chicken," Sandy said, grinning. "Look at it this way, Kris. We've *made* Botany our own and we're going to keep it ours and that means having a next generation to bequeath all our hard work to. I like this planet . . ."

"Now!" Kris reminded her wryly, feeling a bit sheepish over her outburst.

Sandy shook her head. "No, I did from the start because I could be myself here and what I knew was damned helpful. Back on Earth," and she jerked her thumb over her shoulder, "I was considered 'fringe,' or 'weird' and 'antisocial,' nonconformist and definitely an oddball. Hell, here I'm running generals and admirals through my hoops as a town manager. Sure beats the hell out of being 'tolerated.' And I'm not the only one has found a real home on Botany. I think you have, too, even if it means giving up nine months to producing a baby."

"I hadn't thought of it all quite like that . . . I mean, *your* situation. I mean, back there as opposed to all the things you've done here. There's one matter that hasn't

been taken into consideration, though,'' Kris added.
"The Farmers.''

"Yeah,'' Sandy said in a thoughtful drawl. "But we'll
worry about that when we need to. Right now . . .
Oops,'' and she stopped, looking in the direction of the
entrance.

Zainal was there, looking around, and spotted Kris
and Sandy. She got up. "Good luck,'' and she left with
a wink and a grin.

Kris wasn't sure she was ready for Zainal to join her
just then. Sandy's disclosure had really shaken her.
She'd have to sort this all out in her head. Disregarding
the unsolved and unknown Farmers, she had to admit
that having kids on Botany would give the colony sta-
bility, not to mention a morale boost. She was amazed
that even someone who'd been as abused as Patti Sue
could now contemplate getting pregnant.

She found very little consolation in knowing that she
wouldn't have to have physical contact with the male
parent, although that route struck her as cowardly, if not
downright cheating some guy out of . . . could she call
it "a good time''? Isolated from what "society'' was
available on Botany because of the scouting expeditions,
she'd had little contact with other guys. Mostly she and
Zainal had worked with other pairs, like Sarah and Joe,
and Whitby, who had attached himself to Leila though
they seemed an odd couple.

She had known, sort of peripherally, that the Sixth
Drop had contained a group of women who had, at first,
been totally ostracized by the other women in the camps
to which they were assigned. She had noticed and commented on it to Sarah, who took some relish in telling
her that these were "ladies of the night'' who had been
picked up in one of the German cities along with the
actual demonstrators. Apparently Germany tolerated
brothels but insisted that the occupants have periodic
medical examinations to be sure they did not transmit

sexual diseases, so these girls were "clean." With a larger ratio of males to females on Botany, there'd been endless requests of the available women for sexual favors, on any terms. Some of those terms put the offenders up in the stocks to cool off. The arrival of the professionals had been greeted with considerable interest by camp managers. So the women had been given the option of continuing their previous profession if they so chose. When assured such practices would be considered "work hours" for community benefit, all but two had decided to continue. It was stipulated that they would still have to take their turn at the less glamorous chores of the camps, like KP and latrine. They were, however, excused from sentry duties. But they, in turn, had laid down strict regulations about how they could be treated by clients and the number they would be willing to accommodate. Proper respect was the first requirement— from the female population as well as the male.

The puritanical among the Botany women refused to admit that the oldest profession had a place on this planet. But they could not refuse to admit that a lot of guys went around camp in much better humor and with fewer snide remarks directed at the so-called prudes. There were a few intolerant women—like Janet and Anna Bollinger, who studiously avoided them—but the rest did as requested and treated them with due civility.

"You look worried, Kris," Zainal said as he straddled the bench before settling down beside her. "Isn't the soup good today?" he asked, noticing her unfinished bowl.

"Yes, it's good," and she hastily picked up her spoon, though the soup was now only lukewarm.

"Sandy says something to worry you?" He looked concerned.

"Woman things," she said, avoiding an explanation.

"Mitford says you will have to bear a child for the colony. Maybe two."

"What!" Kris dropped the spoon in the soup, splashing it, and then became furious at such sloppiness, mopping hastily with a wad of fluff.

Zainal regarded her with a very level gaze, one corner of his mouth twitching. He leaned closer to her. "Was that what Sandy was saying to you?"

She hid her face from him. "So Mitford had the nerve enough to tell *you*? And not me?"

"Man-to-man stuff," Zainal said, and she could just see him grinning at her out of the corner of her eye. "You know you cannot have a child by me. Is that why you stay with me? So you do not have a child?"

She glared at him. "I stay with you because I'm in love with you, you . . . you . . . brass-head," she replied in a low and intense voice.

He covered her hand briefly with his, squeezing her fingers. "You are young and strong. You will be a good mother."

Kris gulped. "No, I won't. I'm not the least bit maternal—motherly!" She blurted the denial out, daring him to object. "I'd make a lousy mother. I'm not ready to have kids. I'm too young."

He gave her a long look. "It is not something all Earth women do? Have babies?"

"Not all by any long shot," she said grimly.

"I see," he said slowly. "It is not because you don't want to offend me?"

"I'm the faithful type. I don't want any man but you. Even if you can't have children," she replied in a tight voice, looking down at the soup, which now had a thin haze of congealing fat on it.

"You do not need to sex another man. Mitford explained it to me."

"That's even worse," she told him with gritted teeth, rolling her eyes.

"I wish to see a child from you. Choose Mitford. You like him!"

"WHAT?"

She half rose from the bench in agitation and those by the hearth looked over at them. She dropped back to her seat, hand over her face. She was as close to tears as she had ever been since coming to Botany. The trouble was she did like Chuck Mitford, very much, and if she hadn't gotten so incredibly tangled up with Zainal, she might have tried to come cn to the sergeant. She had never once done so, nor had Mitford come on to her at any time: maybe she hadn't been mistaken that he'd've been interested in her if she hadn't paired off with Zainal. Of course, he had kept her so constantly in Zainal's company that finally sexual tension had been inevitable.

Zainal put an arm around her. "Do not be this way, Kris. It is no big deal."

"No big deal?" She whirled on him, pushing his arm away, and had the satisfaction of seeing him recoil slightly from her expression. "No big deal!" She started to get off the bench but he held her down, exhibiting far more of his strength than he had ever used with her.

"You are not a silly woman, Kris Bjornsen. When it is time, you will have the child and I will help you. Do not make it such a big deal."

Then he got up and so startled her that she grabbed for his hand. Had she lost face in his eyes because she was, indeed, being somewhat silly? If he didn't mind, she shouldn't?

"Your soup is cold. I get you hot."

She was nearly light-headed with relief and nodded acceptance of the courtesy. She was relieved, too, that she had a little time without him beside her, to sort out incoherent reactions and irrational emotions. When she put her hands to her face, they were icy cold. Or were her cheeks burning hot with outrage and embarrassment? Whichever, she needed to cool down and stop acting so stupidly. She started at the point where Zainal had said that he did not mind her having sex with another man. He even wanted her to have a child. Did all Catteni women have children whether they wanted to or not? Then she coped with his choosing for her the man she respected above all the others. That suggested a sensitivity in the big Catteni most unusual for his species. Or was Humanity contagious? She knew *he* admired Mitford, too. Or had he and Mitford discussed a putative father of Kris Bjornsen's compulsory child? Which she doubted. Mitford wasn't that sort of man. And she couldn't really see the sergeant and Zainal exchanging man-to-man topics.

He returned with a bowl of steaming soup and a watchful expression on his face and, oddly enough, sympathy in his yellow eyes.

"Thanks, Zainal," she said, spooning up soup and blowing to cool it. "I did overreact there, I think."

"I love you, you know," he said in a sort of off-handed manner which would have exacerbated her already jangling nerves if her remnant of common sense hadn't made her realize that such an admission was also very un-Catteni. He covered her free hand with his. "It is not an emotion I thought I would live as a man to have."

And that caught her hard, right in the guts. She dropped her head to his shoulder, weeping as quietly as she could. She knew he had had two children; even the chosen had the right to produce heirs on Catten. He'd never said a word about the woman, or women, who had borne them. So he had not allowed himself to love? Because he knew he was chosen and would not live long "as a man"?

"Why do you cry . . . now?" He was utterly puzzled.

"For you. Because you can love me."

"It is not hard to do."

She could hear the ripple of amusement in his voice and, dashing the tears from her eyes, looked up at him, with as good a smile as she could present.

"Eat your soup. We have work to do soon," he said very gently, and she loved him even more deeply than ever.

CHAPTER 8

The Eosi Mentats had deliberated: had examined the reports from both satellites with infinitesimal attention to detail. With each fresh review, their agitation grew. Two separate concerns were identified: Firstly, the Eosi were not, as they had assumed, the only highly intelligent species in the galaxy, and why had they never encountered the Others when they had been assiduously exploring this arm of the Milky Way? Secondly, how did the Others arrive at a technology so far superior to their achievements and how soon could they match and then surpass it?

Mentat Ix called to their attention the brief glimpse its shell had had of a comunit. Logically, an investigation should be made of the extant equipment for insights into the construction of the machinery situated on the colony planet.

Mentat Ix was assigned, with two younger Mentats which had technological skills and inventiveness to inspect and analyze the installations. The warship AA1 would take them there and also provide guards against any demonstrations by the indigenous population, who were known to be volatile.

As the superb new warship reached the ionosphere of the subject planet, its new propulsion system developed a fault, an oddity indeed, which resulted in a shock wave passing over the vessel from bow to stern. Gauges on detection equipment went off the scale for a nanosecond, then returned to normal positions, and the engines resumed operation as if they had never faltered. System analyses were run and damage reports undertaken, but no fault was found in any department of the AA1. Even the Ix Mentat was confounded. It liked that no better than the other shocks this wretched backwater system had given it.

The captain activated every safeguard provided by this latest example of Eosi-Catteni engineering and technology as he continued into the atmosphere of the third planet. There were no more life-forms detected than there should be, according to the numbers of prisoners sent there, and the numbers of lesser creatures previously assessed. There were 2,003 fewer humans than the records of removal but there would have been some casualties both in transport and since landing.

The Eosi had stipulated that they land at the point where most of the drops had been made, easily identified by the wrecked transport vessel.

Teams of guards trotted out of the AA1, to make a quick surveillance of the immediate area and the wreck. They were halfway across the field when they were suddenly attacked by aerial creatures. These were shot down with the accuracy for which such crack troops were famed. And identified as indigenous life-forms, previously recorded by the original survey team.

Reaching the wreck, they reported signs of intense heat and fire damage in the propulsion section. That, of course, was consonant with the reports from both the Drassi in command of the transport and the rescuers who had subsequently lost their lives in the second accident.

"Third," Mentat Ix corrected the captain.

"Lord?" the captain asked nervously.

"The scout ship also disappeared after landing on this planet."

"My pardon. I didn't know of that incident, Lord."

"*I* do." And that was that.

"Odd for three . . ." and the young Mentat Co paused thoughtfully.

"Yes, three is odd." Mentat Ix nodded for the captain to continue his investigations.

The team commander then added that only the shell of the wreck remained. It had been gutted.

The Mentat Ix irritably observed that protocol had not been observed in this instance: even a transport should have been blown up so that nothing could have been salvaged from it. It was unfortunate that both Drassi captains had lost their lives in the subsequent explosion of the KDL.

"There may well have been little of any value left," it finally remarked, dismissing the problem.

"There is a concentration of metals not far from here," the captain said, for that report had been hurriedly brought to him.

Ix nodded and a flick of one finger informed the captain that he was to dispatch a reconnaissance team.

They returned with pictorial evidence of a large installation: barns, sheds, piles of rectangles that appeared to be crates in collapsed form. And many different machines.

"Farming machines," the captain said, for he had some familiarity with agricultural procedures.

"What season is it on this place?" the Mentat Se asked.

"The weather is cold but not excessively so. A winter, perhaps?" Co suggested.

"Farm machines are dormant in winter," the captain remarked.

"Bring one here."

"Perhaps the Mentats might prefer to see them in their . . . ah . . . normal surroundings?" the captain suggested. That made more sense than hauling large and cumbersome units about.

"The air is pure?"

"Yes, Lord," the captain said. He was hoping to get a few lungfuls himself and, if he could get the Mentats off the AA1, he had ordered the life-support officers to flush out the ship with the cleaner planetary air.

The Mentats were conveyed effortlessly there in the captain's skiff, which was commodious enough for three Mentats and necessary crew. They saw nothing impressive in the facilities built into the cliffs. Nor in the machines that dutifully awaited the timely resumption of their preprogrammed duties. In fact, the machinery was almost depressingly simple in design and function when compared with the orbital and the massive ship that had stunned the Ix on its first trip to this solar system.

"None of this suits our purpose or forwards an understanding of the mentality of the makers," Mentat Ix said, although it found no fault with the sun or the freshness of the air. "When the colony is established, I may even take control of this planet."

Mentats Co and Se exchanged discreet glances and followed their senior back into the ship. Despite the failure to find anything of technological significance, Ix did not issue any immediate orders, retiring to its own quarters to meditate.

Eventually Ix sent orders to the captain that the skiff must be readied for a second exploratory trip. It took the other Mentats with it. Ix showed the pilot where it wished to land. It also required the pilot to hover when the glyphs carved into the hillside were noticed.

"The message is in Catten," Mentat Co said.

"Yes, the renegade Zainal was here." The Ix Mentat gnashed the teeth in its host's mouth in a most unusual fashion, then peremptorily gestured for the skiff to be landed where once, as Lenvec, it had settled to remind a brother of duty owed.

There was nothing on the site, merely more fields with hedgerows: nothing certainly that would have accounted for the chosen's escape. And only faded traces of where the scout ship had landed. The Ix Mentat turned its head in the direction from which the humans and Zainal had come.

"Take us there!" and it pointed.

The skiff took off and shortly came to the deep ravine which, at a low hover, not only showed visible evidence of human occupation but easily detected in the intricate cave system a considerable number of life-forms. Several emerged to observe the aircraft. The skiff's detection equipment picked up the use of comunits but on a frequency which could not be directionalized before the signal cut off abruptly.

"They have more of those hand units," the Ix Mentat said superciliously.

"Does the Mentat wish to land and speak to the humans?" the pilot asked, as more emerged from the caves.

"I have no interest in pests." The Ix had been more closely observing the signature of the humans than anyone realized. Primarily it searched for the unmistakable signature of a Catteni-life-reading and that was not visible outside or inside the caves. Deep inside the Ix's mind, one pathetic whimper trembled.

"The humans appear to have moved about a great deal," Mentat Co said, "if these," and it flicked a long nail at the screen where more clusters showed at different locations, "are indeed human pulses."

Ix Mentat regarded Co with some interest. "Moved where?"

"On the smaller continent adjacent to this one. Many human life signs registered there as we overflew it."

"Return," Ix Mentat said, and sat back, impatient to reach the ship and order it to the second continent. The Catten signature might be found among the other concentration of humans.

As the AA1 lifted, having left a substantial declivity across most of the field with the weight of its visit, the Ix Mentat entered the bridge and stood behind the officer responsible for the life-form detection.

"Set for Catten sign," the Ix said, clicking its long nails together in a tattoo that had the Catteni officer cringing with nervousness.

The AA1 made the next continent in a shallow curve. It had not yet reached even the intended altitude when the screen gave off a brief blip—registering the presence of a Catteni. It vanished so quickly that the duty officer wondered if it had been a legitimate sighting. The Mentat was taking no chances and ordered the vessel to circle the point, a prong of land extending into the narrow channel between the two landmasses. But nothing registered again on the screen.

"An anomaly, perhaps," the Co suggested blandly, after sufficient time had elapsed to have done several orbits about this wretched planet.

"Perhaps," the Ix replied irritably, and signaled to continue across the water.

The greatest concentration of the lesser, human signatures was found around the northern bay.

"They've infested the place," the Co remarked as the babble was screened for any sign of Catten.

The Ix pondered a long while as the AA1 held its position, using great quantities of fuel to do so. Then, with an abrupt gesture, the Mentat Ix ordered the captain to return with all possible speed to Catten.

The captain wished to do so as well, anxious to be rid of his Eosi passengers, and he gave the necessary orders. And was nearly bounced from his command chair as the forward motion abruptly ceased. The engines were still running, their pulse beginning to reach up to a whine of frustration, as the ship met an impenetrable obstacle.

"There's some sort of barrier, captain," the helmsman said, looking at the opacity which held them motionless. "It's all around the planet."

"Destroy it," the Ix said with an agitated wave of its long arm.

The captain ordered a full barrage of all forward weapons, certain his firepower was sufficient to the task. The ship rocked and crewmen covered their eyes at the resultant flashback.

"I see a lessening in the opacity directly ahead," the navigator said, trying hard not to think of how futile this brand-new ship's much vaunted weaponry had been.

The captain called for more power and the ship moved slowly, slowly, slowly, pushing through the barrier it had been unable to destroy. Then, all of a sudden, the ship plunged forward through the obstacle, knocking to the deck many who were not holding on to something, including all three Mentats.

Although several officers sprang forward in an instinctive effort to assist, the Mentats snarled away any help and slowly got to their feet, glaring around them.

"Turn!" the Ix ordered the captain. "I want to know what that barrier is and how it could impede this ship."

The captain gave the order to the com board to switch to the stern view screen. Nothing happened.

"I asked for the view astern," he roared but, while the communications officer cringed from his captain's anger, all his attempts to access the rear views came to nothing.

"There is no response," he said.

"Damage report," said the engineering officer, "indicates problems with the arrays, sir. It is an external problem.''

"Fix it!" the captain said, bringing his fists down on the armrests.

Orders were forwarded. And the Ix rattled its long nails with far more irritation than the captain dared show.

"Well, then turn the ship around so that the forward view screens can enlighten us. I must examine that obstacle," Ix said, making a small tight circle with one finger.

In getting free, the full power of the AA1's engines had carried them a considerable distance before that maneuver was completed. The captain muttered unhappily when he saw how far they were from the misbegotten Bubble, and an unhappy silence ensued in the bridge until they had returned close enough to examine the phenomenon. During that time, a damage report suggested that every protuberance of more than twenty centimeters and all the more delicate arrays had been snapped off. And indeed, as they neared the opaque Bubble, it was obvious in the forward view screen that every last one of the missing parts was embedded in the Bubble, outlining the less fragile silhouette of the AA1. And the Bubble completely enclosed the planet, just short of the two satellites. The orbital continued its programmed circuits but there would be nothing on its tapes but an endless view of the Bubble.

"It admits sunlight," the science officer said, relieved to find something positive to report, for he had to add that its composition was totally unfamiliar.

"Examine it thoroughly," the Ix said, looming over the technician, expecting answers.

The Catteni, one of the top men in his branch of the service, used every technique available to him at a station that was supposed to have all the latest improvements for its duties, and could find nothing further to report. Finally he spread his hands to admit defeat. He dared not look above his head at the Mentat, so he did not see the blow that crushed his skull like a melon.

The Ix stormed from the bridge, its juniors behind it, and the captain told the helmsman to return to the original course back to Catten. Then he gestured for the corpse to be removed from the science station.

"Hell, I don't know what it was," Marrucci told the others gathered in the bridge of the KDL. "Never seen anything like it—pushed all the gauges off line and it looked . . ." and he paused, "for a split second, as if deep space got lit up."

"Now let's not lose perspective here," Scott began, and then stopped.

Beverly whistled under his breath. "I *know* it can't be technologically possible," he began slowly, "but then a lot of stuff we've been seeing recently is so far beyond what we'd generally consider science-fictional that maybe we can stretch that a little bit further and think it's possible to put a barrier around an entire planet."

"There's something out there now that wasn't there earlier," Scott said, leaning on the edge of the scanner board and staring at it. "Even if it only shows up like a mist or a veil or an opacity."

"There *was* a *Star Trek* episode I saw as a kid," Marrucci remarked almost apologetically, "called 'The Tholian Web' and it was about building a lattice to keep the *Enterprise in.*"

"So how did the *Enterprise* get free?" Beverly asked without a trace of irony.

Marrucci thought for a long moment and then shrugged. "I can't remember. But I can see the web being spun around it and they knew they only had so much time . . ." He trailed off.

"So, are the Farmers keeping us in? And why did they let the Eosi ship in and then out?"

"It blew a hole in the web and got out?" Marrucci asked, looking around the bridge for any other explanation. "That might explain that flash, the Eosi blowing it open."

"There's no hole in it now," Scott said, standing up again but not taking his eyes from the screen. "And why was the Eosi ship here in the first place?"

"Looking us over?" Fetterman suggested. They'd all been alerted by the Deski sentries here at Retreat Bay when the ship had overflown them. Then the group at old Camp Narrow had informed them that the ship had landed in the Drop Field. Discreet observation had followed, and reported, every move, including the skiff arriving at the abattoir and the subsequent removal to the field near Camp Rock, and Worrell had reported the skiff hovering over Camp Rock. And, in detail, what he had seen *in* the skiff.

"I saw three . . . giants . . . in the skiff," Worry said, his voice shaky. "They were staring down at us and I've never seen such nightmares. They were . . . sort of Catteni but no Catteni is that big and glows. The heads are all distorted and the features sort of caricatures of Catteni. Not even Catteni deserve that sort of fate. I'm glad Zainal missed out if that's what he was avoiding!"

"I concur with what Worry says." Leon Dane came on line. "I've never seen anything like that, not in Sydney or in any of the material that we commandeered during our operations in Australia. There's a disease—elephantiasis—that causes something that looks similar. But the gross enlargement of the head isn't at all like an encephalic abnormality. . . . No wonder ordinary Catteni are frightened by the Eosi. They scared the shit out of me just now."

Shortly after that report, the warship was seen to pause just over the channel, where it circled for a long time. But time enough for those at Retreat Bay to complete the camouflage around the KDL and Baby, which were now housed in the big cave.

"You don't think they've been looking for Zainal, do you?" Mitford asked. "He'd've been about there," and the sergeant pointed to the area that had attracted the Catteni hover, "in the Tub."

"What effect does several fathoms of water have on Catteni detection scans?" Marrucci asked those around him.

"Zainal might know but let's not call and ask him, huh?" Mitford said.

No one could anyhow, since that was when the Eosi warship met the immovable opacity and the brand-new worry about whether they were sealed in or others sealed out.

Having completed its programmed task, the Bubble-drone assumed its monitor facet and observed the approach of a small spaceship which had just taken off from the subject planet. It had, of course, observed the arrival and landing of the same craft earlier but, as it was not programmed to take any action at that point, it continued its primary assignment, extruding the material that would form the protective barrier.

However, when the spaceship did not heed the initial resistance of the barrier, it accessed its emergency instructions. In that brief period of time of adding scope on its activities, the spacecraft displayed force which had to be disseminated quickly through the barrier to diffuse the effect. The further efforts of the spacecraft to pass its confines weakened the barrier. Then the instructions were available and the barrier assisted the expulsion of the hostile craft. The substance of the barrier caught on and held protuberances and smaller exterior parts of the exiting body. But the overall integrity of the Bubble remained intact and the subject planet was now safe from external dangers, of which the spacecraft could now be considered one.

Since there had been an attack, the orbiting mechanism initialized its message segment and programmed it with a full report of the proceedings. Once the message segment reached the point at which its hyperspace drive could safely function without a backlash affecting the integrity of a solar system, it made its quick passage back to its home base.

This time its purport was quickly examined by entities able to deal with the subject matter.

By the time Zainal and Kris drove out of the water at Retreat Bay, they were aware of the excitement of those they passed, who waved vigorously at them as they made their way to headquarters in the big cave. That was where they found Mitford waiting for them in his little runabout.

"The consensus of opinion is that they might have been looking for you," Mitford told Zainal. "Get in, the pair of you. Let the others unpack the Tub."

"We just made it into the channel when the ship passed overhead," Kris said, taking a seat. "We were well started when we heard the reports about the landing in the Drop Field, and Zainal here," and she gave him a little grin, "put the pedal to the metal and headed toward the channel as fast as the Tub would go. It wouldn't have done for them to spot it when it's supposed to be shards in space with the rest of the KDL." She glanced at Zainal.

She'd said nothing to him about her other suspicion, which Mitford had voiced, that the ship might be looking for him. At least, not until the skiff was reported landing where Lenvec had, and where they had hijacked the scout vehicle. That was when Zainal started driving faster than was safe over the rough terrain. He was racing to the channel, to get as deep as the Tub could safely go. That was when she knew Zainal was really worried. Now he seemed amused by the incident and shrugged off Mitford's report.

"Worry saw three Eosi?" Zainal asked, his yellow eyes sparkling with an almost demonic glitter.

"Yeah, and they scared the shit out of him and Leon Dane."

Zainal's smile widened with irony. "They are frightful. It was only with great effort that I did not embarrass my father and all my line by losing water." Then he gave his big shoulders one of his characteristic shrugs. "But only the first time."

"Is that what you would have become if you'd gone back?" Mitford asked, not quite meeting Zainal's eyes.

The Catteni nodded once, slowly. "So they came back? And looked at the machinery in Narrow, and at the field and at Camp Rock, and didn't find Catteni-life signs. But they have gone. There was nothing on the screen when we got out at the bay. What happened? I wish to hear more."

"There is more to tell, too, that you wouldn't have seen underwater. The brass-heads are waiting for you," Mitford said with a big grin, stopping the air-cushion by the stairs at the KDL's open hatch.

They climbed in.

"Good news, sarge?" Kris asked, remembering those last few klicks before the Tub immersed itself. Zainal's expression had been so grim, so . . . frightened? She didn't like to think of anything frightening Zainal even if she knew very well that the Eosi did. Did he suspect the ship might be searching for him . . . still? Especially if the others did. Could his brother, Lenvec, still be conscious enough to make an Eosi search him out and take revenge?

"Well, sort of good news," Mitford said with an odd twist to his smile. "Tell me, Zainal, could that warship scan underwater?"

"I hope not," Zainal said, and Kris, watching him closely, saw his jaw muscles tighten.

"If it's any consolation, I don't think they can because otherwise they would have found you, if you're what they were looking for," Mitford said. "They did spend a lot of time circling the channel on the other side, about where you would have submerged."

"We cut it pretty close, I think," Kris said, her eyes on Zainal.

"But they have gone away," Zainal said with a satisfied nod.

"They've gone. With a bang," Mitford said. Neither Kris nor Zainal had time to question him further because they had reached the bridge where Scott, Beverly, and Marrucci waited for them.

"Glad you made it here safely, after all," Scott said in welcome, but he gestured for Zainal and Kris to join him at the big screen. "Gino, replay the Catteni ship's departure, will you?"

Marrucci, grinning from ear to ear, tapped in the necessary keys as if he'd handled Catteni equipment all his professional life.

Zainal echoed the gasp Kris gave when she saw the blip of the Catteni vessel stop short.

"How could it hit a wall in space?" she asked. Only then did she notice the barely visible skin of the Bubble. "That's what stopped it?" She turned first to Beverly and then Scott and Mitford, and finally to Zainal.

He was shaking his head but his eyes were gleaming with intense satisfaction.

"It circles the planet?" he asked.

"We have reason to believe so. But watch," Scott said, holding up one hand, fingers wide to give his eyes some protection from the flash.

"Wow!" Kris said, blinking to clear the afterimage from her eyes. "What was that?"

"The forward blasters of the ship firing at once,"

Zainal said in a very odd tone of voice. "And it isn't enough?" He continued to watch but a half smile turned the corner of his mouth and he began to chuckle. Now he folded his arms across his chest and, still chuckling, watched as the Catteni warship slowly pushed its way through the obstacle and became invisible. "Ah!" He dropped his arms. "That is very interesting indeed," he said, turning to Scott.

"Yes, we think so," and Scott settled himself on the edge of the screen control panel. "We think they were looking for you . . ."

"I told them," Mitford said, seating himself at the next work station.

Scott shot him a glance. "Could they have been?"

"For what purpose?" Zainal lifted one shoulder negligently. "I speeded the Tub so they would not see it out in the open. They might have seen it submerging, if they had the scanners in the right direction. If they came, it was to see what their orbital saw. It was in place when the whiz-ball came over, and it was also there when the big one sent down all the new machines. The Eosi looked at those, did they not?"

Mitford's expression was one of relief and Scott regarded Zainal with a look close to embarrassment.

"They come to see what's new on Botany," Zainal repeated, showing his teeth in a full grin. "Not for me."

Kris allowed herself to relax a trifle. She'd forgotten all about the fact that the Catteni orbital would have sent reports back. Of course that's what they had come to see! Zainal didn't enter into the matter. He was dropped and he stayed.

"So, do you think the Farmers erected that space barrier?" Scott asked, his eyes intently on Zainal's face.

"Who else? Since the warship had to blast its way out," Zainal said. "The watch did not report anything happening in space?"

"Just that the Catteni orbital seemed to have developed a shadow,'' Marrucci said. "I was watch officer when the Catteni arrived. There was nothing, nothing there then.''

''Is the shadow still with the orbital?''

Marrucci grinned. ''Can't see that far anymore.'' But he did call up the log for that period and showed them the tiny shadow behind the orbital.

''If that's the gadget that did the trick, why didn't it move fast enough,'' Mitford said in a low grumble, ''to keep the Eosi from getting in at all?''

''Maybe it just took time to spread out,'' Beverly suggested. Then he turned to Marrucci and added, ''Even that Tholian Web took time, didn't it, to enclose the *Enterprise*?''

''The *Enterprise*?'' Kris exclaimed in surprise. ''The Tholian Web? Oh, I remember that episode.''

''D'you remember how the *Enterprise* got free?'' Marrucci asked hopefully.

''No,'' she replied sheepishly.

''You're no help.''

''Enough,'' Scott said, making a cutting gesture to stop their levity. ''This episode has no happy ending. This planet is now enclosed.''

''To keep us in?'' Kris asked softly, and knew the others had the same question in their minds. ''Maybe they want to be sure their machinery stays intact. Even if they can't differentiate between us and loo-cows, they surely will look at a warship that big with some uneasiness.''

''But the Catteni ships were coming in and out of here like yo-yos,'' Mitford said.

''But the Farmers weren't alerted to the change in . . . tenants, shall I say?'' and Scott gave a mirthless smile, ''until that homing device was sent off . . .''

''By the way, whose bright idea was that?'' Beverly asked, frowning.

''It got a reaction, which is what we wanted,'' Mitford

said, declining to name a name. Which, Kris felt, was more forbearance than Dick Aarens deserved.

"Not for—how many months was it . . ." Beverly asked, "before the whiz-ball arrived?"

"Seven," Zainal said, "and then only three weeks until the big ship arrived to replace the machines."

"What I can't understand," Kris said, "is why that scan of theirs hasn't apparently taken any notice of the existence of a new type of life-form on their planet? Loo-cows have six legs, noticeably, and we have only two. Surely that was noted somewhere?" She raised her hands in a puzzled gesture.

"And the barrier did let the Catteni warship out," Beverly said in a puzzled tone.

"For which I, and I'm certain, Zainal, too, is very grateful," Kris said in an undertone. Beverly shot her an understanding smile, his eyes flicking over Zainal beside her.

"Indeed," Scott said, clearing his throat nervously.

"Very grateful," Zainal added in a low, fervent tone, leaning back in his chair, stretching out his long legs, and giving a sigh of relief.

"But why did it?" Scott asked, pursuing the puzzle.

"Because the ship used weapons against it?" Zainal asked.

"That is a possibility, of course, if the Farmers are pacific by nature," Scott went on. "But we don't know that, do we?"

"We know by the valleys," Zainal said, "which were to keep something in, or something out. But not to kill it. Only now we are kept in and danger is kept out." He pointed to the screen where the Catteni ship's departure was on replay. "I think the Eosi have been given much to think about."

"But where does that leave us," and Scott glanced around those on the KDL's bridge, "in relation to the Farmers?"

"Remember that we all felt we'd been scanned?" Mitford began, making sure he had everyone's attention. "Okay, so the whiz-ball orbital did an inventory and the supply ship dropped off what was needed to fill in the gaps. Let's say that, like all the Farmers' stuff, it was programmed to expect certain life-forms and recorded a great many more of an unidentifiable sort. Maybe that's why there's a bubble around us, until the Farmers can come and have a closer look with something that isn't programmed."

"You're just hoping that's the case, Mitford," Scott said. "It would vindicate everything you originally aimed to do. Attract their attention and their help." When Mitford nodded, he went on. "Only your plan's gone aglae, as the Scotsman said."

"Not much aglae, sir. Not yet, at any rate."

"It would if the Farmers decide that we're some sort of malignant life-form which has contaminated their planet."

Kris glared up at Scott, appalled that he'd say such a thing. Then she paused and amended her thinking: that he'd say what possibly everyone else feared. His expression gave no apology for his blunt speech.

"No," Zainal said into the dismayed silence Scott's observation caused. "No," he added in a stronger tone, and sat forward, clapping his big hands to his knees to emphasize that denial. "The Farmers are cultivators, a race that protects. The valleys prove that to me. The scan could have killed a malignant life-form but did not. The barrier could have destroyed the warship. It did not. But it let it out. We will prove we are cultivators, savers, protectors, too. When the Farmers come . . ."

"You think they will?" Marrucci asked, his thick eyebrows raised in hope of a negative response.

"I think they will but I will not wait until they do," Zainal said with a wry grin on his face. "I will not worry until they do. I will live well until they do."

"I think I agree with you on that, Zainal," Beverly said.

"Me, too," said Marrucci.

"I may have reservations, Zainal," Scott said, "but worry is futile, especially," and now he flung out both arms in a gesture of resignation, "when faced with a far, far superior force."

"This planet has a great potential," Beverly said in a quiet, affirmative voice. "Let us make as much of it as we can and hope that the Farmers see us as cultivators and, perhaps, useful tenants."

"Amen to that," Marrucci added, and made the sign of the cross.

Kris ducked her head respectfully even as she reached for Zainal's hand. He did not mention Phase Three but, by the way he returned the pressure of her hand, she knew that he had not forgotten it.

CHAPTER 9

While the brass-heads, with Peter Easley, Yuri Palit, and Chuck Mitford, visited the various communal mess halls set up around Retreat Bay and farther inland to counteract rumors and explain what had happened, Zainal and the flyboys discussed a quick run in the scout to examine the Bubble. Bert Put, Marrucci, Raisha, Beverly, and Vic Yowell were dying to see the phenomenon. The argument had been that, if the satellites could no longer see what they were doing on the surface, there was no harm in making use of the aircraft for exploratory purposes. And one of the first things to be explored was the Bubble. "As close as one could get to it."

"Or in it," Kris had added, staying in the background but determined to go along for the ride for a variety of reasons. She'd learned all she could about the new equipment and had driven the Tub often enough to have gotten the hang of the Catteni-size finger pads on the control boards. She might never learn to pilot, but there were always other duties during a flight for which she felt herself well qualified.

She also had a feeling that Zainal had no intention of

giving up his plan to "hitch a ride" on the next Farmers' vehicle that darkened Botany's skies. How he could achieve that goal she hadn't a clue, and he was giving her none, though there were times when he stared blindly out at nothing with unfocused eyes, and she knew him well enough to know that he was turning over ways and means of doing it. Considering how quickly the supply ship had made its deliveries, would he have time enough to reach it before it took off again at its incredible speed? The scout was equipped with a tractor beam and she suspected that's what he hoped to use to secure himself to the exterior. But what if he got knocked off when the Farmers' ship accelerated or activated whatever it used to travel the immense distances they were now convinced it traversed?

She kept hoping that when his plans were completed she'd be part of them. For all the good friends she now had on Botany, she did not wish to be left here by herself. Especially since Zainal's presence protected her from importunities. Already she'd had several distressing interviews with men who wanted to be on her "paternity" list. They professed themselves willing to forgo a natural conception but they wanted her to bear their child.

She had managed to thank them for their interest—when she really wanted to clout them as hard as she could—and told them she would consider their offer. And made sure to stick closer to Zainal's side than ever, even though it meant stopping work on the quarters they were building. She did what she could without his help—until guys started showing up with offers of assistance . . . and the paternity requests.

Then Raisha discovered she was pregnant and deferred to whoever wished to take her spot.

"I've been up and it was wonderful," she said, her eyes shining with the memory, "but I don't want to whoopsie in free fall, thank you."

That condition was becoming widespread, Astrid, Sarah, and the three girls who had been Catteni decoders all announcing their pregnancies. She kept as close to Zainal as she possibly could, even sitting through repeated instructions at the scout's control board to avoid the "infection." No wonder so many individual quarters were being built in the bay area.

There was no problem filling Raisha's place and Bert magnanimously offered to step down, too. Beverly and Marrucci went over the credentials of all those who volunteered for the flight and selected Antonio Gedes for Raisha's spot, but Zainal insisted that Bert remain, having had some experience with the craft and in space, while two other pilots, Alejandro Balenquah and Sidi Ahmed, were added to the flight list.

"Not that we're ever likely to go far," Balenquah said gloomily.

He was swarthy, with deep-set black eyes that surveyed his surroundings with reserve. Kris wasn't sure she liked his noncommittal posture when here he was being offered what half a dozen less qualified men and women would have killed to get. Well, not would have killed, but definitely envied.

"Look at it this way, mate," Bert Put said, also displeased by the man's attitude, "you never know, do you? Did you ever think you'd drive a ship in space again? Well, you're doing it now, and here."

"I guess," and Balenquah altered his attitude. He was actually the quickest of the three new men to become easy with the unusual equipment and the finger pad boards.

The flight had been planned in spite of severe reservations from Reidenbacker and Ainger. They were ground personnel, Marrucci had remarked privately to Kris, and suspicious of air and space maneuvers. If the satellites were no longer visible on the screens of the KDL and the scout, then it was two to one that the SATs couldn't see within the Bubble. It was therefore not only safe but a wise precaution to see what the barrier was like up close.

"Not to mention the fact that you're dying to go up again," Kris said, and he grinned, more boyish than ever despite having reached the rank of colonel in the air force.

"You got it, Bjornsen," and he cocked a double-jointed thumb at her, making the rest of his hand into a mock pistol before dropping the thumb. He also had a habit of cracking his knuckles when he was nervous, a routine which fascinated Zainal, who could not, to Kris' relief, duplicate the action. Having one person do it in the confines of a pilot compartment was enough.

Zainal also wanted to see if he could locate a Farmers' satellite, or whatever was controlling the Bubble.

"If they spy on us, it is good. They want to know more before they come."

"That's *your* interpretation," Kris said.

He regarded her with his yellow eyes and a slight smile on his lips. "And what is yours?"

She thought for a moment and then laughed. "Yeah, we could very well be a mouse run."

"A what?" Zainal asked, puzzled, so she suggested they take a break from house building while she explained about laboratory mice and labyrinths to test intelligence and learning ability.

"To add to whatever that scan of theirs discovered about us."

"But we do what we want," Zainal said, still puzzled.

"Maybe we just think we do," she replied, just now identifying that possibility.

"Scott would not like to think someone else commands him," and he chuckled as he got back to his feet and reached for another brick.

"No, he sure as hell wouldn't," Kris agreed, and laughed as she rose to join him. "We've got just enough mortar mixed for another course," she said, scooping up a trowelful. "I'm getting quite adept at this."

Then she remembered Sandy Areson's remark that plastering was like feeding an infant and that she'd use the same skills when she had one of her own. She tapped the next brick in place with such force that it split in half.

"That's the fourth one tonight," she said irritably. "Maybe they need to bake them longer or something."

Sandy was in fact in charge of the brick firing, so Kris knew it was no fault of the manufacture. Brick making was another chore shared throughout the community. But there was something soothing about shoveling the wet muck into the molds and knowing you were building your own place from scratch—including the ones on your arms, hands, and legs, collected in the process of building.

Still, it would be a nice place, when it was finished. She and Zainal had picked the spot together, on that first trip. They had a splendid view of the bay, with enough clear ground around to plant vegetables and berry shrubs, with a stand of "young" lodge-pole trees behind them. After months of barracks living, nearly everyone on Botany wanted privacy and the bay area certainly afforded that.

The Narrow Valley mess hall had been disassembled, loaded aboard the KDL, and reassembled on a height above the bay. Smaller "offices" clustered around it on the natural terraces and levels below and above it. The hospital was the only other large single structure and Leon Dane announced that the medical staff did not have time to build a separate maternity wing. He was, however, training midwives for home births since he was certain all the babies would decide to be born at the same time.

Private accommodations spread out around the bay in all directions, at first built from the lodge-pole tree timber before the brick manufactory got production up to a useful level. Those involved in cutting timber made the interesting discovery that even the smallest of the lodge-pole trees that had grown down into the plateau were at least a thousand years old.

"They have rings, just like trees on Earth," said Vigdin Elsasdochter, the environmental specialist in charge of responsible logging, ready to show the section she carried around with her. "And tight rings to indicate the climate has not changed much throughout the millennium: no drought, no bad winters, no hot summers. Some of the larger trees may be ten thousand years old."

Once again the question was brought up of how long the Farmers had been in possession of the planet. Especially since the "new forest" of "young" trees had been seeded by the much older ones. Even Worrell refused to worry about it.

"I got other more important things to worry about," he'd said one night in the mess hall. "Like allocating glass to people who want to have picture windows and stall showers! Of all things," and he'd flung a hand toward the bay, "as if we don't have a great big bathtub out there."

Those who had been in the building trades on earth, like the Doyle brothers, were kept busy offering advice, showing novices how to do things he'd learned, Lenny said, "at me da's knee, so to speak." Some of the Asians had the most trouble since they had been accustomed to different building materials. After assigned chores were done and the evenings gradually lengthened, everyone worked on their homes, and lent a hand to neighbors for jobs that required a gang.

While some of the brass-heads were living in the cliff hangar and bunking down on pallets in their offices, all of them had picked out sites but keeping track of work assignments for nearly ten thousand people and aliens took most of their time.

"Someone has to do it," Mitford remarked when Kris complained that the admiral seemed to be the unelected head of everything. "And hell, Kris, I might have run the battalion to all intents and purposes, and managed to whip us into some sort of order there at the first, but he had an aircraft carrier and they carry ten thousand. He's used to dealing with that kind of numbers. I'm not. I was only too glad to hand him the can, you know."

Mitford remained in charge of exploration and mapping, attempting to fill in the spatial map with the details necessary for further expansion of the farming and ranching. "If you can call loo-cows ranch animals."

Knowing that the sergeant was truly happier on reconnaissance in the Tub, Kris decided not to harbor any ill feelings toward Ray Scott. There was no question that he was working all the hours God gave the day here on Botany. And some days he seemed almost agreeable, as if Botany was mellowing him. At other times, she was certain he disliked and distrusted Zainal, and her by virtue of her association with the former Emassi officer. He vacillated between extreme cordiality when deferring to Zainal's knowledge of some matters and total dismissal of Zainal's opinions. He didn't have command all his own way, which somewhat mollified Kris, and she supposed that having run an aircraft carrier, he had the requisite experience. She had occasion to be grateful it was Scott who issued most of the orders, rather than Geoffrey Ainger, whom she didn't like at all. He was *so* British that he was almost a caricature of a ranking officer, and she knew he considered Zainal a dangerous commodity. She got along well with Rastancil, Fetterman, and Reidenbacker; John Beverly was the nicest of the lot because he always looked straight at her when he asked or answered questions. And Easley, but then he was as his name—easily to get along with. In fact, meetings seemed less tense when he was involved, and often more productive. He had such a knack for gently redirecting tensions and making suggestions that kept discussions going around, instead of stopping at Ray Scott all the time.

Which brought her back to the present and the meeting Scott and Rastancil had called them in for. They wanted Zainal to check the more mountainous terrain that had not yet been explored during the flight. The number of orbits had expanded from a quick flight up to the Bubble and back down to five days of circumnavigating the planet.

"See if there are any blind valleys here on our continent or deposits of minerals. We could use more lead, copper, zinc, and tin, if this continent has them."

"I believe it does," Zainal said. "The miner, Walter Duxie, has copies of the original spatial survey maps."

"Duxie? Do I know him?" Scott asked over his shoulder at his ever-present aide.

"Yes, he agreed to leave the other place and supervise mining here," Beggs murmured. "Stocky man, balding, forties, English."

"Ah, yes, get them for me to see," and Scott turned back to Zainal and Kris.

She wondered what Beggs' description of Zainal was—and of herself. Then she decided she didn't want to know.

Two days later, Zainal was satisfied that those accompanying him on the Bubble Mission, as its participants named it, were sufficiently trained to put what they had been learning into practice. He announced a dawn takeoff and dismissed them, suggesting that they all relax for the rest of the evening. Not that he intended to follow his own advice, because they were ready to put the shakes on the roof on their two-room cabin. Kris decided she needed to be so thoroughly tired she couldn't stay awake, because she was far more excited about the trip than she let on.

Zainal had just finished setting the piles of shakes in order and was steadying the ladder against the gable end when Mitford, Worry, Tesco, Sandy Areson, Sally Stoffers, and the two Doyles arrived, hammers in hand and with a second ladder.

"Can't have you breaking something the day before the Bubble," Mitford had said gruffly.

Kris smiled gratefully. Zainal might have learned the rudiments of construction but she was terrified that he'd fall through the rafters, or break them, and he wouldn't let her go up on the roof by herself to nail the shakes.

"You can't help," Kris said flatly to the two women.

"Heard about your design with my buff bricks," Sandy said. She was puffing a bit from the walk up the hill and had brought along her own stool. She put it down facing the front of the cabin and nodded approval. "Didn't realize we had so much color variation. . . . Maybe it's all you novices mixing your own batches."

"I liked the buff so that's what I made, and then added more buff to the red ones," Kris said, observing the effect objectively. They'd put the darker bricks around the door, window ledges, corners, the chimney, and the hearth surround. They had a back door, too, out of the smaller room, so they had easier access to the latrine. And a sleeping loft, which had become a popular idea, especially among those families that were increasing. "I think it looks good."

"Does at that. I can help hand out nails, too. Brought you my handy-dandy nail apron, too." She handed over the object and, laughing, Kris tied it about her waist, while Sandy started filling the three commodious pockets with the nails. "Is Zainal going to fill that big mouth of his with nails?"

Kris chuckled. "No, Lenny already warned him about

swallowing nails. Even a Catteni gut couldn't handle a mouthful. He's got a pail.''

Zainal had the ladder in place now, and before he could pick his pail off the ground, she was up the ladder, a bundle of shakes and the hammer in one hand and the other helping her up the rungs.

"Hey," Zainal protested.

"You'd never know he was Catteni," Sandy said conversationally to Sally, "unless you had to look at him."

Sally smothered a giggle as Zainal made as graceful a climb up the ladder as Kris had. Mitford and Lenny Doyle appeared on the roof from the other side and then the hammering began, echoing in the little dell and picked up by the rat-tat-tat of other hammers on other roofs.

With so many to help, passing shakes and replenishing the supply of nails, the cabin was roofed by the time the sun went down. Then Zainal passed around beer while Kris served up tea from the kettle in the fireplace.

"Looks bigger somehow, with the roof on," Kris remarked, glancing up at the rafters and taking a deep breath of the fragrance of the new wood of the shakes. They could have had slate but Mitford thought shakes were nicer and easier to put up.

They lounged about outside until first moonrise and then the guests left.

"We'd better hike to the hangar and get to bed in the scout," Kris said, moving toward the doorway. They had no door yet.

Zainal stopped her. "I want to stay under my own roof, which I have built . . ."

"Helped build," she said, teasingly.

"Tonight," he finished, and gestured toward the pile of blankets which she hadn't noticed in the rush to get the roof done.

"That would make the evening complete."

"Not quite," Zainal said in a low voice, drawing her

into his arms. "It is good to have our own place. Very
good indeed."

And that should have been an idyllic time for them. Except that when she got up in the night, between moons,
she didn't want to disturb the soundly sleeping Zainal,
and on her way back from the latrine she tripped over
the leftover bundle of shakes and broke her right arm.

She was furious with herself for being so clumsy and
for losing her chance at going on the mission.

"Why couldn't I have broken the left one? I'm right-
handed," she said, weeping more from disappointment
than pain as Zainal carried her to the nearest available
air-cushion, one of the flatbeds, and drove her the rest
of the way to the hospital. Both bones had been broken,
although Leon Dane comforted her with the thought that
it wasn't a compound fracture. That would have been
nasty with their limited facilities.

Then he poured her a tot of the grain alcohol that was
currently in use as a painkiller. They hadn't quite got a
decent smoky taste to it but she wouldn't complain.

"This is quite nasty enough," she said, as Zainal held
her against him while Leon maneuvered the bones back
into place. She fainted after, not during, and regained
consciousness while he was fixing the last of the bandages into place around the splints.

"I would like to have immobilized it in plaster, only
we haven't got that kind yet," Leon said. He poured her
a smaller tot, "to help you sleep," he said.

Then he led Zainal, who carried her, to an otherwise
empty ward. Zainal set her down gently by the window
and then moved the next bed against hers.

"Let's not make a practice of that," Leon said, caught
between severity and amusement at Zainal's preemptive
rearrangement. But he put out the solar-powered light
and closed the door quietly behind him.

Kris could almost have wished that Zainal had let her

suffer on her own, but the whiskey had dulled the ache in her arm and the warmth of his body, and his concern, comforted her so that soon enough she was asleep.

He was gone in the morning, when the noise of the scout's takeoff woke her. The bed had been put back in its proper position. It was dawn and he had blasted off on time. She wondered who had taken her place and then didn't want to know. She tried to go back to sleep but couldn't with the ache, so she got out of bed and, with a blanket draped around her, went in search of someone to help her make a hot cup of herbal tea. Maybe that would help the ache in her arm.

What helped her arm was a more judicious shot of the grain whiskey in the tea.

"I can't spend the next few weeks drunk as a lord," she said to the attendant in the hospital's kitchen.

"Ah, the ache'll ease off," Mavis, the duty nurse, told her, grinning. "At least we've got a decent tipple to help. Now, let's get back to your room and I'll help you dress. Can I bring your old coverall up to your cabin when it's clean? And have a look round it while I'm there? Cumber and I are building, too, and I like to get a notion of what others have done. Did you use bricks or timber?"

Mavis was deft in the dressing and kept Kris' mind off her awkward and painful arm as she helped.

"Stop at the pharmacy and they'll give you a bottle— for medicinal purposes," Mavis said with a grin, and pointed toward the right door. "I'll call for a ride but you may have to wait . . ."

"I can perfectly well walk . . ."

"You can perfectly well not," said Pete Easley, coming in the hospital at that moment. "I promised Leon I'd collect you. Got your bottle of medicinal? Sit there while I grab one. I know where they stash it," and he went into the pharmacy and was out again before Kris could take a seat. Then, with his hand under her left elbow, he escorted her out to the runabout.

"Mitford lent it to you?"

"For you, crippled as you are, Mitford is ready to do a great many things. Besides," and Easley looked down at her with a devilish grin, "he promised Zainal he'd look out for you."

"Hmmm, how kind," she said in an acid tone, knowing just what might be going through Zainal's mind in asking Mitford to be on hand.

"You could take another day in the hospital, you know," Easley said, his eyes intent on her face.

"I'm not sick," she said peevishly, and walked ahead of him to climb into the runabout.

The space on the driver's seat was not very wide, though it usually accommodated two people easily. But not one with an unwieldly cast and a brown bottle of hooch. Easley ended up sitting slightly canted so he wouldn't inadvertently bump her. She felt clumsier than ever and definitely out of sorts. She couldn't be hung over from what she'd had last night but she'd've given her eyeteeth for an aspirin. Then she remembered how Zainal laughed at all the eyeteeth she'd given away, and somehow her mood improved.

"He got off all right?" she asked.

"Right on time. Laughrey took your place."

"Laughrey, the former Concorde pilot?" Her good humor increased. She liked Laughrey and he'd be in heaven, literally as well as figuratively. "At least it wasn't Scott's little pipsqueak . . ." She would have hated it if Beggs had gotten the empty chair.

Pete Easley laughed. "The guy's good at what he does but Scott only tolerates him because it keeps him out of other people's hair. He's a natural yes-man but he's got an eidetic memory."

Early risers waved a greeting at Kris and Pete, some of them pointing to her arm and signaling "Tough luck.'' She wasn't sure how to respond to the sympathy, so waved back, smiling. She glanced skyward, knowing that Baby was probably over the other hemisphere about now.

"Could I sneak onto one of the bridges, d'you think?''

"Only when you've had some breakfast. You're white as a sheet,'' he said, pulling in to park at the mess hall.

So she had breakfast, which Pete Easley brought over to the table where he had sat her, one not visible from the door.

"Don't think you need condolences right now,'' he said, sitting so he blocked her from casual glances.

"Is news of my accident all over the bay?'' she demanded, her mood swinging back to annoyance again.

"Well, there had to be an explanation when Zainal showed up with Laughrey. We all know how keen you were to go on the mission,'' he said. "And you know how news goes through Retreat.''

"Hmmm, yes, indeed I do.'' She grimaced then because even to herself she sounded cranky.

"Don't worry about it, Kris,'' Pete said. "I'd be a lot crankier.'' And he escorted her back to the runabout without too many people commiserating with her.

"I think I'll take you home, Kris,'' he said, making the turn toward her cabin where he should have turned toward the hangar. "You still don't look like yourself.''

"I'm not,'' she agreed. "I am definitely *not* myself.''

But she also didn't want to go to a cabin that was empty of Zainal. She tried to think of the things she could do one-handed and came up with very few. Even dishwashing required two.

"Look, Kris, they won't reach the Bubble for a couple more hours. How about I drop you off at your cabin and come get you in time for that? Okay?''

"Yeah, that sounds pretty good,'' she said as he slowed the runabout right at her front door. She was getting out when she realized the doorway was no longer empty. "Hey, how did that get there?" and she pointed to the brand-new addition.

Pete grinned. "Lenny Doyle brought it down at first light. He thought you might prefer to be miserable in privacy."

She was delighted with the surprise, and worked the latch up and down.

"If you pull the string to the inside, it's like locking it," he said, and demonstrated.

"Like the pioneers used to do," and she grinned as she experimented, pulling the latchstring in and out.

Pete gave her a gentle push inward. "Get some rest now. And I'll be back for you."

He shut the door and she pulled the string in again.

"Thanks, Pete," she called, and heard his cheerful "No problemo" and then the whispering sound of the air-cushion driving off.

Someone had also tidied up the bedding, and increased the fluff content of the mattress. She blessed whoever had done her that service. She nudged one of the stools across the flagstone floor with her feet, knocked it over and kicked it into place by the bed, uprighted it, placed the bottle on it in handy reach, and sat down on the bed to take off her boots. She wouldn't sleep, she knew that, but she took a pull on the bottle before she lay down.

A determined knocking and someone calling her name roused her and she sat up, knocking her arm painfully.

"I'm coming, I'm coming," and she discovered it wasn't easy to get to one's feet with an arm in a sling. When she opened the door, Pete Easley was leaning on the frame, smiling broadly.

"You did sleep and you look one hundred percent better," he said, but he took a pocket comb, one of those carved out of loo-cow bone, and ran it through her hair.

"That's better. C'mon. We've just time to make the hangar before they make the Bubble."

When they entered the KDL's bridge it was crowded with an avid audience, but Scott made peremptory gestures for her to be let through and then installed her in one of the seats.

"You'll be interested to know," Beverly was saying from Baby's piloting compartment, "that the Bubble does not register on any detection equipment. But it's visible . . . as you can see."

Which they did, as from Baby's perspective. They could also see the scout ship on the KDL's screen, with its nose a scant ten meters from the barrier.

"We will poke it," Zainal's voice said, and Baby drifted into the opacity of the Bubble and bounced slowly backward.

"Here, let me adjust the screen a bit so they can see what the warship left behind," Marrucci said, laughter rippling through his voice.

"We'll need a touch of reverse for a proper view." That was in Laughrey's amused baritone. He chuckled openly as the view screen of Baby slowly swung to starboard and then slowly reversed.

"See what we mean?" Bert Put said, and Kris could just imagine the grin on the Aussie's face. "Lost every array they had and every mast they had."

"Outlined forever in the Bubble," said Balenquah. "Madre de Dios, the Farmers make some clever stuff!"

"Can you make any analysis of it?" Scott asked.

"Can't if sensors can't pick up anything," Bert Put said. "Not unless we go out and see if we can cut a patch of it."

"No," Zainal said. "If you wish, someone will go outside but we will not take sample."

"Affirmative to defacing it, Zainal," Scott said. "But I'd like an EVA inspection of it."

"I go," Zainal said, and immediately there was protest from both Baby and the KDL observers.

Kris discovered her left hand on her lips, to keep from adding her protest. Then she conquered her fear.

"He's the one to go, Ray," she said firmly. "He knows the gear and the ship. No one else has checked out for a space walk, have they?"

"I have," Bert Put said, "but not with this equipment. Zainal'll be just fine, Kris. He's already suiting up."

Zainal's EVA suit also had its own camera, so after a nervous wait, the view was transferred to Zainal's helmet eye and they saw the shimmering veil of the Bubble as he slowly approached it. They could see his hands reaching out to prod it gently, and the reaction of even that light touch as he floated away from it.

"Can you put your helmet on it, Zainal?" Scott asked, receiving a note from the engineers watching the space walk.

Slowly the Bubble filled the camera screen and was placed right up against the material. Nothing of the black space beyond could be seen through the fabric and it was smooth.

"Like a balloon's skin," Kris murmured under her breath.

"That's how I'd describe it," Scott said.

Then Zainal pulled back. "There are no flaws, even around the debris from the warship."

"Could you make it to that spot?" Scott asked.

"He's at the end of the tether right now, Ray," Beverly said. "We've got all the photographic material you need for examination of that flotsam. No need to risk Zainal for it."

"Agreed," Scott said indifferently. "Thank you for effort, Zainal."

"No problemo," said Zainal's deep voice as his helmet turned and took in Baby's bow and the windows into the pilot's compartment.

Kris' mouth went dry. He was a long way from the ship even if he was slowly returning to it. She felt some-one's hand close reassuringly on her shoulder and she glanced up at Pete Easley. She gave a sigh and con-trolled the flutter in her stomach. The break began to throb again but she decided to ignore it: the pain wasn't there. She had no time for it.

Then Zainal was back inside the scout and his camera turned off. She breathed a sigh of relief, oddly echoed around the crowded bridge. Which, she realized, was just a bit too crowded for her and she rose from her seat, glancing appealingly at Pete.

"Thanks, admiral," she said, nodding to the others she knew among those on the bridge.

A way parted for her as Easley conducted her off the bridge and then off the KDL. Her knees were near to buckling as she stepped down the ladder, hanging on with her left hand. And her arm ached despite her efforts to make it stop.

"There're sandwiches and tea," Pete said, showing where a trestle table was burdened with lunch items. "And I know where they keep the hangar's hooch," he added.

"This isn't like me," she said, peevish again.

"No, it isn't," Pete said equably. "But you're al-lowed. Sit. I'll be right back."

He doctored a cup of tea and brought more sand-wiches than she thought was fair, but she polished off two and had two cups of hooched-up tea. The ache in her bones subsided.

"D'you want to go back in and see the next show?" Easley asked.

He was really being very nice, Kris thought, but she shook her head.

"Then I'll take you back to the cabin," and he cupped her left elbow though he'd parked the runabout very close to where they'd been sitting.

He was really quite a nice guy, she thought. She wondered who'd snap him up as the father of a child, or children. He was a good head taller than she was, and rather more athletic than you'd think with that pose of indolence he usually affected. Not bad-looking, either, though nothing as toyboy–handsome as Dick Aarens was. Or Yuri with his Slavic cheekbones and snapping black eyes. Neither of them was a patch on Zainal though.

The comunit buzzed and Pete answered it. "Oh, you have? That's great. . . . I'm taking Kris home. She needs to rest. Okay? . . . Fine. See you. . . . No, they don't know what the Bubble's made of . . . except it's the biggest damned balloon ever made. Over."

"Yeah," and she giggled, "it is the biggest damned balloon ever made and we don't know who blew it up."

Pete grinned at her and she knew she was acting silly, but it was better than being peevish.

"I love that door," she said as the runabout stopped in front of it. "It's the best front door I've ever seen. Zainal will be so pleased. Say, how much hooch did you pour in my tea?"

"Only enough to stop the ache in your arm. It *has* stopped, hasn't it?"

She looked down at the clumsy white extrusion. "You know, it has."

Pete swung the door inward and she had taken the first step before she realized that the inside was different.

"My God, what's been happening with my back turned?" she demanded, swaying a bit as she turned toward Pete.

He took her good arm and led her inside. "Well, we were going to wait with the shivaree until Zainal could be here, too, but with you hors de combat, as it were, Sandy, Lenny, Ninety, Chuck, Sarah, Whitby, and Leila thought maybe now would be the right time to bring the stuff in."

"Stuff?" She blinked, trying to focus on first the table, with six glasses, almost symmetrical in manufacture, and a pottery set—which looked like Sandy's best designs—two pots, one large, one small, and a cast-iron skillet. There were benches around the table and at one end a chair big enough to fit Zainal. She put her hand to her mouth in surprise. But when her startled gaze flicked past the opening to the smaller room and saw the wooden bedstead with carved posts and the huge puffy fluff mattress that covered it, she burst into tears.

"Now, now, Kris," Pete said in consternation, and, pulling her against him, began to stroke her soothingly, saying a lot of things that she didn't really hear because the generosity of her friends and the team was so overwhelming.

Then he was holding one of the glasses to her lips and urging her to drink. She did because she hated to be such a baby when everyone was being so nice to her. And then her knees seemed to give way and Pete picked her up—as easily as Zainal could—and deposited her on the bed, arranging the pillows behind her and urging her to finish the drink.

"The bed—it's so marvelous . . . and they all know I've wanted a really, really, truly thick mattress . . ." And she clung more firmly to Pete, as the only steady thing in a rapidly whirling world.

She felt arms around her and, out of habit, forgetting that Zainal was off in space, she put her face up to be kissed. And it was. And so were her cheeks, and her neck, just where she liked it, and she was kissing the masculine face, slightly stubbled, which surprised her because Zainal didn't grow a beard but she needed comfort right now and the kisses were very nice indeed and she couldn't resist returning them . . . nor protest, even with her right arm feeling so heavy and not quite hers, when the coverall was slipped off and when she felt the warm skin next to hers. This was all somehow inevitable and, in the end, quite enjoyable.

She woke up with a terrible hangover and discovered, the hard way by accidentally banging her right arm as she tried to sit up, that it was still in a splint, though the throbbing was muted. The struggle just to sit only made her head worse.

She remembered being in the KDL's bridge, and coming back and seeing all the lovely gifts and crying, and sitting down on the bed, and Pete Easley.

She sat bolt upright, collapsing almost immediately with the headache and trying to remember more. And realized that indeed she did remember more. It hadn't been Zainal she'd made love with last night. It had been Pete Easley! And she'd enjoyed it far more than she should have. In fact, she could almost—not quite but almost—regret that her scruples required her to honor the bond that had grown between herself and Zainal as if it were a legal one. And that meant no jumping in the sack with anyone. Well, there were extenuating circumstances involved last night that would never recur. Furthermore, she'd keep far away from any of that "medicinal," inhibition-destroying alcohol. As much because of the headache she had as to what it did to her self-control.

Well, she thought philosophically, and chuckled. At least I remember enjoying it. Then she sighed. She hoped their next meeting wouldn't be awkward. Or that she'd have to explain to Pete that last night was it! She wasn't about to two-time Zainal. Even with someone as good in bed as Pete Easley. Some girl was going to be very lucky! She made another injudicious movement and thought longingly of a cool compress on her forehead and maybe the back of her neck.

Maybe a hair of the dog? She pushed back the blankets and noticed that Pete had neatly laid her coverall on the stool in easy reach, her boots beside it.

Yes, the bottle of medicinal spirits was on the table, and the glass he poured for her, with a good inch in it. Had he had some before he left? Whenever he had left, and she did briefly worry that his departure might have been noticed. Well, if it had, it had. She lifted the glass and knocked it back, shuddering at the taste. It was remarkable she'd been able to drink any of it.

She made a slow way to the hearth and, holding her head very still, lowered herself, spine-straight, to light the fire laid there. Another considerate touch by Mr. Easley. And the kettle was full of water.

One of these days, they would have water piped into houses, but that was in the future.

She went back to the table, to inspect the gifts she remembered vaguely having seen earlier, now sunlit from the small side window above the bed. Its slightly wavy glass sent a prism of rainbow light onto the table. Then she realized how the sun was shining in, from the east. For they faced the cabin south! Good Lord! She'd slept the rest of yesterday and an entire Botany night? No wonder her arm didn't ache as much.

The headache had begun to ease off by the time the kettle had boiled. She took herbs from the little pot on the mantel and made a cup which she took to Zainal's chair to drink. It was a comfortable chair, and she eased into its contours. It'd need a cushion or two. . . . No, she couldn't see Zainal sitting on a cushion, but the wood, when she felt it with her left hand, had been rubbed smooth, smelling only vaguely of the vegetable oil that had been used to give it luster. She wondered who had made it.

Then she absorbed the construction of the table—a three-inch slab of the slate which was quarried nearby, set on sturdy, slightly tapering rounds of lodge-pole trees, with notches spiked through the slate at the corners, keeping the top firmly in place.

There was a tentative knock on the door.

"Coming," she said, and saw that the latchstring was inside. She must have come to long enough to do that when Pete left. She opened the door to Mavis Belton from the hospital, a clean coverall in one hand.

"Oh, do come in," Kris said. "Kettle's just boiled. I was having a cup to get over my hangover."

"How's the arm?" asked Mavis, with a grin.

"Not as bad as yesterday, that's for sure. Come in, come in."

Mavis did, but only after a careful look into the main room of the cabin. Then she saw the furnishings and exclaimed with surprise, running her finger over the surface of the slate slab and admiring the sturdy lodge-pole legs that held such a weight up.

"Not something you could tip over easily," she remarked, stroking the chest and then Zainal's chair. "Big enough even for him, I'd say."

"He'll be delighted with it. He looks so uncomfortable on stools, with his legs sticking up like Arnie Schwarzenegger on a kindergarten chair. Here's your tea, and I'll just steal Zainal's chair. I can rest the splint on the arm."

"I just ended my shift but I thought you'd like to hear that Baby's doing fine in her orbitals."

"I saw them reach the Bubble and Zainal's space walk," Kris said. "That was before Pete Easley plied me with so much liquor I must have passed out."

"I think we're going to have to alter the recipe. That particular distillation is double potency. I told Leon and Mayock they'd better cut it more."

"They should," she said, rubbing the back of her neck. "My hangover's hung over for sure."

"Sit out in the sun. It's a lovely day." Mavis rose. "May I look around? Inside and out?"

"Sure, but watch that pile of shakes on the way to the latrine, will you?"

. . .

By dinnertime, when Mitford came by in the runabout to take her down to the mess hall, she had completely recovered. But she took him to task and demanded to know who had done the furniture she'd found in the cabin on her return from the hangar.

"Whose idea was that table? Not even Zainal could tip it over, and how'd you get it down here?" she asked.

"We were going to do it while you and Zainal were gone, surprise you on your return." Chuck Mitford said with a sly grin at her. "But with you on the sick list, seemed a good idea to put up the bed . . . and then what was a bed without a table and the chairs?"

"Well, it was very, very much appreciated. Especially that thick mattress on that wide bed! Drunk as I was, I appreciated that!" Then she caught Mitford's odd expression. "Oh, yes, Pete Easley got me high as a kite just in case you hear rumors that I was drunk. I was. I slept through an entire Botany night without so much as moving. Mavis came by this morning and said they were going to cut the last batch. I said they'd better . . . it was damned near lethal. Who made the bed?"

"Oh, the Doyles and me. I cut the timber and Lenny did the posts and showed me how to make the joints and stuff. He and Ninety did the table and the chair. Said it was the least they could do for the guy that kept them from becoming frozen steaks in a Farmers' freezer. Joe and Sarah did the mattress and pillows, Sandy Areson the pottery and glassware of course, Whitby the benches. Coo traded for the pots and the skillet. No big deal."

"No big deal?" she exclaimed, and a faint reminder of her hangover made her head ring with the loudness of her voice. "You furnish our cabin and it's no big deal. It's a real big deal to me," and she leaned over and kissed the sergeant on the cheek before she knew she was doing it. "There. And don't blush like that,

Chuck Mitford. I do appreciate what you all did and, besides, no one saw me kiss you.''

She giggled when the sergeant lifted one hand half-way to his cheek and then dropped it quickly back to his lap. He was still red-faced.

"You finished your cabin first. You'll have a chance to help others furnish theirs when they've built," he said in a gruff voice. "By the way, stood a tour on the KDL and the mission's going a-okay. Not a wrinkle on the balloon as far as they've gone. Seamless. All the tech heads are scratching their arses over what was used.''

"What's the general feeling? Or is it too far away to bother the claustrophics?" she asked, trying not to resent her absence . . . and Zainal's.

"I think people are glad. The Deskis evidently had a wild night of dancing, singing . . . if you can call that warble singing . . . and Coo says there are giants pro-tecting us.''

"Did he see the Eosi?''

"No," and Mitford shook his head. "And, frankly, I'm just as glad I didn't. Worry's still having nightmares and I think that's why Leon made the latest hooch so strong. Hoooo-eee!" He let out a long whistle. "You can blame them for getting you drunk, not Pete Easley. Which reminds me. Officially you're on sick leave, Bjornsen, so don't get any ideas about doing anything with that busted wing until Leon gives you the okay. Got me?''

"Yes sir, sergeant, sir," she said, saluting repeatedly with her left hand.

The makers and donors of the furniture were saving spaces for them at a table in the mess hall. Kris lavished praise and gratitude on all for making a cabin into a real home, promising to do as well by them, when their cab-ins were up, as they had by her. Then the conversation devolved to Baby's mission and Mitford, sipping what he assured Kris was a well-watered jolt of hooch, brought them up to speed.

The monitor also tracked the small vessel in its exploration, especially the examination at the barrier, and followed its progress until it landed safely again on the western continent.

CHAPTER 10

Baby returned safely and with sufficient masses of information to keep all the brass-heads, engineers, miners, and Aggies busy. The mission crew took a longer time to get themselves back down to the surface, they were so high on the experience. Zainal's course had used a minimum of fuel and won the plaudits of the aviators and astronauts. Everyone on board had had instruction from him on how to fly Baby and a little chance at maneuvering.

"We may not have flight simulators, but what're they against the real thing?" Balenquah demanded. "Too damned bad we can't go anywhere in the KDL. Zainal says it's much easier to pilot—had to be since Drassis flew that series. That whole caper of capturing the KDL was a waste of time."

"No," Bert Put said, evidently rather fed up with Balenquah's opinions, "it got us extra fuel, a new bridge console, and a lot of tools we'd have a hard time duplicating."

"Oh, yeah, forgot about them," Balenquah replied.

"Well, if we have to shift population, it'll be handy enough."

"There'll be flying in the KDL," Marrucci said, "maybe only mine and grain runs, but we're not totally grounded, you know."

"We are for any *real* space work," the man went on, talking himself into a morose state.

Zainal rose then and muttered something about having to see the admiral and took Kris from the table. Glancing back just as she and Zainal left the mess hall, she saw that others were departing from the table, leaving Balenquah on his own.

Zainal had been struck dumb with amazement when he saw the cabin. The door—which he admired even before he opened it, with Kris barely able to contain her excitement at what lay beyond it—had required his attention: admiring the detail, the latchstring, which gave him great amusement, pulling it in and out.

Then he entered the room and saw the table and the chair, the pottery and glasses, which Kris had put on the mantel, having no other place to store things—yet. Lenny had promised to teach her how to do mortise-and-tenon joins in wood and make herself proper chests and drawers. But the table and the chair shocked him, with one knee raised for the next step, and he stared and stared, and then inarticulately tried to ask her who, how, where these things had come from.

As she replied, interspersing the explanation with giggles for the surprise yet in store for him, he examined everything, even trying to lift the slate-topped table. He sat in the chair, got up, turned it upside down to see how the legs had been fitted in, and the stringers, and then righted it to sit in it again, stroking the armrests with his big hands.

Maybe Catteni didn't have tear ducts or never cried but Zainal's eyes were certainly full of fluid and though he tried to speak, he kept shaking his head, speechless.

"I've saved the best for last," she said, and taking a hand that was attached to a body reluctant to leave the chair that had been made to fit him, she led him to where he couldn't miss the bedstead.

He had an immediate response to that: the very devil of a look in his full eyes, as he swooped her up into his arms and carried her, for all the world the way John Wayne had treated Maureen O'Hara in *The Quiet Man,* and demonstrated how much better he could perform on a resilient surface.

Mitford took her off the sick list when he wanted their team to find a pass through the western hills to the far shore: he let her go along. He knew very well that she'd be better employed marking klicks, which she could do with her left hand, than left at Retreat, fretting that she was useless.

While that was being organized she spent some time making bricks, since she could fill the molds left-handed. She owed Sarah and Joe for their hand in the Great Furniture Surprise. When some loggers were injured—two badly—she sat in the ward with them, checking pulses and temperatures. There were no blood pressure devices and no thermometers, so it was all hands-on. She also fed Boris Slavinkovin, who had broken both arms and most of his ribs when the rolling log took a shortcut over his body. Being fed by a one-handed aide didn't embarrass him half as much, he told her, because it didn't tie up a whole human who could do jobs other than feeding him. Then he asked her if she could teach him better English since he was now stuck in bed and had to do something.

Ex-teachers had gotten together with an ex-cartoonist and created a language primer for those who wished to learn English. There were fifty copies in print, thanks to supplies on the KDL, and they were well worn by the time Kris snagged a copy for Boris.

Leon and Mayock managed to dilute the potency of their distillation so that it not only had the faint aftertaste of a Botany nut variety but did not cause such speedy and legless inebriation.

The only person whose metabolism could cope with the previous grain whiskey was Zainal, so rather than water down what was left (which Leon felt was a crime), they gave the remaining keg to him. The first time he sampled it, Kris told him about Pete Easley getting her drunk on barely two half glasses of it and the hangover she'd had the next day. That reminded her that she hadn't seen as much of Pete Easley as usual. But she thought nothing of it, going to her stints at the hospital or the brick factory.

Then they were ready to leave on their exploratory mission and it was a great relief to all the team to be back together again and out on their own.

"One can get too accustomed to the comforts of home," Sarah announced, settling back in her seat on the big air-cushion truck. "Though I wish we could have started the cabin before we left. And thanks again, Kris, for all those bricks. Worry's put his name in for a hundred and so has Jay Greene. We should have enough by the time we get back."

"We do appreciate the ones you did for us, too," Leila said in her often inaudible voice. She was holding hands with Whitby, while hanging on to a strap with the other.

She looked a bit white, Kris thought, and wondered if she, too, was pregnant. Sarah was, and was very cocky about it, taking it in her stride like any modern woman.

"Sure thing, Leila. Kept me out of mischief," Kris said.

And actually, kept mischief away from her, for any of the importunate men who tried to charm her found themselves also making bricks, if that was where they caught up with her, or feeding a bed-bound patient, which was scarcely a romantic setting for the sort of offers they hoped to make.

Boris Slavinkovin put in his bid and she had to threaten him with her absence at mealtimes if he kept it up.

"You'll have to sometime, you know," Sarah said bluntly.

"Oh, I will, I will," Kris said airily, and did not meet Zainal's eye when he glanced at her beside him. "Ah, that's another klick, isn't it? We've gone one thousand plegs again." She added a slash to her sheet.

They found a way through the hills, through twisting but connecting ravines separated by banks which the air-cushion could manage easily. They marked the more accessible routes with 0's in the blue, almost luminous paint that was a recent innovation. (Red and yellow had already been produced from local vegetable dyes.) The cul-de-sacs were marked with an X. For some reason, Zainal found the procedure very amusing and wouldn't tell her why. They did not find any blind valleys or night crawlers but they did find a new variety of rocksquat and some avians that were almost as good eating as chickens, though some, caught closer to the sea, left a fishy aftertaste in the mouth.

They made their way down the coast until the rocky terrain was impassable even for the remarkably maneuverable vehicle. They were headed back, up the eastern coast, two weeks later when Kris experienced some fleeting nausea first thing in the morning. For a couple of days she was sure it was caused by the ripe soft fruits that flourished in the almost tropical weather that far south. She ignored the minor discomfort until one morning when Joe was replacing the splints and bandages on her arm. The bandage material came from the legs and arms of Catteni coveralls, cut in strips, softened slightly by much washing and use, and adequate for their purpose. Her arm was sweating so much in the heat that she was glad to change the wrappings with the extra roll of bandage that Joe had in his medical kit.

"Arm's healing well," he said, feeling the breaks with careful fingers. "I can feel the thickening of the bones where they've knitted."

"Doesn't hurt anymore either," she said, though she sighed as he replaced splints and bandage strips.

He gave her an odd sideways glance. "Trip's done you good. You were looking a little off color before we left."

"Which reminds me. . . . Anyone else having trouble digesting that pink-fleshed fruit we had last night?" she asked.

Joe was not only medic but botanist.

"No, but we didn't gorge on it either. Why? Got the runs?"

"No, a touch of indigestion, I guess," and she shrugged it off, but Sarah had overheard her query and joined them, peering into her face with an intensely disturbing grin on her face. "So?" Kris demanded when Sarah didn't explain.

"Breasts hurt? Had your period? How long have you noticed the nausea?"

Defensively, Kris crossed her arms over her breasts and, as if Sarah's comment had been a curse, they were tender. She didn't dare change the position of her arms as her mind raced to the conclusion Sarah had obviously just come to.

"I can't be pregnant," she said, jerking her chin up. "I've never—"

"Never what?" asked Sarah with a sly expression on her face.

Kris closed her eyes, remembering the potent hooch she'd had for her arm, remembering Pete Easley offering more, and more, and enough so that she had . . .

"I'll kill him," she said, meaning it fervently. No wonder he had kept out of her way. Just wait till she got back to Retreat. She'd—

"Is something wrong with Kris' arm?" Zainal asked, and Kris wanted to seep into the ground like a night crawler.

"Nothing, nothing's wrong with my arm," and she shot to her feet, glaring at Sarah and Joe.

"No, but she's pregnant," Sarah said, gleefully.

Kris hauled back her left arm to punch Sarah but Zainal caught her around the waist.

"You had to go blab it!" she shouted, trying to reach Sarah, who had nimbly danced out of her way, with the grinning Joe moving into position to protect his mate, hands out in a placatory move.

"Now, Kris, don't go off half-cocked," he said as Leila and Whitby came running over to see what could possibly have happened.

"Kris is preggers, too," Sarah crowed.

Then Zainal was holding her so tightly to his chest, leaving her feet dangling above the ground, that she had to hang on to him for balance.

"Thank you, Kris," he murmured into her ear, and all the fight went out of her.

She hung limply against him as his arms around her assumed a kinder hold, a loving one. There couldn't be many males on any world that would thank a woman who got pregnant by another man.

"You're welcome. I think," she added, and squirmed to be released. When he put her back on her feet, she apologized to Sarah and Joe with as good a grace as she could manage. "I wanted to be sure," she said mendaciously. "It could have just been the ripe fruit."

"So, tell us who the lucky guy was?" Joe asked with the familiarity of an old friend.

Kris chuckled, deciding on an entirely different course

of action that meant she couldn't publicly go after one sweet-talking lothario of a Peter Easley, but neither would she confirm it to him or anyone . . . unless of course the newborn gave some clue to its paternity. That would serve that so-and-so right. Taking advantage of a girl in her condition . . . and yet. . . . She suppressed any recollection of an incident that would result in a lasting and visible proof.

"That's for me to know, and you to guess," she said, delighted to be able to pay Sarah back for blurting out what Kris would rather have kept secret.

The long trek up the Eastern Coast went well, all other events considered. Everyone settled down to the fact of her pregnancy. At night Zainal held her against him with a tenderness she certainly had not expected of him: enough to make her eyes water and make her wish, with all her heart, she might have transcended the barriers of species biology and been pregnant by him.

By the time they got back to Retreat Bay, she felt better than she ever had in her life. She had to see Leon about her arm and he was very pleased with its progress. He wanted her to keep the splints on anyway, since she insisted on working, but she could use her right hand now. He also confirmed her pregnancy and had the grace not to inquire further.

"Actually, you're lucky you're here on Botany. Doesn't take as long," Leon said with a wry grin.

"What do you mean, it doesn't take as long?"

"Average pregnancy is two hundred and sixty to eighty days. But it'll only take you two hundred and twelve point eight Botanical days to gestate." When she blinked in confusion at him, he grinned and added, "Thirty-hour days don't change the development rate of a fetus but it sure alters the *days* you stay pregnant."

"Oh!"

"Most of my OB patients find that comforting."

"I'll remember that."

Word of her pregnancy got around and she could find additional comfort in the fact that her "admirers" went elsewhere with their persuasions. And when she saw Pete Easley across the crowded mess hall one evening, she merely gave him a cheerful wave and left him wondering. She did like the man, in spite of that dirty trick. He'd been drinking that day, too. Maybe she was assigning his solicitude to exterior motives because he'd been drinking as much of that hooch as she had. How could she fault him for getting drunk and doing what was natural enough? Pregnancy was also mellowing her.

The temperature was definitely warming up and bushes were blossoming, spreading a heady smell that the inland breeze wafted down to the bay area. The agricultural teams had plowed during their absence and sowed the fields with seed purloined from the now deserted Bella Vista camp in a special trip of the KDL. As no ship had come to collect what was left of the grain, the KDL did, for the supplies brought across the channel were low.

The silos were swept clean for this year's storage.

On the continent that had been evacuated, the machines had been plowing, too, and many of the fields sown. Some wit among the Aggies set up a competition, one-sided though it was, as to the growth and health of their crops versus the Farmers' and the resultant yield per acre. The Aggies had already elected to use fields the same size the Farmers had, since the arable land seemed to divide into such sections: another clue that this continent might once have been farmed, too. The rustled loo-cows grazed the less desirable fields and the hillsides.

About the time the crops were a good six inches high and thriving, a most unpleasant discovery was made:

there were night crawlers again. Not many, but enough to let them know that there was a resurgence of the menace.

Astrid put forward the theory that the loo-cows excreted internal parasites that had a second cycle as night crawlers. There were a few who agreed with her, but it made for an interesting argument in the evenings, and had those with wooden floors in their huts replacing them with thick slate or flagstones. And many of those who had not sited their dwellings moved nearer the better-traveled areas. No one walked out at night on any field and the sentinel positions were either made of stone or set high above the ground on stilts.

This was, however, a very minor setback. Compost heaps were hastily shifted to stone tubs, and the disposal of noxious wastes was no longer a problem. Not that anyone wanted night crawlers in a latrine. Since such facilities no longer had to be dug, it became a punishment chore to do the late-evening dumps, far enough from the rapidly expanding community to reduce the hazard of night crawler infestation to the populated areas.

Spring lasted months but the fine weather assured the Aggies of excellent crops, as good or even better than what the Farmers were cultivating. The varieties of tubers and pulses occupied half as many fields as the grain crops, and caves were found to store the harvests rather than having to search ever farther afield for the edibles. The night crawlers were not attracted to vegetable matter unless it was mixed with bloody substances, so these crops were not disturbed. The rocksquat compound flourished and it was discovered that baby rocksquats were far more delicate in flavor and texture than the adults.

Evening classes in various skills were given. The nights that Admiral Ray Scott threw his first successful pot, or Bull Fetterman completed a set of six dining chairs, or Marrucci managed a creditable mortise-and-tenon drawer for his chest remained landmarks in the assimilation of the disparate ex-professionals into true Botanicals.

There were failures, as Mitford put it: people who refused to do their share of work or felt themselves put upon by "authority" to always have to do the less glamorous tasks. Judge Bempechat gave each offender three chances to redeem him or herself in the eyes of the community. Then the unrepentant had a one-way trip back to the old continent, where they could fend for themselves, with cup, blanket, knife, and hatchet. After the expulsion of the first dozen or so, delinquency was reduced significantly.

Once a month, the two valley prisons were visited. The Turs disappeared one by one until the valley was empty. The Catteni eventually put up shelters, and when they asked for supplies, like nails or meat as a change from a fish diet, these were provided. But nothing that could provide them any assistance in escaping. Zainal doubted they would try.

"They are Drassi and Tudo. They have enough to eat, a place to sleep, and that is sufficient."

"I can't imagine anyone not wanting to better conditions," Marrucci had said, for he was often in the pilot's seat in one of the two small airships that did the run. "I mean, when you consider we're damned near city size with our own distillery . . ." Marrucci was hoping to add wine to the spirits and had already been south for the soft fruits as a basis for his "cordial."

"They like it the way they have it now," and Zainal shrugged.

"D'you think the Turs did escape?" Marrucci asked.

"Who cares?"

"You got a point there."

.   .   .

The tub went regularly to the mines with supplies for the men and women working there, to rotate personnel and bring back ore. The judge often gave a month's sentence at hard labor for misdemeanors, and only one ever found mining an enjoyable occupation. He stayed on.

For evening entertainment, those with any talent provided shows, managing to remember enough of a musical comedy or even a play to put on abridged versions or invent dialogue and action to add to what they remembered. Decks of cards were manufactured from the heavy wrappings on stores in the KDL and Baby. The cards didn't shuffle well but that didn't keep the players from betting an hour's work or a special bit of scrimshaw to make it interesting.

Gold had been found but it was decided, not without heated debate, that barter made a better system for a small community like theirs where everyone was expected to work community hours, not pay to get out of the labor. Among the diverse trades of the colonists, there were several jewelers. They would contract to produce jewelry for those who found gold, and even a few gemstones, and decided among themselves what was fair payment in grams of the metal.

Iri Bempechat had taken on several assistants as legal advisers in disputes, most of which could be settled by compromise. The ex–military personnel had formed a lower court but their decisions could be appealed, leaving Judge Bempechat to give the final verdict on an issue.

"We don't need a formal government," Beverly had said one evening, when the topic came up again in a mess hall that was more crowded than usual due to an unusually heavy fall of rain. (It was the beginning of many such rainfalls, which limited themselves to nighttimes.) "Why complicate what has been working rather smoothly?"

"If it ain't broke, don't fix it," Mitford called out, and got a good laugh for the old army axiom.

"We have a form of government, actually, though most of you don't realize it. We just don't have elected officials or a nominal head of state. Nor do I believe one is required," Iri said, his cultivated and mellifluous voice reaching to the farthest corners. "Those of us with special expertise have taken on the duties required to ensure peace and tranquillity. Community hours handle public services, such as they are, and the rest of us work where we can be useful and at our previous professions for the most part, even in the limited fashion due to the constraints of supplies. I suppose we should thank our lucky stars that we have so many skills among us. Practically every walk of life is represented. Our alien associates," and he gestured to the Rugarians, sitting in their usual group, and the Deski, who were more apt to mix in with humans, "have supplemented us in many ingenious ways. I think some of us may have a chuckle comparing what we used to do with what we're doing now, but frankly, I think it's been beneficial as well as instructive. We're all doing very well indeed. And able, for the most part, to do what we do the way we want to. Certainly without any bureaucratic interferences and certainly without a thread of red tape. You don't know how happy that makes me!"

Good-natured chuckles greeted that sally.

"Why indeed should we fix something that isn't broken?" he added, raising his hands in appeal.

"Yeah, but what happens to our pleasant utopian dream when the Farmers come?" Balenquah asked, glancing around.

"Leave it to Balenquah," an anonymous male voice said.

"What does *that* mean?" the pilot asked, rising from his chair and staring around, trying to discover the source.

"It means," Marrucci said, reaching across the table and hauling Balenquah down, "you're out of order, off course, and being a pain in the arse again. You're alive, you're sure kicking, you're even flying, and if that isn't better than starving in a Catteni prison for blowing up their freighter, you're gone in the head."

"Don't say another word," Beverly put in from a nearby table, "if you want to fly again."

"That's just what I mean," Balenquah said. "We need a formal government, so you know who's got the right to give orders."

"That's enough out of you, Balenquah," Scott said, seconding Beverly's admonition.

"You're not an admiral of anything here, Scott," Balenquah said.

"Oh, boorrring," drawled one of the "ladies" from two tables over. And she yawned ostentatiously, which made the others at her table howl with laughter.

"You are, you know," Marrucci said, shaking his head at Balenquah, who had colored with such open ridicule, "a real bore with all this gloom and doom and I'm obviously," and now he turned to look at the ladies' table, "not the only one who thinks so."

Balenquah rose, his right arm cocked, but even before Marrucci could rise to defend himself, Scott had nodded to the man beside him and they rose and captured Balenquah's arm and were hustling him out of the mess hall and into the rain.

"Add bouncer to my list of new-world occupations," Scott said to Beverly as the two returned to their seats.

At their table, Kris found herself sharing a bit of Balenquah's pessimism. The problem of the Farmers *was* just beneath the surface of everyone's thoughts, despite the fact that most people carried on as if there were not that threat hanging over them. Zainal kept insisting that the Farmers were benign. He could give no other reason for that than the way this planet had been tended for thousands of years, if the new forest of lodge-pole trees was any indication.

"And it has been months since the Bubble was blown up," he reminded her, as they walked back to their cabin when the rain had stopped. Flagstone pathways had been laid around much of Retreat Bay now, to hinder night crawlers, although walkers automatically stamped hard every third step.

Kris let Zainal do it for them both as she didn't like jarring the baby she could now feel move, in little flutters, within her: normal activity at five months. Sarah kept complaining that her little dear kicked like a soccer star, but she was eight months along. By now, almost every female of childbearing age, including the Deski and Rugarians, was expecting, which meant that Retreat Bay would have a baby boom of 2,103 new souls. Anna Bollinger may have given birth to the first human baby on Botany but there had since been thirty-four born to women who had been captured pregnant. Now the new crop—which had been plowed on Botany, as someone had remarked in a biblical fashion—were reaching term. Patti Sue was first, and prideful about producing a son for Jay Greene.

Kris didn't know which she wanted, apart from being healthy and not too much resembling its sire. Somehow she couldn't ask Zainal what his preference would be. And yet, he would act in loco parentis to whatever she produced.

Most of the pregnant women carried on in their specialty as long as possible: and Kris, Sarah, and Leila were no exceptions. In fact they had arguments with the sergeant that he was assigning the team the "easy" trips. So he organized Zainal to take Baby to the smallest continent—really more of a very large island than a continental landmass—to circumnavigate it, the coastline being the only part that was green.

"Bit like Australian outback," Sarah remarked as

Zainal guided Baby crisscross the interior. "Like Null-arbor. Nothing for klicks! Not even mulga or brush . . . sand and rock," she added in disgust.

"Hmmm, yes, I see," Joe said, without explaining his cryptic remark as he gazed out the starboard side in the pilot's compartment. "Real rock!" He pointed now to a rocky ridge that ran obliquely across below them, like vertebrae, with dips and spires. "Dinosaur bones."

"Hmmm, that's what they do look like," Kris agreed.

Whitby insisted that they land and spend one night at the base of that range, where the spatial maps indicated one of the ore deposits. "We should know where copper and zinc are and that's what is down there. If the lodes are near the surface, it might be advantageous to take a week or so to work up a cargo."

So they landed, and it was hot.

"Just like home in the dry," Sarah said ecstatically, throwing her arms back, her gravid belly out, and turning her face up to the sun.

"Good way to get sunstroke," Joe said, and slammed her reed-weave hat on her head. "We are not, I repeat, we are not delivering you prematurely in the confines of Baby."

"Having the baby in the Baby?" Sarah was off on a fit of the giggles.

Whitby, Leila, Joe, and Zainal went off to try and locate the ore, laden with bottles for samples and soil. Sarah and Kris, who found the heat especially enervating, found what shade they could in the lee of Baby by digging out enough soil under the landing vanes to sit on blankets. Kris dozed off while Sarah dragged her hands through the scattered rocks, trying to find interesting ones.

Sarah, too, dozed off and they were both awakened by the laughter of the returning prospectors. Each carried some sort of dead animal resembling a large rat.

Kris recoiled when Zainal plunked three brace beside

her. The pelts caught her attention because they were mottled in soft sandy shades.

"Camouflage? From what?" she said, venturing to touch the nearest. It was rough with dirt and sand.

"Burrowers," Joe said succinctly, "but they test edible. We thought we'd give them a try. Live on insects, of which this continent has a multitude. I saw twenty-five varieties and caught," and he held up several bottles tied together to prevent breakage, "only a few for closer examination. You never know what might be useful." He grinned wickedly. "Or tasty. And nutritious."

"How would you know? You never hunted outback with the aborigines," Sarah said.

"Neither did you."

"But I did a paper on the ones the aborigines favor," she replied hotly, and they were off again.

The desert burrowers—Kris declined to think of them as rats—were skinned and, after Joe did further tests on the equipment in Baby, were cooked in the galley and served as part of the evening meal. The flesh was different in texture and taste from anything else that Botany had provided: sort of nutty and sleek. Almost difficult to bite into.

Twilight brought out their natural predators, batlike creatures who swooped on long triangular wings from rocky aeries to catch the burrowers. The cooler air encouraged a different set of insects to appear, ones that bit and itched and forced everyone to take refuge in the scout ship. But not before they saw the desert burrowers in action, making incredible leaps into the air to catch their meal on tongues that elongated to make the capture, and seeming to disappear from sight the moment they heard bat wings above them.

"We've some like that on ol' Earth," Joe remarked, watching from the scout.

The men were in general pleased with their prospecting and had marked the areas with the blue paint, though

Whitby and Joe argued about its durability in the unre-mitting sun.

"Well, we'll wear-test it good, then," Joe said, shrug-ging. "And we've the coordinates anyway."

Zainal made for the coast in the dawn light the next morning and, keeping the Baby at a low altitude, made a touchdown in those spots that looked different. This tropical area displayed fruits and nuts, not unlike citrus and coconut, and samples were gathered of everything, including a different variety of insect life. Kris found the smell of rotting vegetable and fruit unsettling but said nothing until the reserved Leila murmured a complaint.

"There're sort of plateaus up ahead," Whitby pointed out. "Maybe cooler up there, with an offshore breeze to keep the gnats and nits away."

Kris disliked using pregnancy as an excuse to avoid any task, but she was glad enough to let the men rig a shelter of the thick-fronded vegetation on a height over-looking a rather lovely white-sanded bay. (On inspec-tion, the white sands contained particularly vicious biting insects, so the charm of the area was considerably diminished and Sarah and Kris could lounge in comfort above that nuisance.) There were even smaller fronds to use as fans and the breezes were cooling and pleasantly scented with whatever was blooming farther inland.

Leila took off to explore with Whitby but she came back, her face and bare arms blotchy from contact with plants they had had to cut their way through.

"The sap which zapped me," Leila said as Kris and Sarah washed her arms and face, "is very sticky and Joe is hoping we've found a rubber substitute."

"The hard way," Sarah said in a droll tone of voice. "Is this helping?"

Leila gave a little sigh. "Only as long as the wet's on me."

"What wouldn't we give for a decent antihistamine!" Sarah said fervently.

"We've chemists enough . . ." Kris said.

"And only the one microscope, which evidently isn't strong enough to do much, so it's back to old trial and error."

So, since trial wet compresses helped, more were made of bandage strips in the first-aid kit and wrapped around her arms and laid on her face and neck.

That was when Sarah's baby decided to arrive. In fact, did before his father and the others returned, though Kris immediately called a Mayday for Joe over the hand unit.

"I must've miscounted," Sarah said apologetically to her midwives when she realized her labor had begun. "This business of thirty-hour days and seven-month pregnancies."

"Nonsense," Kris and Leila retorted in the same breath. "It isn't as if we don't know what to do," Kris added, though her mind was revolving in a panic over all the things they didn't have on board the scout that might be needed.

None were as Sarah's fine lusty baby took the minimum of time in arriving. Both mother and child were all cleaned up when the father leaped into the clearing, red-faced with exertion and badly scratched in his effort to get back in time. Then Whitby and Zainal were congratulating him and Sarah, and admiring the baby. Kris had her eyes on Zainal, wondering if human babies were in any way different from Catteni newborns.

"Small," Zainal muttered, knowing some comment was needed.

"Small?" exclaimed Joe indignantly, as his son squirmed in his arms in reaction to the sudden loud noise.

"He's not small at all," Leila said emphatically, and startling the rest of the team since she rarely contradicted anyone. "He's eight pounds and a few ounces. And healthy!"

"And I feel fine," Sarah said. "And it's so good to

do this," she added, for she was sitting up, arms around her knees, a position she hadn't been able to assume for several months.

"How big are Catteni babies if you think this one's small?" Kris asked, deciding she'd better straighten Zainal out before he could be disappointed in what she produced.

Zainal measured a distance with his hands.

"I pity the females who have to carry *that* much around," Sarah said, shaking her head.

"Bigger head, quite likely, and bigger bones," Joe said sagely.

"He's healthy, that's what matters," Whitby remarked in a definitive tone.

But young Anthony Marley caused the team to leave the insalubrious area and head back to Retreat Bay. Sarah tried to talk them out of an early return because she and Anthony were fine and the reconnaissance could continue, as far as she was concerned. Joe was having none of it, wanting both wife and child checked over by the medics.

Leon Dane pronounced Sarah in excellent postnatal condition and Fawzia Johnston, the pediatrician on duty when they returned, said that young Anthony was as healthy and normal as any mother could wish. The Doyle brothers, who now spent more time as carpenters and joiners, instructing others in the art, presented Sarah and Joe with a cradle for the infant.

"Working all the hours God gave Botany to keep up with the demand," Lenny said, after duly admiring young Anthony and congratulating the parents. "You know, this place is getting more like home all the time, with the babies arriving." He looked melancholy.

"You miss your own?" Sarah said, putting a sympathetic hand on his arm.

Lenny's face brightened into a grin. "Sort've, but who's got time to think of what we left behind with so much to do where we are!"

CHAPTER 11

Zane Charles Bjornsen arrived on Botany at dawn exactly 222 days after conception. He was a long child—in that he did resemble his father. He came with fingernails that had to be cut soon after his birth or he'd've scratched his fair face, and a mass of very dark hair.

He was not, as Anthony Marley had been, red, wrinkled, and an object only his mother could love.

"Zane is a perfectly good name," Kris had told Zainal. "One of my favorite Western writers was a Zane Grey. And I admire Chuck Mitford."

"But he is not the father." Zainal did no more than raise one eyebrow at her, tacitly asking the question she had refused to answer.

"No, but I see no reason I . . . we . . . can't do him the honor of being godfather."

"Godfather?" Zainal's lips twitched. "Oh God, oh God . . . ?"

"Not that sort. The deity that Father Jacob reveres, the real God."

"There is one?"

Zainal had trouble believing in the Almighty, though the several ministers who had been dropped were trying to establish services. The Protestants had no problems but Father Jacob did, since he had none of the accessories properly required to say Mass. He fretted about their lack and how he should manage without them.

Marrucci proved to be a devout Catholic and did his best to console the good father in one of those role reversals which continually happened on Botany.

"If God is everywhere, then He's here, too, padre, and He'll accept the worship of the sincere, dedicated to Him. The earliest Catholics had no altar or relics, and communion was bread and wine. We got them. We got the dedication. You say the words and I'll be altar boy."

Mitford was both pleased and alarmed to have a child named for him.

"Everyone will think he's mine and he isn't," the sergeant said at his gruffest. "Not that I wish he weren't, Kris," he added hastily. "I mean, I'd've been honored if you'd wanted to but . . . well, hell, you know what I mean."

"Yes, I do, Chuck."

"So who is the lucky guy?"

"Remember that hooch Leon and Mayock made, about the time I broke my arm?"

"Yeah, I do," and Mitford looked surprised, then scowled deeply. "You mean you got raped and never reported it?" His fists clenched as if he held the neck of the offender within them.

Kris patted one such fist gently. "I don't know about any rape. But I do know I was very, very drunk."

Chuck frowned. "Pete Easley took you back to your cabin, didn't he?"

"He may have, Chuck, but I don't recall a thing and perhaps that's as well, don't you think?"

"No, I don't."

"Can't do anything about it. But maybe when Zane grows up, we'll know for sure. Zainal couldn't care less."

"No, he couldn't, and you know, the way he's taken this hasn't lost him any points."

Zainal was at that moment changing his foster son's fluff diapers. The reeds which produced the useful material were being cultivated everywhere they would grow around Retreat Bay.

The sticky sap that had been such a problem on their last reconnaissance trip had been harvested and, poured into a mold, made a reasonable facsimile of waterproof garments for baby use. They could be washed and reused four or five times but gradually dissolved, often at the wrong time.

Mitford grinned, watching the anomaly of a Catteni Emassi acting the nursemaid.

Twenty-one hundred and three new lives had been expected, and all but five made it: two human babies were stillborn; one of the Rugarian young lived three days and died but even the one Rugarian who understood his species' needs could not give a reason; a fourth was unfortunately strangled by the umbilical cord during delivery; and the fifth, a Deski, was malformed when it hatched and did not survive.

The promised crèches were opened and every female had the right to leave her youngling in the general care for her day's work or whatever community service she performed. Sometimes it was crèche duty. Kris started the fad of the papoose board, dredging that up from reading Westerns and historical novels about Indians. It worked well for babies up to three months, and for shorter periods after that.

"I said you will be a good mother," Zainal said with a touch of smug pride, when she showed him how she could carry Zane around.

To Kris' astonishment, she didn't find caring for Zane as onerous as she had expected, and that had little to do with Zainal's enthusiasm for the child. She had never had anything so completely dependent on her, so trusting, and so precious to her. Once or twice, she wondered if she was being unfair to Pete Easley by not telling him. But he and one of the Swedish Aggies had made bricks together, which was equivalent to becoming engaged on Botany. If Kris caught him looking very carefully at her son, she ignored the query in his eyes and babbled on about how good a father Zainal was, until even Pete Easley got bored.

The baby boom sparked a lot of investigations and experiments—a fine powder for talcum, an ointment for diaper and other minor rashes, a way to weave some of the vegetable fibers into cloth for proper baby clothes, and a spinning wheel to make knitting yarn out of loo-cow hairs. The creatures had grown longer coats for protection during the colder weather. These were collected—before the night crawlers could get them—and spun, then washed and/or felted.

The crops grew lush and green on both continents. The Catteni continued to do nothing in their valley. The miners excavated tons of iron, copper, tin, zinc, lead, gold, and silver and occasionally some unusual clear stones which the jewelers thought a variant of tourmaline. But then, no one was looking for gemstones or in the places where rubies, emeralds, sapphires, or diamonds—which would have been useful for their hardness—might be found.

Bone was more useful, and the heavy bones in the four rear legs of the loo-cows were scrupulously cleaned and dried for carving.

Zane was just five months old when the Deski sentinel startled everyone on the south side of Retreat Bay with a warning warble. For such a slender species, with no great lung space, they could make a god-awful amount of noise. The baby was teething, so Kris was awake, trying to soothe him. Zainal's comunit buzzed and he shot straight up in bed, alert, unit to his ear before she could take a single step to intercept.

"What?" He was on his feet and, hopping about on one foot, listening as he pulled on his coverall. Even in such a ridiculous pose, Kris admired his physique. If only Zane could have osmosed a single gene from his foster father . . .

"It's down," Zainal added as he closed the hand unit and concentrated on dressing himself as fast as possible.

"What's down?"

"The Bubble." He had both boots on now and was starting for the door.

"I'm coming, too," she said.

"Not like that!" He raked her with a disapproving look, for she was draped in a blanket.

She thrust Zane at his father and dressed as quickly as he, retrieved the blanket and two spare reed pods, and was inserting the baby into the sling she usually carried him in even as she settled into a passenger seat of the air-cushion truck. Zainal spun the control wheel and the vehicle charged off into the pale light of dawn toward the hangar. Lights were coming up throughout the settlement and occasionally someone called out, "What's the matter?" when Zainal was identified at the wheel.

"The Bubble is just down?" she asked as they sped along.

"Deski heard something, not like anything else they have heard," Zainal was saying, "and warned the bridge. The bridge watch had already seen something on the screen but couldn't make out what."

"The Farmers?" Kris asked, scared to the pit of her stomach as she jiggled her son. Motion always put him to sleep, even with teething as he was, and even this short trip worked its magic on him.

Those alerted were arriving on air-cushion, running as fast as they could and often faster than the basic push bikes that had been developed for short-distance transportation. Pneumatic tires were still to be perfected but the iron rims did well enough on the flagstone and dirt tracks and were speedier than walking.

All the lights in the hangar were on, and the hatches on the KDL, Baby, and the office were open. Runabouts were parked helter-skelter.

Zainal guided Kris to the office, which was nearest. The bridge there would show just as much as the ships' would and there'd be more space for her and the baby. In such little matters, Zainal always considered her and Zane.

Scott, Beggs, Fetterman, Yowell, and Coo were in the office and Scott waved Zainal in urgently.

"A full orbit already and it's not large. Not small enough to be a programmed orb but moving too fast for us to get an accurate picture of its dimensions or shape."

"That," and Coo pointed to the trail left by the orbital, "is not heard. Something landed." He spoke with more force than a Deski generally did. He'd probably been repeating it to Scott. Now Coo stabbed his spidery finger at the Farmers' command post, the one Kris, Zainal, and the others had investigated well over a Botanical year ago: where Dick Aarens had deliberately activated a homing device.

"Then what . . ." and Scott irritably followed the course of the orbital with one finger. Just then its track shifted to a north/south orientation. Even as they watched, it completed several circuits of the large globe of Botany. "What is that?"

"We will know . . ." and Zainal paused, eyes watching the progress of the orbital on the screen "about now."

They felt the tingling zap of a scan. He chuckled.

"Ohmigod," Fetterman said, sitting down as if his legs had given out.

Kris had felt it course through her and Zane squirmed slightly against her in his sling. She felt his cheek, wondering if the scan could have been too much for so small a body, and then Zainal's reassuring touch to her back.

"I will volunteer to go," Zainal said.

Kris barely prevented herself from saying, "Oh, no you won't," before Scott lifted both hands in a refusal, his eyes not moving from the screen. The comunit bleeped and he toggled it open.

"We were just scanned?" It was Beverly's voice.

"Coo says they landed at the command post."

"Nothing's showing up there," Beverly said.

Coo nodded emphatically, reaffirming his report.

"Fek agrees," Beverly went on. "Haven't we established they use matter transmission?"

"Oh, oh," Yowell said, and he stumbled backward to collapse on the nearest stool, his face a study of conflicting emotions: hope, fear, anxiety, and confusion.

Coo's head turned toward the office door and he rose to his feet, raising one arm to point straight ahead.

"They're here?" Scott asked.

Kris gulped, her arms automatically tightening on Zane. But as soon as Zainal moved, she was right behind him, ahead of the others who had hesitated just that split second longer before acting. If their destiny was coming to them, she wanted to see it.

As they left the office, she glanced over at the KDL and saw Fek's unmistakable shape in the hatch, then Balenquah's stocky frame silhouetted briefly in the hatch light, followed by Worrell's slightly stooped figure, the tall erect one that was probably Rastancil, and the slight frame of a woman whom she didn't recognize and Slav. From Baby came Mitford, Easley, Yuri, and Judge Bempechat.

They converged, forming a semicircle facing outward.

What happened before their eyes did not resemble anything from a *Star Trek* program. No colored lights or beams or columns. Nor any other special effect Kris remembered from all the science fiction films and videos she'd seen. And yet . . . something was out there, forming a solid mass which moved toward them, a nimbus around a darker interior. Something which even by the dawn light looked larger than the tallest of the waiting humans.

Then it wasn't taller and seemed to spread out. She recognized the distinctive spider-legged form of a Deski. Beside her, Coo gurgled once and stiffened. With her free hand, Kris reached for Coo's long fingers and gripped them. She had Zane's face shielded with the other. Zainal had shifted his body so he overlapped her in partial protection. But most of the forms that coalesced out of the mist, only it wasn't mist, were human in appearance as the details of face and appendages became obvious.

"They're shape changers," she whispered. "They're changing into us?"

Coo sucked breath in, a slow sound. Terror? Apprehension? Defensiveness? Kris tightened her grip, not knowing if she was giving, or seeking support.

"Shape changers?" Scott hissed, eyes never leaving what was in front of him as he leaned slightly in her direction.

"There's a Deski and a Rugarian and the rest are humans. But not as many of them as there are of us."

When the transformation was complete, and there was no doubt that these visitors showed representation of the three species facing them, each group regarded the other.

"There's no Catteni." Kris' comment was barely audible. But the omission caused a little giggle to escape her which she hastily suppressed. If these were the Farmers, and every evidence pointed to that assumption, for who else could have lifted the Bubble, then they weren't all-seeing and perfect. Somehow that gave her a lift of confidence.

But no one was saying anything and the tension was mounting. So, if the visitors weren't showing immediate aggression, maybe they should be treated like visitors, all eight of them. *We outnumber them,* she thought, *though outnumber is all we do, considering what they just did.* It was so silly to just stand there, looking at each other.

"Hello," she said, making the word friendly and inquiring. She stepped around Zainal and inadvertently pulled Coo with her just as Judge Iri Bempechat took a step forward. She knew she had a silly look on her face as she looked at the judge for a sign as to what to do next.

Whether she was impertinent or not she never did find out, but the judge grinned fleetingly at her—so she felt she hadn't done anything really wrong—and he held out both hands, the (she hoped) galactic indication of being unarmed.

"We have hoped that we would meet you, and explain our presence on a planet which you have clearly used for many thousands of years," he said, inclining his upper body slightly forward in a gesture that was as dignified as it was hospitable. "I realize that you do not understand what I'm saying but I hope the sincerity with which I speak will be apparent. We do realize that we have trespassed on your property but we were brought here against our volition and cannot return to our own worlds."

As the judge spoke, Kris felt the very slightest of pressures against her forehead and at the back of her neck. Zane gave an odd little movement and she jiggled him gently, stroking his back in a reassurance that usually quieted him.

"We moved to this continent because you are not farming it now. We did not wish to interfere with your installations here. We wish to stay. With your permission. If it is at all possible, because we do not have sufficient transportation to leave here. Can we try to make you understand? Somehow?'' He opened his hands toward them again, with dignity and entreaty.

''It is understood,'' said a voice remarkably like the judge's.

Whoever had spoken had done so so quickly that Kris hadn't seen any mouth moving. Then she realized no one had spoken. The voice was right in her own head. Zane moved restlessly again.

''We have come to meet with you. Do not be afraid. We do not injure. We do not kill. We do not inhabit. You are very young, all of you.''

''Young species?'' Iri Bempechat asked, amused.

''Yes,'' and one of the males used his mouth to enunciate the word, though she still heard it more inside her head than in her ears. ''Very young.''

Judge Bempechat smiled. ''We humans are. I believe the Deskis,'' and he gestured toward Coo, ''have lived much longer than humans,'' and he pointed to himself and then to Kris.

''We have seen the Deski and passed them by. They do well as they are. Why are so many here? Why are three . . . no, five . . . species here on this planet?''

''We were dropped here. We have to stay,'' the judge said in a wry voice, flashing a glance at Zainal.

''Because the others, like this one,'' and now the spokesperson gestured a well-shaped hand toward the Catteni, ''have put you here against your will to make a colony of this world.''

''I see that we will not have to tell you much,'' Judge Bempechat said. ''You read the thoughts in our minds.''

''Such as they are.'' There was a kindness rather than a condescension in his tone that was sounding less like an echo of the judge and more obviously like a reflection of this speaker's personality.

"We try to improve," the judge said, inclining his upper body respectfully.

"A very long, hard process that is eternal. But you are not."

"And you are?"

"In essence."

"Not as the Eosi are," Zainal said.

The entity turned his head to the new speaker. "We are not familiar with either the name or your mental image of these Eosi."

"That's the best way to be," someone remarked softly, and for a moment Kris thought it had to be Mitford. It sounded like him. Or maybe Yowell, since the sergeant was in the central group, and Vic much closer.

"We seek your help to escape from the domination of the Eosi over my people, the Catteni, and these other species," Zainal said, gesturing urgently at those around him.

"Such a process includes species injury, which we do not condone."

"Even if injuries continue to be perpetrated on innocent species who have no protection against the superior force?" Judge Bempechat asked.

"If force is used, there is no reformation of the desires which caused force to be used," and the entity's face now reflected a gentle reprimand.

"How do you avoid force then?" Scott said, speaking for the first time.

"There are ways. Learn them."

The figures began to dissolve.

"How are you called?" the judge asked, taking a quick step forward in an effort to prevent their leaving.

"You have named us Farmers. It is appropriate." The spokesman smiled in the most benign way.

Kris mused that this entity would have been well cast as Jesus Christ.

"He is not among you?" was the thought inserted in her mind.

"Don't leave," Zainal said, also stepping forward, one hand raised, "not yet. How do we avoid force when it is used against us? How do we free ourselves and our friends from Eosian domination?"

"Are we allowed to stay here? On your planet?" Kris jumped forward, startling Zane awake. He let out a yell.

One of the Farmers glided forward. The legs moved but the female—she appeared subtly feminine to Kris as she approached—did not make contact with the ground in an actual walk.

"They observe well." Again a thought was inserted in her head as the being reached her and looked down at Zane. Despite Kris' attempts to soothe him, the first yell segued into soft, fearful crying. Not that she blamed Zane for reacting to the tension, the disappointment, and the fear that clogged the air around him. Certainly those were her feelings.

"We have so much to ask you. So many questions," Easley said beseechingly.

"This is your child!" the female said, and she turned back to Kris.

Kris could no more have refused to display her son than she could have resisted the contractions that had expelled him from her womb. She turned Zane, his face reddening in baby distress, toward the entity. The entity bent over him, slid one graceful, almost transparent hand over his face, and he instantly switched to smiling contentment, burbling charmingly up at his newest admirer.

"There are many new young here," she said, and Kris thought she sounded envious. "We are!"

"Then we may stay?" Kris asked earnestly.

"You stay. We will observe but we do not interfere."

"May we leave?" Zainal asked, making a sphere with his hands.

"It is for your protection," the first speaker said.

"We are grateful," Judge Bempechat said, shooting a warning look at Zainal.

"That is more than the others were." The thought crept into Kris' mind, and the female reversed her glide to rejoin her group.

The instant they were all together again, they disappeared.

Like zap! Kris thought, as her son gurgled happily in her arms.

Everyone started talking at once then, the main argument being that they had learned very little, and who had made the judge the spokesman, and why hadn't more questions been asked while they had the Farmers' attention? And who did Zainal think he was, demanding assistance from obvious pacifists?

Scott called for quiet. Judge Bempechat said in a humble tone that he had certainly not intended to speak for everyone but suddenly was speaking. Balenquah railed at Kris for her stupid "Hello."

"Well, we couldn't ask them to take us to their leader, could we?" she responded, "and keep your voice down around my baby!"

"Were you going to give him to them?" Balenquah demanded.

"Don't be such an idiot. She wanted to look at him," Kris said, and walked away from the egregious pilot. She'd thought Aarens was obnoxious, but Balenquah opened up a whole new category of insufferable.

"NOW LISTEN UP," Scott said, raising his voice over the babble. "We are allowed to stay. That is the most important fact we needed to know, wasn't it?"

As he spoke, the sound of excited voices and the hum of air-cushion vehicles nearing the hangar could be more clearly heard.

"Hey, they came. We can stay," Lenny Doyle was shouting as he jumped from the air-cushion and ran into the hangar. "They just appeared outside the mess hall and—'' He broke off, being close enough to see expressions. "We *can* call them Farmers," he finished, his words trailing off. "They were here, too?"

Worrell, Leon Dane, Mayock, and two nurses were next, piling out of the air-cushion flatbed that doubled as ambulance. Their faces were wreathed with the elated grins of people big with news, which faded as they, too, realized that their experience was by no means unique.

"How many shape changers came?" Kris said into the silence.

Then the main comunit was buzzing as all lines into the office seemed to go off at once.

"Rather unusual mass hallucination then," Dane said wryly. "Should we compare notes? We can stay, or so they said, and we can refer to them as the Farmers . . ."

"Since that is appropriate," the judge added in a tone much like Leon's.

"Did we all ask the same questions?" Leon asked, looking at Scott and then Zainal.

"We'd better compare notes," Scott said, "after we've answered those calls. Kris, Yowell, Zainal, help me with these . . ." and he gestured to the busy com board.

"How *many* were there?" Kris asked when there was time to review the astonishing simultaneous manifestation of Farmers to all major groups on Botany. Even the miners had had a visitation of ten.

No group of Farmers had been larger than those they had confronted. The five people on watch at the command post had been approached by three; those at the mess hall, where the majority of people had been having breakfast, had counted thirty. The hospital had been favored with fifteen.

"All at the same time?" Leon asked, astounded.

"Fifty at least, and they could not all have fit in that orbital!" Beverly said.

''That depends on how much space shape changers need,'' Kris remarked.

''If they appeared to all of us, why didn't someone find out more about them?'' Scott demanded, exasperated. ''We all had the chance to make the confrontation substantive.''

''We all had the same chance,'' Rastancil said, ''but I sure couldn't get my wits to work fast enough, nor did I notice you asking leading questions, Ray.''

Despite the way Rastancil phrased it, Admiral Ray Scott took umbrage.

''Nonsense,'' Kris said, ''they've had a lot more practice with third-kind encounters than we have. We're young, we are,'' and she giggled. ''But you really think we'd get direct answers from a species that has the technology they have? We're far too young to deserve more than the few minutes they spent here with us.''

''Let us look at the positive aspects of that confrontation,'' Pete Easley said, holding up a restraining hand to Scott, who seemed to be the one most offended by the lost opportunity. ''We now have permission to stay. I got the distinct impression,'' and he turned to Zainal for confirmation, ''that we may even be able to get through the Bubble but others, like the Eosi, won't be able to.''

Zainal nodded.

''I'd like you to organize a flight to test that, Zainal. Today, if at all possible,'' Scott said, grasping a point he could understand and react to. ''I don't know if that advances your Phrase Three plan but...'' and he shrugged.

''What did they mean, 'That is more than the others'?'' Kris asked.

Scott, Zainal, and the judge regarded her with surprise.

''When you asked to have the Bubble removed, Zainal, and the judge said we were grateful for the protection, one of them said, 'That is more than the others were.' Didn't you hear it?'' Kris glanced around. "Was I the only one?''

"What else did you hear, Kris?'' Judge Bempechat asked, smiling at her in a way that suggested that he might have had private thoughts inserted in his mind, too.

"They envy us having children,'' she said, looking around. And caught Pete Easley's eyes. He smiled at her and *then* she remembered the female's remark: "This is your child!'' And the female had been looking at Pete, not at Kris.

The truth will out, won't it? Kris thought to herself, and nodded. She had been mean not to tell him before: depriving him of that knowledge out of spite. He smiled back at her, a really happy smile, before pointing at Scott, who was repeating a question aimed at her.

"I'm sorry, Ray, what did you ask me?''

"What else did you 'hear' that we didn't?''

"I dunno,'' she said with a shrug. "I never thought I was telepathic. I thought we were all hearing the same things. Did anyone else besides the judge and me get special treatment?''

"I heard plainly that they will be examining this quadrant for sentient species which have developed since their last visit,'' Zainal said, looking around.

"Last visit?'' Pete Easley exclaimed. And whistled.

"They have been at Deski world,'' Coo said, rather proudly.

"You come off better than we humans do, then,'' Judge Bempechat said, grinning broadly.

Kris noticed that Scott had been about to speak and the judge had forestalled the admiral with a much more diplomatic comment. Scott closed his mouth.

"I think,'' the judge went on, reaching for pen and paper, "we had best organize that astonishing interview as best we can recall it. And insert whatever we individually may have heard with the public comments.''

''Good idea,'' Leon said.

''We might have more in the composite than we got individually,'' the judge said. ''We must ask the miners to do the same, and those at the command post. Everyone who met our shape-changing Farmers.''

Zainal left at midmorning, with Marrucci, Balenquah, and Beverly, to fly to the Bubble and see if it permitted them to pass.

''More importantly, come back,'' Kris said stoutly, when Zainal told her they were going.

It took most of the day to transcribe the various interviews, and more information *had* been exchanged when it was all written down on paper.

''I wonder. Are they doing this sort of rehash on their way back home?'' Kris said at one point in the painstaking reconstruction of who had said what, when and where.

''I doubt it,'' Rastancil said. ''They picked our brains quite easily, so they'd probably all know what went on everywhere else.''

''Probably as it was being done,'' Worry said with a sniff. Most uncharacteristically, he had a distinctly unworried expression on his face.

Almost everyone—or at least those who worried about special problems—had been given ''private'' information. Leon Dane, fretting over medical problems for which he had no treatment and waiting for a chance to ask for advice, had been told which specific plants to find, and, ''like some sort of a superblast into my head,'' he got the method of refining and the beneficial dosages to use.

''We've already tested most of the plants as being either noxious or damned well fatal. But, of course, minute and diluted dosages of dangerous substances have often had therapeutic value if properly administered. I just got a short hard course in the local botanical resources. Seems there's a shrub, located on that dry continent, that can provide a general anesthetic, but they would prefer us to use our one lone acupuncturist. She's to teach others her skills.''

"They liked us making bricks," Sandy Areson said, "and I now know where to get five different varieties of clay . . .''

"And I was told what other bushes have seedpods like the fluff which we can use to spin into cloth," Janet said. "He was so like Jesus Christ."

"Who is with us," Kris added.

"What did you say?" Janet was indignant.

"'He is not among you?' was what I heard," Kris said.

"And you will note," Janet went on, drawing herself up with great dignity, "that they appeared to us in human form. So we now have confirmation of the Almighty's appearance. Human!"

"That's because you had neither Rugarians nor Deski in with you at the time," Sandy Areson said, but she spoke without her usual irreverence for Janet's overt religiosity. "We had both Deski and Rugarians because that's who were having breakfast with us humans."

The sentries at the command post had been kindly informed that their presence there was no longer needed. The miners had been assured that the Farmers did not object to the use of mineral and metallic resources. The loggers had been asked not to cut down the oldest trees and were given permission to thin the other varieties grown on the second farmed continent, as these were softer woods, more suitable for "the making of useful artifacts."

Universal had been the permission to remain on the second continent, acceptance of the term "Farmers," and conveyance of the fact that they did not condone "species injury."

"They were sad to see us so far from home," Coo admitted.

"And?" Judge Bempechat prompted when it was obvious Coo had been told more than that. "Did they suggest returning you home?"

"Not now," Coo said. "We are better here." Then he smiled in his fashion. "Much better here."

"We, too," Slav added. "No one safe with Catteni." He drew his brows together and managed to suck his lips inside his mouth, indicating great displeasure. "Farmers not see danger?" he added, looking from the judge to Scott, Worrell, and those still left in the office.

"Not if it causes species injury, which they do not seem willing to commit even on territorially aggressive races like the Catteni . . ." the judge began, and when Kris cleared her throat, "I stand corrected, my dear . . . like the Eosi . . . who command the Catteni subordinates to do so without compunction."

"Hey, he's there, and I think he's doing it," shouted Bert Put.

Everyone in the office crowded around the screen to watch the minute speck that was Baby. The speck disappeared. Most cheered and clapped at this verification of the tacit Farmer permission. Kris, however, held her breath.

"I wouldn't," Easley said, who was standing next to her. "He could be out awhile."

Inadvertently Kris met his eyes and exhaled with a weak smile. She had been trying to avoid any conversation with him.

"So much hooch that day I honestly don't remember what I did, or that I did," he continued in a low voice. "He's a good baby for you?"

"Couldn't be better," she said, looking fatuously down at the sleeping Zane. "Thank you." And then she added, to keep him in his place, "I think."

Pete Easley chuckled wryly at her amendment and

gave her shoulder a squeeze before he moved away. She would almost rather that he had stayed because the wait was a long one. She bet anything that Zainal was making sure the Eosi knew he'd been outside the Bubble, probably spinning the scout on its axis around the orbital as well as the geosynchronous satellite. Just like him! Although what she thought he could accomplish, she wasn't sure. She was certain, however, that he did have some sort of a new Phase Three plan. And cocking a snoot at the Eosi was part of it. Of course, that blew the painstaking false trail he had laid to get them to believe he was elsewhere in the galaxy. But wasn't he taking an awful risk for all of them? What if the Bubble would give way to the Eosi warship now?

In her arms, Zane sighed and snuggled closer to her. No, she thought, he would do nothing to jeopardize his son.

"Ah, he's back inside!" Bert let out another loud crow, which caused Zane to stir uneasily. "Heading home!"

Relieved that Zainal had succeeded, Kris decided that she could now leave discreetly. Zane would need to be fed when he woke this time, and changed, and she'd run out of fluff pods. She was tired, too, with all the excitement of meeting the Farmers, and then the rehash of who had heard what and where. Once she fed her son, she'd have time for a rest before Zainal touched down.

The orbital duly recorded the emergence of a small vehicle from the protective veil: its emergence, its brief run around the fixed satellite, and then its insertion. Nothing could be recorded past the obstacle, but this brief flight was enough of a phenomenon for the orbital to send an immediate message to its home base.

The report, when it was received, went immediately to the Ix Mentat, who was enraged. Very quickly the vehicle was identified as similar in design to the scout ship in which Zainal was supposed to have exited the system.

"Removing the markings fools no one," the Ix said. "And if a scout, with limited power, can penetrate that obstacle in both directions, so can we!"

The warship, the AAI, plus its sister ship which had just passed its test flights and been commissioned were supplied and crewed for the fastest possible return to the system in question. Twice the firepower of the previous visit would certainly punch a hole through whatever it was that had impeded their exit and then refused to readmit the AAI.

"This time Zainal will return for appropriate punishment," the Ix Mentat said, turning over in its mind the sorts of physical abuse that would wreak the worst pain and humiliation on the chosen who had failed to present himself at Eosi command. It savored scenes of dismemberment, of flaying alive, of the application of noxious substances to the few tender portions of Catteni anatomy.

Meanwhile, the impetus to reach new heights of technological development extended to every single Eosi. They had been idle too long, complacent in their mastery of seven solar systems, their exploitation of the riches available to them, but with so many worlds still to be discovered and turned to Eosian advancement and enjoyment. They were on the threshold of a new era in Eosian domination! Let no one curtail their pleasure in achievement. The galaxy would eventually be theirs!

When attacked by the might of Eosian naval strength, the barrier remained impervious to any combination of the missiles, beams, and force available: the attack was useless against the barrier, and the bombardment of weapons of all kinds proved insufficient to pierce it. Only those on the planet remained unaware of the attempt.

Throughout the Eosian-dominated systems, captains and governors were apprised of this unexpected insult. Word filtered down to the suppressed on Rugarian, Deski, Ilginish, Tur, and Terran home worlds and on the compulsorily colonized planets. Hope was reborn! Reborn and thwarted by the savagery of Eosian frustration, which now focused on extracting some means of penetrating the barrier from whatever source that might come. The Eosi had been unpleasant at any time; now they turned vicious. All effort was aimed at combating the first real test of Eosian supremacy since the Mentats had sloughed off their corporeal forms to find a type of immortality by using the strong Catteni bodies.

And still the barrier remained impregnable.

So the Ix Mentat sent every available scout out, far beyond previously explored sectors, to find any trace of those whose advanced technology prevented it from achieving the revenge it now craved.

CHAPTER 12

Baby slipped through like an eel," Marrucci said, grinning broadly as he wiggled his clasped hands in demonstration. "Mind you, Zainal had us at dead slow and that might be the trick. Come charging at it and it bounces you back as it did the first time we nosed around."

"I think we were a little speedier reentering," Beverly said on consideration.

"We could have blasted the Eosi orbital. Baby's armed. Blown it out of the skies as a warning," Balenquah said, sullen as ever. "We should have, you know! Proven we can do something positive against their surveillance! And we didn't get so much as a whisker sensor stripped off." He added a "Ha!" of satisfaction before he wandered off to grab some of the sandwiches set out on the table and left the office.

"Glad you were along, general," Marrucci said softly. "That guy grosses me out."

"He is a good pilot," Beverly said, but without much enthusiasm.

Scott leaned across his desk, gesturing for the two to

do the same. "Is what Balenquah said accurate? You weren't beyond the Bubble long enough to be seen by the orbital?"

Beverly grinned. "Of course we were. Zainal even booted us past the geosynch sat. That was Zainal's main object in seeing if he could breach the Bubble, to get the exit, and reentry noticed."

"Won't that just make the Eosi madder'n ever?"

"Frankly, I hope so. With Farmers protecting us . . ."

"Now, wait a minute," Scott sat bolt upright. "What makes Zainal think they will if we pull damn fool stunts like that?"

"If you're on the top of the pile by many light-years, you don't need to do 'species injury' to maintain the position—not with the technology the Farmers have. But the Eosi don't. That'll piss them off, according to Zainal, and I think he's right. If they keep trying to storm Botany, won't the Farmers object?"

"Damn Zainal. He's going to get that Phase Three of his started one way or another." And there was a touch of admiration in Scott's tone. "But damnation, he should take us into his confidence on such decisions. We have to consider the good of the entire community. And where is Zainal? I need to do more than debrief him now."

"Oh, he dropped us off and went on to check the Catteni valley, to see if the Farmers visited them. I thought you knew."

"Me? I certainly didn't suggest it." Scott's frown deepened. "That damned Cat!"

"Frankly, Ray, I'd like to know if the Farmers did appear to them. Mind you, I'm comfortable enough here on Botany, but there were a lot of things left undone on Earth and I'd expected to have a major part of their doing," Beverly said, giving a final nod of emphasis.

"A soldier's first duty is to return to his unit if at all

possible?'' Scott said with a slightly condescending smile.

''You got it. As far as I'm concerned,'' and Beverly folded his hands together, ''I'm not stopping until Earth is free of the Eosi. A lot of us here feel the same way. And I suspect more than you'd guess would back Zainal in an attempt to get active Farmer support.''

Scott considered that and sighed. ''If we could . . .'' Then, in an altogether different voice and with a rueful smile, he added, ''Not that I haven't learned some very valuable lessons here on Botany.''

''We all have,'' Beverly agreed with a wry expression, and he looked down at the calluses on his hands.

When Zainal returned, he immediately reported to Ray Scott that the Farmers had appeared to the Catteni and scared them so badly, two were still in shock. The others refused to believe that they had not been visited by Eosi and pleaded with him to take them to a safer place.

''I told them these were not Eosi but the true owners of the planet and if they tried to leave the valley, worse would happen to them.''

''What would be worse than Eosi?'' Scott asked with a snort.

''What they do not know is always worse,'' Zainal said with one of his shrugs. ''They will never leave the valley.''

''Had they been trying to?''

Zainal gave another shrug. ''No. The Drassi has authority over them only on the ship. They will do nothing.''

''You stayed long enough outside the Bubble to let both satellites have a good look at you?''

''As John told you,'' Zainal said.

''Tell me, Zainal,'' and Scott made himself lean back, as if totally at ease, ''is it wise to aggravate the Eosi this way? How can we be sure the Farmers will protect us if we taunt our enemy? We know very little of their philosophy and society, or their technology, except that it is superior to everything any of us have seen.''

Zainal grinned, and the look in his eyes was menacing. ''Right now, the Eosi are very worried. Some other group is more advanced than they are. They will not stand for that. They will be doing two things: searching for the Farmers and trying to take as large a technological leap forward as they can.''

''Yes, but are they capable of it? I mean, matter transmission such as the Farmers used is a huge step forward, I would think,'' Scott said.

''Wars have a habit of improving technology,'' Beverly said. ''We should know that better than most, Ray.''

''A lot of good our improved technology did us when the Catteni landed,'' Scott said with a bitter laugh.

''Did they ever track down the subs?'' Beverly asked.

Scott glared at him, tilting his head at Zainal.

''Whose side is he on, Ray?'' Beverly said.

''My own,'' Zainal said with a grin. ''I go home now.''

Kris was asleep and she roused briefly when she felt him slide under the blankets beside her.

''You've planned Phase Three, haven't you?'' she murmured, and before he could admit that he had, she was asleep again.

Zane woke them as night was falling, ready to eat and play awhile.

''Well, you have, haven't you?'' she said, nursing the baby by the fire while Zainal sat in his big chair, watching the process as he idly stroked one chair arm.

''I have what?''

''Planned Phase Three.''

He grinned at her. ''It is only logical to complete what Mitford started. To get the Farmers to notice us and come to see what we have done to their world. That

Eosi came is very good. We upset *their* plans and that
has needed doing for many generations.''

"Don't tell me other Catteni have wanted to do away
with the Eosi?'' That surprised her.

"It has been talked of, privately,'' he admitted, and
the stroking turned to a drumming of his fingers. "I was
on Barevi to speak to . . . a group about a plan.''

"You were? And I ruined all that for you?'' Kris
flushed with chagrin. "Did you mention that to Chuck?
Or anyone?''

Zainal shrugged. "No reason, until now.''

"Is that why you wanted to be able to leave the
planet?''

"I am thinking that to have a base for those who resist
the Eosi would be a very good thing.''

"More Catteni here?'' Kris could think of several
hundred people who would object to that. Or maybe they
wouldn't, now that it was pretty well established in people's heads that it was the Eosi who were masterminding
Catteni activities. The problem with that was that so
many Catteni *enjoyed* far too much what they did to
subject races.

"That would cause trouble if it was known,'' Zainal
agreed, instantly following her thought. "There is that
desert continent. No one goes there.''

"That's true. And if folks didn't know there were
Catteni . . . but you can't keep something like this from
the brass-heads, Zainal. They trust you now. They
wouldn't—''

"Do not worry, I respect their trust. I will tell them
if I think I can do what I wish now to do. I would need
much assistance from Beverly, Scott, Easley, Yowell,
Bert, Raisha. We must rescue more from Earth, too.''

"The transport ship?'' She startled Zane and had to
comfort him.

Zainal nodded. "On board the KDL is much we
would need. The star maps, the codes . . .''

"Wouldn't the Eosi change codes? Just in case you get loose?"

Zainal shook his head, his yellow eyes dancing in the firelight.

"Drassi learn too slowly to do that quickly."

"So you must move more quickly, and soon. Is that right?"

He nodded. And her heart pounded in fear for him.

"You're planning to infiltrate Earth?"

He gave his head a quick shake. "Barevi is safer for me. Many coming and going and we can find out much information from new prisoners. And 'transport' those we need."

"You, Emassi Zainal, can just walk in and demand the worst of the prisoners and they'll be handed over to you?" Anxiety made her sarcastic. "You with a crew of—"

"Deski and Rugarians, and friends hidden from Emassi and Drassi eyes."

"I didn't know Deski and Rugarians crewed for Catteni."

"They will not be the entire crew, only the ones most seen," Zainal said. Then he rose, in a smooth graceful movement for such a big-boned man, and began to pace. "We are not transport ship. We are from mines at K'dasht Nik Sot Fil," he said as he paced. "We need certain workers, strong, with perhaps some mechanical experience. We get what we need—and certain things Botany needs . . ."

"And no one will be the wiser?"

"The gray skin stuff? How long will it last on a man's face?"

"I don't know," she said, but she was beginning to see just how he would be able to cope. "But you can take as much as you need with you." She ran over in her mind those who had been fake Catteni when the KDL was captured. "But won't the Eosi be watching everything? What if they've already seen the scout getting in and out?''

Zainal chuckled, pausing by her chair to stroke her cheek, looking down at the hungry baby.

"I hope that they have."

"Yes, but you can't meet them sneaking out the back door, can you?"

"Bert Put goes up and takes a quick look to see if . . . the shore is clear?" He lifted his eyebrows in query.

"Coast is clear . . ."

"Good, and I take Catteni speakers, too." Now he started pacing again, rubbing his hands together as he thought out loud. "Have you forgotten all Barevi?" he asked in that language.

Startled, she replied in the Barevi affirmative. Could she go with him? Did she want to go with him? She certainly didn't want to stay behind. But Zane?

"Chuck would be useful," she added. "And Jay Greene . . ."

He had paused by her and looked down at Zane, who had nursed himself to sleep. "I need you, too."

She almost burst into tears, her heart so full of love for both, her responsibilities pulling her in two directions at once.

"Sandy has more milk than a cow," she said, not daring to look at Zainal just then. She added more briskly, "And this is the sort of situation we set up the crèche system for, isn't it?"

She heard Zainal tap out call numbers. "Chuck? Are you free to talk over an idea this evening?"

Chuck Mitford immediately said they had to talk this over with the brass-heads.

"Only a few of them, at that," he added, grinning and rubbing his hands together because Zainal had included him as the crew foreman. Chuck hadn't even taken that as a slur because he was indeed the build and height of many Catteni. Handsomer than most, however, as Kris could not resist saying.

Scott had to be consulted—especially as Chuck wanted him to play Catteni, too. And John Beverly, Gino Marrucci, Ninety Doyle, Dowdall, Mack Su for his electronics knowledge, Yuri Palit, and several others who had been in the original commando group because they had some knowledge of Catteni.

"I don't see why we can't go straight to Earth," was Scott's first objection.

"I do not have codes for Earth . . . KDL is Barevi-based. I figure that we speak with latest transports from Earth . . ."

"What about stealing another ship with the right codes?" Marrucci wanted to know, flexing his fingers as if already settled in a cockpit and about to take off. "I sure would love to get back to good ol' Terra Firma."

Zainal grinned. "That is also a possibility. If one just happens to be ready to fly."

"You can't leave the crew around . . ." Scott began.

"There are other valleys here," Zainal said. "The KDL can get in and out of Barevi with no problem. That is important. I know I can get supplies that we need with no problem."

"We get to make a wish list?" Rastancil said, brightening.

"No, a *need* list."

"Medical supplies?" Chuck asked, hopefully, taking his pad and pencil stub from his pocket.

"If we can find any," Zainal replied, reminding Mitford that Catteni medicine was rudimentary at best. "Good steel we can get," he added, knowing that the fabricators needed better materials to form proper surgical instruments.

Chuck wrote "steel" and underscored it.

"This time we have clean Catteni uniforms to wear?" Yuri Palit asked, wrinkling his nose.

Zainal shook his head. "You must smell like Catteni, too, and you don't." Yuri made a grimace and sighed. "Wear what you have on voyage, *then* change at Barevi," Zainal added with a grin. "Now," and he took out the sheets he had worked on to show Chuck, of the Barevi spaceport and its environs, "we must know where to go and you must learn what to answer to questions. If you walk fast as if you know where you're going, that you are taking a message, no one will question. So you must *know*!"

They readily agreed to that, but, along with the language lessons, came questions, especially from those who had not been enslaved on Barevi and were unfamiliar with it. That was where Kris came in because she had flitted all over the city with her owner.

"Can't we just steal flitters and not walk everywhere?" Dowdall asked.

"You may *rent* flitters," Zainal corrected him. "We must fit in or be noticed. If we fit in right, we can come back again."

"Hey, I like that," Ninety Doyle said, grinning. "There's a couple of Tudos . . ."

Zainal pointed his pencil at Ninety. "You will be good Tudo and follow your Drassi's orders."

"Yeah, sure, boss, gotcha, boss Drassi," Ninety said good-naturedly, tugging at an imaginary cap and nodding agreement.

"Chuck, can you remember the exact layout of where slaves were held?"

"Can do, have done," and Chuck, too, took out a sheet on which he had earlier drawn an outline. "We better learn some Catteni symbols, too, you know . . . to follow hall markings . . ."

Preparations took ten days, with long learning sessions for those who were chosen to take part. The selection was restricted to those whose physical appearance was closest to Catteni, who already had some knowledge of the language and some experience with Barevi. Scott, Marrucci, and Yuri did not but they could be paired with those who did, like Chuck, Ninety Doyle, Dowdall, and Mack Su. Coo, Slav, and Pess were a bit nervous about going but they would be required to contact their own ethnic groups for what news they had. Kris was an essential addition for her knowledge of the city and familiarity with the flitters. The legs of one Catteni uniform had to be lengthened to fit her but, with her hair skinned back with the gray mud that would disguise Terran locks and with the gray powder makeup, she passed well enough. She also knew enough Catteni and Barevian lingua to hire flitters and bargain properly. Someone not bargaining with Barevian shopkeepers would immediately be suspect. On both the KDL and the scout enough Catteni scrip and coin were found. Zainal then told them that the habit was for ships to charge to their number, and the charges would be sent back to a central bank to make payments.

"And we'll be long gone before the reckoning," Doyle chuckled, rubbing his hands together in anticipation.

"What happens, Zainal," John Beverly asked one morning during the planning sessions, "if someone recognizes *you*?"

All at the table, and Sandy Areson was sitting in that morning to explain about the gray makeup, turned toward him.

"I am dead," Zainal said, shrugging off that consideration. "No one will expect to see me, especially in Drassi uniform," he added.

Sandy tilted her head and then, rising and reaching across the table, turned him by the chin from one profile to the other.

"No problem," she said. "We add cheek pads so he looks fatter, another in front, and some lines down his face to make him look older, and his own mother wouldn't recognize him.''

"What is this? Pads?" Zainal asked, somewhat dismayed.

"I used to do makeup for our theater group, Zainal. Trust me. You won't recognize yourself. I'll bring some over to the cabin and show you," and Sandy added when she saw other skeptical expressions, "you won't know him either. Trust me.''

When she demonstrated to Kris and Zainal later that evening, it was remarkable the change those few alterations made.

"I'd slump if I were you," Sandy remarked. "Drassi are small men and don't walk proud like an Emassi, you know.''

Zainal grinned as he thanked her, a grin that was substantially altered from his normal one with the pads in place.

"Take them out," Kris said when Sandy had left. "I'm not sharing this cabin with a total stranger. A very unattractive total stranger, I might add." And she gave a shudder of dismay until he had removed the pads and looked himself again.

The arrival of the Ix Mentat and its two juniors at the Catteni main Earth spaceport in Texas, near what had been Houston, caused major security problems. Its reason for coming caused consternation, since the military governor was somehow sure that he would be forced to honorably end his life because he had not been able to reduce the rebellion of the indigenous population, despite the severe measures he employed. He had scrupulously followed orders sent to him by the Mentats on Catten but seemed no closer to dealing with the tides of revolt and producing the wealth available from the planet than he had been in the first months of occupation.

When High Emassi Bulent learned the sort of equipment the Mentats had brought with them, he turned ashen, until he also heard that the mind probes were to be used on humans, not on ineffective Emassi.

Therefore he listened intently to the Ix Mentat's wishes, organized the search, and rounded up as many of the required subjects as could be found. Some could be proven dead; others might well have been already transported, since they had resided in the fifty cities originally depopulated in the first wave of Catteni suppressions.

Bulent could almost feel sorry for the men and women rounded up and crammed into the open slave pens, for the summer heat was intense, though he himself reveled in such temperatures. There were casualties from the heat and the crowding. He had the unenviable task of explaining to the Ix Mentat that humans could not endure the solar rays that Catteni hides could, particularly humans in this upper age group as most of the new prisoners were. So they were moved to a huge shed that had been cleared of its exhibits.

Bulent's staff then had to assign numbers to the types of specialists the Ix wished to interrogate in order of rank within the science humans had practiced.

The Ix, Co, and Se made trial examinations on lesser-known individuals with varying results. After four deaths with little information retrieved from the bursting brains, the instrument had to be recalibrated. It had originally been used to upgrade Catteni mentality by expanding cerebral and cortical areas and stimulating certain centers in both lobes. The result had been the intelligent Emassi subset of Catteni who had originally been primitive and little more than upright animals. But what could be enhanced could also be withdrawn. That was the purpose of using the equipment on the humans.

The actual examination could take up to half a day, if the initial information plucked from the more accessible areas of the mind looked interesting. That is, if the subject was worth treating carefully. Otherwise an hour's viewing would suffice but the subject rarely recovered much personality and memory. Incontinence was a frequent problem and some retained insufficient intelligence to feed themselves. These were quietly disposed of.

In more judicious use of the mind probe, the Ix and its juniors gained the codes to private files in research laboratories, but much of the material dealt only with human concerns. The Mentats found top-security codes but they weren't interested in the politics, considering them very commonplace and predictable in the extreme—though there were one or two ploys that the Ix might use if the need arose.

Among its victims were the remaining heads of state who had not met with either transportation or execution, revealing the names of more important officials whose brains were full of sometimes amusing if petty details. Some investigations were more fruitful, leading the Mentats to find out what particular scientific studies were in progress and where. This was what the Ix had been searching for, and it gave the High Emassi a list.

The High Emassi Bulent sent his minions scurrying to find these people: often they returned empty-handed with stories that the named persons had died or had possibly been transported, but certainly could not be found. Several of these, the Ix decided, must be found unless proof of death could be established beyond doubt. So Bulent dispatched his best people, including several of the renegade humans, with instructions and promises of titillating rewards for success, to make a thorough sweep of known hiding places and refuges.

The Ix exhausted all avenues to discover what little the humans had learned about the galaxy, the universe, their incredibly primitive methods of star travel, as well as theories that, over its millennium of existence, it had already investigated, and implemented or discarded.

The resultant human chaff that remained alive from these sessions was loaded on transports and sent to Barevi, to be sold as slaves for whatever use could be found for the near-mindless.

Then the Ix closed itself in its vessel and began to sift carefully through all it had learned, in the hope that perhaps there might be even one theory that could spark its high mentality toward a viable line of research.

On the off-chance that they could hijack another ship, Bert Put and Balenquah would come along as auxiliary pilots. It fell to Raisha, then, to pilot the scout to the Bubble and see if the coast was clear. Beverly and Marrucci had plotted the next five windows available that would avoid the orbital satellite, so it only remained to check on the absence of any Catteni ships in the general area.

Kris found it both hard and easy to leave Zane in Sandy's charge. She had been able to partially wean him and he was already eating pureed foods. But Sandy promised she would not stint him. And Kris could trust her. Pete Easley put in an appearance when she brought Zane to the crèche, feeling treacherous and unnatural because part of her was dying to go on this adventure and another part would miss her darling son terribly.

"He's a good size, isn't he?" Pete remarked to no one in particular as Kris started to hand him over to Sandy. He was awake and in one of his giggling moods, the kind that are hard to ignore. "Here, give him to me," he said, and gave Kris no chance to refuse.

Being the adaptable personality he was, Zane had no problems with being passed around, and gurgled as happily up at Pete Easley as he would have at Zainal.

Kris, watching the transfer, suddenly realized that Pete was telling her he intended to watch out for his natural son during her absence. His proprietariness was both welcome and disturbing. But should the unthinkable happen, Kris knew that Pete Easley would assume responsibility for Zane, and, she had to admit, he had a right.

With a cheery wave at him and a farewell hug and kiss for Sandy, Kris left the crèche, her conflicting emotions gradually easing as she focused all her attention on the mission.

Raisha took off in the scout to test the space beyond the Bubble just as Zainal aimed the KDL at the "back door." She poked the prow through the obstacle long enough to get a reading that there was nothing immediately visible in space. Zainal eased the KDL through the Bubble just above the southern polar region. He wasn't the only one to expel a gust of relief that the maneuver was unrestricted and the KDL allowed to exit. Then he aimed the ship toward the nearest of the five moons, and using that to hide his trajectory surveillance, made all speed to that point. Once there, he plotted the course out of the system and to Barevi's.

Even at the speed the KDL was capable of making, the journey would take three weeks. So there was more time in which to perfect their Catteni roles, and learn to automatically respond to orders and queries. The meager library of the KDL did contain spaceport plans for those planets under Catteni domination. These were enlarged for study, especially by Bert and Balenquah if the chance of a second hijack was feasible. Scott was not yet committed to that objective.

"He wants a warship," Mitford confided to Zainal and Kris. "Firepower."

Zainal considered that. "It might be possible to steal weapons but even Catteni keep guards on warships. We don't have enough for crew. Maybe another time."

Chuck and Kris gawked at him in surprise and he grinned back.

"Who was it who said, 'Think big'?"

"Dick Aarens?" Kris suggested.

There were also maps of Barevi town which augmented the memories of those who had spent time in it. And how much a flitter should cost to such and such a destination. How to argue with cheaters, how to act if accosted for a fight.

"Catteni always fight," Zainal said. "Work off anger that way. Avoid at all costs."

"Hey, it's easy enough to topple a Catteni," Yuri said, and proceeded to demonstrate a jujitsu maneuver on the unsuspecting Zainal. One moment the Emassi was on his feet, the next flat on his back on the deck, looking both surprised and annoyed.

When Yuri offered him a hand up, he ignored it but he was smiling when he got back on his feet.

"Teach us!"

So jujitsu, karate, and other forms of martial arts were included in the daily training sessions.

"It is better we do no . . ." and Zainal grinned, "species injuries."

"As if the Farmers would know or care," scoffed Balenquah.

"*We* will know and *we* will care that harm has been done," Zainal said, making his position plain to the surly pilot.

"You're a fine one to talk," Sev Balenquah replied at his most contentious.

"I am finer than you to know," was Zainal's retort.

At this point Mitford, who was sitting next to the pilot, jabbed him so roughly in the ribs that he was winded.

"There's a brig on this ship," Beverly said. "D'you want to spend the rest of the trip in it?"

"Have it your way," Balenquah said, and, pushing away from the table, stalked off.

When Beverly would have called him back, Scott shook his head.

"We'd better watch that one," Marrucci murmured to Beverly. Both the general and Scott nodded. "Can't figure out what's wrong with him. And he's even gotten to fly again."

Everyone took turns in the galley, leaving the Catteni food stores alone since they were even worse in taste than the bars supplied to transported prisoners. The KDL had originally had three freezers: two medium-size and one large storage type. That was now in the mess hall, while one of the mediums was in the hospital. But the remaining one was adequate for the journey since Zainal expected to restock perishable goods from the markets at Barevi. Surprisingly enough, the Catteni galley had the equivalent of a microwave heating device so that the prepackaged soups, bread, and meals that the mess hall had contributed to the mission could be reheated.

By the time the first contact was made with Barevian planetary authority, they had all perfected their skills to the best of their abilities. Even Balenquah could spit out appropriate answers. Despite his more glaring personality defects, he was a natural linguist and Zainal hoped to use him to accompany Kris on her buying missions.

"He glowers just like my old boss," Kris said, "typical nasty Tudo. Whoops, not Tudo, Foto," she said, correcting herself. She had known "Foto" before she was aware of the distinction between Emassi and Drassi.

When hailed by the Barevian perimeter guards, Zainal, posing as Drassi Kubitai, barked the responses and Kris understood every word he said and every word the duty officer said. The KDL was officially the KDI, since the KDL would be listed as missing. There was no problem in the code.

"Sloppy," Zainal muttered under his breath, thankful though he probably was that this was the case.

He elected to overfly the town to give everyone the aerial aspect of it and help orient them, giving a description of each area on his way to their appointed docking facility.

Mack Su was the putative navigator and Yuri the engineer. They both had immediate work to do, checking in with the port authorities: Matt Dargle to handle the paperwork and show the log which Zainal had created for them, while Yuri organized refueling, watering, and the usual docking procedures. Zainal paced about the dock area to be sure they encountered no immediate difficulties as the various teams disembarked for their assignments.

Coo and Slav went off first, pretending pathetic eagerness to be away from the Drassi, while Pess stayed on board with Matt, Bert, and Beverly. The latter two should not be seen. Pess and Matt had basic Barevi and some Catteni so they were the best ones to stay behind and prevent unauthorized entry. Ninety and Dowdall would see if there were any humans in the slave markets. Zainal, Mitford, and Scott would go into the center of Barevi and have a meal and some drinks and hear what there was in the way of gossip. Then, when Mack and Yuri had finished their details, Yuri and Marrucci would combine with Kris and Balenquah to get supplies in the market. Some could even be charged to the ship so they could use what Catteni money they had for other things, like the "plursaw" additive the Deski needed. The original shipment was running low and there were new Deski babies in need of it. Zainal had made up a shopping list for them to display, as most Tudo couldn't read or write more than their own names, and signed it "Drassi Kubitai." He also made Kris practice the glyph for "Kubitai" in case she had to sign chits for orders.

Kris was scared to the nails on her toes in the heavy Catteni boots. They were a bit large for her, although that only made her plod in a more authentic Catteni gait.

She'd probably get heel blisters in spite of fluff-padding the toes but she marched as smartly as the others did out of their berth and onto the main dock staging area. There were few Catteni lounging about, watching Rugarians and Deski shift crates, loading and unloading material at other berths. The ship, berthed three places beyond the KDI, looked like another of her class, still so new she had few meteor pockmarks, or dinges, on her hull and all of her paint looked fresh.

Marrucci caught Kris in the ribs with his elbow, looking at the ship as a possibly hijackable victim. She grinned and mouthed "No way, José!" at him. He kept grinning.

They saw no Terrans at all once they were out of the main facility and looking about for flitters. Zainal had said there were always a few waiting for possible passengers. They approached the first, its driver a wizened old Catteni whose face was badly scarred. Balenquah gave the orders, as sullen as a Catteni, and shoved everyone on board, his fingers lingering a little too long on Kris' hip as he did so, grumbling about wanting to get this duty over with. He squeezed himself next to Kris on the hard, wide seat, his thigh pressing against hers in a way that made her want to punch him good. She could do nothing now but sit there and endure his attentions. Had the man no wits about him at all? Didn't he know she'd never let him get away with such nonsense? Wait till they got back to the KDL . . . no, KDI, she must keep that alteration firmly in mind. With the maneuvers of the flitter in and out of traffic, Balenquah must be enjoying the ride, rubbing constantly against her leg. Marrucci caught her eyes once and gave her a look that meant he had not missed Balenquah's ploy.

Then they were over the open market area, their driver skillfully avoiding arrogant ascending flitters in the fashion that had always caused Kris near heart failure in her slave days. They got down safely enough and the driver grabbed the fare Balenquah offered and then flung his craft aloft, out of the way of incoming craft.

"Don't push me around, Balenquah," Kris said in an undertone as they moved off.

"Who? Me?"

Marrucci prodded his back, telling him, in Catteni, to talk right, then asked Kris, also in the language, which direction to take.

"Here is food market for Deski additives. We buy enough, they deliver."

"We buy plenty," Marrucci said. "Where?"

Kris had been looking around and spotted a crowd of Deski. "There!"

"Deskis! Huh!" Kris wasn't sure if Balenquah was acting in character or just being his charming self.

On their way, they passed a booth selling the alcoholic beverages only Catteni could stomach, but Balenquah insisted on stopping to sample one, saying he was thirsty.

"Not good," Kris said, frowning because that was the best way to prove to Balenquah that he *should* try one. All were swill but let him find that out.

Laughing and jostling her, he pointed to the amber bottle and a large glass, Even the stall owner looked surprised. Guffawing, Balenquah clapped Kris so hard on the back that she nearly lost her balance, but, knowing what was to come, she stood firm and waited.

Balenquah was even stupid enough to try to knock back the entire portion. He should have watched another Catteni who was sipping cautiously. As the raw liquid began to burn down his throat, his eyes bulged and his grayed skin turned red enough to startle her, but somehow he got most of it down.

"Told you not good," Kris said, deepening her voice. "Better over there!" And she pointed to the corner where her master used to take a drink on market days. She left Balenquah to recover from the pilth—ah, she remembered the name of that particular poison—and strode on toward the Deski. She was also keeping on the alert for any bands of Catteni swaggering around the market area just looking for trouble. Marrucci waited with Balenquah while Yuri moved out in step beside her.

"Good on you," he muttered in English, and she elbowed him. "Agreed," he added in Catteni.

They could both hear Balenquah hawking and spitting behind them, and gasping as his system tried to cope with the Catteni equivalent of antifreeze. It certainly smelled like it. The pilth had also affected Balenquah's vocal cords and he was reduced to gargling unintelligible words when he and Marrucci joined them at the Deski plursaw stall, for that was all this merchant sold. She argued over delivery charges but then added more for an immediate delivery to the KDI. This was actually the most urgent of the supplies they were after. The next was salt: enough to use to preserve meats. Sugar was not a commodity known to the Catteni, so she was to get enough vinegar for pickling. These were easy, since she'd dealt with kitchen supplies and knew where to find them. At the same stall, she was astonished to discover what looked like rolls of cinnamon bark in a sack and a keg of nutmegs: the spicy scent of them was so familiar. She lifted a piece of curled brown bark high enough to her nose to be sure that it was indeed cinnamon—though what it was doing on Barevi was beyond her.

Then, in the gravelly voice she affected for Catteni words, she asked, "What's this?" of the stall-keeper, dropping the bark curl indolently back into the bag and brushing her hand off on her uniform as any Catteni would.

She understood only half of what he said, catching that it was from Terra and used in cooking. She should try some. She pretended indecision until Marrucci tapped her shoulder and came to her rescue.

"Drassi Kubitai likes new things. Try it."

That's when they lucked out because the two commodities were so unusual and suspect that the stall-keeper had been unable to shift any and was feeling he'd made a bad purchase. So the bargaining began in earnest, but in the end she got the spices, the full keg and the sack, and had him throw in a large bag of peppercorns which he also hadn't been able to sell. Kris had no problem getting him to deliver to the KDI and could barely contain her delight in finding the seasonings. The mess hall would bless her forever. She also got gallons of vinegar of a good quality.

In the next rectangle over, Kris found fabrics of all kinds, colors, and patterns and materials, some of which she recognized as Terran manufacture, which both pleased and upset her. The Catteni must be looting the Earth right, left, and center. She suppressed resentment and went about bidding for whole bolts, in different shades and weights for children's clothes. The local weaving industry would suffice for any females who wanted something to wear that wasn't made over from Catteni coveralls, but the kids' needs were different. Kris bought enough to make the shopkeeper ask if she was a trader.

"Drassi is," she said as if she thoroughly disapproved, pointing with no real attention to what she was buying. The last shop also sold needles and indifferently she threw a handful of packets on the counter and made the shop owner scrawl a receipt for her. "Drassi requires." Which was all she needed to say. "Deliver by sundown and will get extra," she said, winking as she had seen her steward master do from time to time.

Then she looked around for her shipmates and found them near a fruit seller's stall as Balenquah tried to restore his throat lining.

"I told you no good," she said, and took a gorupear from the display pile. She turned her head slightly so the stall-keeper would not see that she did not have Catteni-size teeth as she tore off the tough peel as any good Catteni soldier would do and spat it out on the street. One thing sure, she never thought she'd be eating these lovely winy fruits again. My, she'd come a long way from that forest. She pointed to a net of the pears, asking the price.

"Four," she said, and then began haggling for a discount, just like in the old days. She got them at a good price—enough for everyone to enjoy on the way back to Botany—and tied the nets together, slinging them over one shoulder. Yuri and Marrucci were watching her. "Tell you later," she said in Catteni. "This way."

They went through another arcade, doors open to display and wares of the more permanently sited merchants, to where she thought she'd find ironmongery. The mess hall had also asked for some big stewing pots and cooking sheets. That sort of thing would be there, and sure enough, she acquired five cauldron-size kettles and some huge baking tins. She also saw other items that were definitely Terran in origin, like the fabrics. If there was so much looting on Terra going on, maybe they'd be lucky enough to find medical equipment. Leon Dane had patiently drawn out the tools he especially needed. If she did, they'd basically filled today's list. She wanted to be out of the market area soon. Once the guard changed, there'd be all kinds of gangs of them off duty, drinking and looking for trouble: any trouble. She wanted to get out of the area before the guards arrived.

Knives of the fine size and shapes Leon Dane had wanted were indeed available, in one of the arcade stores, but at a price higher than Zainal had estimated. She bought what they had funds for—bundles of scalpels, lancets, and the retractors, small-headed hammers, surgical saws. It looked from the display as if Earth hospitals had been thoroughly looted. Still, she bargained so hard that the trader wanted to know why she needed such Terran things.

"Terran? What's that?" and she pretended to try to find the name on the scalpel's handle.

"Where you been?"

"There and back," she said with an indifferent shrug.

"Make it fast," Marrucci said in an irritable tone, and jerked his head over his shoulder at a gang of Catteni entering the rectangle at the far end, six abreast and brushing past everyone and everything in their way.

"Pack them. We have other business today," she said, and managed enough saliva to spit into the gutter with. Turning her head, she was able then to gauge the speed at which the gang moved. "Get Bal to a flitter," she told Marrucci. "Yuri stays."

She didn't trust Balenquah if those Catteni muscled him out of the way.

"What takes you so long, Foto?" she snapped at the storekeeper, who was making quite a job of packing the tools, but then the blades were very sharp.

Marrucci did get Balenquah out of the way: thanks to the pilth, he was in no condition to argue much. She had just got her hands on the packet from the shopkeeper when Yuri was bowled into her, knocking her into the shopkeeper's cabinet, causing half his stock to tumble about and several pieces—since the cabinet was open on his side—to stick into him. He was howling with pain and rage as he plucked sharp objects from his thighs.

Yuri reacted, ducking under the first swing of a squat Catteni guard and then kicking out at the assailant's kneecaps with a double strike that had the guard howling with pain and dropping to the ground. The shopkeeper shouted for help and grabbed at Kris, almost tearing the precious package from her hand. But she twisted her arm down and up and freed herself. When he came around the cabinet, bleeding from the cuts, she got him square in the guts with a karate kick, thrusting him backward and into another glass-fronted cabinet. She heard him scream as a shard of glass penetrated his backside, but she didn't stop.

"Out of here," she yelled in good Catteni, fright thickening her voice as she grabbed at Yuri's uniform just as he flipped another Catteni to his back.

Several of his mates, reacting to his groans and curses, started after them but Catteni are not good runners and Yuri and Kris had very good reasons to run as fast as they could.

They nearly ran over Marrucci, who had come back for them, and so they all made tracks to the flitter where Balenquah slumped, victim of the pilth.

However, the state of him—or rather the smell that emanated from him, added to the bruised gorupears that had split open in the nets Kris had been carrying over her shoulder—made the flitter driver waste no time in getting them back to the dock. When they arrived, the merchandise had, too, with Pess, a cloth bolt in each arm, dealing with the loading.

"Did the plursaw come?" Kris asked, racing up the extruded gangway.

Pess grinned and nodded, speaking Barevi. "First thing. See me, ask questions. I say Drassi orders. Don't know *what* he orders."

Well, she could hope no one heard her speak in English. Marrucci and Yuri were angling the unconscious Balenquah out of the flitter. She went back to pay the driver.

"We the first?" she asked Pess as she helped him stow the cloth away, making sure that the needles had been included.

Pess nodded. "What's wrong with pilot?"

"He drank pilth," she replied. Then grinned as she added. "I told him it was no good."

Pess smiled broadly and she managed to look away

from that yawning cavern of greenish gum without giving him offense.

Beverly and Bert Put came out of hiding and, though they seemed somewhat distracted, listened to their adventures, chuckling over Balenquah's mishap. They approved her purchases, especially the spices, salt, vinegar, and pepper.

"We had to quit because there was a roving band of Catteni looking for trouble," Yuri said. "We'll go for the electronics tomorrow," he added, looking at Kris for confirmation.

Kris shared out the gorupears and they all agreed that the fruit was very tasty indeed. "We can keep the pits and start our own bushes back on Botany," she said, and was looking for something to store them in as she asked if there was any word from the other parties.

"Zainal reported in when he and Mitford reached the restaurant. So did Coo and Slav," Beverly told them. "But they had upsetting news."

"How upsetting?"

Beverly and Bert exchanged anxious glances.

"It's not going to get any better waiting," Kris reminded them, but a sick feeling started in her stomach.

"There are large numbers of Terrans here now, waiting to be shipped out."

A pause.

"What's new in that?" she asked.

"Coo says they're damaged," and Beverly tapped his skull. "They sit or stand and do not speak."

"*What*?"

She, Yuri, and Gino reacted simultaneously and stared in horrified consternation at Beverly.

"Coo says he heard their minds were taken from them."

"The Eosi have mindwipes?" she whispered, appalled.

"Does Zainal know?" Marrucci asked, equally shocked.

"Coo says everyone talks about it—quietly. Even the Catteni. Zainal will also hear."

Marrucci swore inventively and without repeating himself. Yuri looked pale under his gray face paint. It was cracking around the natural creases of his face and, absently, she reminded herself to tell him to powder up before he went outside again.

"Zainal won't do anything drastic until he can check with you, will he?" Kris asked Beverly. "What do the Eosi intend to *get* out of minds? They wouldn't know about us."

"Coo said they are older men, mostly, some women . . ."

"Scientists, I bet," Kris said, and Beverly nodded sadly. "Oh, God, what did we start?"

Beverly covered her hand with a reassuring grip. "We started a rebellion, Kris, as we wanted to on Earth, and couldn't. But Zainal knew how and has."

"But the cost!" She gripped her hands together, holding in the pain of guilt.

"When was there ever a war without casualties?" Yuri said in a bleak voice, absently doodling with the water spill on the table until it was spread out in a Rorschach blob.

"What about Ninety and Dowdall?"

"They say the pens are full of humans. They also heard about the zombies," Beverly said. "They're on their way back, too, before the guard changes."

"Dowdall remembered that, did he?" Kris said, nodding with satisfaction.

Zainal, Scott, and Mitford returned in a silence that spoke more profoundly of the tragedy than words. The first thing Zainal did was remove the cheek and chin pads that disguised him.

"We managed to get into one compound," Scott said, slumping into a chair and taking the glass of hooch that Kris immediately poured for all three. "I recognized a few faces from articles and newspapers. You'd probably recognize more, John, Gino. The ones I could identify were top people in quantum physics, organ transplants, and laser applications."

"Lasers can be used as weapons," Kris murmured.

"Eosi have such already," Zainal replied, also speaking in a low voice.

"Will they . . . recover?" Kris asked.

Zainal shook his head but added, "It depends how long they were subjected to the probe. The Eosi have little pity."

"Other news is good, though," Scott said shaking off that dispiriting vision. "Earth continues to rebel and Catteni are looting on a massive scale."

"I wondered about that," Kris said. "I bought nutmeg, cinnamon, pepper, salt, bolts of Earth-made fabric and needles, surgical equipment: no doubt part of that loot. I hadn't enough money with me to buy everything Leon said he needed. Do we have more to spend?" she asked Zainal, who nodded.

"No electronics?" Scott asked, perturbed. "We need them more than surgical tools."

"If the Catteni have looted as thoroughly as it looks like they have, we'll find all the Terran electronics we could possibly want. But we encountered an off-duty squad," Kris said, and Zainal grunted. "And left."

"We did, too," Dowdall said. "The spaceport's full. We were lucky to get a berth."

"Any damage?" Zainal asked.

"Not to us." Kris grinned. So did Dowdall.

"Where's Balenquah?" Scott asked, looking around.

"Sleeping off a full glass of pilth," Kris replied, still grinning maliciously.

Zainal roared with laughter.

"I told him it was no good," Kris said as Yuri and Marrucci chuckled.

"Serves him right, too," Marrucci said, but Kris gave him a look and he didn't elaborate.

"Did you get the Deski plursaw?" Zainal asked. She nodded.

"At a good price, too. I got as much delivered as I could. Pess has most of it already stored away. 'Drassi says,' " and she smiled at him for the efficacy of that cryptic explanation.

Coo and Slav returned then, Slav with a cut over one eye and Coo with visible abrasions down one side of his slender frame.

"Trouble?" Zainal asked, on his feet.

Coo held up one hand reassuringly. "Catteni gang. Hate aliens."

"They hate anyone," Dowdall said forcefully. "Here, lemme fix that cut for you, Slav," and he took him over to the cabinet containing the few medical supplies they had. Slav endured the ministrations though the brown Catteni antiseptic stung like fire—even for Catteni.

"Bad news," Coo said, joining the others at the table.

Mitford fixed herbal tea when Coo politely refused to drink the hooch already on the table.

"They're after your people, too?" Scott asked.

Coo shook his head. "We do not make machines."

"My people must work in noisy places," Slav said, scrubbing his chest hair in agitation. "We are strong."

"You Earth no good working," Coo said, grinning. "Too much trouble."

"We make trouble," Slav said, "if word is given." And he looked pointedly at Mitford.

"All suppressed minorities rebelling at one time would be difficult for the Eosi to handle," Scott said, immediately savoring the notion.

Zainal, however, snorted and shook his head. "More species injuries."

Scott slammed one fist onto the table so hard the hooch bottle jiggled. "Damn it, Zainal, there're already species injuries, on my people. You saw the state of them. How many more will be put through the same torture? Then sold off as mindless zombies and die who knows where."

Kris had never seen Scott so emotional, but then, she could only imagine the horror of seeing brilliant people reduced to imbeciles.

"The Eosi look for ideas from your people," Zainal said, and there was no doubt from the perturbation on his usually inscrutable face that he felt for the victims and agreed with Scott. "When they find none they can use, they will stop."

"When . . ." demanded Scott, stretching the "n" out to stress the urgency, "will that be?"

"I heard nothing today. Tomorrow we can go elsewhere and listen, and maybe ask."

"And all those . . . those desecrated people?" Scott asked, grieving so keenly that Kris saw tears in the admiral's eyes.

"We can do something about *that*," Zainal said firmly. Then he turned to Kris and Marrucci. "Tomorrow early get the wire, the plastic, the electronic supplies needed. Be ready to move if I arrange . . ."

"What are you arranging?" Mitford asked, though the look on his face suggested to Kris that he already had a suspicion.

"What can be done to help. The Farmers do not *like*," and Zainal emphasized that word, "species injuries. We show them what can happen."

"We'll bring them back with us?" Scott began, his expression brightening for a scant second before common sense overruled that possibility. "How can we possibly care for so many damaged people?"

"We will somehow," Kris said so fiercely that Scott recoiled. "How many are there?"

"Hundreds," Scott said, waving a despairing hand about.

"Not all are damaged," Zainal said. "But they *will* die in mines and fields with no care given."

"We can't leave them if we *can* take them," Dowdall said firmly, glancing around the table for agreement. Even the two Deski and Slav were in accord.

"Zainal, did you notice the other ship of this class a few berths down from us?" Marrucci asked, his eyes sparkling.

Bert Put, who had been silent through most of the discussion, sat up, an expectant look on his face, watching Zainal.

He nodded, a grin turning his mouth up in one corner. "I maybe go see guard tonight, drink a little pilth."

"No," Mitford said with an evil grin, "he'd be used to that. Take some of the hooch."

The next morning as they breakfasted, Zainal had good news from his evening's interview. Most of the KDM's crew were on shore leave, having just completed a wide swing which had included Earth. In fact, they had brought two deckfuls of the brain-wiped humans to the slave marts and loot that would soon be available in the Barevi markets. Only two crewmen were on board, taking turns on watch. They were not happy about that duty but expected to be relieved in another two days. As was standard practice with Catteni ships, the KDM was already refueled and stocked. The crewmen said they were slated for another trip to Earth: to collect cargo as the Catteni invaders were systematically clearing warehouses and storage facilities, whether the items were useful or not.

"Whatever the Eosi hope to find on Earth, they have not," Zainal said. "Not even information. They may even be pulling out."

"What?"

"Leaving Earth?"

"Hurrah, we socked it to them and they couldn't take it."

"No rush," Zainal said, raising his hands to indicate caution. "Your Earth may never be the same."

"Then we improve it when we get back home," Beverly said, a fierce expression on his face.

Zainal pointedly said nothing. "I also learn that the port manager is very busy with so many ships going in and out."

"Which means he's not checking on individual ones?" Beverly asked.

Zainal nodded. "We come at a lucky time."

"Let's leave lucky, too," Mitford said gruffly. "If we get all the stuff we need, can we leave tonight? I got a gut feeling we're crowding what luck we've already had. On our way back, I spotted just too many of those roving gangs charging about drunk. Glad we weren't on foot."

Everyone looked at Zainal. He hesitated and then nodded. "Sooner is better than later, but first," and he held up one finger, "we do not go back empty."

"Hey, if there's only two crewmen aboard the KDM, couldn't we hijack it?" asked Gino, eagerly.

Mitford made a disgusted sound, dismissing the notion, but Scott leaned forward eagerly.

"Could we?"

"I think it would be very easy. Gino can be captain. Balenquah . . ." and Zainal looked around for the man.

"He was sick all night," Mitford said sourly. "He's no use to us at all, I never did have more than a sip of pilth and that was enough to make me avoid it."

"I told him it was no good," Kris repeated, with an innocent expression on her face.

"Which made him all the more eager to try it, huh?" Mitford asked, giving her a dirty look.

"He deserved it . . ." Gino Marrucci began, but Kris kicked him under the table. "Sullen bastard that he is," the pilot said in place of what he had started to say.

"All right," Scott said, getting back to the jobs at hand, "we find out what we can about the . . . disabled. Right?" He looked at Zainal, who nodded. "You got yesterday's list, Kris? So today escort Mack Su, Ninety, and Marrucci for whatever electronics we can acquire . . ."

"We'll find plenty," Kris said, scowling. "I only had a quick glance but everywhere I looked I could see things that had to have come from home."

"Good," Mack said, "that means we'll have a good chance of finding what we need. We've done as much as we can with the Farmers' material. But we could do a helluva lot more with familiar components, couldn't we. Dowdall?"

"Also get more hand units." And Zainal tapped his Catteni comunit. "We need all we can get, or make."

Kris handed him a pencil and the thin plastic that the Catteni used for notes. "Make us out another shopping list, Drassi Kubitai!"

Zainal grimaced. "I do not know the Catteni shapes," he admitted wryly.

"No word for 'spare parts' in Catteni?" Mack asked, grinning.

"Ah, yes," and Zainal deftly created the glyph, adding tails and squiggles to it. "That means anything to repair electronics." He peered at it. "I think."

"Have we completely contaminated an upright Catteni lad?" Mack asked with one of his displays of whimsy.

"Absolutely," Zainal agreed heartily. "Let us make . . . con . . . con something plans . . ."

"Contingency plans?" Kris asked.

"Them. In case there can be two shipments of humans to mines or colonies or wherever they plan to send them. We are ready to go and take the problems with us," Zainal said. "I call in to Chuck, I tell him where to bring

KDM. Then, sergeant, you will take more hooch to guard on duty. The other will be sleeping. You will know what to do. Then Gino, Beverly, Coo, Pess, and Slav get aboard as crew. Bert, Gino, be ready to bring the ships where I tell you." He flipped through the pile of maps and charts and found the one he wanted. "Here are slave pens, but you must go around the city, not overfly."

"Don't we have to clear takeoff with the port authority?" Gino asked.

Zainal slapped his forehead and sucked breath in between his teeth.

"After we secure the KDM, I can come back and do that, Zainal," Mitford said. "Give me the words for 'slave compound' in Catteni. I only know Barevi."

"Use Barevi if you need to," Zainal said, rocking one hand to indicate that the port authorities would know both. Then he rose in a decisive manner. "Good luck." And he gave the thumbs-up signal, grinning when his eyes fell on Kris.

"Right back atcha," she said as everyone else got to their feet. "And watch your face paint if you start to sweat, you guys. And, for godssake, remember to keep your caps down, shading your eyes. No Catteni I've ever seen has blue ones, much less brown."

"Slav, Pess, Coo, you guard ship," was Zainal's final order as he made for the hatch.

Kris, with Dowdall, Mack, and Ninety, got the last remaining flitter outside the port. The driver grumbled that the market wasn't open yet.

"Shop I go is," Kris answered in Barevi. "Drassi says so."

That ended any further inquiries from the Catteni. He had no left hand, a hook attachment replacing it, but a flitter was easily driven with only one. Did only disabled Catteni get taxi licenses on Barevi?

As the craft made its way to the market area, they all noticed smoke rising from various places.

"Many fights?" Ninety asked in Barevi, grinning but remembering to keep his lips over his teeth.

"Many," replied the Catteni in his own language and in a sour tone. "Nine ship gangs. Biggest fights in weeks."

Which meant the survivors would likely be sleeping off pilth as well as any injuries from the fighting. Or hiding out for the requisite twenty-four hours. Luck was again with them, she hoped, and didn't dare hope too loudly.

Much of the first marketplace that they overflew—the one they had shopped in the day before—was a wreck of tangled stalls, debris, and shopkeepers sorting for what might still be salable. As they crossed over the line of apartments separating the two, she saw that streamers of fabric, probably from some of the shops she had visited, festooned the area.

"Boys had lots of fun," Ninety muttered, and got Kris' elbow in his ribs for speaking in English. He rolled his eyes in apology but the driver had not heard.

There was not quite as much damage in the third rectangle, the one they had directed the flitter to. Possibly because there were fewer drink and food stands in this one. But one section seemed to have been leveled. Kris just hoped it wasn't the very one they needed the most.

"Another ticco if you wait," she told the driver in her gravelly Catteni voice. She was getting so she could do it whenever she needed to, though her throat was a trifle sore from all the rough-voiced bargaining she'd done yesterday.

"Just one ticco?" he complained.

"Wait and see," she said, leaving it up to him. She handed him a smaller coin and pointed to the stand selling hot drinks and the almost indigestible bread Catteni baked.

That sweetened him sufficiently and she walked off with the others, to find the spare parts.

Four shops which displayed boxes spilling loose chips in their grilled windows, were not open. They came upon a fifth on the long end of the rectangular market area and the shopkeeper was sweeping up components and/or chips with total disregard for the damage done. Mack and Dowdall winced and Kris hissed at them for falling out of character.

"You selling?" she asked, acting the stupid Catteni Tudo.

"What does it look like?" the shopkeeper replied angrily, gesturing at the havoc within and without. He ranted on, switching from Barevi to Catteni in his fury.

Kris held up Zainal's glyphed note. "You got some?"

The shopkeeper paused long enough in his description of what he would do to the gang who had smashed and kicked his stock into garbage and, eyeing her suspiciously, then turned his attention to Mack and Dowdall, who were lovingly picking up this and that which had not been damaged.

"Got everything needed for repair. And then some . . . if it hasn't all been smashed."

He put down the broom and led them through the shop, palmed open a rear door and showed them unopened cardboard boxes, all bar-coded and listing the contents in English, French, German, and either Japanese or Chinese . . . Kris couldn't tell the difference.

"Ah, many unhurt," she cried. "Drassi wants."

"All?" The shopkeeper was both delighted and suspicious.

"Drassi Kubitai trades," said Dowdall, winking as he began removing boxes from the shelves and stacking them in the center. His eyes were so alight with success that Kris yanked furiously at her own cap to warn him. "Kubitai pleased with us," he said in Barevi, turning his face away.

"Not all, but samples to show. How much?" Kris began, tapping the boxes Dowdall had chosen and to which Mack was adding selections, breathing heavily with excitement but remembering to keep his head down. "You deliver?"

"Ha! When I must clean this and lock up before they come back again?"

"Kubitai wants comunits, Drassi?" Mack asked, returning from a back shelf with a crate. "And wires?"

Kris pretended to look at the list. The shopkeeper pointed to the right glyph.

"Here, stupid," he said, his yellow eyes turning crafty as he suspected he might be able to do her on the prices.

"I count well," she said, jerking her cap to shade her eyes but looking fiercely at him. "I be Drassi soon. You see."

"Ha!" was his reply, but he began to move the chosen boxes toward the front of the shop. "You got transport?"

"Flitter," she said. "I call it over."

She had to go get the flitter driver, who had indeed been treating himself to a meal on her coin. When he saw how much was stacked out in the litter in front of the smashed shop, he shook his head.

"Call another," she told him, pointing to his control panel. "Drassi Kubitai very happy with us. We get long shore leave." She strutted back to the shop to find Dowdall who was looking anxious.

"Won't he suspect when we order so much? And check out the KDI?" He spoke in a barely articulated whisper.

"He probably has, and if the port authority has time to answer him, will know which berth the KDI has," she murmured back, and, then, seeing the shop man out of the corner of her eye, punched Dowdall in the arm. "Work! No work, no leave!"

However, greed—and possibly the call to the dock to verify that a KDI with a Drassi Kubitai was in port—moved the shopkeeper to encourage the large order.

Kris bargained in earnest with him, as part of her character as not so stupid Tudo messenger. She had no idea of what the parts would have cost on Earth but Mack was slightly agog at the range of the merchandise. There were even laptops still in their packing cases. Now what possible use would the Catteni have for such items? They couldn't even read the manuals, much less figure out what the icons meant. She'd had enough trouble with her 286 IBM clone at college. She noticed a dozen units along with all the other parts, plus tool kits and several cases of floppies. She devoutly hoped she wouldn't have to explain why those were among her purchases. She only knew so much Catteni and Barevi.

She haggled and finally made her mark on the collection of glyphs that spewed out of his electronic equipment. She also added the glyph for Kubitai that Zainal had shown her, grateful for his forethought.

Then they all loaded the boxes into the flitters. Their driver had estimated the cargo space required and called in two, not one.

All the way across the city, Kris forced herself to cheerful thoughts, terrified that something might happen and they'd be caught by an army trap or port patrol or some other unexpected glitch. But they made it safely back to the berth, and started unloading. Mitford, Gino, Slav, Coo, and Pess hurried out to speed the process along, Gino whistling under his breath at the range of their purchases.

"Catteni can't whistle," Kris said inside the safety of the ship.

"Ooops."

"Any word from Zainal?"

Gino shook his head, trotting back down the ramp, muttering unintelligible noises that could be muffled

Catteni curses and adding "Drassi says" in a grumpy tone.

They were nearly finished unloading when Balenquah staggered into the open hatch, his gray face paint smeared with rivulets of sweat, his hair mud rubbed off overnight on the pillow, looking not at all like any Catteni.

Mitford recovered first. "Sick! Get back! Dow, Nine, get him back!" The two hauled the pilot back out of the way and he had time for only one muffled protest before someone knocked him out. Mitford rolled his eyes at Kris, who was facing the stunned flitter drivers.

Taking her clue from Mitford's remark, she shook her head, feeling quite ill suddenly, too.

"Very sick. Terran sick," she said, still shaking her head and making her wobbly legs carry her back down the ramp. There were only a few more boxes to be stored.

"Dockmaster knows?" the one-handed Catteni asked, his murky yellow eyes suspicious.

"Dockmaster says keep him on board and take him back to Terra," Mitford said, keeping his face away from the Catteni. "Leave him there."

"Drassi say we leave today," Kris added for good measure. "I take shore leave back there! Told Bal no good there."

She gave the drivers just enough to satisfy them, not so meager a sum as to annoy them yet not enough to be considered a possible bribe. She mentally blessed those awful shopping journeys with her Catteni steward for knowing the difference.

With them safely off the dock area, she marched straight to the bottle of hooch and poured herself a stiff one. Dowdall and Ninety joined her, silently taking the bottle from her hand.

"We tied him in," Dowdall said. "Goddamn stinking arrogant bastard nearly blew the whistle on us."

"He might still have," Mitford said, holding out his hand for the bottle, "I'm not sure the one-handed guy bought the explanation."

"Yeah, but why would he suspect Catteni-dressed soldiers to be anything but Catteni?" Kris said, reaching for reassurance.

"There is that," Mitford agreed.

"Is it safe?" whispered Beverly and Bert Put from their compartment.

"For now," Kris said, sitting down because her legs had never felt so kneeless. She buried her head in her hands. "I never want to go through another moment like that."

An urgent buzz from the com board on the bridge startled all of them. Beverly and Mitford tried to make it through the door at the same time, with the sergeant twisting his torso edgewise to allow the general through first.

"Schkelk?" Beverly asked in proper Tudo response as he keyed open the ship's unit. "Oh, thank God." Craning her head toward the bridge, Kris could see him visibly relax. For just one moment—then he straightened and urgently beckoned the others to come in. "Yes, yes, I got you. What does 'forty-seven' look like in Catteni, for God's sake? . . . Oh." He had grabbed up a pad, which Mitford now held firmly for him, since he had the hand unit. "Thick upright, two crossbars, three downstrokes, and a small right-hand square within the end two right-hand downstrokes. Got that. That's for the KDI?" Beverly began to smile and heaved a sigh of relief that seemed to permeate his whole frame. "Thank God," he whispered. "Okay, so there's just a change in the final figure, a circle rather than a square between the two right-hand downstrokes? . . . Got it. Be there as fast as we can get permission to quit the dock. Watch for us."

He toggled the line closed.

"Contingency plan is now in operation. Mitford, grab another bottle of hooch and go visiting. Gino, Coo, Slav, Pess, Ninety, lounge outside like you're bored. We're going to rescue us some folks. And God grant there's some spark of mind left to them. We're clearing the prisons."

"I know how to work the levels," Kris said, and grabbed Ninety by the hand. "I'd better show you. Let's hope they're the same as the wreck's."

The controls were sited in the same place by the hatch, although they looked in far better working order.

"And will they be drugged and all?" Ninety asked anxiously.

"I hope so. They'll survive better if they are," Kris said, deliberately not thinking about that process and the bodies that would shortly inhabit the four levels of shallow deck. "Take a peek outside. Ninety, just in case we have unexpected visitors," she said, shoving the comunit from her belt at him.

CHAPTER 13

For a contingency plan, hastily organized and speedily executed, it went very well. But there were other Catteni around on the dockside now, shifting cargoes or watching the Rugarians do so. Bert Put's height would make him stand out like the proverbial sore thumb. So he got wrapped up in blankets and Dowdall and Slav carried him over to the KDM, grumbling about Drassis and their crazy tradings back and forth. Then returned to the KDI.

"Piece of cake." Mitford said when he returned to the KDI. "Front and center, Bert, general. We're about to shift ass off this sinkhole."

"What about Zainal and Scott?" Ninety asked.

"We meet them at platform forty-seven and forty-nine when we pick up our passengers. Now I gotta log on to port authority and get clearance."

While Bert settled into the captain's chair, Beverly took the engineer's place as Mitford made contact with the port authority. Kris watched as his shoulders stiffened and he rolled his eyes.

What now? The glitch she had been expecting all

along that was going to betray them? She fretted, knees getting wobbly again.

"Sick?" Mitford exclaimed in Catteni, and swore with unexpected fluency in the language for emphasis. "Yes, Terran sick." He sounded disgusted. "We dump him with others. They not see," and he managed a very evil chuckle. "Kotik. Ten."

He whistled when he closed the switch. "That driver was suspicious. Let's get out of here before anyone comes to look at our Terran-sick soldier. Take her no higher than a thousand plegs, Bert. That's our assigned level."

Mitford gave Kris a good luck sign, and, grabbing another bottle of hooch, leaving only two for the journey home, he sauntered back to the recently hijacked vessel.

Bert initiated the undocking procedures, starting the siren to warn the crew back inside, closing the hatch when they reported all in, starting the engines, just as if he'd done it all his professional life. The KDI lifted easily, and Bert made the course correction and they could see the spaceport steadily receding. On the small thrusters that were permissible in such crowded airspace, it seemed to take a long time to circumnavigate Barevi town, strewn before them and out into the nearby forests and fields. They could see where big land-moving equipment was knocking down trees and scooping up great mountains of rock and dirt to clear more space. Doubtless, Kris thought bitterly, for the masses of products they were importing from a pillaged Earth.

Flitters darted in and around, and each one that seemed to choose a trajectory in front of Kris made her catch her breath.

"They can't see in," Bert said, to reassure her. "And I'll turn this seat over to you immediately if we are hailed. Wouldn't you like to drive this beauty for a while?"

His banter made her relax but she stayed right beside his position in case they had to execute a quick shift.

They did have a little trouble deciding which platform they should dock at, since there were only minor changes in the basic glyph that Zainal had given them. But as they cruised at the slowest possible forward speed, everyone on the bridge identified the number at the same moment, and could even see the KDM's platform just beyond.

Below were the slave pens, similar to the ones Kris had been in when she'd been forced aboard the transport that had landed her on Botany so many months ago. There were acres of pens, spreading out from a huge rectangular building. Not all the pens, however, were full or in use. Only four. She couldn't see who inhabited the ones beyond platform 49 and hoped she wouldn't ever know who or what they had had to abandon that day.

Bert neatly sidled into the platform, cut the engines, and opened the hatch. Kris took her station at the controls and suddenly Zainal strode up the ramp, spitting out the disfiguring pads, muttering under his breath, and snarling up at her, but winking as he passed on his way to the bridge. Kris managed a very subservient "Yes, Drassi," and saw the first of the pathetic transportees.

She nearly burst into tears at the sight of the expressionless faces, the dead eyes, the automatic motion that no intelligence motivated. She did manage to alter the decks to the lowest one as the loading process began.

Half the time she had all she could do to keep from bawling out loud, getting some relief by snarling at the Catteni who drove these poor souls up the ramps. Most had their blankets slung over their shoulders, one hand holding the packet of ration bars to their bodies, the other the treacherous soup cup, now emptied of its contents. She told herself over and over that she was rescuing them—they'd soon be safe, they'd soon be cared for—and she wondered how on earth they would manage all these walking dead at Botany, where there was so much hope and life and a future.

She shifted blindly when the first level was filled. Several of those trudging like sheep up the ramp staggered and fell. It was all she could do to keep herself at the controls and not go help them up, but that would have been out of character for the Catteni Tudo she was pretending to be. She was *not* going to cause a glitch. She was rescuing these people. She was doing all she could.

She shifted to the third level and then it was filled up. So was the air around her with little sobs and cries for pity from those in the lower decks. The drugged soup couldn't put them out of their immediate misery, and hers, soon enough.

It was Zainal who carefully removed her hands from the controls when the ramp retracted and the hatch clanged shut. He helped her back to the wardroom and poured her another shot of hooch.

"We're almost out of it," she protested.

"You need it now, Kris," he said. "I hadn't realized what you were in for. I'd've done it myself—"

"No, no," and she shook her head, "not a Drassi captain." Then she put her head on the table and began to weep.

"They're all asleep now," Zainal said, gathering her up in his arms and against his chest, stroking her hair.

"Zainal?" she cried, raising her tear-marked face, "did we get them all?"

"All we can cram on board. A few spare Deski, Rugarians, half a dozen Ilginish and some Turs for good measure."

"We need Ilginish and Turs so badly, don't we?" she quipped, trying to control her weeping.

Ninety and Beverly stood in the doorway. Zainal nodded at them to enter and both poured a hefty tot from the bottle.

"We don't have much left," Kris said inanely.

"It's medicinal, my dear," Beverly said, and she thought he looked awful under his coffee-colored skin. "Dowdall says the KDM's on a parallel course. There's incoming traffic but we're cleared to leave the system and doing it with all possible speed." He let out a long sigh and knocked back the rest of the hooch. "You're relieved, Bjornsen. I don't want to see you on deck for two full shifts."

"Aye aye, sir," she said, managing a weak smile and limp salute.

Zainal helped her stand and guided her back to her compartment. He had to lift her up into the upper bunk but his hands, as he covered her with the rough Catteni-issue blanket, were very gentle.

They answered several challenges over the next two weeks, until they got to the less trafficked area leading to the Botany system. Most were more or less standard ship-talk which Zainal handled on the bogus KDI and Mitford on the KDM.

They also talked about how they could integrate the people they had rescued into the Botany colony.

Kris found herself regarding Admiral Ray Scott with amazement: under all that naval braid and command training there was a man with unexpected compassion. And a high moral integrity. She wasn't the only one who kept reassuring him that there was no way those folks could have been allowed to depart on Catteni slave ships.

"Hell, Ray," Beverly said the second evening, "it isn't as if there are more of them than there are of us! So we'll need to hunt more often and plant a few more fields. If we have to, we'll form a crèche situation for the ones who can do nothing for themselves. We don't even know just how badly some of them were mind-wiped. There may be something there that some of our pysch people can revive. For all of that, maybe just being among humans again . . . begging your pardon, Zainal . . . and good food and attention will bring some round."

"Almost everyone's got some kind of house now. We can give them shelter, food and . . . a lot of caring," Dowdall said, clearing his throat. He was another one who didn't let emotions overwhelm him.

"And we shall inform the Farmers," Zainal said.

"You think they can perform some sort of a psychic whammy and replace what got wiped?" Dowdall asked.

Zainal shrugged. "It is possible, since their science is so much better than ours. Why not such healing?"

"I think that's asking for too much of a miracle," Ray Scott said, although the brief flare of hope in his eyes at the mere suggestion of a possible restoration was not lost on anyone at the table.

"We shall inform them," Zainal repeated.

"Speaking for myself," Kris said, "they can't be any more trouble than a baby and we can handle one more in our house, can't we, Zainal?"

He nodded. "If he or she doesn't get upset seeing a Catteni around."

"Well, I think," Kris went on staunchly, "it's important for everyone to know that there's at least one good Catteni in this universe!"

They were nearing the heliopause when Zainal mentioned, quite casually, Kris thought, that it was just possible that they might have a little trouble getting the second ship through the Bubble.

"Why?" Kris asked. "They're alike as two peas in a pod."

"There are two and only one went out."

"The KDL was pregnant when she left. The KDM is her daughter," Kris said, surprising herself with such a whimsy. The others around the wardroom table laughed politely.

"It *is* a problem," Beverly said.

"Why?" Scott wanted to know. "If we proceed slowly, as we did getting out, just nudging past the Bubble."

Zainal was not convinced.

"Too bad we can't call downside and get Raisha up in the scout to poke a hole for us," Bert said. "We could go piggyback, maybe," he suggested, and then canceled that notion with a whisk of his hand. "Too risky."

Zainal agreed with a skeptical twist of one shoulder.

"Fine thing if we get these folks right up to the door and can't wedge 'em in," Dowdall said.

"There *has* to be a way," Scott said, looking at Zainal for inspiration.

"If there is, we find it," the former Emassi said.

But it was obvious that everyone on board the KDL worried about it for the rest of the journey through the solar system to its third planet.

"Engines," Kris said as she sat on the bridge watching their approach to Botany.

"What?" Scott demanded. He looked up from the final course plotting that would escape both the satellite and orbital observation.

"Would there be such a thing on board as a tractor beam?" she asked Zainal.

"A what?" He frowned, unable to find those words in his now very large vocabulary.

"Something to pull another ship along, a ship with no power."

"She's got it!" Scott said. "Does the KDL have one?"

It took a little time for Zainal to understand exactly what they meant, but when he did, his grin was broad.

"Not a tractor beam but is possible to connect," and he jammed both fists together. "One ship hull is negative, the other positive. Very easy to do. I tell Bert.''

They had not allowed themselves many intership broadcasts on the off chance that they might be overheard. But so close to Botany, they could risk it. The orbital might pick up some of what was transmitted, but not enough to give any alert. Not unless there were Eosi hiding behind the moons.

''Oh, he means magnetize the hull,'' Bert said, catching on. ''Okay, give me the procedure.''

The light bump as the KDM magnetically sealed itself behind the KDL was felt by everyone. There was also a certain tingling in the air. The KDL would be pushed through the Bubble first, propelled by the KDM. All watched nervously as the Bubble's smooth skin got closer and closer and behind it, a luminous half-moon, was Botany. Bert had slowed to the barest possible forward motion while Zainal, in the fore, guided him. The nose of the KDL prodded the Bubble, which gaped wide enough to admit the ship. All of the KDL was shortly inside the Bubble and they felt no resistance, nor any sudden disconnection of the KDM.

''We did it!'' crowed Bert on the open line. ''We did it! Now how do I separate us? Just kidding.''

Then Rastancil opened a channel, demanding to know were they all right. What was the other ship doing on his screen? ''What have you guys been up to?''

''Well, we needed it to complete our . . . rescue mission,'' Scott said, suddenly dropping from the high of successfully penetrating the last obstacle to home. ''We couldn't just . . .'' and his voice faltered then continued firmly, ''leave them there on Barevi.''

''Rescued? Who? What?''

''You'll see,'' Scott said almost angrily. ''Some of them are pretty bad. Have all the medics on hand and anyone else with any nursing experience we've got. Especially the psychiatrists. We've some more Catteni prisoners to go to the valley. So have Raisha stand by to fly 'em out. Then we'll need another valley for a bunch of Turs we had to bring along, too. She ought to have guards with that lot in case any wake up prematurely.''

"Medics? Psychiatrists? What sort of casualties are they?'' Rastancil sounded alarmed.

"You'll see soon enough,'' Scott said in a terse voice, "and we'll need a good nutritious soup or something easy to eat.''

He disconnected, a brooding expression on his face.

"It'll work out, Ray,'' Kris said, laying a hand on his arm. "You'll see.''

"Botany can take on any challenge,'' Dowdall added with the pride of a First Drop survivor.

When the two ships landed in the big field in front of the hangar, Rastancil had mobilized transport, medical staff and enough personnel to assist in unloading the sleepers. Jim Rastancil, Geoffrey Ainger, Bob Reidenbacker, Bull Fetterman—in fact all those who constituted the Council—waited patiently for Scott and Zainal to descend from the KDM, which landed slightly ahead of its sister ship.

"This should have been a unanimous decision by all Botanists,'' Scott began, nervously finger-combing his hair back from his forehead or rubbing the back of his neck.

"It was sure as hell unanimous with all the Botanists there,'' Beverly said firmly.

"Hell, yes,'' Dowdall, Kris, and Mitford added in unison.

"Who? What?'' Rastancil asked, surprised to find Scott hesitant.

"The ones the Eosi mind-wiped,'' Scott said flatly. "They were about to be shipped off God-knows-where as slaves.''

"Jesus! Of course you had to bring them here," said Rastancil. "Leon, Mayock, front and center and let's get them out of there," and he charged up the ramp with the medical personnel.

Kris slipped ahead of him to her post at the deck controls.

"All right, now, let's do this efficiently," she heard Bull Fetterman roaring. "Move that big sled up, stretcher bearers up front. Someone get blankets ready as makeshift . . ."

The cargo hold doors parted and, although several people choked over the rancid body smells that wafted out, they walked on it and stopped.

"God in heaven . . ." Rastancil whispered, staring at the human debris, crumpled in small heaps, though some had managed to lie flat before the drug overcame them.

"And I thought we had it bad," Leon murmured, kneeling beside the first unconscious body, feeling the neck for a pulse, his eyes ranging around the deck.

Kris had turned on what lighting there was.

"Stretcher here," Leon said, pointing to the man and then moving inward, to the next prone body. "Mayock, we'd better do a triage."

And the rescue operation began its final phase.

Sixteen hundred humans, fortunately not all of them mind-wiped but many with abused bodies and minor injuries, were disembarked from the two ships. And two hundred Deski, one hundred and fourteen Rugarians, ninety Ilginish, and twelve Turs.

The Turs were left on a lower deck, which confined them should they wake before Raisha returned from taking the Catteni to their new accommodations. The two crewmen from the KDM had been secured in its cheerless brig throughout the trip, seeing only Coo or Mitford in his Catteni role. They were told that their ship had been commandeered. One of them protested such treat-

ment every time food was brought: even protested the
good food he was served because it wasn't what he was
accustomed to. The other Catteni slept almost the entire
time, rousing only long enough to take care of natural
needs and eat. They were blindfolded before they left
their cell so they would have little to add to what information the other captives might have.

With so many hands to help, Leon's triage teams separated those who needed the most attention from those
who needed only rest, good food, and reassurance. By
then, quite a few were regaining consciousness and
could be offered water and a soup, hastily brought from
the dining hall. Even without formal orders, there was
suddenly a carer with every victim in a response that
certainly gladdened Kris' heart. Scott should have had
more faith in the community's generosity. It wasn't as
if he hadn't seen examples of it with every new drop
the Catteni made.

Some awakened and were utterly passive: their empty
faces expressionless. They had to be helped to drink,
though they could manage to swallow or eat once food
was put to their lips. Others woke, screaming or sobbing
helplessly, and that was nearly as heartbreaking even if
it gave an indication that some vestige of the original
personality might remain.

"Just keep talking to them, folks," Leon called out.
"Let them hear English, see human faces around them.
Feed 'em, but don't let them gorge."

"Who knows when they've had a decent meal,"
Anna Bollinger muttered, trying to keep the bruised and
battered woman beside her from gulping down the entire
cup of soup. "Just sip it. There'll be all you need."

"Gawd, it's like a disaster scene, an earthquake or
something," Joe Latore said, helping his male victim to
his feet since the man was trying so desperately to stand.

"What in hell are you doing, Zainal? Taking pictures of people right now."

"I show the Farmers what Eosi do to people. I show the Farmers what humans do to help," he said, bringing the taper in close to the vacant eyes of Joe's man.

Then Zainal turned the camera to include the woman Leon was treating for body lacerations that covered every inch of her torso. He went from her to a group of three whose faces were devoid of any expression, eyes dulled and unfocusing.

Those who could be classified as walking wounded were sent to the homes of volunteer carers, with instructions for basic care.

"Like a bath!" someone remarked loudly. "Wonder what I'll find under all that dirt and . . . yuck."

Everyone volunteered to help almost to the point of being disappointed when all the victims had been assigned a place.

Leon and the other medical staff gave general directions for emergency care. "Keep them warm, give them plenty of fluid, but limit solid food until their bodies can adjust. Let them sleep all they want. But don't let them go off on their own. We'll set up evaluation conferences and see which might respond to rehabilitation."

"Can you manage, Leon?" Scott asked earnestly.

"You better believe it, Ray," Leon replied sharply. "In fact, we can and have managed it," and he swung his arm in a broad gesture across the all but empty field. "Who knows? Good food, fresh air, plenty of friendly faces . . ." he added with a wry grin, "and good trauma skills, we may even effect a significant number of complete recoveries."

"You really think so?" Scott looked ready to accept any reassurance for the responsibility he had off-loaded on the colony.

"Sure do!" Leon said in such a positive tone that

Scott finally relaxed. "No way you could have left them! Any road, they're better off with us."

"They are, you know," Kris said. "You look beat, Ray."

"I should take one in with me. My house is finished," and Scott stared after the last couples leaving the field.

"We'll switch people around, Ray. I'll make sure you take your turn," Leon said ironically. "Now, my prescription for you, Ray Scott, is get some rest. You, too, Kris. You left a baby in the crèche, or does that seem years ago?"

"It does, you know," she said. She'd been too busy to give much thought to Zane. But he was happy where he was: one of the crèche girls had told her that he'd been just fine.

"I believe it. Get on up to him, now," and Leon gave her a little push in the right direction. Then, when he saw Kris glancing about her for Zainal, he added, "He was following the final load on the sled the last time I saw him."

To her delighted surprise, she met him just short of the crèche, with Zane in his arms. He shrieked with joy on seeing his mother and, almost overbalancing himself out of Zainal's arms, reached out both hands for her. Zainal let the exchange be made, one hand holding the recording camera tight against his side.

"I saw you filming," Scott said, altering his direction to join them. He even managed a tired smile at the enthusiastic way Zane was hugging his mother.

Zainal patted the camera, nodding. "Such evidence is needed to show the Farmers how the Eosi treat humans. You will help me write a report, Ray?" And when Scott nodded wearily, Zainal added. "What words do not say, the film will."

"You'll use one of those homing capsules the Farmers have in the Command Post?"

"The Farmers do not approve the species' injury.

Once they see what Eosi do, we will hear from them again.''

"What if the Farmers can live with that?" Scott asked bitterly.

"That's what we'll have to find out, won't we?" Zainal said, but the tone of his voice told Kris that he wouldn't rest until he had completed Phase Three, no matter what it took.

There was considerable discussion about whether or not the Farmers would be able to play the pictorial record when Zainal, Kris, and the former movie cameraman had finished making it. Baxter, however, did still photographs that were indeed worth a thousand words of explanation and these were carefully inserted in the message tube.

The homing device had no trouble penetrating the Bubble on its way to its destination. Its departure was once again noted by the orbital and the geosynchronous satellite as well as its abrupt disappearance just past the heliopause. The event was immediately sent to Eosi headquarters for distribution.

The Ix Mentat, just returned from its almost futile investigations on the rebellious planet, was so contorted with rage that its juniors feared it might lose connection with its host. It had only just received a report from Barevi, citing the disappearance of one of the new transporter vessels as well as over two thousand slaves, destined for the mining colony at Ble Sot Fac Set, which had been expecting replacements for unavoidable casualties in a major shaft collapse. When the report got to the composition of that shipment, the Ix Mentat came closer to self-extinction than any of its peer group in their long history.

Its recovery from such a seizure was slow: its host had suffered bodily injury and had to be repaired, an

almost unheard-of complication in an Eosi-Emassi sym-
biosis.

To calm their senior, Mentats Co and Se issued orders
that an installation was to be built on the innermost
moon of the subject planet: a second orbital, programmed for a slower rotation, would provide constant
surveillance and prevent the recalcitrant population from
effecting another covert exit, since it was now obvious
that they had two, or more, spaceships.

When the Mentat Ix recovered fully from its incapac-
ity, it began to organize the largest expedition ever
mounted by Catteni forces. It would wreak the most horrific vengeance on that recalcitrant planet that had ever
been mounted by Eosi Mentat. Afterwards, there would
be no opposition left in the galaxy that could subject an
Eosi to such humiliation. But first, they must find the
weapons or the method to breach the barrier around the
colony planet. A planet, the Mentat Ix stoutly told all its
colleagues, which was undoubtedly the cause of all the
problems recently encountered by Catteni and Eosi alike.
Once it was destroyed, the Eosi could resume their normal activities and enjoy their conquests unopposed.